My Father's Enchanted Garden

Vee Dowdy

Cover Design by Phillip D Tovar
Cover Images by Vee Dowdy and Phillip D Tovar

Publisher may be contacted at:
Gray Wolf and Kitty Cat Enterprizes
PO Box 342388
Memphis, TN 38184-2388
graywolfandkittycat@earthlink.net
website: graywolfandkittycat.com

CIP Data
Dowdy, Vee
My Father's Enchanted Garden/Vee Dowdy-1st Edition
ISBN 978-0-9818255-2-6
Subjects: 1.Fiction 2.Idaho 3.Action and Adventure

This is a work of fiction. All the characters and events in the
novel are fictious. The Botanic Enchantment is a creation from
the author's imagination. The author has used general Idaho
geography, floral, animals, or historical knowledge to the best
of author's ability. Historical figures, Edward Bonner and
Sylvan Ambrose Hart, are well-known historical Idaho figures.

Thank you to my family and friends who have supported and listened as the adventure progressed. A special thanks to my parents for all that you have done and continue to do.

For my husband, who is my knight in shining armor. You are my anchor when the winds around life are a gentle breeze or hurricane force.

Thank you, Vicki! For your guidance, suggestions, and wonderful conversations about life. We appreciate you taking this journey with us. I'm blessed to have wonderful friends such as you in my life.

Phillip, you took a rough idea and turned it into magic. Thank you for the work and for being patient while working with family!

Saturday

Callie heard a twig snap down the trail. She noted that something heavier than a squirrel or deer made the sound. She slipped into the trees. A message had asked to meet the following day. No one was supposed to be in the middle of these woods.

A lone man appeared in the clearing and studied the path. A cellular phone vibrating sounded like a foghorn in the silence. Callie could have reached out and touched his shoulder if she'd been on the other side of the tree.

The stranger answered the phone softly, "Hello."

After listening, the woodsman said, "Yes, I'm at the rendezvous a day early. Tracking my phone is not cool."

Callie could hear the conversation even though the phone was not on speaker. She recognized the caller's voice: Solomon.

"Asher, I bought the phone. Technically, I am tracking my phone. Put the speaker on."

Asher did, and Solomon said tiredly, "Callie, I am sure you can hear me. Don't shoot Rorke."

Callie stepped around to stand behind the man. "Why not?"

Surprised, the man whirled to find Callie training a gun on him. She recognized Rorke Asher, but her face never expressed recognition. Rorke's face displayed brief admiration. He was not one who surprised easily in the wilderness.

Solomon spoke to Callie and Rorke. "We were supposed to meet tomorrow for a private talk, but today is fine. Callie, Rorke Asher owes me a debt, and I've asked him to watch your back. I told Rorke about your father's car accident and the inheritance to be distributed on your twenty-fourth birthday."

Callie directed the question to Solomon. "There is nothing to substantiate a claim that my father's death was anything more than an auto accident. Did you explain that the consequences of involvement could be injury or death?"

Rorke entered the conversation. "Would you lower the weapon? Medical treatment is pretty scarce in the area."

Callie ignored Rorke and told Solomon, "Don't waste calling in a favor or debt. I'm perfectly capable of standing on my own."

Solomon would probably ignore her words, and Callie silently departed the clearing.

Sunday

Callie drove home from church and was feeling thankful for many things in her life. One was not meeting Rorke in the woods today. She'd not slept well, and hiking around Caribou-Targhee National Forest didn't sound appealing. The drive wasn't far in relative terms, but she looked forward to a day of rest.

One of her biggest blessings was her father's planning skills. He'd bought 300 acres near Inkom, Idaho. There was access to the major thoroughfares through Idaho, Interstate 15 and 86. The roads followed routes used by the pioneers who stopped to make Idaho home or went on to Oregon or California. When her grandfather died, Callie's father, Nigel, had his mother, Rosa, move in with them. The first step was to build a family house in a neighborhood that bordered Nigel's land. Over the next five years, they built efficiencies to rent.

Callie used to wonder if her father ever slept. He was continually working on something. After her grandmother moved in, the only argument Callie heard between them was about money. Gran wanted to know if Nigel was into illegal dealings to support his family.

Nigel's answer was one of the few times Callie heard her father raise his voice. His tone was defensive and annoyed at being questioned. Investments, hard work, and networking were the reason they had the money. Nigel attended college on scholarships and grants. While going to school, he saved every penny possible and did not start a business in debt. Botanic Enchantment, his flower and plant business, was privately owned. Her father believed in using every possible free resource and didn't feel the need to buy new equipment. Nigel recycled, repaired, or made do with what was available.

Nigel also had no problem allowing companies of his choosing to experiment on his property within reason, and he made sure to oversee every detail. Access to the greenhouse was under strict conditions. One of the experimental designs was the golf cart looking type work vehicle. The transport ran on hydrogen combustion, or water, and biodegradable fuel. Most people were familiar with biodegradable fuel as biodiesel. Hydrogen, or water, comprised the backup system. The transports weren't fast, but they did the job for short distances and hauling.

Callie could walk from the house to the greenhouse office, and she loved the stroll through the property. The location was ideal for reaching various stores or activities in a short time. Restaurants or malls were about twenty minutes away. The university was about the same amount of time down the interstate as well. Grocery stores or gas stations were nearby.

Her grandmother had arrived home from church services before her, and the two ate lunch together. As they finished, chimes from the security system sounded. Callie checked the camera to see who had come to visit. She recognized Rorke Asher and studied him in the sunlight. The dim, wooded clearing had not given her a clear view for scrutinizing details. She was about five-two in height, so she estimated that her new friend was roughly six feet tall. He had black hair, brown eyes, and chiseled facial features. The toned muscles were from hard work.

Rosa smiled at Callie. "Stop spying and answer the door. I'll make coffee and pull out a pie."

Callie nodded and settled her face into a neutral expression that she used when facing the world.

Rorke grinned at Callie. "Hello again. Rosa Rivera is expecting me about renting an efficiency."

"Oh, great!"

The visitor looked confused at the sarcastic tone, but he saw that Callie wasn't looking at him. She was gazing over his shoulder. A second man parked behind Rorke and strutted up the sidewalk.

Callie whispered to Rorke. "If a confrontation bothers you, come back in a little while."

Rorke shrugged. "Might as well meet the locals if I plan on staying."

A handsome, refined-looking gentleman joined the pair.

Callie made introductions. "Rorke Asher, this is Beau Dew."

The two men stood in front of her, and she had a vivid, visual contrast. Beau's skin was windburned from fishing out on the water. His fit, trim figure was due to gym workouts. Blond hair was highlighted and trimmed regularly by a professional. Summer dress shirt and pants appeared to be pressed and right out of the closet.

Rorke shook hands, and Beau made small talk as the three walked into the kitchen. Rosa, in her mid to late sixties, rinsed dishes in the sink. Her long grey hair was braided and wrapped to make a bun in the back. She personified the image of a grandmother: lined face, spectacles, wrinkled hands, and an air of no-nonsense.

Callie announced, "Gran. Beau showed up as well as Mr. Asher, the new tenant for Efficiency Number Six."

Beau made himself at home after pouring a cup of coffee. Gran waved at Rorke and then the pot to see if their guest wanted some. Mr. Asher negatively shook his head.

6

Rosa Rivera, also known as Gran, dried her hands and asked, "Are we going to play nice?"

Beau answered, "Yes, ma'am."

Callie crossed her arms and leaned on the counter. "Depends. We're on round four, and three strikes are more than most men deserve. Beau insisted that he was going fishing with buddies and ended up at a strip club."

Beau smiled benevolently and responded good-naturedly. "I did not lie. We never specified the type of fishing. Callie, the past makes trust hard for you. The issue of dating, much less a marriage proposal, isn't happening any time soon in your situation."

Callie stilled and controlled her voice. "My answer was clear. Marriage needs more to a relationship than business. I hope you find a woman who isn't bothered by the lack of love in a relationship. After our last discussion, I figured that a doctor's visit was in order. Here are the papers from the physical exam. Doctor's ran tests from pregnancy to genital warts, Aids, venereal disease, or other sexually transmitted diseases. You'll be happy to know everything was negative."

Beau did not redden with embarrassment, and his expression never wavered. "Safe sex is a must in today's times, but a doctor's visit is a little overkill. You and I are not the types to rely on romantic feelings in a relationship. A business proposal is the best you'll receive in a lifetime."

Gran entered the conversation. Her tone was not angry or defensive. "Beau, that is enough. Rinse out the mug and go trout fishing."

Callie waited until Beau was gone to let out a long exhale. "I have work to do at BE."

Rorke asked, "BE?"

"Botanic Enchantment, the business my father started. Sometimes, we call it The Greenhouse."

Gran chastised her granddaughter. "Running and hiding won't help. Stay while I chat about the rental. Mr. Asher's application, background check, and deposit have cleared."

"Mrs. Rivera, please call me Rorke."

"Call me Rosa or Gran. Does anyone want some pie and ice cream?"

Rorke perked up. "Yes, please."

Callie glanced at Rorke and tried not to show her surprise at his enthusiasm for pie. "Aren't you going to ask what kind?"

"No, ma'am. I'll eat pretty much any edible food."

The older woman's weathered face lit with a smile at Rorke's enthusiasm. "Let's discuss a few housekeeping details. Callie and I are not of the same race or ethnicity, but she is my granddaughter. Do you have a problem with the issue?"

"No, but my curiosity is ready to burst. Why did Beau make the wisecrack about dating much less marrying?"

Gran took a bowl of pie that Callie handed her to pass to Rorke and answered. "Here's a short version of family history. I am Hispanic. My husband was black. We couldn't have children. A zero sperm count, not race, was the problem. Our choice was to adopt six children who had difficult circumstances in life. Callie's father, Nigel, was the oldest. He went off to college, fell in love, and the young woman became pregnant. They married, had a baby girl, but the mother died in the hospital. Nigel never remarried. The only lady he ever brought to the house was Dusty.

"Dusty and Nigel had a strange bond, and the lady shows up every so often. I think Dusty wanted stability and distraction from her own life. The woman was not responsible with money or ideas. She always had a get rich scheme. If you meet, I suggest running as fast and as far away as possible."

Rorke guessed. "Sexy and manipulative?"

Gran nodded in agreement. "Yes."

Callie finally entered the conversation to announce, "Dusty will show up in the next month or so to see if my father's estate distributes the rest of the money. I am sure that she'll have a crazy idea or several schemes she wants us to finance."

Gran rolled her brown eyes and continued. "My husband died of complications from a stroke when Callie was eight. I sold the farm to help pay for medical bills. Nigel saved every penny he could over the years. My son loaned me the money and helped build the rental properties. We have built sixteen rental units over the years. Nigel died when Callie was thirteen."

Rorke finished his pie and ice cream. "Would you mind if I ask what happened to the other five children?"

"Two boys live out of state and work in management. One of the girls married and is raising three children. Mer, the youngest, draws cartoons for computers."

Callie explained, "Mer does video graphics."

Gran ignored the interruption. "Thessa died of an overdose."

Rorke rinsed his bowl and felt the air pause with emotion at Thessa's name.

Gran looked out the window. "We don't know the details, but Thessa became mixed up with Dusty. Thessa was arrested and died of a drug overdose six months later."

Callie explained. "No one knows for sure if Thessa and Dusty were doing anything. Dusty is not a great example of responsibility. My eleventh birthday is a good illustration. Dusty talked my dad into letting us attend a heavy metal concert with Uncle Mer as a chaperone. Dusty disappeared, reappeared, and wanted us to go to a party after the concert. Uncle Mer might have stayed, but I was eleven. He brought me home. You'll recognize Uncle Mer immediately. He dresses in black leather, boots, and eyeliner."

"Interesting family."

Gran smiled. "We each have our crosses to bear. Do you have questions about the additional clauses to the standard rental agreement?"

Rorke returned the grin. "No, ma'am. If I were younger, maybe. Responsibility has become my middle name in the last few years. I'll have a beer or wine occasionally. May I ask why there is a clause about respecting various religions?"

"Is there a problem?"

"No, ma'am. Curious. I have friends who are practicing Muslims. During Ramadan, if we eat a meal together, we don't eat until after sunset."

"I was raised Baptist. Callie goes to a Catholic Church, and we have a Hindu family renting. I have enough responsibilities in this life without debating names for the afterlife."

The house phone rang, and the caller identification read Burnly. Burnly was a general contractor whom Gran hired to do maintenance on the property. Burnly asked for Callie. A tree had fallen on private property. The family wouldn't be able to pay until insurance processed the claims. Burnly agreed to remove the tree, put a temporary patch on the roof, and take payment after the insurance check cleared. The hiccup was they needed to borrow BE's tree removal equipment. Callie told Burnly to text her the address, and she'd bring the equipment.

When Callie hung up the phone, Rorke put his plate in the sink. "I suppose that you will take the equipment and stay. If you want, I'll tag along and do what I can to help."

Callie stalled on an answer. "I keep telling Gran to have her hearing checked. She turns the volume to the highest setting, which hurts my ears. I hold the receiver away, and everyone hears the conversation. Do you have experience with tree removal?"

"Spent two summers as a logger. My labor costs dinner with more pie."

"Fine. Wear clothes that you don't mind getting dirty or torn. I have safety gear and padding."

Callie went to change, took a phone from her nightstand, and dialed Solomon's direct number. "Rorke's here. How much of my life did you share?"

"I provided details about Nigel's auto accident and investigation. Time for secrets is over, and I trust the man. That should be good enough for you. I have told Rosa what I found on the background check as well."

Callie felt her face heat with anger and embarrassment. "Geez. Gran did a great job of playing clueless if she had prior information about Rorke. Do you have to do an extensive and intrusive inspection of every person that I meet?"

Solomon did not react to the sarcasm. "Yes. I like Rorke better than Beau. Thank you for telling me about the reasons for going out to dinner ahead of time."

Callie snorted. "I didn't seem to have a choice. You feel obligated because of a promise to my father. I can manage my life without an overbearing, bossy dictator's help. I wish you had a project, other than me. You tend to smother from the shadows."

Solomon made a sound that Callie found disturbing. She didn't think that she had ever heard the man laugh. The noise of his strange chortle lingered in the air as she disconnected.

The young woman looked at herself in the mirror and felt the weight of the world pressing down on her. Solomon had no idea that trying to help could be her undoing. The adage about one seed or grain of sand tipping the balanced scale one way or the other popped into her mind. That tiny, solitary number. One!

One night changed the course of a thirteen-year-old's life. One revelation from a father to a daughter. One dying to protect his family and friends. A child promised to live bound her to a responsibility where lives were the price of failing. One year turned into ten years of overseeing her father's task to keep everyone safe. Every moment revolved around balancing the scales from the shadows. The shadows where she lived were even darker than the places that Solomon lurked. She was tired, weary, and craved normal. Gray streaked her sandy blond hair. Green eyes rimmed with black circles from lack of sleep. Worry lines permanently creased her forehead.

Callie ran her fingers over her father's picture and spoke as if he were standing beside her. "Life is spinning out of control. Solomon promised to look out for me, but he is too dedicated. I pray that he doesn't get us killed.

"The individual lives of your old friends, my friends, and our family are about to become tangled into a messy, complicated ball. Keep praying and watching over us. I'll try to find a method to make sure the enemy doesn't start cutting our lives into tiny bits of nothing."

Chapter

Callie parked along the curb and checked out the situation. A tree had fallen against the outer wall and sliced off a corner of the roof. Most of the massive trunk rested on the roof support.

"Would you hand me the camera that's at your feet?"

Rorke reached down and passed over the camera, and Callie said, "Cleanup will take most of the day. Let me see where the family is in the process. I am hoping the insurance representative has already been here. Are you sure about staying after seeing the mess?"

Rorke's eyes glittered at the opportunity of helping, as well as tackling a challenge. Callie found the owners of the house looking bewildered. She introduced herself and took charge. After looking over the paperwork from their insurance company and taking pictures, she handed out hard hats, eye protection goggles, and breathing masks. The tree was anchored and not moving so the area was safe.

The family had not been home when the tree fell. Damage appeared to be confined to a corner bedroom, outer wall, and a part of the roof. A pipe in the attic had broken when the tree came down. Water had soaked most of the belongings in the room, but someone had turned the water off.

The damaged room belonged to Lilac. The girl was outside, where they were collecting items to sort. When Lilac's bedding came to the driveway, the girl began to cry, seeing her special bedtime friends soaking wet and bedraggled. Callie reassured the child that her stuffed animals would be fine with a good bath and trip through the dryer. She asked to take the pony and bird home with her. Callie would return the next morning as good as new, and Lilac agreed.

Callie gave Lilac a sleeping bag, but the girl was hesitant. She admitted to wetting the bed and was afraid of an accident in the middle of the night.

Callie knelt and looked Lilac in the face. "Lilac is a strong name. Our state, Idaho, thought Syringa was an important flower. The Syringa, a Lilac, is the state flower. You are strong and important too. My grandmother says that a washing machine is one of the most magnificent inventions in the world. The appliance washes out dirt, stains, and accidents without much fuss. Our machines are sleeping bag size. A friend of mine lets me buy sleeping bags for five dollars. Contractor bags will protect the carpet, floor, or bed, and they cost about 27 cents. Between the sleeping bag and trash bag, I think my budget will be all right."

Callie went to the truck and took a plastic trash bag from a box in the back. A cut down the side seam and the bag was large enough to spread out under the makeshift bed. Then, she took her phone and texted Burnly, who had only seen the outside. His crew would need a couple of plywood sheets, materials to shore the inner wall, and plastic sheeting. Hopefully, the plastic would help keep the water damage from spreading through the walls or floor.

Rorke approached Callie to find out how volunteers could help.

Callie explained. "Anyone who wants to help should wear clothes that cover their arms and legs. There are gloves on the tailgate. We'll need to haul as much as possible to the street for the city to collect. I'll go ahead and start on the roof without Burnly. Liability covers me with the chain saw, but no one else."

"Do you have an extra chain saw? Good Samaritan laws protect me today." Callie nodded her permission.

"There are spikes for the shoes in the back of the truck."

Two hours later, Rorke took a sip of water and felt arm muscles he hadn't used in a while protesting, but the tree was void of branches.

Callie noticed him sweating and offered him a bottle of water. "Drink and take a break. We finished the hard part."

Rorke sat a moment and watched Callie adjust the safety strap before beginning to cut v shapes in the top of the trunk. The two stopped when the tree was clear of the house. Callie told Rorke that the rest could wait until the insurance was processed. Another work truck pulled up with a middle-aged man driving.

Callie was putting away gear and greeted the newcomer. "Hey Burnly!"

"Hey, girl. We would have been here earlier, but there was an emergency call about busted pipes. The couple had no idea how to turn off the water to the house or at the street. How's Rosa?"

"Gran's fine. Burnly, meet Rorke. Burnly contracts with Gran to repair, paint, and do general maintenance on the property. I haven't caught them smooching yet, but my guess is they've been a couple for a while."

"Don't be cheeky, young lady. Our relationship is none of your concern. Are you all right with the Beau situation?"

"Yes."

Burnly studied Rorke and asked, "What brings you to town?"

"Teaching literacy theory at the university."

Burnly gave Rorke a quizzical look.

Rorke grinned. "Means my classes will consist of any subject the English department wants to assign me."

A truck with four workers pulled alongside the curb, and Callie asked, "Do you have enough to cover everyone's wages today? The renters in each unit have paid rent for the last three months, and everyone is current on payments."

"We are covered financially through the winter. Finished and received payment for major work at two companies. You look tired. Go home, clean up, and have a good night's sleep."

Callie and Rorke went home to let Burnly's construction crew begin securing the walls and roof.

Gran was working in her office. Callie knocked on the open door. "I'm home. My plan is a shower and bed unless you need anything."

Rosa told Callie to go to bed. Gran studied the documents on the desk and thought. Rosa knew Solomon did not trust many people, and he vouched for Rorke. Callie and Rorke had dropped everything to help another in need. It didn't matter that they had things going on in their lives.

Callie displayed a spark of emotion that her grandmother delighted in seeing. The girl had built high walls around her heart, and she liked Rorke. Her granddaughter might lower her emotional defenses. Callie had never been in love with Beau, even though they went on a couple of dates. Rosa never received the full story about Beau. Her granddaughter wouldn't share or volunteer information until she was ready to talk.

Gran saw Lilac's bird and pony beside Callie's backpack. Once upon a time, children came to the family due to various circumstances. Each child had or found special items to cherish as their own. Gran was a master at repairing or mending old, torn, beloved friends. Three hours later, the pony and bird were clean, fluffed, and ready to be snuggled.

The following morning, Callie found Rorke at the kitchen table. He finished the food, thanked Rosa, and went on to the university.

Callie poured a glass of juice. "This was going to be a catch-up week before classes started, but my schedule may change. Dr. Wither called me last night and asked me to be at orientation."

"Why?"

"You are aware that I've been a graduate assistant for the last couple of years. I defended the thesis for my master's degree last spring with three classes left. Last fall, Dr. Wither asked me to teach a general botany class. The teacher quit the day classes started, and I became the instructor for 300 students. Overseeing BE takes time. This semester, I

13

am taking my last courses, supervising four work-study students, and instructing. Rorke might be causing me additional work."

Gran tilted her head and asked, "How do you know the culprit is Rorke?"

"Gossip runs like wildfire on campus. Rorke sent an email to the head of the English department. He wants to give paper tests and take roll manually instead of using the university system. He'll have to juggle a compromise. I incorporate the old and new system, which fulfills the squares for everyone. Dr. Lite, Dean of English, contacted Dr. Wither, my department head. They think I might be a good mentor."

"Mija, I sense that you are angry toward Rorke."

"I am tired and annoyed at men in general."

Gran's eyes changed to concern. "Are the nightmares back?"

"Yes, and don't worry. The reason is the same every year. The anniversary of dad's accident is coming up. Gran, you put your life on hold to take care of me when Dad died. Do you regret the decision to take care of me?"

Gran put plates in the dishwasher. "No. I would make the same choice. I've had a good life and known real love. The world is not fair, and people are people. No matter what happened in the past, we had our blessings. One is you. Would you like to talk about the real reason you went out with Beau?"

Callie played with her fork and sighed. "No, but I do have a concern. There will be a huge transition with me turning twenty-four and taking over full responsibility of BE. Dusty usually shows up around my birthday, which is not long after the anniversary of dad's death. My concern is that she may try to pressure you. Dusty looks at life differently. During our last conversation, she thinks that the inheritance is taking over BE, the rentals, and putting the house in my name. The woman refuses to listen to my explanation."

"Your father made arrangements for the future and put a management team together. If anything happens to me, you may remain in the house upon my demise."

Callie looked horrified. "Thank you, but I will be fine without the house."

Gran explained the rest of the concern. "Yes, but the renters will need your presence and reassurance. Mr. Pica is one tenant who could end up on the street instead of a new place. The man was one of the first tenants and is still renting. Have you decided on what to do about continuing school to earn a doctorate?"

14

Callie made a face of disgust at Gran. "No, and I see you trying to hide a sly smile. Please don't badger me about having a party for finishing my master's degree."

Gran's grin turned into a sigh. "One day, you have to make peace with life and celebrate milestones in life."

"Are we back to discussing Beau?"

Gran peered intently at her granddaughter. "No, but what changed your mind about going out with Beau?"

"Promise not to judge or be upset."

"No."

Callie issued an exaggerated moan. "I deserved that. The answer was Granddad. I'd been back for two years working at the university with the agriculture department. One night after sitting at the bar and drinking water most of the night, I came home and hung up my keys next to the tractor set.

"When I was little, Dad would help you bring Granddad into the house on Wednesday. Granddad went to the bar while you were at bible study. One morning, I asked Granddad why he went drinking, and he laughed."

Callie looked up to see her Grandmother tearing up, but she waved to keep going.

"Grandad informed me that his life and family were good. He married for love and didn't settle for the first woman who came along. Love meant compromise, and he would never risk losing a wonderful thing. Drinking was his one vice. He wasn't lying, cheating with women, or stealing mortgage or food money to drink liquor. Granddad told me that he worked hard, provided for his family with a minimum of debt, and raised six fine children. A couple of times, he thought he might go to jail for murdering one. Dad had come in, and Granddad stared hard at him. Guess there were stories about Dad's shenanigans growing up. I didn't mean to make you cry."

Gran dabbed at her eyes under her glasses. "I have no delusions about your granddad. He was a good man. Never violent or mean. He had good reasons for the liquor, and drinking was his way of coping with life."

Callie diverted the subject of the conversation a second time. "Did my Dad ever date anyone after I was born?"

"Nigel was never one to talk about or show his feelings. We adopted him at the age of ten, and we never knew anything about his family or background. Nigel agreed to use whatever name we chose. The boy excelled in science and plants. College was a blessing on so many levels.

15

Nigel was able to find a path for himself. One night he showed up on the doorstep. The boy was a mess and asking for help. He had a baby girl and had no idea what to do. An announcement of having a wife, now departed, and a baby was a huge shock. Nigel uttered the only words I ever heard about his past. He swore that his child was never to be raised by strangers if he died. We took you out of the car, and Nigel slept until Sunday."

Callie finished her last bite of food. "Thank you for sharing."

"Thank you for having the self-worth to tell Beau goodbye. There are some nice gentlemen at church I could call."

Callie huffed. "Please don't. My heart isn't broken or crushed. Solomon informed me about your conversation regarding my life. The two of you need to stop meddling."

Chapter

The doorbell rang without the security chimes sounding. Gran turned off the security system again. Callie sighed and checked the camera before going to the front. Rorke stood at the door.

Callie opened the door and asked, "Did you become lost?"

"No. Dean of English, Dr. Lite, called. He and Dr. Wither are meeting us here. Dr. Lite refused to explain the conference's reason for the conference, but he sounded too gleeful for a Monday. The two will arrive in an hour."

Callie glanced at her watch. "Gran is in the kitchen. Would you let her know? I need a quick shower."

Callie showered, dressed in a pants suit, and did her makeup. She decided to forego the jeans and shirt for an official meeting. Callie went down the hall toward the kitchen and heard Dr. Wither's voice come from the kitchen. The conversation stopped her from stepping in.

Dr. Wither's asked, "Ma'am, would you feel better leaving if we promised to keep an eye on Callie? Take the offer and mend the fences before the lady dies. You'll return in time for Callie's birthday."

Callie wondered what lady? What trip?

Gran answered, "My concern is Callie and the anniversary of Nigel's death. She's not sleeping. Something other than BE and schoolwork is worrying her."

The next part of the conversation threw Callie's thinking processes. "Rosa, Dr. Lite is talking to Mr. Asher outside. I normally see you when the family is present, and we have a few minutes alone. I want to talk about Nigel but rather not let Callie know that I am discussing her father."

"Go ahead."

"The subject has never come up, and Nigel was like a brother to me. His death was difficult. I never liked the fact that it was ruled as a hit and run accident. The investigators looked into Nigel's life to see if someone had a problem with him. His childhood came up during the investigation, but no one could answer the questions. Callie officially takes over BE next month. Is there anything in Nigel's past that could cause problems for Callie taking over the business?"

Callie felt ill. Why did Dr. Wither know so much about the accident?

Gran had the same thought. "How do you know?"

"The authorities questioned anyone with a connection to Nigel. The problem was Nigel's personality. He never shared much, even with the

17

people closest to him. As far as I knew, Nigel didn't speak about his life before the adoption. What do you know?"

Callie could hear her grandmother stop washing pans and think before answering. "The two boys didn't have any known family, and very few details were available. The boys refused to tell the authorities their names, and they didn't have birth certificates or paperwork. We would have taken both boys, but Nigel's brother ran away before we arrived. The authorities helped us with a birth certificate, and Nigel told us to pick a name. He agreed to take my husband's first and surname with junior for adoption. I think Nigel's brother appeared every so often to check on him."

"Why?"

"Nigel was a handful, but he worked hard and followed most of the rules. We watched him sneak out to the woods every so often with food that he'd saved from meals. My husband and I never confronted the boy because he never took anything but food and returned before morning. I'd always make easy travel dishes and extra when I saw the boy squirreling food away. If you discover additional information, let me know. I'll try to help."

Callie knew the words about helping meant Rosa finished discussing the topic.

Callie entered and asked, "What is going on?"

Gran answered to divert the topic from Nigel. "My mother is dying, and she wants to mend fences before her death. The family has arranged for me to come home. The doctors gave her about four weeks, and she wants me to visit."

"I. Whoa. Back up. Your mother?"

"My parents kicked me out for marrying outside the Hispanic community and never spoke to me again."

Callie asked, "How did they find you?"

"My sister and I continued to correspond."

"Do you want me to go with you? I've defended my thesis. Dr. Wither could find someone to teach my classes."

Gran looked sideways at Callie. "Mija, if I went, you would have to stay and manage the place as well as work. Dusty may show up before your birthday looking for money."

"Don't worry. I learned to keep my mouth closed and money out of reach. Where is the original Casa?"

"One of only about four Spanish words you can say, but the answer is Vermont. Is that your only question?"

"No, and I know more than four Spanish words. You'd wash my mouth out with vinegar if I blurted them. If you want to take the trip, we have support."

"I'll think about the trip." Gran was closing the subject with those words.

Callie knew that answer but asked, "Where are Dr. Lite and Rorke?"

Gran replied while picking up her coffee cup to leave. "Outside talking about literature. I'll let them know you are ready."

Callie blocked the door. "No. Stay."

"Don't sass me. I am not a puppy."

"Gran, whatever is happening, you should hear."

Rorke and Dr. Lite entered the kitchen with tumblers of coffee. Gran had already offered the group something to drink, so Callie remained silent.

After introductions, Dr. Lite explained the nature of the meeting. "Plants have been used for healing and have been written about in literature for centuries. Idaho's branch offices of the Drug Enforcement Agency, Federal Drug Administration, Department of Agriculture, and an independent homeopathic company want to put together a book of Idaho plants used for medicinal or therapeutic purposes. When I say the Department of Agriculture, we are specifically referring to the Forestry Service. The state level will take the lead on the project because the focus will be on the state. Part of the concise, understandable description is to include the plant's use in literature. The grant stipulates that the work is to be done by graduates working toward advanced degrees. Students will author the book, and any advisers will be named as editors. The two of you have been chosen to be the leads on the project."

Gran's news unsettled Callie's stomach. Now, she felt the nervous feeling turn to knots. A part of her hoped that her blinking and breathing remained even. The entire scope of the unexpected project left her completely unbalanced.

Callie asked, "Not to play devil's advocate, but what about liability? Say a family buys a plant, but the blooms are poisonous. A child eats the flower because it's colorful or pretty. Reflect on Beethoven, the musical composer. He may have consumed too much Willow Bark, which damaged his liver and led to his death."

Dr. Wither expounded. "Supposition. Willow Bark has been used for aches, pain, and fever, but aspirin is derived from a different plant. The process of production creates less Salicylic acid and gastric issues."

Callie grinned. "Oops! I forgot your doctorate was on medicinal plants."

Dr. Wither glanced at Dr. Lite who nodded to go ahead and share.

Dr. Wither imparted the rest of good news. "The program will pay for tuition, books, fees, and a living wage. If our university doesn't offer the doctoral or master's class, we will coordinate with another university."

Rorke added. "Not to be picky, but my position is a little unorthodox. I have an undergraduate degree in literature, but my master's degree is geography. The university hired me on the condition that I work toward a master's in literature. I am on a waiting list for the three recommended classes."

Lite smiled. "We will make sure the paperwork is above board. There is one small detail. Due to today's political climate and liability, you must pass a comprehensive background check. The preliminary was completed through the university."

Callie chuckled drily. "That knocks me out, but there are students who would be great for the program."

Gran became annoyed at Callie's attitude, and her tone showed. "Why? You've never been arrested."

"A clearance implies that you are not a security threat."

Rorke developed a slight pained look and diverted the conversation to his concern. "Ah, that implies the process started weeks ago. I wasn't offered the teaching position until about ten days ago. My previous job required two weeks' notice but allowed me to leave early for orientation. Is there a backup plan if we don't qualify for the program?"

Dr. Lite leaned back in his chair with a twinkle in his eye. "Are you referring to the juvenile record?"

Rorke returned without a defensive tone, but the sarcasm was distinctive. "Thank you for bringing up the subject in the presence of my new landlord."

"Relax, young man. We would not bring up the topic unless we had facts and permission to proceed."

Gran tried to provide reassurance. "I doubt what happened is a shocker. We fostered some children but could only adopt those classified as difficult. Times have changed, but children still test the boundaries. Callie's rebellion is nonexistent compared to her father, aunts, and uncles. My husband had to collect one son from the drunk tank, and he was thirteen years old."

Callie asked, "Which uncle?"

Gran ignored the question and locked her eyes with Rorke as she spoke. "Don't worry. I am sure that the story isn't worse than any other I have already heard."

20

Rorke looked down at his hands and tried to find the words. "My parents dropped me off at school one day and disappeared. I went through the foster care system and started working at fifteen. I turned eighteen with a few months of high school left. A local college had accepted me, but my foster family didn't have the resources to let me stay. I built a treehouse on public land and lived there until the end of summer. Local authorities found me. Charges ranged from trespassing to building without a permit. I ended up in juvenile court even though I was eighteen."

Callie asked curiously, "What was the outcome?"

"All charges were dropped after probation, and I transferred schools as soon as I could."

Gran said, "Rorke, don't worry about a place to stay. You found a way to solve the problem without hurting anyone. The system has changed over the years, but age is still one of the problems facing families and children in the system. Any assistance stops at the age of eighteen because the person is considered a legal adult. Everything from medical expenses to food to housing is affected. Medical is available but expensive."

Callie looked at her grandmother with interest. "How do you know?"

"When you left for college, I joined a support group. Talk to families on the computer, phone, and church. I'm still certified for foster care, but I haven't taken in children since you returned. My role is more to advise or offer an ear to listen."

Dr. Wither stood up. "Callie, don't worry about attending orientation since we've met about the program. I have to go and prepare for today's meetings. Rorke, I'll probably see you later."

Dr. Lite left as well, and Callie peered at her grandmother. "I've been back from college for two years, and you never told me about the support group."

"None of your business, Mija."

Rorke asked, "What are you calling Callie?"

"The word means daughter in Spanish. If I say Mijo, that is the word for son. If I consider the trip, would you be comfortable supervising the rentals, running the business, and starting this book project?"

"Yes. Dad might disapprove of me living alone with single men on the property, but he was rather protective. As a teen, a strict and protective father was unfair, stupid, and dumb. I'm still upset that I never could wear a bikini to the pool, but time, age, and maturity helped me understand. No matter what I said or did, I never questioned that he loved his family. Besides, I'm sure that Solomon will be his normal,

21

irritating guardian self. He loves to keep track of my every move and lurk in the shadows."

Tears rolled down Gran's face, and Callie hugged her.

Rorke looked a little pale and turned to Callie, who didn't look much better than he felt. "Am I paranoid, or were we just steamrolled into a life-altering project and additional schoolwork?"

"Manipulated and conned are better descriptions."

Rorke looked at his watch. "I have to leave to attend orientation. If there is anything I can do, let me know."

Callie mentally processed the two conversations until her grandmother gathered herself.

When Gran's tears stopped, Callie asked, "When is the last time you saw your sister?"

Surprised at the change in conversation, Gran answered, "The day I left. Before cell phones, we wrote letters. Today, computers and cellular phones make communication easy. We talk daily or every few days."

Curious about her grandmother's family, Callie asked, "What is her name?"

"Consuela."

Callie didn't press her grandmother on staying or going. "Dr. Wither told me that I was off the hook for orientation. I owe Rorke dinner for helping with the tree. Want to go to a sit-down eating establishment that has a menu?"

"What are we celebrating?"

Callie sent Gran a sly look. "Nothing in particular. I don't feel like leftovers or fast food. Mr. Burnly is welcome to join us."

"I'll think about it."

Callie hugged her grandmother and went to work at the BE. She was glad for uninterrupted time to work in her beloved greenhouse.

Chapter

Rorke finished orientation, and he drove Callie and Rosa to the restaurant. A server came over to ask about drinks, and they requested tea. When the tea arrived, the waiter asked if the three were ready to place their order.

After ordering, the waiter commented. "A young couple taking an older person of a different race to dinner is wonderful."

Rorke sat stunned at the words, and his face began to turn red. Callie smiled benevolently, and Gran placed a hand on Rorke's arm with a wink.

When the waiter disappeared, Gran smiled. "Don't mind the clueless comments. I've seen the world change drastically in my lifetime, but religion and race are issues that create emotional responses instead of respect and understanding."

Rorke asked, "Are past experiences the reason for the renter's clauses?"

"Nigel is the one who set up and built the properties. He researched, planned, filed the permits, and made sure everything was built and ran smoothly. I only have to maintain or upkeep what he started."

Callie peeked sideways at her grandmother. "Would you tell us about your family and the trip?"

"Why the interest in my past?" Gran looked uncomfortable for the first time.

Callie was trying to gain any information about her grandmother. "Love. Think of the lives touched by past decisions. The fact you and Grandad ran away and married brings us here today. Granddad made sure to let us know that he did not regret his choice. The two of you survived and flourished. Neither of you gave up. You remained together, and love endured.

"We'll be fine, and you may phone every day. Visit and bring me back lots of pictures with stories, along with a family tree."

Gran smiled with reflection. "I have not heard anyone utter a picture request in years. I have no idea who started the tradition, but you took the matter so seriously. Every picture had to have a report."

Rorke entered the conversation again. "Where does your family live?"

"Vermont."

Rorke didn't hide his surprise. "Idaho is a long way from Vermont."

"Where we live, it's warmer too. My husband and I budgeted our money. Took the train as far as we could and bought a farm."

After dinner, Callie was tired and went to bed. The nightmares started, and she woke up tangled in the sheets. Sweat soaked the bed. Waking fully before trying to move, she tried to be as quiet as possible. Gran needed her sleep.

Callie continued to have nightmares ten years after the death of her father. The week of the anniversary was the worst. Quickly, she put on a new set of sheets and padded down the hall to throw the sweat-soaked linens in the wash.

Gran's voice sounded from the kitchen, and she spoke in hushed tones. "Callie's independent, stubborn, but insulated. College helped her grow, but her lack of exposure to normal life concerns me. Right or wrong, Nigel protected and sheltered her beyond what is considered normal. We guessed that his childhood played a part in his strict rules."

Rorke's voice came from the vicinity of the table. "What was Nigel protecting her from?"

"No clue. Nigel was closed about his past and personal life. I never understood his relationships, especially with Dusty. Nigel refused to share his problems. I am trusting you with one of the most precious items in my life. Hurt my granddaughter, and there will be nowhere to hide from my wrath."

"I will do my best, but don't underestimate Callie."

Callie decided to start the wash in the morning and went back to bed. Her thoughts would not settle. Dr. Wither and Gran believed her father's accident was intentional.

The young woman tried to sleep but couldn't. She tried to relax by listing flowers. A trick that she'd devised in place of counting sheep. Finally, she dozed.

***

Dragging herself into the kitchen, Callie found that Gran invited Rorke to breakfast.

Callie declined the eggs and fixed a bowl of oatmeal. "Gran, should we give Rorke the Ring of Protection?"

Gran looked confused and then smiled. "Ask Rorke."

Rorke glanced up from the newspaper, "Ah, I don't know whether to ask when two women are smiling at me like cats rolling in catnip."

Gran explained. "Nigel was a single gentleman with a young daughter. He wore a wedding band when teaching or making deliveries to keep the average student from pursuing more than an academic relationship."

"Average?"

"A few looked at a relationship with a married person as safe or even a challenge. Could the married be seduced into breaking their vows and start an affair? Every so often, a student tried to exchange sex for a better grade. Callie didn't want her father lying, so she made me take her shopping for a protection ring. The ring symbolized the promise to the family and not a marital union."

Callie opened a box, took out a silver ring on a chain, and glanced at a sheet of stationery folded inside. "He wrote the words of the promise out and laminated the paper at some point. I am not sure that the ring would fit, but you could wear the jewelry on a necklace."

Rorke asked, "How do you protect yourself from unwanted attention?"

"I lay out the rules and don't bend when the subject is personal space or professionalism. A few disgruntled people have called me cold, distant, and paranoid. I've also heard ice queen and prickly."

The doorbell rang, and Callie needed to start double-checking that Gran set the security system. The chimes announced a visitor instead of the alarms.

Dr. Wither entered, laid thick folders on the counter, and poured himself a cup of coffee. "I stopped to drop off paperwork."

The box on the counter caught his attention, and Wither asked, "Is that Nigel's protection ring?"

Gran asked, "Should I be ready to hear scandalous gossip?"

"No, ma'am. We were having dinner, and Nigel was wearing the band. He forgot to take the ring off and explained his promise. We were best friends and could bare our souls without worry. We called each other for advice or reassurance. We didn't feel so alone dealing with unfamiliar issues. His stories about Callie were a little more entertaining than those about my children. My wife laughed about a bastardess for years."

Gran chuckled delightedly. "I'd forgotten about that word."

Callic crossed her arms and pretended to pout. "I don't think the incident was funny. The teacher made me take a makeup test during recess."

Gran shared with Rorke. "The school called me because Nigel was at work and unreachable. One of the boys in Callie's second-grade class called her a bastard. Callie explained in a matter-of-fact voice that males without a father were named such. She was a girl without a mother, which made her a bastardess. Luckily, I was able to speak to Nigel before dropping Callie at the flower shop. Callie was indignant about missing her test and told her father to call the school immediately. He had to talk to the administration before Callie could return."

Wither laughed. "Nigel phoned me after hanging up with Rosa. Callie had never been a problem student, and she didn't instigate the argument. His first reaction was to beat up the boy's parents. He had no idea how to proceed or what to say."

Rorke commented. "Not to cross swords, but the correct term is bastard for male or female."

Wither glanced at his watch and finished the coffee. "I have to go to work. Meetings start soon." He tapped the folders. "Don't wait until Thursday night because the application is rather long."

After Wither disappeared, Gran sat down and spoke to the couple. "The plane ticket to Vermont is for this evening. It won't leave me much time to pack or prepare."

Callie grasped her grandmother's hand. "What do you need?"

Gran peered intently at her granddaughter. "I am not sure. My biggest concern about taking a trip is leaving you. Sunday is the anniversary of Nigel's death, and your birthday is not far behind."

"I'll stick to my yearly routine and be fine. Take flowers to church and go out to the cabin for the day."

Callie's calm demeanor didn't fool her grandmother, and Gran warned. "Stay out of trouble and keep the place in one piece until I return."

Callie ignored the tone and asked, "Do you want me to call Auntie and Uncles?"

"No. I'll inform the family of the situation."

"Be ready to answer lots of questions. Think about having Uncle Mer loop everyone, including me, together for a conference call."

Rorke left for the second day of orientation, and Callie headed to the university as well. A friend, Ms. Pickle, was picking Callie up and dropping her off at the campus. The two ladies carpooled when possible so that they could visit. Today was a day where they could ride together. Her parking pass had to be renewed for the upcoming year. Callie didn't have enough in the checking account to pay for the parking fees until payday.

Pickle dropped her off at the edge of the campus, and Callie walked to the university greenhouse. The twenty-minute stroll allowed her a chance to think.

A part of her was happy to continue pursuing an advanced degree because she loved her work at the campus. Discovering that research and teaching were a part of her nature didn't surprise anyone. Nigel centered on horticulture or the art and cultivation of plants. He loved the science of plants and passed along the passion. Her earliest memories were listening as he shared every piece of knowledge possible.

Callie's focus in Botany centered on a plant's anatomy, classification, and place in the overall picture of life. Her thesis was on natural water filtration and a plant's role in the process. The research centered on using natural flora to clean impurities from the water: Iris, Cabomba, Water Lilies, and Hornwort. She'd finished and defended her thesis but needed to complete the last elective classes required for the degree.

Something bothered her about the book project, but she wasn't sure the reason for the concern. Time would tell, and she hoped that Dr. Wither would share the paperwork and contracts. Paranoia made her want to check the documents with various lawyers. Her first thought was a lawyer named Ms. Nod. She was a trusted confidant and handled her father's estate. The woman's specialty was family and inheritance law. Ms. Nod could explain or translate the legal terms in the paperwork, and she never charged Gran or Callie the full amount for legal fees.

Callie had received permission to build a small workplace in the university greenhouse. The glass enclosure felt cozy and warm. When she finished at the university, the office could be dismantled in less than an hour. A separate building housed the research labs.

Inside her office, Callie filled in most of the application forms and locked the folder in the desk. Then she made her way to the administration building and Wither's office.

Wither was turning on his computer when Callie knocked, and he invited her inside. "Would you like to close the door?"

"Same answer as always. No. If anyone wishes to join the conversation, come in. I gather that you didn't want to share the proposal until it was rejected or accepted. I have a feeling that important details aren't being shared?"

"We haven't ironed out specifics, so please, don't share yet."

Callie promised not to betray the confidence.

Wither explained. "I have faith in your abilities. You will be teaching an introduction to plant biology. The class will include Rorke. Conversely, you are taking his Intro to English Literature, which is comprised mostly of visiting students. The class will count as an elective, and you'll be able to take the second elective as an independent study. You'll graduate on time."

Callie frowned and shared a part of her concern. "Long term projects with large amounts of human interaction are challenging for me. My favorite activity is to dole out assignments and supervise. What sort of group enrolls students to take a random class about plants?"

"Ask the representatives who will be here on Saturday. My excitement about the project led me to devise a list of 500 plants. We'll narrow the list later."

"I haven't accepted nor been cleared to participate."

Wither tried another tactic. "What would be a good bribe?"

Callie made an exaggerated disapproval face with her eyes rolling. "Ah, I don't do bribes, but the offer tells me how much the project means to you. May I read the proposal and acceptance?"

"Have you made an appointment with Ms. Nod to look at the materials?"

The young woman's face went from eye-rolling to surprise. "Should I be concerned that you know so much about me?"

Wither forwarded Callie several emails with documents in response to her request. "My association with Nigel started before you were born, and we have weathered many life events together. One is that each of our wives died well before we were ready."

Wither leaned forward in his chair and drummed his fingers on the desk. The young woman peered closely at her mentor, colleague, and friend. Wither was trying to convey a message. The man was tapping his fingers on a piece of paper. Looking at the letters, Callie noticed his hand moved around to spell the word who. Her father and his friends used a code that they had developed to communicate silently, and she had learned the system over time.

Time to play twenty questions, and Callie asked, "Subject switch. Who exactly proposed the book project?"

"We were approached by a third party. The estimated donation to the university will be about a million and a half dollars."

"No wonder Dr. Lite was so happy."

Dr. Wither smiled and warned her to be careful with whom she shared such an opinion. "We are all delighted. Be aware, Dr. Lite is active in politics around the state."

"How does Rorke fit into the equation?"

"No idea. Your colleague did have the best scores on the state geography and literature exams."

Callie pinched her nose. "Could the entire project be a fishing expedition? Could we be in someone's Venus Flytrap?"

"I have been around long enough not to discount anything. Coincidences are adding up, which bothers me. If you need anything or have any concerns, call me."

Chapter

Callie went back to her desk and worked on the applications. After finishing most of the forms, she took her badges and headed to the laboratory building. She checked in at the security desk.

Hal, the head of security, smiled as she signed into the building. Callie's demeanor was more relaxed and open with Hal. The gentleman was head of security and not her supervisor or teacher. They had known each other for a long time, and she trusted Hal.

"Hey, Ice Queen. Congrats."

"Is everyone else aware of the program?"

"Probably. Government agents came to visit for security upgrades. Updates will occur over the weekend, and the workers are not to interfere with ongoing routines."

"Seems to be a lot of work for one project on plants. It's not like we're working with dangerous specimens."

Hal smiled and handed Callie a set of forms. "These have to be filled out by Monday. Do you want to start and tell me about Mr. Dew? We hear you kicked Beau to the curb. Are you ready to let my wife set you up on a date?"

"Geez, word travels fast. My hands are full dealing with other issues. We found out that my grandmother has family in Vermont. They threw her out for marrying my grandfather, and she never told us. Her mom is dying and wants to make peace."

Hal looked slightly surprised, but the practical man asked, "If you are staying alone, are you carrying a weapon?"

"Yes, sir, but not on university property. Elsewhere, yes."

"Seriously, have you practiced lately?"

Callie admitted, "No. Haven't had time."

The former policeman announced with a no-nonsense tone, "Tomorrow is Wednesday and my day for lunch at the range. Dr. Wither and I usually meet to practice, and he stays to teach the safety class. Plan to accompany me. I don't want my favorite plant lady to end up as worm food."

Callie always had a hard time remembering that Wither's hobby was riflery. The man had won many shooting contests, taught gun safety, and sponsored the local trap team.

Callie didn't provide a firm answer. "I'll have to let you know later because I don't have my schedule. Everyone is supposed to lock their phones in a locker at the security desk, but could you keep mine handy?

Gran may call with details on her trip, and Uncle Mer may try to loop everyone in on a conference call."

"Sure. I have the new yearly teaching assistant's rules. I'll put the papers in the locker. Remember to sign and return the top copy. You tossed dirt on the documents last year and tried to clean off smudges. Ink mixed with dirt does not easily scan into the computer."

Callie spent the next few hours repotting plants, watering, and fertilizing. The phone on the desk rang, and Callie answered. Hal informed her that Rosa called Callie's cell. Removing her gardening gloves, Callie walked down to the front desk where Hal was chatting with her grandmother.

Callie took the phone, and Gran asked, "Could you come home? Ms. Nod has legal documents for you to sign. If a water heater bursts or a fridge dies, you'll have to buy a replacement. Then, could you take me to the airport?"

"Sure. Um, have you spoken to the rest of the family?"

"Yes. Mer wants you to set up a new group on my text button."

Callie agreed but stayed silent about her grandmother's refusal to enter the modern age. Gran didn't like texting. A phone was for talking, and a computer was for email. Callie disconnected.

Hal offered. "My replacement is here for the next shift. I'll walk with you to the car."

"Thank you, but I'm good. I need to go to the greenhouse to collect my stuff."

Hal knew that she hadn't bought the parking tags yet because he supervised parking passes as part of his job. Hal had known Callie long enough to understand how she thought. She wouldn't admit to not driving to the school. Hal didn't mind dropping her off on his way home. Then, Hal watched Rorke entering the building and decided to manipulate the couple to spend time together. Callie didn't need to be alone, but Hal was wise enough not to say that aloud.

Hal nodded, and they shook hands. "Hey, Rorke. We're the last stop on the new instructors' list. We'll deal with logistics tomorrow. Do me a favor? Take Callie home and then drive the ladies to the airport."

Callie groused. "Great! Figures that you know about Rorke as well. Stay and do the paperwork. Gran has not been so far away from home and shouldn't travel by herself. She's staying a month, and I could take the rest of the week off. The map apps estimate that the round trip would take roughly four days. I could plan on five to take a day between arrival and departure."

The young woman was reluctant to let her grandmother travel away from home by herself. Rorke grinned at Callie's sudden reversal on encouraging her grandmother to visit Vermont.

Rorke commented. "A little separation anxiety is normal. Tagging along would not be healthy for you or Rosa. Rosa will be fine. She's independent, wise, and competent. Where did you park?"

"Ms. Pickle and I carpooled. She drove and dropped me off."

Hal saw Callie's jaw set with stubbornness and directed the couple to a golf cart. "We'll take the campus limo to Rorke's truck."

Callie's mind was elsewhere, and she remained silent while Hal and Rorke talked.

When they arrived at home, a stately and confident woman sat at the kitchen table with a printer, laptop, and several stacks of paper. The woman's black hair was pinned stylishly on top of her head. Brown eyes behind glasses watched Callie coming inside.

Callie plopped her purse on the counter. "Hello. Here is a quick introduction: Rorke, Nod. There is a whole series of documents that I need you to look at for me. I'll pay your normal rates to expedite the process. I would like to understand the contents before next week. We may have to talk on the phone."

Nod looked startled at the announcement. "Why?"

Rorke supplied an explanation. "Callie is experiencing apprehension about Rosa traveling. I'll go help Rosa with her bags."

Callie glared daggers at Rorke, but Ms. Nod distracted her. "Rosa told me about the offer at school. Sounds exciting."

Callie's attention turned to the project. "I think someone is taking advantage of the system. Two million dollars, at a minimum, is being sunk into the program. No one, especially the government, pours that sort of money into a book about plants."

Nod thought aloud. "The money could be used as a tax shelter. Someone could also be lobbying for something. Callie, what else is going on? You have on your serious, thinking face."

"What do you know about any secrets in my father's life?"

"Wow! That was a serious shift in subject matter. Callie, digging into Nigel's past is emotionally difficult."

"Why?"

Nod looked down at a piece of paper and paused before answering. "There are questions and answers that could be difficult. How about having lunch Friday afternoon? I should finish filing papers by noon, and I'll figure out what to say. Be very sure that you want to discuss the subject."

"Well, if I wasn't curious before, I am now. Thank you for helping at the last minute."

"A client canceled, and Rosa always has yummy treats with coffee. Your birthday is so near the anniversary of Nigel's accident. How are you doing?"

Callie smiled. "Has your staff started the betting pool for when Dusty will make her appearance?"

"Yes."

"May I place a wager?"

Nod eyed Callie with interest. "Yes. Judge Walrus is keeping the tally of wagers because he doesn't gamble."

Callie laughed. "I've never met Judge Walrus, but that name is too wonderful. People tease me about my name, but Walrus is worse."

"Judge Walrus has a great sense of humor, and he oversees family court matters. He knew your father and is aware of your name."

"Put me down for Monday. Give her a week to figure out that Gran is gone. She'll socialize with friends on the weekend, travel Monday morning, and begin a siege. I'd even bet that she doesn't remember that the anniversary of the accident is Sunday." Callie paused. "Nod, did my father ever fall in love after meeting Dusty?"

Nod answered. "No. My take on the relationship was an attraction of opposites. Dusty isn't mean or spiteful. She never learned the value of money. She's merely immature, self-absorbed, and cares too much about appearance."

"My father used to tell me roughly the same thing. A part of me never understood his attitude. No matter how the woman behaved, he was gracious, nice, and forgiving of her antics."

"Callie, sign the power of attorney. You are taking responsibility if anything needs repair or if anything happens. Rosa needs a physical presence and actual signature to deal with bills or take care of property damage while she is away."

Rorke rolled two bags through the door. "We are ready."

Callie asked, "Gran, are you sure about flying?"

"Yes. My nerves are a little fluttery, but Mer constantly flies for his job. My sister is meeting me, and I'll follow her to the hotel from the airport."

"There is a two-hour difference in time zones. When does the plane land?"

"Nine o'clock, which is seven here."

Rorke suggested. "I'll take you to the airport. If your granddaughter drives, she may detour to Vermont."

Nod smiled encouragement. "Rosa, returning home under the circumstances is not easy, and reconciling is a huge deal for both parties. Add me to your texting group. I'd like to know everything is all right."

Later, Callie sat in Rorke's vehicle with tears running down her face. She'd waited to cry until her grandmother waved from the gate side of security and disappeared.

When Rorke asked, "Where would you like to have dinner?"

"Anywhere is fine."

"You would change the offer if I decided a place where one had to dress in formal wear to eat lobster and steak."

Callie wiped her eyes and tried to grin at the attempt to make her smile. "Correct. Revised offer. Pick a normal place."

"Where is a restaurant with decent steak?"

"There is a place near the university. Food is good. I don't know about the service because my schedule is usually busy. I call, pickup, and eat later."

Callie's phone vibrated with a text, and she immediately clicked on the icon. "Gran's flight was called, and she's about to board." A weight lifted off her shoulders with the knowledge that her grandmother was all right.

Rorke found the eating establishment.

When the two were seated at a table, Callie asked, "What do you think about the book project?"

"No idea. I Haven't had much time to think about the overall picture."

"Dr. Wither shared that the university is clearing close to a million and a half dollars. Something bothers me about the whole deal, and the feeling has nothing to do with paranoia. Hal shared that the government is modifying the lab's security system. Who cares about security for a plant book?"

Rorke shrugged and didn't seem a bit worried. "Part of me stopped trying to understand bureaucracy. Someone could be concerned about the environment or drugs. Opioids and medical marijuana are hot topics these days."

"Yes, but we aren't working with pharmaceutical derivatives."

"You are overthinking things. Thank you for being polite but put your phone on the table. Stealing a look into your purse every two seconds is driving me crazy. It's nice that you care enough to worry, but a plane taking off and landing will not go faster looking at the screen."

Callie studied Rorke while she took a sip of her water. "Who worries about you?"

33

"Me? I have friends. They have families, which should be and are their first responsibility."

Callie's phone chimed with the song "Waltz of the Flowers," from Tchaikovsky's The Nutcracker symphony.

Switching off the alarm, Callie asked, "Would you mind dropping me off at the greenhouse after we eat? I have to reset the alarm and see what the raccoon dug up."

Rorke didn't mind, and their conversation shifted as the two spoke about hiking and camping. Rorke shared his aspirations of traveling to visit places written about in books. One area both spoke about visiting was the Mississippi River. Rorke talked about riverboats, and Callie shared her knowledge about the various environments and vegetation. When the dialogue ended, neither felt the need to fill the comfortable silence between them.

Chapter

Rorke had not been to the Botanic Enchantment and wasn't sure what to expect. Callie told him to ignore the GPS and provided directions. They'd take a right off the main road instead of left. They were coming to BE from the opposite end of their neighborhood.

The place was a genius of design. There was a flow to the landscape. The greenhouse didn't blare that it was a business built beside a residential neighborhood.

A passerby would see a beautifully maintained lawn with a cottage set way back from the road. Yet, there was an inviting, festive, eye-catching aura about BE. A picket fence painted barn red ran around the front and side yard. The driveway had an elaborate archway over the front entrance. Several signs announced that one was entering the Botanic Enchantment.

Turning into the driveway, Rorke found that the wide road split into three. A sign directed delivery trucks to the right. There was not a road sign to what was to the left. The winding road seemed to lead to the back of the property.

Callie saw Rorke looking at the gravel switch-back design to the left and explained. "We landscape the drive to show off various flower beds, garden ideas, or patio designs. When winter comes, we deck the place out with yard decorations to add color.

"I'm crossing my fingers that a deal with an outside company goes through. Nod and I have been working with a garden and outdoor supply company on a contract. The company would rent part of the front area and set up samples of their products. One of the sketches was a gazebo with flower boxes. They'd bring in customers to buy flowers, and I would not have to maintain the front as much. The company is in desperate need of space and not in a position to create or expand. The trade would be beneficial to everyone."

The driveway that went straight led to a parking lot, and he realized that the cottage was an optical illusion. They had come in from the south, and the front was a facade. The front door leading inside was on the east, or right side, of the building. A visitor would park and not have to walk around.

Rorke studied the building's pretend wall, and Callie provided a background for BE. "My father mowed lawns, landscaped for businesses, and did any type of yard work possible. He worked for flower shops and made deliveries. He bought the land while in college and before I was born. The maintenance shed was the first building. It's out beyond the tree line to the left. We store the large equipment like mowers, dirt haulers, and tree baskets.

"After Dad graduated and felt financially confident, he opened BE. He built the cottage as his business office. The land to the west was beginning to be developed and zoned as residential. The Mention family owns the land on the other side of the fence to the tree line. They incorporated the area as a farm to keep from dealing with zoning codes. Their house and barn are a couple of miles to the northeast, and we don't see one another much. If the family ever decides to move or sell, I have the first option of buying the land."

Rorke eyed her. "I hope you have that in writing."

Callie smiled. "Yes, but I doubt another person would make an offer. A developer would be crazy to use the land."

Rorke watched a van pull into the drive. "What is the front wall?"

"The wall is constructed with supports and painted glass panels. I'm very thankful that the design is etched into the glass. The paint is on the inside, so the painter is working with a mirror image. My head hurts thinking about trying to put the right color in the correct space. Each panel has a removable pane of glass and a protective layer. If a person leans on the glass or bumps over a vase, the mural is safe."

A pleasant-faced, plump woman climbed out of a delivery van that parked beside Rorke's truck. Her brown hair was secured in a twisted kind of knot at her neck. Even in heeled boots, she was shorter than Callie's five-two frame.

Callie hugged the woman in greeting and made introductions. "Ms. Pickle, meet Rorke Asher. He'll be teaching at the university and renting number six."

Smiling brightly, Ms. Pickle shook hands. "Nice to meet you. You'll love staying at Rosa's place. My family has been in the area for about twenty years. I moved to the rentals to be out of the house and start college."

"Pickle is in horticulture, and the sole reason Dad's company was able to continue after he died."

Her friend turned scarlet at the compliment and countered. "I only helped. Nigel taught me to cultivate seeds, care for the babies, and to arrange flowers."

Callie waved the words away and added. "Ms. Pickle is also the reason I could attend college. She managed the place while I took classes. When I finished my degree, Pickle opened a flower shop in town. We help each other out. Today, she discovered a raccoon found the corn stalks, and I need to repair the aftermath of its feast."

Pickle smiled. "I don't have the heart to call animal control because they might hurt it. The little guy is only looking for food, but our nocturnal guest defeats the raccoon defenses regularly."

Callie teased, "I think the raccoon and Pickle have developed a love/hate relationship."

Pickle moved on to business. "The semester starts Monday, and fall is usually busy for school and flower shops. Do you need extra help?"

"No. Five students who worked part-time at BE last year are looking for extra money. Their waivers and tax papers are on file as well as updated. Each one has no problem with Mr. Pica supervising when I'm not present."

Pickle's smile faded. "Are you positive about the new business model for BE? I could find another intern for the shop and scale back my hours."

Callie didn't have to have Pica's help, but she wanted to keep Pica busy. Her other reasons were her own. "We're good. The shop is your dream, and the place is doing great. Pica has been renting here for years, knows our system, and is semi-retired. The man needs an outlet for the transition."

Pickle decided not to voice any other misgivings about Mr. Pica. "How are you doing?"

"Dealing. You?"

"I miss Nigel even after a decade. He took a chance on me, and I owe him everything."

Rorke entered behind the ladies into a room filled with color. Flowers and plants of various shapes, sizes, and colors occupied every shelf, corner, and counter.

Pickle turned to Rorke with a wide grin and shining zeal. "Isn't the reception center beautiful?! These are silk, plastic, and other non-perishable materials. Pictures are two dimensional. Showing is much more efficient and fun. When a client has no idea what to order, we narrow down the choices without compromising the health of flowers and plants."

Callie loved her friend's passion for plants. "I'll go take care of the raccoon mess. The plants and flowers for today and tomorrow are in the pickup area. If you need anything else, let me know. Still planning on attending Girls' Night Out on Friday?"

"Yes." Pickle collected the flowers she needed and went onto her shop to make floral arrangements for the following day.

Rorke followed Callie out an adjacent door, which led to a sidewalk running parallel to the parking lot. The path led the way to a greenhouse.

Punching a code into a keypad and using a biometric sensor, she waited for a hum and entered a second sequence.

The foyer was a one-story open room with lockers along the back, a sitting room, and a wash area. Restroom signs pointed to men's and ladies' rooms to the left. A counter with sink, microwave, and fridge was off to the right.

Callie spied her guest's uncomfortable footwear. "Ah, you're in dress clothes and shoes. We have a mile or so walk. The cart is faster but takes time to pull out and start."

"Are bare feet a choice?"

Callie grinned with excitement at showing off her treasured greenhouse. "Sure. The walkways are paved through the section where we are going. Past the compost pile, the paths change to rocks or steppingstones. I would be careful stepping off the side or tripping. If you fall into certain clumps, there are cacti with needles."

Rorke sat on a cushioned chair and took off his loafers. "The floor is unusually smooth. What is the material?"

"My father used an adobe mixture for filling in the frame. The final layer is a waterproof plaster.

"Building codes are different for greenhouses, but dad designed the place to comply with existing regulations at the time. I have the architects and contractors' names, but we've never had a problem with the structural integrity. The place has withstood wear and tear over the years. I've had to make minor repairs, replace water lines, and fix or replace the glass. Luckily, we've never had anything more serious than a worker backing a cart into the pond."

"Love to see the schematics one day."

Callie took a bottle of water from the fridge and offered one to Rorke, who declined. While Callie changed shoes and put on a work apron, Rorke studied a map posted on the wall. Five separate sections were labeled: Foyer, Tropical Paradise, Fairy Garden with Turtle Pond, Hidden Wonders, Hello and Farewell.

A sign underneath offered a caution. Birds, bees, and other wildlife are present.

The young woman advised. "Don't let the diagram be misleading. My father had a wicked sense of humor, and even BE's name has meaning. He built more than a greenhouse. A true botanic garden could be considered a work in progress. Plants are collected, cultivated, preserved, and displayed with their botany names. He has done so in the greenhouse. Thus, the botanic in the title. I've made sure to place signs with the front yard displays.

"Our Tropical Paradise has nothing to do with a tropical environment. The Fairy Garden is an area by the pond and computer office. Hidden Wonders is an area where we keep very fragrant plants and has foliage that has taken over. Unless there is a problem, I have not had time or reason to cultivate the area. Hello and Farewell is our propagation, planting, and germination zone. We also cut and prepare plants or flowers for departure there."

Callie led the way through the doorway to where the greenhouse opened into a world in and of itself. The one-story expanded into two to three stories high. There were even various containers hanging from roof supports. One couldn't tell due to the sheer number of plants. The roof and walls were constructed of plexiglass.

She was correct in that Tropical Paradise had nothing to do with sand or the beach. Tall vertical shelves occupied much of the space. Rorke studied the closest stand.

"Callie, do those shelves rotate?"

She smiled and answered. "Yes. No idea if my father used someone else's design or developed his own. Each shelf can go around like a Ferris Wheel. The mechanism locks so that the shelves won't move and accidentally tip over the pots or containers. There is an option to move them electronically, but I don't usually share that choice. Rather not have a novice playing around with electricity near the guttering system. Guttering has to do with channels and water."

Rorke eyed Callie and asked, "Do you ever go in and not come out?"

Callie laughed delightedly. "My family accuses me of doing that all the time. If you ever need directions, look for the black bicycle flag. Each flag is on a pole, which shows a map and points the way to the main exit. There are also fire escape doors with directions on the paths per fire department regulations. Lastly, look up. Exit signs with arrows to show where to exit. We make sure the signs are not covered, so people don't get lost. Past our destination, the greenhouse changes."

Rorke thought that Callie was exaggerating about a mile, but she wasn't. The winding path would disappear until you walked forward.

Rorke asked Callie about the running water that he was hearing. He was slightly concerned that there was a leak. "Running water sounds stronger than what should be flowing through the hoses for misters, sprinklers, and watering."

Callie thought and offered. "If you don't mind dirty feet, I'll show you the atrium after dealing with the raccoon. The area with the turtle pond is the best part of the greenhouse."

She found the spot where the ringtail had dug through a bottom row of plants and visited a compost bin stored underneath the benches.

Callie studied the area and whispered, "Rorke, be a chap and stand by the flowers that look like white miniature roses. Don't make a sudden noise or quick movement. I'll do minimal cleanup to make sure the plants stay healthy."

Her friend did as she requested. The roots seemed intact, so Callie carefully and quickly packed the dirt. Quietly, she led Rorke back down the path.

Rorke fell into step with Callie and waited to make sure their voices wouldn't carry to the sleeping marsupial. "Spotted the raccoon curled up in a nice bundle of weeds."

"Those weeds are rushes. Unless in their den, raccoons tend to stay in a place for one day and move along the next night."

"You're a regular encyclopedia of trivia."

"Mainly of plants and critters that like to invade a garden."

"Squirrels? Birds?" asked Rorke.

"Some. They coexist and don't eat much."

A glass wall at the end of Tropical Paradise led to the Fairy Garden. The partition was not solid and had ventilation holes cut from ceiling to floor. Some gaps were large enough for birds, bees, or other wildlife to come and go as they pleased. The unique part was that the openings were many shapes and sizes but not large enough for a child or adult to climb through. There were colorful images on clear areas, so birds wouldn't fly into the glass. Large industrial fans provided airflow in a north to a south pattern. There were also windows in the outer walls that could open or close near the ceiling for outside ventilation.

The path turned to packed dirt as they went through a second doorway, and Callie asked, "Are you up to going a little further?"

"Sure."

Around a bend, Callie stopped to let Rorke go ahead. The landscape changed drastically and opened to be more of an atrium. The structure rose to roughly seven stories tall with metal supports crisscrossing the entire ceiling.

Callie announced proudly. "These are my favorite five acres."

Rorke blurted. "Five? The building cost alone must have been a small fortune, and trees are growing in here."

"Yes, along with lots of other species. We have four separate water systems that originate at the pond. Storage tanks for rainwater run along the outside and underground. We don't fill all the tanks in case torrential rains cause flooding, and there is a runoff system. A lazy river runs through a channel system that supplies the entire greenhouse with water. Most of the pipes are open with an average depth of 24 inches. The sprinklers and misters are an independent system. Lastly, the pond itself has ten different waterfalls to act as pumps to keep the water flowing. The largest one is about twenty-five feet high by the outer wall. When I was little, this was my playground. Aunt Thessa was older than me, but she never turned down an invitation to a fairy tea party by the pond. The playroom that my father built for me is now the computer room.

"There are a couple of storage rooms along the east wall. The first floor is for the carts. The second and third stories contain gardening equipment, pumping supplies, seed storage, and miscellaneous items. I used to get upset that we had to use stairs or electric lifts to haul what we needed. Dad explained that the construct was for a reason. Plants that needed sunlight, but more shade, could grow in a more natural state. As I learned more about environments, I understood the reasoning."

Rorke agreed with Callie. "The place is beautiful. I understand why I saw a couple of bicycles in the foyer. How do you maintain this place without help?"

Callie laughed. "I don't. We hire high school and college students. Most of the college students are in botany and need work experience. Additionally, we have roughly thirty part-time, permanent employees who rotate throughout the week. They want extra money but don't wish to work forty hours. We don't open BE on Sunday. After church, I'll prepare loads, catch up on accounts, or enjoy the gardens. If the need arises, we'll contact core employees for special events. During the holidays, we hire seasonal employees who want the hours or extra money. I teach classes and give tours to gardening clubs."

"Tours?"

"Remember, botanic is in the name. Cultivating, preserving, and displaying is part of our purpose. We have flower beds in the atrium that you won't find in an average home garden. Another example is the water plants living in the pond. A few are not native to Idaho or our climate. Later, when you are wearing shoes, I'll show you the rest of the turtle pond. Half the island is inside, and the other half is outside the atrium. Near the island is a channel that flows around the outside wall to a pool. A family of wild ducks lives on the island. They may come and go as they please.

"We keep the water flowing and turn on a heater in the winter. Water streams around to a mini-volcano structure made of rocks. The volcano is a combination of outer wall and waterfall. Pipes run water up the middle to supply the flowing water."

Locking up, they found an unknown vehicle pulled up behind Rorke's truck. A woman was waiting and climbed out. She was dressed in a business suit but looked younger than Callie.

Callie asked, "May I help you?"

"My name is Special Agent Valley of the Federal Bureau of Investigation. I'm to escort you to a meeting."

Callie looked confused. "Meeting?"

Rorke ordered. "Callie, get in the car!"

Rorke's tone annoyed rather than scared Callie. "Why?"

"Now!"

"Fine! Bossy!" Callie closed the door, watched, and listened to the conversation outside of the truck.

Agent Valley understood Rorke's concern. "Mr. Asher, I'm going to hand over my badge and identification."

Rorke took out his phone and placed a call. Callie listened as Rorke described the petite woman with brown eyes and a scar near her collar bone.

The interesting part about the agent was that she had purple hair, and Rorke asked, "Is there anything distinctive about the woman to verify her identity?"

Rorke must have verified Valley's credentials because he hung up and told Valley. "I am driving Callie to the meeting. We will follow you."

Rorke climbed into the driver's seat, turned to his passenger, and chastised. "Do you always climb into a stranger's car without checking their identity?"

Callie shrugged off the accusation. "The lady is an agent. Why is her hair purple?"

"Undercover assignment before today."

Chapter

Twenty minutes later, they pulled into the parking lot of an office building. Rorke climbed out and opened the door for Callie. Agent Valley waited outside and told the couple to proceed to room 101.

Rorke stilled in surprise at the agent in charge. Then every muscle tensed. The reaction reminded Callie of a deer surprised in the woods. Every muscle ready to flee or fight.

A tall, muscular man in a rumpled suit greeted the couple. "Hello, Ms. Rivera. My name is Pend Isley. I wanted to talk to you privately before word spreads further. An official decision was made today that will affect you, me, and Rorke. Lines of professional and personal relationships are about to blur, and I try to stay far away from blurred lines."

Callie guessed. "News about the book project?"

"Yes, but the situation is more involved. Eight months ago, Fish and Wildlife intercepted a shipment of counterfeit goods which included plants and seeds."

Rorke interrupted. "I am lost in one sentence. Counterfeit flowers?"

Callie answered instead of Isley. "There are plants which are difficult to grow and cultivate. Scientists have looked for ways to improve aspects of science. New strains of seed to be disease resistant or pest-proof. Cheaper varieties to sell to the consumer. Medical plants and spices are hot topics."

"Spices?"

"Take a Saffron Crocus. Saffron spice is made from flowers coming from the Middle East, Spain, and Italy. A pound of true spice takes about 80,000 flowers and sells on average for about $1300. Problems include an environment to grow and extracting the spice from that many plants. The return on investment is not worth the effort. A counterfeiter might sell a spice with a minimal amount of Saffron mixed with fillers. The compound might smell, look, or taste similar, but the profit would be huge. The flower is also used for dye."

Rorke looked disgusted. "Geez. Who pays that much for a plant?"

Callie shrugged. "No idea. Go ahead, Agent Isley."

Isley rubbed his face as if he were trying to wipe away the lines of tiredness. "The shipment held several crop seeds that were diseased or old. A portion of the shipment was destined for research at a pharmaceutical company that studies homeopathic cures. My understanding is diseased or old seeds could do a lot of damage to the research."

Rorke asked, "How big was the shipment?"

"Three truck loads. The experts believe that a counterfeit ring is running several billions of dollars of fraudulent goods. Items run the gambit from olive oil to purses to furs. FDA, DEA, Agriculture, and genuine companies have a vested interest in finding out the who, what, where, and why. Internal sources stalled on finding answers. Today, an official plan was approved. The scheme involves you and the project. After contacting Solomon, I am recusing myself because of my relationship with Rorke."

Callie paled and asked, "Solomon?"

"Ah, you know Solomon!"

Callie explained. "Yes and no. I have never met Solomon in person, but he calls at least once a week to see how Gran and I are doing. Mostly, he asks intrusive questions. What did he say to you?"

"The man's advice was to hand over the case. Use my relationship with Rorke to keep abreast of what is happening. Rorke knows the outdoors. He's worked with various groups, as well as forestry employees, as an outdoor guide. I am sure the job choices were a rebellious excuse to escape my supervision."

Rorke quipped. "Good guess! The main reason was the salary paid the bills."

Callie studied the two men. "Why is there such tension between the two of you?"

Isley explained. "Are you aware of Rorke's treehouse?"

"Yes."

Isley looked slightly surprised that Callie knew of the treehouse, and he skipped to the outcome. "Somehow, I was assigned to make sure a young man met his probation challenges. The case was out of the ordinary. I was to make sure he dismantled his treehouse and finish his college degree. Best way to ensure the conditions was to become roommates. When Rorke was able to transfer to a college closer to my work, we shared an apartment. The young man attended classes, and I usually kept my opinion quiet about his friends. Then, a girl with suspect friends entered the picture."

Rorke made a disgruntled sound, but Isley continued without pause. "The girl and her friends weren't great influences. Rorke wouldn't listen. A friend of mine advised me that life had to teach. Mission accomplished. There was an incident, and we never saw Rorke's girlfriend again."

Rorke accused. "An incident? You slept with my girlfriend and made sure of my timely arrival."

"Ms. Rivera, before labeling me a horrible human being, hear the facts. The young lady and I did not have sex, but the point was made before clothing came off. The demonstration was so the young man could see the error of his ways. The girlfriend, who was over 21, ran with a bad crowd."

Sulkily, Rorke admitted. "I don't like shocks." He nodded to the older gentleman. "Isley might be a horrible roommate, but he is very good at his job."

Callie asked, "If Rorke graduated and finished his degree, why are you concerned about a current connection?"

Isley explained. "The court made me Rorke's guardian, which means we have a relationship that started years ago. Working together might be construed as favoritism."

Callie made a joyful sound and smiled widely. "See! There is someone to put down as an emergency contact who cares: Isley."

Rorke's expression turned irate, and Callie pretended not to notice.

Isley brought the conversation back to the original subject. "I want to explain what you both are facing before the authorities officially approach with an offer."

Callie's surprise showed. "Us?"

"Yes. I will start with Rorke. A team constructed an exam to test a candidate's knowledge. A list of fifty qualified individuals were contacted for a written, oral, and visual test regarding geography with writing and literature skills. Rorke scored the highest."

"Callie, your selection was twofold. We sent representatives to thirty universities in various states who administered a plant identification test to staff and students. Dr. Wither and you had the highest scores in the least amount of time. The twenty highest scoring students took a second test. Callie scored the highest again."

Callie felt her cheeks flush at the recognition, but Isley's next words made her pale as quickly.

"A connection between past and present surfaced: Nigel Rivera. A report surfaced from ten years ago. Callie's father wanted to inform the authorities about an illegal operation. He had proof but died before anyone could follow up."

Callie stated, "The next statement had better not be to accuse me, my father, or Gran of involvement."

"No. Your father, Rosa Rivera, Rorke Asher, Solomon, and I are in the clear. Anyone else on the planet is suspect. You were twelve or thirteen at the time. I must ask. Did your father say or do anything that might help unravel the mystery?"

Callie paused and titled her head in thought. The question brought her nightmares into focus, and she was careful with her words. "The fact he left in the middle of the night after a phone call was strange. If he went out with friends, he made sure I had a babysitter. I argued that I could stay by myself for a couple of hours. Rorke, if the project is a conflict, we'll go home and tell the deans to find someone else. Rorke, you and Agent Isley have a strange, rocky history. Whether Isley has recused himself or not, I'd rather decline than be pushed into an unfriendly work environment."

Rorke uttered in disbelief. "You'd give up a chance at a paid doctorate because of a connection between Isley and me?"

Isley began to shuffle papers on the makeshift desk. "The work environment will be fine. My appearance will be as a meddling guardian. I must stress your roles are expertise and research. Do not play detective.

Callie glared at Isley. "If I find out who murdered my father...."

Isley interrupted. "Don't finish that sentence. You will talk to us and not do anything stupid."

Rorke and Callie returned to the house. Rorke dropped her off at the house and mentioned he was going to a sports' bar for a drink.

"Do you want some company?" Callie didn't want her new friend drinking and driving home.

"No. I want a little space and a large television screen."

Callie suspected that Rorke was meeting Isley. The agent's admission about the report her father filed put a new spin on the situation. Callie wasn't supposed to be aware of the report that Nigel sent to the authorities. Solomon was the only person who knew of her knowledge, but she never shared how the discovery was made. Granted, Solomon probably told Rorke.

Callie called Solomon on the phone from her nightstand.

"Hello." The man answered on the first ring.

Callie sounded more discouraged than angry. "You might have warned me that my father's report had been dug up out of the mothballs."

Solomon answered in an exhausted tone. "If I had time, I would have sent word. The clock is working against me. Are you all right?"

Time would be working against Callie as well. "I'm fine. Did you tell Rorke that I knew my father filed a report?"

"No. The report stayed buried until now. Sharing the details would only put you in danger."

"I think that Rorke is meeting Isley. Are you able to eavesdrop on Rorke using the phone you gave him?"

"Yes."

"Would you set the system up, so I may listen?

Solomon was silent a long time before talking. "I don't think that you have ever specifically asked me for help or a favor. Are you sure you want to blur the line of right and wrong?"

"No, but my trust only stretches so far. I am not happy that you seem to be talking to everyone about me and my life. If the plant project goes forward, I'd like to know if Isley and Rorke are trustworthy."

Callie wished she had an idea of what Solomon was thinking. It didn't help that she couldn't read his facial expressions.

Solomon asked, "Are you sure?"

Callie replied very softly. "No, but yes."

"I'll provide you access this one time. Turn on the laptop used for the house security system, and I'll guide you on the phone."

The young woman had a disturbing thought. "Are you spying on me and watching the house using Uncle Mer's home security system?"

"Yes."

The outer perimeter, kitchen, living room, and office were the only areas that were under surveillance. She'd have to be doubly careful what she put on her laptop.

"I'm telling Mer."

Solomon laughed at her mulish tone. "Child, I have Rosa's permission, and Mer gave me the passwords."

Solomon used a remote program to connect, and her computer showed the inside of a nearby eating establishment. The image zoomed in on Agent Isley, who was sitting across from Rorke. The two were meeting. She could see and hear clearly.

Isley took a sip of iced tea. "You are not an FBI agent, and I like Callie."

"Understood. Status quo. Be eyes, ears, and invisible. I've deniability and no family. Disposable if the situation turns nasty."

Her father's picture caught her attention when she looked up, and Callie's guilt on invading a private conversation was too much.

Callie told Solomon in a conciliatory tone. "Thank you for helping, but I can't."

Disconnecting the line, Callie grabbed her purse and keys. She drove to the sport's bar and told the hostess she was meeting someone.

Agent Isley saw Callie enter and nodded to her. Rorke turned around to see who Isley was greeting. She walked to the table, shifted from foot to foot, and decided to slide into the booth beside Isley. Isley eyed the young woman without comment.

Callie made sure to keep her face composed, but her eyes darted from the table to the floor. "I won't stay. I. I am sorry."

Rorke arched an eyebrow. "For?"

Callie clenched her hands together and paused. Today was not a great example of keeping herself together. Emotion was weakness, and weakness was used to manipulate. Cracks were a way to pry open and crumble a person. Think about stone and defenses.

Isley tried to distract Callie. "When is the last time you slept more than a cat nap?"

The inquiry unbalanced the young woman's thought process. "I'll sleep after Sunday."

"What's Sunday?"

"I have nightmares about car crashes before the anniversary of my father's death. After Sunday, my dreams will return to normal."

Rorke grew impatient with Callie. "Why are you here?"

Callie grabbed her purse and mumbled, "Never mind. Bye."

Outside, she opened her car door, but Beau's voice stopped her from climbing into the driver's seat. "We meet again."

Callie took a deep breath, composed her face, smiled, and turned to Beau. "I forgot happy hour is starting."

"Have you thought anymore to my proposal?" Beau asked, hopefully.

"No. We'd not be a good fit, and you deserve to be happy."

Beau tried to maneuver himself between the woman and car door. Callie was faster, sat down, and closed the door. He had to move his hand away before Callie caught his fingers. She started the engine, waved goodbye brightly, and backed out.

Callie kept her composure until she walked into her room. Sobs racked her entire body as she lay across the bed. No one could see or use the fear, weakness, or guilt against her.

Today, she'd displayed raw emotion and fallen apart twice. Isley's remark about lack of sleep hit a little too close to home, and she'd exposed a crack in the stone. One day brought a deluge of change and new information. How could she keep her promise to her father? She knew the report with the authorities was a layer of protection. Her father filed the report as a part of his puzzle with misdirects.

Could she continue to act as if she wasn't terrified every second? If anyone discovered her extensive knowledge of her father's research, the consequences would be lives. The timing of finding the report was unfortunate because the anniversary of her father's death was Sunday. Emotions were harder to keep in check around the date of his death.

Activity and keeping her mind occupied helped. Her pain had dulled over the years, but there were times when a wave of grief would knock her down. Her grandfather's death was difficult, but Callie had been able to say goodbye. Her father was a different story. The car had burned hot and did not leave a recognizable body. Memorial services were in front of a picture. Then, the cabin burned. Family, friends, and her father's garden were the constants or foci in her life.

Callie finished with tears and washed her face. She went down to the kitchen to heat a kettle of water for tea. An incessant tapping on the window finally caught Callie's attention. Isley stood at the window, patiently knocking on the glass. Great. Gran wasn't the only one who forgot to turn on the security system.

Callie opened the window a tiny crack. "You are lucky I turned off the security system because tampering with the window would activate the alarm. Is everything all right?"

Isley spoke very politely. "Yes. May we come inside? I'd rather not make a scene and have a neighbor phone the police. I have a flight to catch in a couple of hours and should be packing."

"Fine. Come to the back door."

Callie allowed Isley and Rorke inside and walked to the living room. When the three were seated, Rorke apologized for being rude.

Callie shrugged and stated. "Apology accepted. I am sure that you wish to unpack, and Isley may catch his flight."

Isley commented. "Nice move with the car door. A few squashed fingers might improve the guy's attitude. Did you contemplate marrying the oaf?"

"No. Beau spoke of marriage, but he wants a woman who will turn a blind eye to his shenanigans. Beau and I had dinner a total of five times, but dating was never in the cards."

Isley peered at the young woman. "What else?"

"What do you mean?"

"You're a self-confident, intelligent, pretty lady with a decent amount of common sense. The man is below your standards. I assume you're aware of the land and business value of your father's estate?"

Callie found that she was answering many of Isley's questions carefully. "Yes. I receive the business and ten thousand dollars on my twenty-fourth birthday. As to overall value, I let Ms. Nod deal with the accountants and audits. I keep the daily records, but Ms. Nod handles employee pay and taxes. There is enough in the accounts to cover

49

expenses and pay workers. Dad taught me everything he knew about horticulture and botany. I mostly to maintain the garden he started. Each plant is a part of my life, and my concern focuses on the plants.

"My father oversaw the renovation of the house and built the rental properties for my grandmother. The construction was done without going into massive debt. I hope Gran lives a long life, and I may live in the house after she dies. My guess is that Gran's children will sell the place or find a manager." She looked at her watch. "Gran should be landing soon, and she promised to text. Why are the two of you passing looks back and forth? Did the plane crash?"

Isley's gaze swung back to Callie and held her attention with its intensity. "The plane is still in the air. Rorke is concerned that the research could become dangerous."

Callie watched Rorke flinch in surprise, but the young man remained quiet.

"How would the book be dangerous?"

"A connection between the past and present puts you in a no-win scenario. Interested parties may want to find out what you know or believe you could have seen or heard."

Callie shrugged. "Meaning that an ulterior motive was and is to use me as bait. I am of legal age and understand the risk. I agree."

Rorke remained silent, but Callie could see his jaw clench in disapproval at her words. Rorke decided to leave the house instead of arguing.

Isley waited until he heard the door close. "Callie, I'll stay abreast of the case, and thank you for caring about Rorke."

"Rorke? Why?"

"The boy would never believe my words, but he is like a son to me. Rorke rarely reacts with visible emotion, much less with a temper. You made a huge impression and have a connection with him. Here are my direct numbers. Call me anytime."

Callie walked Isley out and found Mr. Pica patiently waiting for Isley.

Pica ignored Callie and spoke to Isley. "Are you the G man? Rorke's father?"

"Yes." Isley did not explain, correct the assumption, or tell Mr. Pica he was showing his age. G man was an older term and a slang term for a government worker.

"Rosa let us know Rorke is staying with Callie while she is gone. Are we able to trust Rorke to be a gentleman?"

"Yes, sir, and I don't put up with funny business. Here is my business card and a few extra to hand out. Don't hesitate to leave a message if you want to voice an opinion or concern."

Callie glared daggers at Pica. "I refuse to have a repeat performance of prom."

Pica patted her on the head like a puppy. "We couldn't ignore the rumors that kids have sex and drink alcohol on Prom Night."

"Oh, for crying out loud. I realize that you have known me since I was about nine, but I am twenty-three and not seventeen."

Chapter

Callie took a long shower. After washing her hair, she stood in hot water until the temperature turned cold. She wanted to return to the greenhouse to work. The feel of dirt between her fingers was a healing balm, but she was tired. Should she crawl into bed or start on some work? The phone ringing helped provide the answer.

Rorke called. "I am sorry about earlier. Isley's appearance rattled me, and his manipulation of events is annoying. Solomon's timing is not a coincidence on talking to me. Both are doubly irritating. I haven't felt this manipulated or bossed around in a long time."

Callie teased, "I've never guessed, but welcome to my club. Solomon's been a thorn in my side since my father died."

Rorke asked, "Could I use the internet to work on a couple of administrative things for school? One is printing a class roster."

"Yes, but I'd wait to do printouts until Monday. Students move into dorms Friday, and there will be a flurry of class changes."

Callie heard Rorke shuffle papers and read his notes. "Why did the speaker advise us to print one today?"

"The answer is to make sure you log in to the system and start learning the program. Be prepared for the teaching schedule to change as well."

"Would you mind if I look at your syllabus? The English department has a general syllabus, but each instructor modifies the document to fit specific class objectives."

Callie offered. "Come on over, and I'll find one for you."

Rorke met her at the back door, and Callie led him to her office. It was like entering a new world. Bright colors covered every inch of the walls.

Callie explained. "Dad hired Chi Pica, who is an artist, to paint four different landscapes with the ecosystem of plants and animals. The murals are from photographs my father took on trips. After he died, I moved to the bedroom down the hall. There are two desks here to make an office. One desk is for school, and the second is dedicated to business."

"Chi Pica? The neighbor?"

"Yes. The man is a bit dramatic, but he means well. He rented one of the first units. Pica and Aunt Thessa fell in love, but their relationship was constant drama. They dated and broke up in an endless cycle over three years. During the last good round, Pica was going to ask Thessa to marry him. Pica's version is that Solomon found out about the proposal

52

and met with Thessa. Whatever he told Thessa put a permanent end to the relationship. When Thessa died, there was only a memorial service after cremation. Solomon made sure Pica wasn't welcome. My dad and Rosa tend to doubt Pica's version because they never cared if he attended. I wasn't there because Dad took me early to say goodbye."

"Has anyone ever talked about why there was disapproval?"

"No, but I was still a girl. Pica and Thessa loved each other, but the relationship wasn't a healthy one. Be aware Pica's feelings border on hating Solomon. Pica blames Solomon if anything negative occurs in life. When my father's friends are at any gathering, Pica acts annoyed or disgruntled.

"I'm aware that Pickle is concerned. She knows that Pica can be bossy and abrasive. Pica semi-retired three months ago and needs something to do other than paint or teach art classes. We developed a schedule where he may supervise a few part-time workers at BE. Each of the chosen staff is flexible, knows the system, and can work alongside Pica with his personality quirks. They have enough sense to play along or finish the activity the correct way later. They let me know so I'm able to run interference."

"That seems to be a lot of extra work for you."

Callie shrugged and dismissed the observation, so Rorke asked, "What are these added drawings?"

"My attempt at adding to the creation. Pica tried to teach me to draw and paint when he saw my embellishments. Art is not one of my strengths."

Callie withdrew a folder from a desk drawer. "Here is a copy of my syllabi and class policies."

The phone rang again, and Callie answered on the first ring. "Hello."

Gran was on the other end. "I am at the luggage return, and Consuela is here with me. Everything is fine. Could you send a text for me? Oh, and Rorke is staying on the couch until Sunday."

Callie made a sour face at Rorke as Gran gave her the news. "Thanks for letting me know. Love you."

"Love you too. Bye."

Callie sent an update text message and scanned the string of replies.

Rorke teased. "See. The plane didn't fall out of the sky."

"Do not let the neighbors, especially Pica, dictate your decisions. Sleep at home instead of the couch."

Rorke didn't argue and made himself a workspace on the couch by repositioning the coffee table. Callie brought in her laptop and sat on the other end to give him room. An hour or so later, Rorke stretched and found Callie curled up sound asleep. He found a quilt and draped it across her sleeping form. The lines of worry and stress were gone, and she looked more her age.

Sound asleep, Callie started waving her hands while dreaming. Rorke's voice invaded her sleep, and she fought to wake up from the nightmare. Disoriented, Callie felt herself falling off of the sofa and warm arms catching her. Rorke's reassuring tone made her feel safe.

Rorke laid her back on the cushions. "You were having nightmares. Try to go back to sleep."

Callie nestled against Rorke as he sat beside her. The young woman stirred drowsily and heard Rorke curse under his breath.

"What's wrong?"

"Emotional entanglements are not in either of our best interests."

Mostly asleep, Callie offered advice. "Do not share who is the center of your attention, or Isley may sleep with her."

"Over my dead body."

Callie's head relaxed into his chest, and the next thing she heard was a phone alarm. Callie started feeling around for the annoying interruption.

Rorke's voice came from beneath her. "Please don't move."

Half asleep, she realized that she had her hand was groping between Rorke's legs. Callie stilled and reddened in embarrassment.

"Oh, Lord, thank you that Gran is gone."

"That is your prayer."

"I've never had to worry about waking up next to a man, much less on top of one. Other than this awkward situation, I have no complaints."

"Are you trying to flirt?"

"No idea. Too early in the morning to function properly, but I have to empty my bladder."

"Put your weight on my shoulder and roll off the couch."

When Callie emerged from the bathroom, Rorke had disappeared. She dressed for the day and packed a couple of different outfits. Hal wanted her to go to the shooting range. Then she'd go straight to her beloved enchanted garden.

After lunch, Hal and Callie returned from the practice range. The woman who sat at the front desk motioned to Hal that a visitor Rorke sat reading and waiting to complete the process to enter the lab area.

Hal attempted to hand Callie a ten-dollar bill, but she pushed the money away. "I don't believe in wasting my money gambling."

"Wasn't gambling. You were a sure winner."

If you want to repay me, don't rise to the bait next time."

Rorke asked, "What happened?"

Callie explained. "We were at the range. A gentleman, I use the term loosely, was extremely impressed that a woman could shoot and hit the target. Next thing I know, Hal had us competing."

Hal praised. "Yep, and she won in front of a crowd."

"What if I had missed the paper and hit the dirt?"

"I would have lost ten dollars, and you would have to listen to where a woman belonged."

Callie chastised her friend and tried to make him understand. "Seriously, Hal, if that guy is at the range, be careful. He's related to Beau Dew. The Dew family owns numerous businesses. Beau and his siblings stay out of trouble because their father buys their way out. A possible expansion to their holdings is an area adjacent to BE property. Beau conveniently introduced himself at the grocery store and invited me out. He probed about the land and decided that I would be a compliant, easily manipulated, and obedient wife. I'm grabbing my stuff and heading to BE. See you tomorrow."

Callie spent the rest of the afternoon sending out orders, pruning, repotting, and inspecting various plants. She updated reminders in the daily calendar of tasks to revisit as she completed each. The list included such things as checking the irrigation pipes for leaks, drips, or clogs. Time management was an important issue when classes started. Juggling business and school obligations could be challenging.

Gran called around dinner time and reassured Callie that all was well. The first meeting with her mother was uncomfortable, but the ice had been broken to allow the healing process to begin.

Gran asked without embarrassment. "Did Rorke sleep on the couch?"

Callie didn't have to monitor her words, tone, or emotions with Gran. "Yes. Evidently, you and the neighbors are not concerned about how the situation appears to the world."

"Child, I like Rorke way better than Beau. Rorke is far more respectable, kind, and polite. If you have sex, there are condoms in my bathroom cabinet. Modern women need to be as prepared as men and take precautions."

"Gran! Oh, Worms! Geez! That!"

When Callie became quiet, she could hear her grandmother laughing. "Mija, your generation did not invent sex."

"I am embarrassed and now suspicious. Why are you so ready to send us on a date?"

"Great-grandchildren."

55

"Ok. That is enough teasing. Send me pictures and juicy details of my new family."

"Touché. Love you. Bye."

Callie could not concentrate after the conversation. She decided to come back later. Driving home, Rorke and Mr. Pica were talking in front of the mailboxes. Callie waved hello but continued to the house. She made a beeline for the master suite. Inside the cupboard were containers of condoms. She pulled out a box and read curiously. Peeking inside, she took the first one. A long ribbon of condoms came out.

Movement in the corner of her eye made her turn around. Pica and Rorke were standing at the doorway.

Red and embarrassed, Callie looked down. "This is not what it looks like. I promise."

Pica smiled in amusement. "What does it look like?"

Callie stuttered, "Gran. She. She's gone through menopause. I mean. Hasn't she? She told me. My grandmother!"

Pica couldn't help himself. The gentleman laughed so hard that tears ran down his face.

Callie asked, "What's so funny?"

Pica took some tissue from a box on the bathroom counter, wiped his eyes, and blew his nose. "I am sorry, but Rosa keeps those for everyone. Safe sex is easy to discuss. Teens, especially boys, aren't as comfortable buying, uh, protection. Girls are criticized or grilled if they decide to try and be prepared. She uses the waterproof ducks outside in the backyard. If anyone needs one, they may acquire without questions or judgment."

Callie went to the window and spied the various garden statues in the shrubs. "I'm not stuffing ducks. You two decide which one of you gets Duck Duty while I go back to work."

Callie disappeared before they could argue or decline the chore. She went to find the keys in her purse and flushed even brighter. A brightly colored string of Glow in the Dark and Extra Sensation condoms was in her hand. She refused to go back inside and shoved the birth control under the seat. Mr. Pica would lock up the house.

Back in the greenhouse, Callie drove through the property while studying every area. Security cameras were great, but a visual inspection made her feel better. Around seven, Rorke called to see if she'd eaten.

Callie had not, but she had another half an hour of work and needed a shower. Rorke asked if she wanted to order take out.

"Sure. How about Chinese? Gran complains about the spices and the large amounts of food in one serving. I never quite understood. She cooks with red chili and green chili peppers like there is no tomorrow. I'll eat any dish from the menu."

"Do you have food allergies?"

Callie stopped the cart. "No. I have to hang up. A plant needs a haircut."

An hour later, she sat at the kitchen table devouring dinner. Rorke ordered four different dishes with chicken or beef. He'd ordered steamed rice, fried rice, and egg rolls to go with the entrees. They ate in relative silence. Between starting the morning in an awkward position and the condom episode, she had no idea what to say.

Rorke finally broached the subject. "We should talk. I'm going to be blunt because playing games is not my style. We are about to embark on a journey that could become dangerous. I don't feel that I must be in a relationship to make my life complete. A female's hurt feelings or relationship drama does not sit well with me."

Rorke paused and tried to find the next words.

Callie thought she understood Rorke's concern. "You're a handsome, smart, and nice company. I find you attractive, but we are about to spend a lot of time together. I'd rather have a trusted friend. Whether a romantic relationship develops or not, a long-term commitment or marriage should evolve naturally. If you are concerned with my relationship with Beau, don't worry. I think everyone, including Gran, thinks I had a torrid affair with Beau, but I have not."

Rorke took in her words and eyed her with a guarded expression.

Callie sighed at his expression. "Stop with the suspicious looks and rolled eyes."

"Casual romance doesn't fit you."

Callie drummed her fingers on the table. Rorke was fascinated because her mouth and eyes were very expressive. She had tried to control her facial expressions since they'd met. When Callie relaxed and lowered her defenses, her face radiated with feeling: unsure, hesitant, angry, and, finally, resigned.

"The observation of my personality is appreciated, and I would never use teasing or love to play with a person's emotions. I leave that to Dusty. She has cornered the market on such behavior. For me, a romantic relationship would be as important as my word. As to Beau, he wanted to marry me to build a grocery store on a piece of land adjacent to BE property."

The bitter, angry tone took Rorke by surprise, given the conversation Sunday. "Whoa! Not the enemy here."

"Sorry. I'm upset at the situation and not you. My mind is trying to figure out how to reassure you without breaking my oath."

The documents Callie tried to hand Beau hadn't moved from where she'd laid them on the counter a few days before.

Callie said, "I still need a shower. Why don't you carefully read the folder that Beau ignored?"

When she reemerged from the bathroom, Rorke was working in her office. Oddly, his presence seemed natural and not invasive.

Rorke smiled in greeting. "Honestly, the information in the folder makes me feel better. I wondered about your judgment of men and dating. Protecting another young lady from a man's attention tracks more with your personality. Ah, I should warn you. Isley thought the interaction at the sport's bar was curious and out of character. The man lives to unearth and collect every piece of a person's private business."

"He loves you."

"Isley is a pain in every part of the body, but he has never acted inappropriately."

Callie laughed. "Sorry. I meant as family. Does defending his character mean that you forgave his behavior with the girlfriend?"

Rorke grinned sheepishly. "Today is the first time that we ever discussed the situation. When I came home, the woman saw me and invited me in to join the fun."

Callie's eyes widened in disbelief. "No wonder you were upset and shocked. You are welcome to finish working, but I should be up at six. Nod wants to have lunch around one."

Callie set her alarm and crawled under the covers. She managed to sleep until about midnight. Tonight, in the dream, she used her boot to break out the cracked window and crawl out. Rorke woke her without being kicked. Breathing hard, Callie clung to Rorke as he comforted the quivering woman.

Settling back in the covers, Callie asked, "Stay? I was able to sleep a little last night."

"Yes, but I am not raiding the ducks for condoms."

Humor helped her relax. "I guess reliving the condoms conversation is going to be my most embarrassing moment for years. Pica texted the group, and Uncle Mer comes home next week. I doubt my uncle has a serious bone in his body."

Chapter

The chirping of the alarm woke her. Instead of turning off the noise, she rolled over and put her elbow in the middle of Rorke's stomach.

Rorke grunted and stopped the alarm. "You need to work on waking up without injuring me."

"No good deed goes unpunished. Thank you for staying with me. I managed to sleep without more nightmares."

"Could I ask you a question?"

"Sure, but I have to use the restroom." When Callie padded back, Rorke looked at her with a somber expression.

Rorke asked, "Why do you trust me? My motive could be to wine, dine, and take the money, land, or business."

"Why believe I trust you?"

"I thought we were past games."

No one ever asked or spoke to Callie about the circumstances surrounding her father's accident. The adults mainly ignored her presence or looked at her in pity. She'd heard people talk to Gran, and they used words like tragic, orphan, too young, and horrible.

Callie started high school. Most of her early school friendships faded with distance and age. A few family friends remained in her life. Friends from college had never met her father, and blended families were not unusual. Experts used the term blended family for a family that consisted of divorced, remarried, or adopted members. There remained stigma attached, but her real friends never cared or minded that her grandmother raised her.

"I will deny we ever spoke if the subject broached. I am aware Solomon was quite chatty about the past, but he doesn't know everything."

"Understood."

Callie paused and gathered her thoughts before telling the story. "The night of my father's accident, he was upset, distracted, and beyond worried. I was thirteen, almost fourteen, and imagined myself mature enough to help. My aunt was about to give birth to her second child, and Gran had gone to stay with the family. Dad sent me to bed and went to the greenhouse. I was old enough to be left alone, but the fact he left me alone was unusual."

Rorke guessed. "You followed him."

"Yes. I hid in the Osage Orange and Winged Euonymus plants. I could hear perfectly but was only able to see a little. Dad met six people that night: Hal Bear, Chi Pica, Dean Wither, Ms. Nod, Uncle Mer, and

Solomon. Solomon was out of my line of sight, and I wish I could have seen the man.

"Dad apologized for interrupting their lives. He'd been researching a criminal organization, and a clueless person saw his pictures. The person was trusted and wanted to help, but an innocent inquiry alerted the enemy to his research. My father reassured his friends that he had not involved me on any level. His only and last option was to protect his family and friends. The consequences would be his life."

"Shit!" Rorke reacted and immediately apologized for cursing in front of her.

Callie smiled. "Your reaction is mild compared to the ensuing commotion. Uncle Mer sent a piercing whistle through the air and told everyone to shut it. Mer made Dad explain what happened.

"Dad had heard about an illegal distribution system. Over a two-year time, he investigated and tracked shipments. His notes included names, places, types of cargo, and dates. A trusted friend discovered his research and begged him to involve the authorities. The person unknowably tipped off the suspected culprits."

Rorke asked, "Why would a person alert a dangerous criminal that he was under surveillance?"

"Uncle Mer asked the same question. The person made an innocent inquiry to help. Nod wanted to go straight to the police and put him in protective custody."

"Good call."

Callie's voice waved with emotion as tears slid down her face. "Dad never argued or raised his voice. I will never forget his expression: sad, resigned, love, and amused. His words will also never fade." She willed her voice to steady and uttered softly. "'An investigation would only hurt what I struggled each day to build. My past will not darken or define the legacy of a future for friends and family. Arrangements are in place. My garden will remain, endure, thrive, and be passed on to my daughter, Callie. We are beyond stopping events. A target has been placed on me by a powerful and connected organization. I have hidden the evidence and research beyond the reach of friend or foe.'"

Rorke wrapped Callie in a warm embrace. "I'm slightly surprised nightmares are the only outward symptom."

Seeing Callie's confused expression, Rorke explained, "A child keeping such a secret is a horrible responsibility. Did anyone ever find the research?"

"Dad told his friends he filed a report with the authorities that held clues to the evidence's location. I am assuming that is the report Isley found."

Callie didn't want Rorke to release her, but she shifted to try and gauge his reaction to the next piece of news. Her question was purposely going to change the subject and throw his thinking process. "Your turn. How did you know my father?"

Rorke released Callie and stepped back as if she'd burned him. "What?!"

"Dad asked Nod to wait. He wanted her help on a different matter. He'd met a young man who had been in the foster care system, turned eighteen, and wanted to attend college."

"The description could describe thousands, and I do not recall meeting Nigel Rivera."

"Dad explained that he'd discovered a treehouse in his travels. The builder was resourceful, cautious, and a good kid but wouldn't last the winter alone. Robinson Crusoe needed a person to care and offer a chance to rise above the system. Dad wanted a particular account to be liquidated and be used to pay for legal fees. Any leftover money could go toward the young man's schooling. Dad had taken care of us. He'd set aside my money for college, and he'd made sure that we would be fine financially. Well, as long as no one embezzled or act irresponsibly with money."

Rorke looked thoroughly shocked. "As far as I knew, no one had a clue about the treehouse until the day the authorities cornered me at the place."

Callie asked, "If you promise not to rat me out, would you like to have lunch with Nod and me on Friday?"

"Yes. How is Solomon related to you?"

"He was in foster care with my dad, and they became friends. Dad spoke to him at least once a week on the phone."

Both were startled when the doorbell rang. Callie peeked around the curtain and saw Isley. Only two other people could remotely turn off the security system: Solomon and Mer. That meant one or the other sent Isley. Isley grew impatient and pounded on the door for attention.

"Ah, that is not good. Isley was supposed to be out of town and knocking before seven. Would you answer the door while I call Gran to make sure she is all right?"

Callie retrieved her cell phone. Rorke agreed but didn't look pleased with starting his day greeting Isley. Conversationally, Callie made sure no one had been hurt or in an accident. More relaxed, she entered the

61

kitchen where Isley was making a pot of coffee. When Isley turned his back to Rorke, Rorke shrugged that he didn't have a reason for the visit.

Callie remembered Isley's remark about her lack of sleep and asked, "When's the last time you slept, young man? You are in the same clothes you were wearing last night."

Isley's tone took on a menacing quality. "If the circumstances were different, I might be impressed with the sassy response. Rorke is in the same clothes as well. At least, he was able to take off his shoes and socks to rest."

Rorke asked, "What's wrong?"

"Nod's practice and Botanic Enchantment were broken into last night. Guess who the common denominator is? Luckily, Ms. Nod's practice is secure. Records and files are not accessible or comprised during a burglary. I am not here in an official capacity and haven't even touched my other reasons. Get dressed and pack for a long weekend. We are attending a meeting before taking a trip to a safe house for the weekend."

Callie countered. "I am afraid that is not an option. We have a meeting Saturday morning. Several orders are due, and classes start Monday."

"Where do you keep the financial records and bank accounts?"

Callie answered. "Current month is kept in a drawer in the house office. Past ledgers are locked in a vault. I take everything to an accountant for taxes. I give Ms. Nod a copy after forms are filled out. Until I turn twenty-four, she is the designated business manager. Employee records go through her office. Uncle Mer and I are the only two with access to the vault."

"Where are the files?"

"The information hasn't been accessed."

Isley pressed Callie for the answers. "Show me."

"No."

Isley stared with his mouth open at her refusal, but Callie stood her ground. "You recused yourself, remember? Hand me a warrant or good reason to share."

"Your life."

"Nope. Has anyone involved the police?"

"No. Solomon called me after he investigated the incident. I am taking the man's word that nothing of value was on site, and no one took anything. I wanted to inform the police, but Solomon refused."

Callie nodded in agreement with her nosey guardian. "If Solomon investigated, he'd study the problem thoroughly. I trust his view on the matter, and we'll deal with business as usual."

Isley turned a shade of scarlet as he tried to control his temper. The opinion went against everything he believed as a lawman.

Rorke intervened in the argument. "Stop arguing! What would you have to be done for you to leave everything until Monday?"

After thinking, Callie listed the chores. "There are six orders to complete, and there is a shipment going out today. Pickle has three weddings, and we need to gather the flowers. Blooms must be cut and put together as close to the day of the event as possible. I can call a couple of employees to help, but there are a few things that I must do myself."

"How long would you need before you could leave?" Rorke moved himself to strategically blocked Callie's view of Isley.

"If I have help, three to four hours. I must stop at the lab and close out the research. The computers must be backed up, locked, and stored before classes begin on Monday. We're not able to access the main servers from remote locations. We also have the meeting Saturday."

"Dr. Lite sent a text. Our Saturday meeting has been rescheduled for Monday. Why aren't you in a panic or meltdown about a break-in at the greenhouse?"

"The flowers in the reception area are props, and my family has weathered far worse problems."

Rorke placed a hand on her shoulder. "Get dressed and put together a bag. We'll settle the business matters before departing."

Callie dressed, started to pack, and realized she had no idea what type of clothes to bring. Did she need shorts or jeans? Were they headed to higher elevations where she needed a jacket?

Heading back to the kitchen, she heard Rorke say, "Don't back Callie into a corner. She's kind and giving to a point but used to doing things her way."

Isley made a disagreeing sound. "A point? She wins the prize for stubbornness. Speaking of complications, be careful of Beau and anyone connected with him."

Rorke asked curiously, "Why?"

"Less than stellar reputation with authorities, and the whole family is suspect. Dad owns several business chains. Publicly, he is a benevolent, caring, benefactor. The mother tries to be a good influence, but rumors are the father rules family and business with an iron fist. Money is for influence and motivation. If a child has a run-in with the law, Dad uses money, threats, intimidation, influence, or a combination to ensure compliance. I never liked men or women using their power to tromp on others. Don't!"

Rorke sounded amused. "Don't what?"

"Accuse me of being a hypocrite. I tried to warn you but never demanded you end the relationship. Both of you were over eighteen and consenting adults, but she was not a good influence."

"You realize we are discussing an event that was well over five years ago. I am over it."

Isley's movements sounded like he was stirring something. "Good because you will probably need my help."

"Why?"

"While you were busy watching Callie drive off, I saw Beau's mask slip. Callie has no idea that she threw down a flag of challenge. Once the man figures out what he wants, he'll stop at nothing to acquire it. If you become a roadblock, there are many ways to remove or eliminate a barrier. The girl may be able to hit a target on the range, but Beau is a whole different barrel of fish."

"Warning noted. Isley, how concerned are you about Callie's safety?"

"Scale one to ten? Twenty. The stubborn streak won't do us any favors if she is not willing to accept help. Callie may know plants, but she's oblivious to real carnage left in a war's wake."

Rorke complimented. "That is oddly perceptive of you."

"I have my moments. How dirty are you willing to become on Callie's behalf?"

Rorke kept a straight face as he decided to annoy his friend. "Do you mean how big a barrier or roadblock? Patience is a virtue, and quick judgments should be avoided. Snap decisions could lead to a lifesaving moment or death."

Isley rattled a frying pan. "One day, you are going to run out of words. If you mess up, I may not be able to protect you. I'd hate for my hard work to end up in the garbage or worse, a grave."

Callie wished that she had the courage to interrupt but decided to retreat and pack. This was the third time that she'd decided not to interrupt a kitchen conference. A part of her felt guilty for not announcing her presence, but it was a shared space. Callie packed and brought her two small bags to the kitchen.

Isley cooked breakfast, so the three ate before going to the greenhouse. Callie met five employees who agreed to help on short notice, and she provided directions. The last order, she'd supervise. Two hours later, Isley was testing Callie's patience. She wanted to turn the man into compost for the plants. Then, she decided his acidity might kill the roots.

A semi-truck arrived with three workers. The driver, Trix, climbed down and greeted Callie with a warm bear hug. His brown hair was long and tied back in a ponytail. A stocky, bearded man with a potbelly, beefy arms, and gigantic smile, hugged Callie in greeting instead of shaking hands. Brown eyes twinkled with a relaxed, calm view of the world. Trix's slow drawled accent had always intrigued Callie.

Trix never said hello but asked a question for his usual greeting. "Are you ready to see the town in the rear-view mirror and visit the world with me?"

"Is there a bathroom in the rig yet?"

"Nope."

"Out of luck. Tumbleweeds are only so big, and my shy bladder isn't up to the task."

Isley stated with an annoyed, impatient tone, "We need to move along."

Callie didn't react with anger. "Trix, meet Isley and Rorke. Ignore Isley. The flowers are giving him watery eyes. The guy has not figured out many of us have businesses to run as well as schoolwork. Wait till he meets Pickle."

Trix made a sound like a guff. "Pickle is a nice, polite lady, but she is all business. I tried to flirt with her one day and found myself holding the thorny end of a rose stem."

Callie smiled. "Pickle is awesome at business and flowers, but she's shy. Our unique sense of humor is an acquired taste. Do you need me for loading?"

"I always need you, babe, but we're good. Paperwork is signed, and I see the pallets and trays are waiting in the loading dock."

Callie turned and asked, "Mr. Isley, would you walk with me?"

Isley waved for her to lead the way and didn't see the glint of annoyed irritation in her eyes.

Alone in the reception center, Callie stood toe to toe with Isley. "Stifle the attitude! Prodding and snide remarks are not going to make anyone work any faster. Be quiet, or stay here and separate flowers. It's not hard. Pick two and see if they match. Make a pile. Then, choose another. If the flower doesn't match, start another stack."

Callie left Isley and returned to the greenhouse. Rorke found her and asked how he could help.

Callie looked at her watch. "Would you mind finding out what each of the workers wants for lunch? Ordering for a large group takes a while and one person to organize. If there is a consensus, here is the business credit card. Place the order under my name, and make sure to keep the receipt."

"That is trusting of you."

"My card has a five-hundred-dollar limit, and I check the balance daily. Plus, I have the advantage. Gran has your information and owns the house that you rent."

Rorke asked, "Requests?"

"No. I'll eat anything but anchovies. Prefer to stay away from berries or nuts unless out on the trail."

"What did you say to Isley on the way back to the office?"

"I told him the choice was to stifle the attitude or sort flowers."

Rorke started to laugh but saw Callie's neutral expression begin to shift to anger, and he wisely went to take care of food orders. Callie collected several pots of small roses and placed them in a wagon.

The smell of fertilizer, dirt, and fresh roses eased the worry and stress. Concerns faded with the gentle breezes wafting through the greenhouse. Annoyance toward Isley lessened. The break-in did bother her, but her flowers were safe. There was no money on the property, and nothing was damaged. Her biggest concern was Solomon's silence. Under normal circumstances, he'd be the first to call and let her know what happened.

Over the years, her father stressed that people were not so different from plants. Every individual, no matter the species or color, was unique and had value. Each plant could be forced to grow a certain way, but distinctive traits would find a way to the surface. If given a positive environment and room to grow, both people and plants would thrive. Sometimes the optimal setting was unknown and had to be discovered. When two or more people or plants had to coexist, they could achieve a balance. There had to be work, compromise, and communication.

Callie had wanted to do her master's thesis on plant communication. Plants communicated but not like people. If thirsty, leaves would begin to droop. The entire group of teachers discarded the idea. Deemed boring, useless, and a waste, plant communication did not bring in research grants or funding. Now, the university and teachers asked her to participate in a project that would ultimately bring funds to the university. The comparison wasn't fair, but she didn't feel like having charitable thoughts.

Rorke's hand on her shoulder startled her. "Earth to Callie. Start answering the phone. It's lunchtime, and the group that Isely wants us to meet is here. Isley was ready to call the National Guard to retrieve you. Instead, Mer told us where to find you and me to escort you to lunch."

Chapter

Callie walked from the greenhouse to the Reception Center. The side door had glass on the upper part of the door, which allowed her to see inside. The image greeting her was almost surreal. A large monitor was set on the counter. The picture showed a white wall with the edge of a desk near the bottom. An unknown person shuffled papers and moved objects outside of the camera's view.

Hal Bear, Ms. Nod, Chi Pica, Dean Wither, Uncle Mer, and Agent Isley were sorting flowers. They had rearranged the furniture to make various piles.

Every so often, someone would ask, "Wither, what is this?"

Wither would glance up from his heap and answer a lily, carnation, rose, or begonia. Callie had no idea how long she stood there until Rorke touched her shoulder a second time. Callie nodded and opened the door.

Callie went to give Mer a big hug in greeting. "When did you arrive? The schedule has the flight coming in next week."

Mer ignored the flowers that fell out of his lap as he stood and hugged her back. "Plans change."

"Love the color scheme against the black leather."

"I do not."

Callie stared pointedly at Isley. "No one is to give Isley access to financials or the property without a warrant. Uncle Mer, why didn't the alarms go off last night? I didn't receive an alert."

Mer looked upset and sheepish. "Normally, I do maintenance during the day, but work has been busy. I was in the middle of an admin update, and the main system was offline."

"Oh, good. Mystery solved. I am still trying to figure out the new additions, and a raccoon is tripping off the sensors near the corn stalks and compost heaps. Mer, I hate to ask, but Isley wants me out of town for the weekend. I usually take flowers to church and leave plants for parishioners to take home for the anniversary."

Uncle Mer nodded. "The Motley Mob knows the drill. We'll take care of the flowers."

"Motley mob? That sounds condescending and mean."

Isley asked Rorke. "Is there anything you are supposed to do for school?"

Rorke answered. "The meeting for Saturday was rescheduled to Monday. New staff is to practice with the system, turn in a syllabus, and begin lesson plans. Teaching schedules are supposed to be posted by noon today."

Callie made a noise and shook her head.

Rorke revised his statement. "The classes that we may instruct are available with a notation that schedule could change."

Isley's eyes glistened with amusement at Callie's mannerism. "A run-in with the system?"

Callie glanced at the dean of her department and answered very carefully. "There's a shortage of qualified science teachers at most levels. Accreditation standards are met if an instructor is almost qualified or working toward qualifications. I had never taught a class alone. The day that the semester started, they assigned me to teach a required General Science with approximately 300 students."

Rorke observed, "You could have declined."

Callie changed the subject. "Nod? My birthday isn't for several weeks. Could we hire one full-time employee before the official turnover?"

"Yes."

Callie turned to Pica. "Would you be willing to supervise a young lady? She's a hard worker, responsible, learns quickly, reliable, but she'll need greenhouse training."

Pica nodded in agreement instead of talking, which was unusual. Pica liked to socialize and have conversations going. Granted, he was in a group where he was uncomfortable.

"Oh, good. Before we start a meeting, I need to make a call and offer Blake the position."

Isley grumped. "Now she learns to use a phone."

Callie pulled her phone from her back pocket and called a number. "Blake, would you consider working at BE full time? We could arrange the hours around your class schedule. I will be out of town until Sunday night, but Mr. Pica agreed to show you the system. You'd not have to worry about safety. Hal Bear runs security for the campus, and he will also be making rounds to secure the place."

Everyone heard Blake's squeal of delight. Callie pushed the mute button so she could listen and hear when Blake finished celebrating. Callie caught Rorke's frown and remembered that Rorke had read the folder in the kitchen. The material in the folder had to do with Blake and Beau.

Rorke asked, "Is hiring Blake a smart idea? The circumstances with Beau might create trouble for you or Blake."

Callie shrugged and took the phone off mute. "Mr. Pica is scheduled to come in at one o'clock. I'll text you his phone number and a photo. He'll pick you up in the company truck and take you to Ms. Nod's office. Make sure to have your driver's license and social security card. Don't worry about the time the appointment takes. While you do paperwork, he'll probably visit an art gallery up the street."

"Thank you! Thank you!"

Callie disconnected, and Pica gave Callie a small grin. "Does that mean you'll buy me a painting as well?"

"I couldn't afford one of your masterpieces, much less one hanging in a gallery. How about dinner for two at your favorite Italian eatery with the fixings?"

A wide smile lit Pica's face as he agreed. "You know me so well. It's a date."

Isley interrupted plans for the Italian meal with a triumphant sound. "I knew it! What's the story with Beau? What charges may I bring up to arrest the arrogant clod?"

"There is no story. Sorry! No arrests for you today." Callie didn't sound contrite.

Nod asked in a very relieved tone, "I don't have to worry about you marrying that horrible excuse of a human being?"

Slightly defensive, the young woman stated. "How many times do I need to say the same words? Beau and I went out for a total of five dinners. His family is contemplating building three grocery stores. One option for construction was the land adjacent to BE.

"Several surveys and environmental studies have been completed over the years. A smart person would never build. Of course, that is unless a financial backer agreed and took a huge, huge risk. Beau decided to broach the idea of marriage merely to have access to a piece of property."

Uncle Mer let out a long breath. "Thank goodness! My niece has not lost her mind."

Isley revisited Rorke's words. "What did Rorke mean about trouble?"

Callie ignored Isley, but Nod asked pointedly, "Is there a connection between Blake and Beau?"

Callie knew Blake would trust Ms. Nod. The family lawyer was good at her job because she could untangle underlying family dynamics. She was fair and honest. Nod would let Blake know she was not alone and a friend if needed.

Callie ignored the subject and asked, "Where's the food?"

Isley stood and stretched, but his eyes glittered with anticipation and victorious glee. "Would you like to eat before or after sharing your secret?"

Callie didn't blink in concern at the implied threat or intimidation until Isley continued. "I am not bragging, but my talent is that I am an excellent investigator. The group gathered here has a closet full of skeletons. Anyone wish to begin?"

Silence reigned in the room.

Isley continued. "Protecting the past and one another is liable to get someone killed. Our conversation will not penetrate these walls, but the time for secrets is over. As the outsider and someone not emotionally invested, I'll start. I could care less if my words offend anyone. Feel free to chime in with discrepancies or details that need correcting. The common denominator in the room is Nigel Rivera.

"Nigel was an extremely shrewd businessman as well as a horticulturalist. He started Botanic Enchantment from very little and built the business slowly. Later, when his father died, Nigel helped Rosa start a new life with the rentals. A way to supplement incomes was to hire out his services as a companion."

Nod muttered several expletives and interrupted. "I was going to broach the matter more delicately when we had lunch."

"I think Miss Rivera is well aware of Nigel's extra income."

Nod sought verification from Callie.

The young woman explained. "Dad shared a little because we were arguing about rules. I insisted that I was perfectly capable of staying by myself. Then, he left a couple of receipts out for a pair of Boston Ferns. He charged the customer eight hundred dollars, which offended me, and I was already mad about having a babysitter. Dad had to figure out a way to explain his role as an escort. The word tends to have a negative stigma attached because of the association to paid sex. My father once attended an opera with a lady because her husband would rather pay someone to sit through the production for him. There are apps now that do the same thing. Pay someone to stand in line or bring take out to the house."

Wither looked around the room and blurted. "How come he never told me? I thought he was one of my best friends."

Nod tried to ease the man's hurt feelings. "No one was supposed to know, and I found out by sheer coincidence. Protecting his past, family, and Callie was his top priority. Nigel was a shrewd individual. He had a gift of being unassuming and invisible. Half of his personality was friendly, polite, quiet, and gentlemanly. The other half was a ruthless, merciless, fierce nature. I saw that person twice, and the transformation scared me."

70

Mer didn't elaborate on the opinion. "I concur. Thank goodness, arguments with Callie about rules didn't begin until the teenage hormones started. Usually, disagreements were one-sided. Callie argued, and Nigel ignored."

Curious Rorke, asked, "What if she broke the rules?"

"Depended. Callie wasn't allowed to wear makeup until high school. One day she raided Rosa's cosmetics. Callie sat down to dinner. Nigel didn't yell or react. He told his daughter to collect her purse. Nigel took Callie to a store and let the saleswoman explain the products. Afterward, he made a deal. Callie could wait for the start of high school, and he'd buy the makeup. If Callie wanted makeup immediately, she bought the items with her allowance."

Callie admitted sheepishly. "I think Dad took me to the most expensive place on the planet. I waited to buy the products, but Gran made me work to replace her makeup. Using the same brushes and sticking my fingers in the different jars ruined the makeup."

Isley put a halt to more stories. "Let's bring the subject back to Nigel. I have updated everyone that the authorities located Nigel's report. If approached, Callie offered to help translate his notes."

Loud disagreement erupted in the small area. Callie went over to the computer displaying the image on the wall.

Callie tapped the screen. "Solomon?"

Solomon's deep voice answered. "I am here."

Callie whispered, "You have remained extremely quiet. What have you done?"

"Kept my promise."

Callie felt the blood drain from her face and repeated. "What have you done?"

"The past needs to be put to rest. Isley recused himself from the plant project, but the break-in at Nod's office and Botanic Enchantment changes the overall picture. We started working on a plan, but there are details to finalize. You and Rorke need to be off-site until Sunday."

Isley went to stand beside Callie. "Would you voluntarily hand over the phone and laptop?"

"No. Gran and I talk each night. There will be orders to fill, and the university is posting teaching assignments."

"Did you hear a word that I uttered earlier about safety?"

"Yes, but I never agreed with the opinion."

Isley did not debate but turned to Rorke. "We've had our differences, but I am proud of the man and person you have become."

"That had better not be an attempt at saying goodbye. I thought you turned over the case to someone else."

"Correct, but I will not speak freely after today. I have a reputation to maintain as an outcast and unfeeling robot. I think you should find a nice lady, get married, and settle down. If you have children, I could breeze in with lots of noisy toys, play grandpa for an afternoon, and leave."

Rorke was stunned hearing the man's revelation and remained rooted to his spot. Isley apologized for his next actions, and Callie's world went dark.

Chapter

Callie's next conscious thought was that her head felt too large for her body. Her mouth was drier than she'd ever remembered.

A woman's voice offered, "The headache is the worst part. Here, drink a few sips of tea. The brew will relieve most of the throbbing."

Callie looked around. A woman with the reddest hair that she'd ever seen sat beside her. Lots of freckles dotted a pale nose and cheeks. Callie wondered how quickly the lady would sunburn if she stayed outside. There was an air of openness and kindness surrounding her.

"Solomon is making food. Don't wander into the kitchen unless you want a face full of skunk spray. The man is serious about cooking and kicked me out of my kitchen."

"What did Isley do to me?"

"A mild tranquilizer. Isley doesn't play well with others. He figured the safest, quickest, and quietest method of transport to the Lodge was you being unconscious."

Feeling slightly better, Callie poured every ounce of sarcasm she could into her words. "How astute of the agent."

"Before you try to stand, we need to talk about what you missed. My name is Lion, and Solomon did not betray you. Isley discovered a recording of Nigel's last phone call and confronted Solomon. The agent put the pieces together regarding the night of your father's accident.

"The call makes more sense if you were at the scene of the accident. That information changed the overall picture. You stowed away in the car. Nigel discovered your presence and called Solomon to pick you up. Nigel left you at the cabin. Solomon and Isley believe that you saw the accident and who killed Nigel."

Callie put the hot tea on the nightstand by the bed and found tears running down her face.

"It's all right, dear. We won't press. Currently, Solomon is more concerned about who Nigel was investigating. My role is to take care of your physical and emotional health over the weekend. We're going to trust one another and put an end to this mess.

After Callie composed herself, Lion had her stand carefully and helped her to the main room. Rorke sat with a young-looking teen with sandy brown hair.

Callie paled and felt dizzy as she tried to take a step. Rorke was immediately there to support her to a chair, and the young man stood to wait for Lion to have a seat.

Lion smiled and said, "Bash, thank you for recognizing my status as an elder and a lady, but please sit. We are here until Sunday, and you may drop the Ms. and call me Lion."

Callie thought the woman's smile lit up and warmed the entire room. Bash turned his gaze to Callie.

Callie knew Solomon was in the kitchen. "Don't stand for me. Where's Solomon?"

Solomon's voice sounded from an adjoining room. "No one comes inside the kitchen when I am cooking."

Callie angrily called. "Then come out here! How could you?!"

"Isley arrived at my office with files and pictures. A copy of the information is here for you to study. Callie, I don't have much time, but I'll explain the plan while the food finishes cooking."

"You never stay in one place and always complain about being late like Lewis Carrol's white rabbit. "'Oh dear! Oh dear! I shall be too late!'"

Lion laughed merrily, and Callie's mind envisioned fairy light. "I love you, child! That assessment is spot on, but no one dares to challenge him on the matter. I've only come across a few people in the world who aren't afraid to challenge Solomon."

Solomon didn't argue. "Callie, five men are arriving shortly. You, Rorke, Bash, and these five men will find the evidence that Nigel hid. Each of you is an experienced outdoorsman and passed a meticulous background check. We do not have much time for the group to meld as a team and trust one another. Since Nigel left a treasure hunt for the authorities, we are performing a smaller scale scavenger hunt. A map in the other room has seven marked spots. Boxes are hidden at each location. The last numbered challenge is the most difficult.

"Lion will provide the gear and details, but the precious lady is not built for outdoor adventures. She is present as a liaison to the outside world and in case of an emergency. Callie, Lion has a phone for you to call your grandmother or deal with work issues. Rorke is in charge. He's an experienced leader and has a natural ability to bring various personalities together to complete a mission. A bonus is that he's already a unit leader in search and rescue."

Rorke looked extremely surprised and not happy at the promotion. "Uh, thanks, I think."

Solomon announced. "Lion, the food is ready."

Lion didn't appear as if she could detain a kitten, much less Callie. Yet, the young woman found herself in a strong but firm hold. Solomon was gone before anyone stepped a shoe toward the kitchen.

Lion's soft, calm voice told Callie. "Isley is on the contact list and asked for a call when you woke."

Callie rubbed her forehead. "Rorke, Bash, or Lion, do you mind if I use the speaker? I feel like a thousand leprechauns are hammering on fairy shoes at once in my head. Shouting in my ear will only make the pain worse."

Receiving nods of assent, she took a deep breath and dialed.

Nod's concerned voice answered on the first ring. "Are you all right? We are still here with Isley. The agent insisted on taking you to a place without communications."

Uncle Mer's voice filled the speaker. "Why didn't you tell us that you agreed to help the authorities?"

Callie reassured her friends and family. "No one has officially asked, and I had no idea Isley would blab."

Nod warned Callie. "Isley told Solomon the plan, and they believe the danger to you is minimal. Be careful! The people involved aren't playing around. Lives are at stake."

"Noted. Before anyone asks, I doubt anything was at the cabin. Literally and figuratively, the place burned to the ground a week after Dad died. The cabin was rebuilt after the fire. A part of me would like to solve the puzzle and find out what my father was doing. The flip side is the investigation. If the criminals are still around, they will want to see what we find. The best and most low-key solution is to stay in the shadows and let someone else do the work."

Rorke suddenly turned on his heel, walked out the front door, and slammed the wooden entrance behind him.

Isley asked, "Did Rorke leave?"

"Yes. What did I miss?" Callie's tone expressed her confusion.

"Nothing. Rorke doesn't like feeling helpless or purposely placing a person in danger. Callie, we are walking a dangerous tightrope without any safety equipment. My position is precarious because I am no long a part of the official investigation. Once we start, backing out is not an option."

Callie reassured Isley, "When the mystery is solved, the past will truly be history."

Isley praised, "Brave but naïve. I'll remain in the loop. Whatever Solomon has arranged on his end, trust him."

Callie asked, "Why?"

"Solomon promised Nigel to protect and look after you."

Callie asked, "Uncle Mer, do you have my laptop?"

"Yes."

"If I am gone until Sunday, there are usually last-minute orders to be shipped out. If extra help is needed, send a message to the part-time help."

Nod said, "Don't worry. We'll take care of BE. You stay safe."

"I love you guys. Bye."

Callie stood and wobbled her way to the front door. Bash and Lion let her move but were ready to offer support. Rorke stood against a porch post and looked out at the stars. Callie used the door frame to keep herself upright.

Rorke heard Callie and stated his opinion. "Your life is worth more than piles of stupid seeds! Why take a risk for dumb plants? You sat and discussed dying at the hands of counterfeiters without a trace of emotion. Where did those gems of insight on Isley or Solomon's plan fall from?"

Callie sighed tiredly. "I may disagree with Isley's, uh, people skills, but he cares. He is attempting to solve the problem and bring the guilty to justice with as little bloodshed as possible."

Rorke finally looked toward Callie. "You need to sit down before you fall over."

Putting an arm around her waist, Rorke let her lean into him. They went inside to join Bash and Lion for dinner. Five men had wandered inside from the back door to join Bash and Lion. Callie saw the newcomers and tried to talk. Instead, she felt her knees buckle slightly. Rorke made sure she didn't fall and supported her to her a chair. The food was on the table, and it smelled wonderful. She was hungry, but her stomach churned with stress.

Lion provided a distraction. "The men are aware Isley tranquilized you for the trip. Why don't you introduce yourselves? Start with Rorke and work counterclockwise around the table."

"Rorke Asher, and I'm trying to figure out how I ended up leading our expedition. I'll do my best. If anyone has an idea or better way, speak up."

Lion prompted. "Still, go ahead."

Still appeared slightly older than Rorke with black hair and the iciest blue eyes that Callie had ever seen. An easy smile graced the weathered face. "Name's Still. More of a river rat than a mountain climber."

Crabbe went next, and the man reminded Callie of a crab with a beard. The man had blond hair with a face reddened by windburn. An angular jawline accented his rosy cheeks. Slender fingers belied the strength one could see in his hands.

Callie knew Bash's name from the earlier conversation, and he told the others his name.

Whipper had a thinning hairline and a face lined from sun exposure. The man was the shortest and stoutest of the group. Callie found his droopy eyes fascinating because he looked asleep. Yet, Whipper was wide awake.

Tort, in contrast to Whipper, was tall, lean, but muscular. His face immediately made Callie think of a hawk. Brown eyes watched the motions of every person. His slightly hooked nose reminded Callie of a beak. Natural sun highlights in honey-blond hair flowed like feathers around his forehead and ears.

Thicke had shaved his head and didn't have facial hair. The man's eyes twinkled under the pair of glasses he wore. Thicke was the only one wearing eyeglasses.

Lion offered a blessing for their food before sharing details of their upcoming adventure. "Before Callie explains counterfeit seeds, let me tell you about the scavenger hunt. There are eight treasure chests at seven locations around the state. The last and furthest away is the most difficult to reach. The boxes must be brought back and opened at the same time for the rewards. You're to sort the gear and make a list of additional items after dinner. Think about what gear or equipment you might need. If you want specific trail food or equipment, let me know."

Callie asked, "Is eight a significant number?"

"Each chest holds something specific for each of you."

Callie asked, "Is there a prize for you?"

"No. My participation is organizational.

"That's not fair. You may have whatever is in my box."

Lion patted Callie's hand. "Thank you, but Solomon has sent me lots of gifts over the years."

"Unconscious people left on your doorstep don't count as a prize."

Lion laughed. "Depends on the individual who appears."

Callie continued her questions. "What does Solomon look like?"

"The man stays out of my sight as well as yours. He calls if he needs something. You may begin discussing plants, dear."

Callie felt her dry mouth and took a sip of water. "If I confuse anyone, let me know. Counterfeit might be a strong word, but the term means fake. I'll use the genus, Linum. Most people know the plant's common name: Flax or Linseed. The plant has been used for various purposes through the ages. Bed sheets, rope, twine, tablecloths, linens, clothes, or other textiles are made from the fibers. Cotton has overshadowed Flax as a commercial crop, but Flax is a stronger fiber.

77

Linseed oil comes from Flax seeds, and the seeds are used as food to feed people or certain animals. Types of food range from health supplements, ground for flour or meal, and a spice. Also, the oil is used in paints, varnishes, linoleum, and inks."

Tort made a face as he'd bitten into a lemon. "Gross. A plant that you eat is also in varnish and paint."

"There are about 200 species of the plant. You don't pick a flower and toss the seeds in a pot. The seeds are in a capsule. Stalks aren't pulled up like a weed with the roots and taken to a weaver. Plants must be cultivated, harvested, and processed."

Crabbe asked, "Why does that matter?"

"Say a farmer buys 70000 pounds or roughly 35 tons of seed. The price is usually by weight, and farmers aren't about to inspect every seed. If seeds are in shell, weight is added. Say the farmer realistically ends up with 20 tons of viable seeds. Less yield for a larger cost. Germination is also slower. Some years, a farmer can harvest several crops in one year. If germination is slow, the farmer does not benefit.

"Take the stalks used for fibers. If the seeds are unhealthy and weak, they're vulnerable to disease or may not mature fast enough to repel weeds. During the harvest, weeds create problems. A farmer sells crops for processing, and weeds add weight. The buyer won't be happy paying for weeds instead of a plant. Be aware that my explanation is somewhat simplistic. My botany knowledge centers on ornamental flowers and not crops. Does anyone have any questions?"

No one spoke or voiced any thoughts. They ate the rest of meal without talking.

Chapter

When everyone finished eating, Lion said, "Don't worry about doing dishes. Study the maps and equipment. Solomon warned me that no one is going to be happy about shoes and clothes. There were comments about breaking in the boots, and clothes should smell like dirt mixed with sweat."

The eight adventurers adjourned to an office area with maps tacked to boards. Callie had never seen so many types of maps in one place. Basic topography and elevation charts were readily recognizable. Others looked to be outlines of specific sections and marked with symbols.

Tables off to the left had eight sets of hiking equipment to include boots, helmets, backpacks, and knives. Each pile had a name tag plate beside the footwear. Solomon was serious about an outdoor quest to include rock climbing and walking.

Callie decided to pack the bag and study the provided gear. The helmet went into the bottom of the bag. Since she didn't have to worry about overnight camping, she put the helmet upside down in the bottom. Some hikers like to secure head protection on the outside for more room inside the pack. Its position allowed for maximum organization of space. Skillfully and carefully, Callie put her pack together. She slipped her arms in the straps to try out the weight distribution in the backpack.

Lion had come in and sat down to read a newspaper after doing dishes, and Callie caught her attention. "Ma'am, I request a real compass. Fancy electronics with GPS, satellite radio, walkie-talkie, and map are nice pieces of equipment, but signals could be spotty to nonexistent in the wilderness. I'd like sixteen spools of Baker's twine. Each spool a different color and 2,300 ft. in length."

Lion wrote down the specifics. "Anything else?"

"Paper, writing instrument, and camera."

"Why?"

Callie answered, "Fall season is beginning, but we are on the clock for the treasure hunt. Certain foliage will be ready for seed collecting. If I have a picture and location, I could come back for samples later."

"I'll check with Solomon."

Callie turned to Rorke. "I promise not to waste anyone's time. I'll keep notes and take pictures during water or restroom breaks."

Rorke said, "You are not supposed to remove anything from the environment in natural parks. Picking nuts, berries, or other food for consumption is allowed."

"I have state and federal licenses to collect seeds for research or propagation. The rangers assigned to nearby forest areas know me by sight."

Crabbe asked, "Nearby? How did you figure out our coordinates?"

"I spent my entire life traipsing around Idaho. We are between Snake River Plains and Sawtooth. More specific southeast of Hailey City and near to Little Wood River." Callie's face lit with impish amusement as she added. "My knowledge of Idaho, and Solomon put a red sticker on the wall map that says: You are here."

The men had been inspecting and packing as well. Their eyes turned to a map tacked to a free-standing corkboard.

Callie asked, "Lion, may I raid the kitchen for food supplies? If possible, I prefer not to eat grubs, worms, fish, or wildlife on the trail."

Lion answered, "Food and water was left in boxes by the kitchen island. Don't you want to help plan the hike?"

"No. Divide up the rations, and I'll pack my share food before we depart. I know each member of the team is familiar with outdoor skills by the way he is inspecting and arranging the gear. I do have a suggestion. If the seven map pins on the wall represent our destinations, I recommend we begin with the furthest north because the terrain will be the greatest challenge. We work the numbers backward, but I am flexible and will follow along."

Rorke asked, "What are you going to do?"

"Isley told me that there was a box of my father's photographs. I'd like to see them."

Lion smiled. "I put the box on the table where we ate dinner."

Callie could hear the conversation in the other room. She had no idea who spoke after she walked out. The speaker wasn't Lion or Rorke because she'd recognize their voices.

"Lord, almighty. Solomon warned me that she is perceptive and intelligent. I pride myself on being aware of my surroundings but missed the map. Granted, the number of diagrams in one small space is sheer overload. Did anyone have an interview with Solomon in person? He spoke to me on the phone."

Rorke groused. "Lucky you. I never had an interview and found out about the venture today."

Callie recognized Crabbe's deep voice. "Still and I have worked with Rorke on the trail several times. He's one of the best."

Still had to be the man who spoke next. "I agree. I've been on the rescue team when Rorke led. Good leader and person."

Rorke's response was too low for her to hear. Callie made a mental note that Rorke was good at not giving away information. Rorke had past contact with Solomon, and Callie wouldn't betray the trust.

Files lay inside the banker's box. The first set was bound together with a rubber band. Tabs were labeled with family and friends' names. Skimming the information, she didn't see new or surprising information. Files on Solomon, Rorke, and Isley were missing. Gran's file intrigued her, and she read instead of scanned.

Rosa was born in Montpelier, Vermont, and her parents had eight children. Her father owned six fishing boats, and her mother was a housewife who did the accounting for the fleet. One of Rosa's brothers took over the business twenty-five years ago. The rest of the data in the profile was not new. A list of the property and tenants were listed, along with tax returns, permits, repair contracts, and insurance. There were no files on Solomon, Rorke, or her.

Callie read the information on her father. School diplomas and various licenses with application were included. One item caught her attention. Her father graduated summa cum laude in high school and college. His grade-point was a 4.4 on a 4.0 scale which meant he took honors classes and received A's.

A search warrant inside the sleeve required Nod to provide family and business records. The assets of Botanic Enchantment were listed. Scanning, there wasn't anything out of the ordinary.

The enclosed sheets were copies of every tax return from the business's established year to the previous year. Behind the paper was an inventory list for each year's audit. A summary of business expenses with the credit card statement was attached.

The final object in the container was a plastic tub. The box was sideways with a sealed lid. Taking off the top, an accident report and citizen's complaint form lay on top of a stack of roughly 300 photographs. Each print was an 8x10 inch color picture.

Callie picked up the first one, which featured a group of flowers. The plants had oval leaves and small flowers in a dense cluster. Her father's handwriting on the reverse side identified the Syringa with the common and scientific name. The information included a date, general location, and characteristics.

The second photograph sent Callie back into the map room. "Lion, may I have the phone? I need to talk to Isley and Solomon. Now!"

"Give me a moment."

Callie returned to the table and balled her hands into fists. Deep breath. Control. No emotion. Composure. No cracks.

Ms. Lion entered. "The two are on the phone."

A bubbling of emotion surfaced, and Callie lost her composure. "You diseased infested fleas! How could you? Horrible cases of blight! The test! That!"

"Did you have Lion use a secure line so you could call us names?" Isley sounded amused rather than upset.

"The test administered to select botanists for the book project used pictures from my father's evidence report, file, or whatever it's called!"

Solomon asked, "How many pictures did you study?"

"One! I recognized the first and only glanced at the second."

"Well, I lost because my wager was three. We had a betting pool on how many pictures you'd study before figuring out the test used Nigel's photographs."

Callie grew rigid with anger, surprise, and distress. People were taking bets about such a serious matter. She regained enough control of her poise to hand the phone to Lion without saying goodbye.

Callie returned to her bedroom. The fact she'd lost her composure bothered Callie more than the pictures. Reacting in a temper showed weakness that anyone could exploit. She'd spied a bathroom in a corner. Closing the door, Callie ran water in the tap until the temperature became warm. She cupped her hands together, made a bowl, and let the water fill up in her palms. Once the water was at the top of her thumbs, she leaned over the sink and splashed her face. Patting her face dry, she went to sit on the bed and closed her eyes. She started to recite a plant list from memory.

Abelia, botanical name Caprifoliaceae, is best used as a border. Abelmoschus, Botanical name Malvaceae, is a deciduous shrub.

A knock sounded, and Callie told the person to come in.

Rorke opened the door. "What sort of soliloquy are you performing?"

"Be glad that I know the definition of soliloquy. Scientific names of plant species are in Latin. I wish you were not around for every meltdown this week."

"I'd say that given the overall circumstances, you are doing remarkably well."

Callie acknowledged the compliment. "Thanks. I'm more embarrassed and upset at myself. Instead of being strong, my entire body feels like someone dumped a ton of bricks on me."

Rorke asked, "May I explain to the men about your father and the case? I'd only share what seems to be generally known."

"Sure. I understand Solomon and Isley's plan. We offer clues and translate the pictures, and they shake the trees to see what falls out. The group has two missions. Help take pictures for the book and secure whatever my father hid. The two have a lot of faith that we'll solve the puzzle my father left. There are two huge holes in the net to trap a criminal. How are we supposed to juggle a book project, exploration group, and continue everyday life? The second is the information. Is a ten-year-old report worth investigating? Who would care?"

Rorke answered, "My guess is exposure. Isley found Nigel's report. Rumors and news would spread with an official plan. The information would leak, especially with multiple agencies involved. Authorities would ask for translation and research. Nothing more and nothing less, but every action will be under the microscope by every interested party. If we discover any items, the discovery is turned over to the proper authorities. You and the team stay out of the problem."

"Would Isley ask you to be a spy and share with a person under suspicion to trap the suspect?"

"No."

"If Isley was kidnapped to force you to tell what you knew, would you cooperate?"

Rorke tried to provide Callie a measure of comfort. "I'm aware that Isley and I would die as soon as the information traded hands. If I even thought of dealing and he lived, he'd kill me for attempting to negotiate a trade. Try not to let the past cloud logical and emotional reasoning."

Callie heard the phone ring, and Lion came into her room. She showed Rorke the caller identification screen. He went to take the phone, but Ms. Lion put a hand up to stop him.

Ms. Lion pressed the speaker function, answered, and greeted in an Irish brogue. "Hello, this is Rorke's Mum answering his phone. How may I help you?"

"Oh, hello, Mrs. Asher, my name is Dr. Lite. I was calling to talk to Rorke."

"Dr. Lite, thank you for taking good care of Rorke. I am so excited about him going back to school, teaching, and the plant book."

Rorke made a face at Lion and asked loudly for Dr. Lite's benefit. "Did my phone ring?"

Lion smiled. "Yes, love. Dr. Lite wishes to talk to you."

Rorke issued a dramatic sigh. "Thank you. You realize explaining family dynamics is going to become old quickly. You are not my biological mother, and Isley is not my biological father."

Ms. Lion laughed. "I need some reason to share with the world what a wonderful person you have become."

Rorke teased. "I doubt that you've ever needed a reason to strike up a conversation to boast about family."

"Oui! Be polite, or you'll be doing dishes."

"I'll be doing dishes anyway. Bye, Mum!"

Rorke went to take the speaker off, but Ms. Lion shook her head to keep the speaker on.

"Hello, Dr. Lite. Sorry about that."

"I enjoy talking to family members. I called for a couple of reasons. We knew our meeting changed from Saturday to Monday, and the time changed to ten in the morning. I wanted to call about another matter. The Dean of Admissions called after looking at transcripts. You're earned credits for the three Master level classes. Academically, we won't offer the next set of classes you need until Spring. Would you be willing to teach four classes with taking the Botany course?"

Callie made a horrible face and wiggled two or three fingers.

Rorke offered. "I am new to the system. Three would be the most that I'd be comfortable teaching. Although, if the class is three hundred freshmen, one might be an overload."

Lite chuckled delightedly. "I wouldn't do that to our newest department star. I'll make sure the classes you and Ms. Rivera are teaching are in the same auditorium. Ms. Rivera will only be teaching the Botany class."

"May I ask why the changes?"

"I don't know the details. Let me know if you need anything or have any questions."

Lion ended the call, and Callie exhaled sharply. "Right! As painful and easy as falling on a spiky cactus. Four classes? Is he crazy?"

"No. Desperate. There are not enough qualified teachers to fill the positions."

Callie rolled her eyes. "Science department is in the same situation. I'm certainly going to hear grousing from the unfortunate instructor or instructors."

Lion asked, "Would you like dessert?"

"Yes, please."

"Callie, I hear the immense worry in Solomon's voice, but I told him that you were strong and smart. You'll wade through the muck and come out the other side fresh as a daisy. Your challenge will be letting people help and trusting in their abilities."

"I appreciate your confidence in me, but life is not guaranteed. What was the tea made from earlier? The drink helped."

Lion shared her secret. "The recipe is easy. One bag of chamomile and a bag of ginger. I'll brew a cup while you eat."

"I don't mind making my tea."

"Not a huge fan of other cooks in my kitchen. You may eat dessert while I make a cup."

The others had dished up various pies and cakes. Callie counted eight desserts. Everyone but she and Rorke had plates with pie or cake at their seat.

Callie asked, "Are these desserts our entire weekend's rations?"

"No. We have a set for each night. Leftovers will be boxed up and sent home."

Rorke took a piece of apple. Stacked plates were on a sideboard, and Callie took two of the largest in diameter. She cut a slice from each dessert to place on her dish.

Tort commented, "Girl, you ate two helpings of each course at dinner. Are you going to eat all that food?"

"If not, we'll put the excess in my leftover box to go home."

Tort looked around the table. "Oh, sneaky. I like it. Anyone want the rest of the carrot?"

Tort took his fork and wrote his name in the icing. No one volunteered. Bash, the youngest looking of the group, didn't bother with later. He took the cherry pie and finished what was left.

Chapter

Callie was not a morning person, especially at five. The sun wasn't up, but she rose, automatically dressed, ate, and added the food supplies to her pack. Her teammates had laid out an eighth of the food by her backpack.

Solomon sent the items she requested, including a compass and a camera that looked brand new. She had hoped that Solomon would send her old, trusty equipment. Learning a new camera while on unfamiliar trails bothered her, but she was grateful to have any device. Twine, paper, and writing implements went into side pockets.

Rorke was wide awake and warned her about the time change. "Our current location in Idaho is on Mountain Time. We are heading up to the panhandle in the north, which is on Pacific Time. Set your watch an hour behind. We are flying out in a helicopter from a regional airport."

Callie frowned in concern at the news. "Last minute charted flights are usually expensive. There are scheduled supply runs to remote areas. Families or tiny communities rely on the locally run airstrips for communication and resources. Some pilots don't mind if you tag along, but you have to know the times, routes, and places."

"Tort and Whipper are pilots, and we rented a helicopter for the day. Rental vehicles are waiting for us at the destination. We decided to work by location and collect the box by Bonners Ferry. We'll begin at the furthest point and work toward home base. We have no idea why Solomon marked the seventh location as the most difficult to retrieve."

Callie finished packing her bag and asked hopefully, "Are we going to the Boundary County Museum? The museum has a nice collection, and there are Kootenai Indian artifacts on display."

"We're going up to the Kootenai refuge. I don't think we'll see any camels at the ferry," Rorke offered the piece of trivia because she liked learning interesting facts.

Callie was continually looking at Idaho history for research, but this piece of information was new. "Camels? Really? I knew mules were used to pack mining supplies, but camels?"

"Edwin Bonner founded a ferry service to take prospectors, passengers, and mules carrying gear across the Kootenai River. An entrepreneur in San Francisco imported and sold camels as pack animals."

Callie visualized the map with numbers in her head. "I noticed that one of our stops is around St. Maries. Are we mining for garnets? The gems are only able to be found in India and Idaho."

"We are traveling through St. Maries but not stopping to prospect."

"How about Coeur D'Alene? Beach? Water skiing?"

Rorke smiled at Callie's enthusiasm while half-asleep. "No. We are not going on a resort vacation, and the food and wine festival is not until April."

"There is more to the Coeur D'Alene than the festival. There are places where the food is good all year."

Rorke advised. "You should take a closer look at our destinations after another cup of coffee. Someone is meeting us with car rentals stocked with extra water, sports drinks, and energy bars."

Callie stifled another yawn. "Geez, do Lion or Solomon ever sleep?"

"No idea. More concerned about where the extensive resources originate."

"If you find out, clue me in. I was always afraid that Solomon robbed a bank to pay for my birthday presents."

Rorke looked a little surprised at Callie's concern. "You don't know much about Solomon, do you?"

"Why are you so surprised? I tried, but he won't even send me a picture. The man has zero social media presence. I read every page of my father's college yearbooks to try and find a picture."

"Ah, I am not about to get in the middle of a family squabble, but Solomon is a respected law enforcement official. He is many things, but an outlaw is not one."

Callie studied Rorke with new interest. "How do you know?"

"We have worked together on multiple occasions. Part of his success is staying under the radar and networking. Solomon is a nosy, bossy busybody, but he is also a guardian of people and places. The man seems to know everything that goes on in approximately 83,000 square miles of Idaho, the six bordering states, and Canada. He has acquaintances and friends on both sides of the law."

"Then he is a criminal in a law enforcement position."

Rorke shook his head negatively. "There are cases where a person in law enforcement must use common sense and discretion."

Callie finished closing her backpack. "Remember, I'm not fully awake yet."

Rorke smiled at her. "Here is an example. An elderly neighbor is growing marijuana without permits. Medical care and doctor visits have run up a huge financial debt. Debt has exceeded its limit, and there is no money for doctors. Marijuana is the only pain relief available. The plants are not grown for distribution or shared with anyone else. Would you, as law enforcement, arrest the neighbor after finding out about the plants?"

Callie thought and answered with a question. "What about helping the neighbor secure the proper documentation?"

"Point of discussion is that the person doesn't have long to live, and resources are hard to acquire."

"Trying to process and think early in the morning is making my head hurt. Could we pick up the discussion later when I am awake?"

"Sure. We leave in ten minutes."

An hour and a half later, Callie stretched and was wide awake. Her watch read five-thirty. She climbed out of the helicopter and told Rorke that she needed the restroom before a car ride. Callie returned to the transport and found their two jeeps loaded and ready.

Tort nodded and shared the plan. "Hope you are awake enough to move quickly. The team planned on being in and out of the area in less than two hours. We have permits to go into the protected preserve. We went ahead and secured permission, permits, and passes to use the access roads as well. Two staff members are riding along to make sure we come out safely. I know the park staff, and they are probably more curious than concerned about us disturbing the environment."

Callie thought. "Normally, special permission takes time and paperwork. How was the process expedited?"

"No idea. Unique circumstances? Do you plan on asking questions the entire day?"

Callie laughed. "No, but I do have one more question. Why did Solomon say that this was the hardest retrieval?"

"We think the task has to do with logging. There is logging gear packed in the vehicles. I doubt we are felling any trees because we will be in a National Forest. The place is also a preserve and refuge."

Callie had not been sure of their reception because the expedition group would be disrupting the ecosystem. Rorke, Whipper, and Tort knew the park staff, who met the team with a warm greeting. As protectors of the area, they trusted the men to respect the land and environment. Callie was not as familiar with the personnel in the Panhandle and began to ask about the area.

The older woman discovered that Callie was interested instead of politely inquiring, and she provided stories about the wildlife.

When the three vehicles reached the destination, Callie wanted to wring Solomon's neck. The man knew Ponderosa Pine trees were her Achilles' Heel.

The park's caretakers were not happy taking in the situation. They demanded to know how and why two containers were strung roughly one hundred feet in the air. No one had an answer for them, and Thicke started to unpack logging ropes.

Rorke asked, "The paperwork given to me does not include a resume. Callie?"

Callie leaned against the hood, eyed the trees, and quipped, "Really? Did you see any Ponderosa Pines around the greenhouse? My knowledge only extends to the information about the tree. The scientific name is Pinus Ponderosa. A few of the common names are Bull Pine, Western Yellow Pine, or Western Pitch Pine. It has a single trunk with scaly bark. The needles grow in bundles of 2 or 3. The pinecones are prickly and contain seeds that are brown and winged. If planted or spaced correctly, the trees make a wonderful windbreak. Turpentine comes from Ponderosa Pines. Would anyone like to know about the root system, preferred habitat, or natural pests?"

No one took her up on the offer, but Crabbe looked quizzically at Callie. "What's wrong? You look like a thundercloud ready to spit lightning."

The young woman made her face relax and sighed. "Sorry. I didn't mean to sound annoyed. The reality of new clothes and shoes is sinking into my body. If our challenges are to climb trees, I'd prefer my trusty, old friends. I mean boots."

Crabbe smiled. "I think each of us would agree, and I'll be ecstatic if our tasks are similar. This challenge is easy. Shimmy up the tree, collect the two treasure chests, and done in less than an hour."

Callie returned the grin and assumed. "If you say so. It sounds like you've had experience climbing trees."

"A little. Thicke and I will go up. Start timing."

Crabbe and Thicke had more than an amateur's knowledge. The two had the safety ropes and harnesses ready in minutes. Callie explored while the two shimmied up the trees. A few minutes passed before Rorke called her name. She answered while adjusting the lens on the camera. Birds scattered at the noise but returned when silence settled in the clearing.

Rorke kept an eye on the climbers while scanning the undergrowth for Callie. She was watching birds gather seeds and attempting to take a picture with the new camera.

Rorke caught her attention from atop the hill and softly ordered. "Don't wander!"

Nodding, Callie continued to take pictures. A few minutes later, she moved and heard Rorke calling her for a second time. After the third time, Bash accompanied Rorke. The young man found a position where he could keep an eye on Callie as well as Crabbe and Thicke.

Callie heard the men congratulating Thicke and Crabbe. She headed back to the clearing. Carefully packing her camera, she followed everyone else into vehicles. Each person had chosen a specific seat, and she took the rear passenger seat. Bash sat across from her, and Still drove. Crabbe slid into the shotgun seat. Callie knew the term derived from the heyday of the gangster era. Nowadays, some called the position the suicide seat depending on who was driving. Rorke drove the second car with Tort riding shotgun. Thicke and Whipper took the rear window positions in Rorke's car.

Approaching Bonner's Ferry, the radio crackled. "Shuttle one and two, this is base. When approaching Bonner's Ferry, stop at the gas station. Two escorts will be waiting to take you down Highway 95 to Coeur d'Alene and Interstate 90. When you reach Route 3, a different escort group will pick you up. You'll be on your own once you reach Route 8 and the gravel road. Radio call signs for the first escort group is Panhandle, and the second is Gold Rush."

Callie reached up by the headrest and tapped Crabbe's shoulder. "Ask why we aren't flying back."

Solomon's voice spoke from the radio. "If I may continue, you're not flying back because the helicopter is needed elsewhere. Callie, if you want treats, buy snacks at the gas station. You may not stop the cars for gathering seeds because you collected plenty at the first location."

Callie felt her face flush. "I did collect seeds but followed protocol. If the caretakers had to verify everything, we could have been there for the rest of the day. Everything is tagged, logged, and legally obtained. I stayed away from the endangered foliage or nesting wildlife. The problem is that Solomon didn't send my permits and documents. I did remember to ask Lion before bed for the paperwork to be collected. How are you listening to us?"

"Radio and wireless."

Tort's voice came through the speakers. "Solomon, for an experimental communications' setup, the range and clarity are good."

Callie commented sarcastically. "Oh, someone else needs the helicopter, so we get to be the lab mice to try out experimental radio signals. Does anyone else want food or drink when we stop?"

Tort was in the second vehicle, and his voice came over the car speakers. "We are good, and there are additional rations in the rear. Callie, the food and coolers are located directly behind you."

Callie grinned. "I guess that I choose the seat. Let's see what we have for snacks."

Crabbe, in the front passenger seat, lowered the visor. He could watch Callie in the mirror and make sure she didn't knock him in the back of the head. He could move or duck out of the way if she swung wide.

Callie grew up in a generation where car seats, booster seats, and seatbelts were mandatory. She'd learned to maneuver and retrieve items from the way back. Quickly, she grabbed and swung the coolers to their seat.

Bash had more to worry about than Crabbe with Callie's aim. Luckily, the young man was agile. He caught the cooler before Callie clocked him in the head.

"Oops! Sorry, Bash! I am not used to anyone in the seat next to me. Thank you."

Organizing three small coolers around her, she started poking through the contents. Callie found a sealed food storage container with her name written on top. Peering inside, she made a humph sound.

Bash asked, "What's wrong?"

"If Solomon thinks that bribing me for forgiveness will work, he is sorely mistaken. Although Baklava is a good start."

Still frowned, "A what?"

"Baklava is a dessert made with phyllo pastry, cinnamon, nuts, and honey. There are various versions, and I love the one with strawberries. Here are some forks."

Callie used a fork to cut the layers. Then she placed a bite on two different utensils to hand to Bash and Crabbe. Still declined to try the dessert while he was driving.

Bash ate the piece and immediately downed several sips of water. "It's very sweet!"

Crabbe opened his canteen of water before trying his sample. "I find the Baklava is rich. Good though."

91

Chapter

Their gas station stop was right after reaching the interstate. Callie checked her watch. Seven-fifteen. She went inside to use the restroom. A few minutes later, she caught Rorke's attention and motioned for him to come inside. They watched Callie place a basket on the counter and talk to Rorke. Rorke shook his head in a negative manner. Callie refused to accept the answer. Rorke returned to the vehicle and started to use the radio.

The men heard Solomon's voice from the dashboard. "Open the glove box. There are gift cards and a debit card for making purchases."

Rorke pulled out an envelope and returned inside. Callie exited with a young couple and their son. The mother had tears running down her face and trying not to show distress. The father looked tired, worn, and discouraged.

Callie motioned to Still to open the hatch.

When the back was open, Callie smiled. "Vance, hop up on the back while I grab the peanut butter. We'll have you fixed up in no time. I'm impressed that you fit ten pieces of bubble gum in your mouth at once. That must have been a huge bubble. I'm jealous. I think that I was in third grade by the time I figured out how to blow a bubble with gum."

Vance peered at the expedition team milling around. "I'm starting first grade, but I've got to go to a new school. We are going to live with Gran and Pop because Dad lost his job."

Callie handed the jar of peanut butter to Bash to open while she pulled on a pair of disposable gloves. "My dad and I lived with my grandparents. Will you have a room to yourself?"

"I don't know."

"My two aunts and I shared a bedroom for a long time. They were older and didn't like me wearing their clothes or shoes."

"Weren't you squished?"

"Not that I remember. What I do recall was Aunt Thessa being annoyed if her boyfriend came over. She wanted to smooch with him in private, but he wasn't supposed to be in the house anyway."

Vance asked, "Did your mom and dad have to share with anyone?"

"My mom died when I was born, and my dad slept in the barn. Dad told Grandad that the cows and chickens were cleaner and quieter than his brothers, Mer and Moose. They built a room in the back for Dad, but it took a little while."

Rorke returned with a bag. One of the items was a comb.

Callie asked, "Mrs. and Mr. Creek, do you want to do the honors?"

92

Mrs. Creek glanced at her husband before answering. "Ma'am, you seem to have experience. Go ahead"

Callie smiled reassurance. "Ice works sometimes, but the oil in peanut butter helps break up the gum. I rather use peanut butter because it's not as cold. Where does your family live?"

Vance took over the conversation while Callie used the peanut butter like a shampoo. Vance had done an excellent job of coating his entire head of hair with gum. There wasn't a spot that didn't have a speck or blob of pink attached. Mrs. Creek handed over paper towels to slide the gum and peanut butter out.

The boy became comfortable with the number of people standing around and asked, "Callie, what do you do?"

"I grow plants."

"How many people are needed to grow plants?"

Callie laughed. "Rorke and I are teaching classes on plants and Literature. We are taking lots of field trips to train for taking our students."

Vance asked, "May I take the class?"

"These classes are for those who are 18 and older."

The first-grader asked, "How come you have to be an adult?"

Callie answered. "I suppose the best way is to show you. I have a picture of Mr. Crabbe and Mr. Thicke climbing. Honestly, I'm not sure I am old enough to climb trees so tall. I was afraid that someone would break their neck. Rorke, would you work the camera while I comb out the gum."

Rorke took the camera and clicked through the pictures on the screen until he found the photo. He showed the family the two men untying the ropes holding the treasure boxes.

"What are they doing?"

Rorke explained. "We had to show that we could accomplish a challenge and bring the containers down."

"That is really, really high." Vance agreed with Callie.

"Yes. I thought the men were fearless, and they climbed like jungle cats."

Vance looked almost pink free, and Callie said, "That should be clean enough to keep the car from being sticky until you arrive. The gas station is also a truck stop with showers. The attendant has keys to take showers. Here is a shower kit for each of you. Make sure to wear the flip flops. The tile is slick and can have a yucky sticky from the cleaner."

Mr. and Mrs. Creek looked slightly startled, and Callie told her companions. "If you want to load up, I'll be ready as soon as I visit the restroom one more time. Drinking lots of water has a downside. Be right back."

Rorke frowned as Callie left him to deal with the last item. "Mr. Creek, Callie wanted you to have these."

Mr. Creek opened the envelope and paled. "We can't."

Rorke sighed. "Sir, please don't argue. I'm stepping in the middle of a family argument and am uncomfortable. Callie and her guardian have a running battle about her birthday present every year. She's mad because he sends money and gift certificates instead of visiting in person. The guardian knows that she gives away the gift to annoy him."

Mrs. Creek sniffled while Vance hopped down from the tailgate. "Do you and Callie have children?"

Slightly thrown by the question, Rorke automatically answered. "No."

Vance announced. "You should have kids. She'll make a good mom."

Rorke recovered quickly and smiled. "Thank you for the input. I agree."

The family walked back inside.

Callie's voice spoke from near the front of the vehicle. "One word or snide remark, I'll find poison ivy and make the rest of your trip miserable."

The men chuckled because they knew Callie's threat was empty, but Tort teased. "Girl, if we can't identify poison ivy, we have no business being here."

Callie laughed. "Good point! I do appreciate you being patient about helping the family."

Rorke tried to emphasize time. "We are all right as long as we don't take a lot of side trips. We are making a two-minute stop in St. Maries to pick up lunch. Here's a menu for the restaurant. Figure out what you want, and we'll radio the order to basc. It will be ready when we arrive."

A lead escort vehicle of the group Solomon called Panhandles pulled onto the main road. Still, as a driver, followed in line as the second car, and Rorke pulled out in third place. Finally, the last transport entered the highway. The escorts turned on the flashing lights and sped up. Callie made a mental note that Still and Rorke were comfortable driving at high speeds and caravanning.

Callie's thoughts drifted to wondering why Solomon thought a police escort was necessary. Time was a factor, but a high-speed caravan seemed excessive.

Callie finally asked, "Still, why does Solomon feel we need to go so fast? We have until Sunday evening, which is three days to collect the boxes. I'd like to visit the cabin before classes start Monday, but I don't have to go out."

"No one consulted us. Sit back and enjoy the view."

"Hard to enjoy the scenery whizzing by at a million miles an hour." Callie tried to relax but changed the subject to ask, "Crabbe, how did you learn to climb trees so fast?"

"My father works for a Salvage Logging and Conservation business. When he traveled, we'd go along. Mom is a conservationist and does educational programs. As my brothers and I got older, we would enter the logging competitions. Our current route is going down highway 95, and you may see signs for one of the big festivals at Priest River. There is a turn off for the area at Highway 2."

Still asked about logging and different parts of the contest. While Crabbe shared, Callie wrote down her request for food and passed the papers to Bash.

Bash had Crabbe pause a moment to ask, "Callie, are you going to eat this much food?"

"Maybe. If I have one or two sides left, I'll finish the rest after we collect the treasure chest at Elk Creek Falls."

Bash decided to draw a line and add his underneath. Crabbe took the paper and scanned the menu without an opinion on Callie's four entrees with sides. Still told Crabbe to order him any dish with chicken.

The caravan did not make any stops. They did slow down around city limits, especially near Coeur d'Alene. When the transports reached the turnoff from Interstate 90, the Panhandles continued to travel east. Gold Rush, their new escort, waited by the exit.

Callie had always been fascinated by the road system from Interstate 90 to Highway 12. Roads with even numbers ran East to West. Odd numbers went North to South. As a girl, Callie told her father that part of Highway 12 should be 12.5 because the road went along the Locksa River. The route headed all four directions at some point on a map. Older, she had a better understanding of how to read maps and reasons for how the system worked.

Much of the mid to eastern part of the state was forest or gravel road with rivers branching out. Her father made her memorize every detail of a map. If she was ever lost, he wanted her to know the lay of the land. Once, Dad made her draw the major roads and rivers. The drawing reminded her of how a drunk spider might weave a web.

Reaching St. Maries, they stopped to meet the person who ordered and collected the food. A woman was waiting with their lunch in the parking lot near St. Joe's River. The team took turns using the facilities. Bash and Tort pumped gas while Still and Rorke went inside to the restroom. The pairs switched. Moving from the pumps and parking, Whipper stored their lunch. No one was hungry yet because it was still morning.

Whipper looked around and asked, "Where's Callie?"

Still said, "She came out of the girl's room."

Rorke mumbled something unintelligible and then asked, "Who has the loudest voice?"

Everyone answered at once. "Tort!"

Tort grinned. "Glad someone noticed."

Whipper teased. "I think the entire state heard you giving directions to Thick and Crabbe in the tree. Well done, though. The instructions were precise, directive, and didn't let a shred of panic invade when the rope started to slip."

Tort called Callie's name. The young woman popped up from a nearby bank where a bunch of flowers grew.

"Are we ready?"

"Yes."

Rorke waited for Callie to put her seeds away and restated, "Callie, don't wander."

"I remained in sight of the vehicles. If I wanted to take a stroll, there were some beautiful tiger lilies about half a mile back on public land."

The two-minute stop was ten minutes. Rorke didn't waste time arguing, and they drove down Highway 3 until the turnoff onto Highway 8. Rorke moved around Still to lead the way down to the trailhead. The Gold Rush escort continued South.

Rorke asked the others not to tell Callie that Solomon was using her as a test subject. The man had arranged for various law enforcement to perform drills for traveling VIPs. State agencies were also watching their treasure hunt to make sure bystanders remained out of the way and safe. The goal was to divert anyone from interfering or being concerned about safety or breaking laws. A prime example was at the refuge. Several birdwatchers called the rangers about their group disturbing the peace, and vehicles were not allowed where the cars went. Rangers could reassure concerned visitors. The authorities supervised the situation, and the park's wildlife was safe.

The average driving time was about four hours from the refuge to the falls. Callie glanced at her watch and read ten-forty-five. It meant that they'd been moving fast. The team had secured the boxes, helped the Creek family, had a rest stop, and arrived in a little over five hours. She started to say something, and Still shook his head not to say a word in the car.

Outside the vehicle, Still whispered. "Radios are two-way. Friend and foe overhear everything. Be careful what you say."

Chapter

They hiked down to the upper falls. Elk Creek Falls consisted of three cascading drops. Callie had been swimming in the falls. She was a good, strong swimmer, so the current didn't bother her. There were times of the year that the flow was too swift for a safe dip. Today was one of the days that swimming would be dangerous.

Water cascaded down into a ravine. The white water rushing over the falls made a beautiful and inviting scene. Yet, the force of nature sent the water careening into a pool with an explosive sound. The entire waterfall from the upper to lower pool dropped about 150 feet.

When the team reached the Upper Falls, Callie slipped behind the trees. The men didn't notice because they were busy studying the map and terrain. Their destination was about halfway down, under the falls, and in the rocks. Various options to retrieve the box were discussed.

Callie changed into a swimsuit. She had a protective coverup for her body and arms. The outfit looked like a scuba wetsuit with the legs cut off. Her water shoes were constructed to traverse wet, basalt rock. Her pack also held waterproof goggles, necessary for seeing while repelling down. She knotted the climbing ropes and plopped on her helmet before donning neoprene gloves. Due to the swimsuit and protective gear, Callie decided the harness would be more troublesome than helpful.

Tapping Rorke on the shoulder, she asked, "I am ready. Which side of the creek would you like the anchor rope? Tort, do you want to call progressive again?"

The men took in Callie's appearance and remained silent. Rorke nodded at Tort to go ahead and answer honestly.

Tort answered, "Sure."

Still asked, "Callie, have you used communications in running water?"

"No."

"These helmets have a two-way radio inside. You'll hear everything we say, and we hear every sound or noise from you."

Callie quipped, "So, don't scream and break someone's eardrum."

"My thought was don't put your head in the waterfall. Water is swift and noisy to the point of deafening. Though yelling could do some serious ear damage as well."

Rorke organized and gave directions to the team. "Everyone but Callie, take a headset and radio. Still and Crabbe, make your way to a vantage point. Whipper and Thick, you have good rope skills. Make your way to the pool at the Lower Falls. Bash and I will anchor from here, but be ready to fish Callie. The water is high and a force by itself. Tort, follow Callie down the trail and try to guide her and us. We won't have a line of sight."

The men found positions quickly. Tort and Callie found a place about halfway down the falls.

Tort shared with the team. "Solomon marked the spot for us. There is a huge yellow ribbon with a sign that says x marks the spot."

Callie asked, "Should I take the side rocks or go under the water?"

Still answered, "Take the side. Going through running water is going to be rough. Are you sure about going down?"

Callie stated in a practical voice. "I didn't put on the harness with quickdraws or carabiners. I also left cams, nuts, hexes, and tricams in the pack. Does anyone know if these treasure chests are durable?"

Solomon's voice came over the headset. "The chest is padded and would survive a tumble down the falls. You, on the other hand, are breakable."

Callie reassured Solomon. "Should have known that you were listening. Thank you for helping out the Creek family."

"You're welcome, but less talk. Pay attention to the wet rocks!"

Callie descended the fifty feet or so without much problem. She had a lot of experience hiking, climbing, and navigating rocky terrain. Tort guided her on where to enter the waterfall and rocks underneath. Cognizant of Still's words about not going into the running falls, she maneuvered between the plunging water and slippery rocks.

The problem occurred when Callie tried to remove the container from the wet rocks. The young woman had good upper body strength, but she couldn't budge the tightly wedged box out from the rocks.

Callie sighed. "Slight change in plans. I'll have to use my knife to pry out the pouch. If it comes loose, I won't be able to play catch without losing my balance. I'm tethering my extra line to the box. The 100-foot length should be long enough for anyone at the bottom to collect the case. I'll be fine, but someone must grab the rope before the chest floats downstream."

Still cautioned that if the current caught any part of her or the gear, she'd go over the edge.

"The only way my position is compromised is if the rope becomes tight on my end or gets caught in the rocks."

Rorke's voice ordered. "Callie, do not anchor that extra rope yourself. Let the line go, and someone downstream will collect it. Then

99

pry the box away, clear yourself. We have you secured from the top and sides. Do not take a chance."

"Letting go of the pink rope now."

A short time later, Whipper announced, "We have our end."

Callie inserted her knife in a small space and wiggled the blade down. Carefully, she used a loose stone to tap the blade further into the crevice. Then, she used the handle like a crowbar.

"Oops!"

Rorke asked, "What do you mean, oops?"

Callie announced. "One treasure coming your way!"

"Callie! Answer me!"

"I broke the knife! These new knives need an upgrade. Coming out!"

Callie was wet, but she didn't have any trouble clinging to the rocks like a mountain goat. Tort held out a hand to help steady her jump from the bank to solid ground.

Tort shared. "Callie is clear, and we are on the trail."

Whipper said, "We have the package and are heading back up. The lower falls have a steep climb back, which means we have a hike."

Callie and Tort returned to the top.

Callie asked, "Could I go back and change? I rather use the towels in the car than my pack towel."

Rorke nodded and asked, "Bash, would you be comfortable being Callie's partner? I realize the lady tends to wander off."

Bash grinned. "Nope. Callie, give me your pack. You're sopping wet and liable to drip on the food."

Their backpacks were waterproof. Callie figured Bash was being kind and giving her a chance to rest. She didn't complain because the exertion had left her tired.

Tort, Whipper, Thicke, Still, Crabbe, and Rorke returned to the trailhead. Bash was sitting on a picnic table eating. Callie wasn't in sight.

Rorke made a questioning face at Bash, who pointed to the tree line. The table provided a perch to watch the entire area. Callie was eating her lunch and collecting seeds. Rorke went to tell her that they were back and join the gathering. Everyone took advantage of the break to eat quickly.

Still looked around after he finished his food. "I suppose my moment to shine is at hand. We are heading back to Bovill to catch a helicopter to Moose Creek. We have a four-mile canoe trip from Moose Creek to Cedar Flats. Normally, the trip takes two hours. We built in an extra hour for organizing and assessing skills. Time is a factor, so we'll be paddling instead of sightseeing."

Callie smiled sweetly as Still stared pointedly at her with the word sightseeing. "Who's not been whitewater rafting, canoeing, or kayaking?"

Callie raised her hand and looked around. "Well, don't I feel singled out? I could stay onshore and take pictures of everyone floating down in the boats. I have no problem driving up and down the road to play shuttle bunny."

Bash asked, "Shuttle bunny?"

"Dad called us the shuttle bunnies when we dropped boaters off and met them at the end of the adventure. I don't remember much, but I do remember having a root beer float at the end. No one would let me have a beer or wine."

Still disagreed, "We stay together. You and Rorke will take a test run down the first rapid. You take the front. If you capsize the canoe, we'll put you in the middle without a paddle for the duration."

Callie looked intrigued. "I have experience with boats on lakes, flat water, and slow-moving creeks. How does a canoe spit a person out?"

Still didn't see anything amiss with Callie's curious question, but Rorke's eyes narrowed with suspicion. Rivers were part of Idaho's life.

Still answered, "There are images that are better seen or experienced than explained. A canoe tipping and spitting out a person must be seen or experienced on a river."

Crabbe volunteered with enthusiasm. "I read the equipment list and call a kayak."

Callie asked, "What is so special about a kayak?"

"The design is akin to a submarine or penguin, and a kayaker is able to become part of the river flow. Snuggle inside the skirt and roll. A kayak maneuvers with sleek precision through a rapid. If you miss a fall or hole, you roll and keep going."

Tort asked Still, "Who's taking the second kayak?"

"Depends on each of our skill levels."

Callie took a piece of paper that Still handed her, and she turned the color printout several ways before asking, "What sort of diagram is this?"

"River Map. The satellite picture was taken at 1 PM yesterday. The shading is the sunlight's azimuth."

Callie frowned, "Why do we care about the sun's position?"

Still answered, "We've had enough rain the past two weeks that Moose Creek is running fast. Increased water flow will impact the

Selway's current. Sun's position with shadows is important for reading the rapids."

Callie had information overload by the time their helicopter landed. There were too many terms to remember. She had no idea there were so many kinds of waves or types of holes. A few words, like throw ropes, were familiar. She knew what Rapid Classes meant. A rapid were classified by how hard it would be to maneuver and run. The higher the number, the harder it was to maneuver the rapid. Still had shared that he didn't care if they decided to use Sneak or Hero Routes. Crabbe made a pained expression, and Callie had to ask why he made a face.

Crabbe explained. "A Sneak Route is the easiest and safest way to navigate a rapid. Conversely, the Hero Route is the most difficult, perhaps dangerous, way down the river. Hero routes are for those with river experience and live for a challenge."

A couple of forest rangers were waiting at Moose Creek Landing Strip. The landing area was upriver from where the creek and river met. There was a ranger station, and it was staffed this time of year. Staff was waiting with the canoes, kayaks, and boating gear. The expedition team hiked up to a lookout point on Tony Point Bridge. They discussed the first rapid. Today the rapid was more of a Class II to III, due to the higher water level.

Still told Callie. "If you fall out of the boat, don't panic and relax. Keep your feet up and turn yourself to face downstream. Try to maneuver yourself to the bank. If you have trouble, someone will toss a throw rope. Grab ahold of the line, and you'll be pulled to the bank."

Each of the members donned lifejackets, helmets, earplugs, and safety glasses. Still and Crabbe took the kayaks down the first rapid to watch and wait. Bash and Tort were paired up in a red canoe to go behind the kayaks. Whipper went with Thicke in a green boat. Both teams made the run without a problem. Rorke and Callie had a bright yellow canoe.

They hit a boulder at the top of the run. Callie felt the list, or tip, of the boat and water rush over the gunnel. She should have leaned upriver. Instead, she instinctively grabbed the gunnels. Water and gravity did the rest. The canoe flipped and spit Callie out into the river.

She relaxed, pointed her feet downriver, and floated. Callie closed her eyes and relaxed. The water carried her downstream, and she didn't hear the men calling her name.

Still swiftly crossed the river in the kayak and grabbed the back of her life vest. The man had experience plucking people out of the river and plopped her on the hull. "Callie!"

Callie opened her eyes, and Still's face relaxed. "Girl! You scared the devil out of me. Why aren't you moving, swimming, or trying to make the riverbank?"

"I was following directions. Relax, face downstream, and float to the riverbank. Here is your paddle. I held onto it. Water isn't too cold, and the scenery is gorgeous from this position."

Still rolled his eyes, and Callie hoped the answer didn't sound too flippant, empty-headed, or brainless. Her goal was to be a competent outdoorsman but slightly distractible. The men knew that she spent most of her time outside but alone. Working as a team would require patience on their part. She understood Solomon's overall plan, but he'd lost his advantage. The enemy had inserted a spy. Fooling Solomon was not easy, and he had been duped. She knew this with absolute certainty. Even after ten years, she recognized one of their expedition team. He'd been in the car that caused her father's accident. Lion and Rorke were the only two at the lodge that she completely trusted.

They rearranged the seating. Crabbe was the only one to paddle a kayak. Still took the stern with Rorke in the bow. Callie sat in the middle without a paddle. The men were skilled at reading the water and paddled four miles in under two hours. They stopped to scout the safest path to run the rapid at each of the Level IV rapids. Their treasure box was waiting at the Wa-Poots Rapid. The box was in a spot inside an S-bend in the run called the Grizzly Saddle. Crabbe and Still discussed which one of them would be better at snagging the chest nestled right before a second, long drop in the boulders.

Crabbe grinned at his friends. "We have three more tries."

Callie asked, "How will we know what happens? We don't have team communications anymore. The helmets are in the cars we left, and there is no way to keep a visual as a boat goes downstream."

Still explained, "The high traffic on the river is enough that canoes, kayaks, and rafts must take turns. This rapid can be dangerous if someone gets trapped. Spotters with radios are at the top and bottom to direct traffic. Lookouts are stationed upstream, on the banks, and at the end to help anyone in trouble. They know that we are attempting to receive a box, and they'll be our communication."

Still had Callie wait while the men started back to the boats. "Callie, the next three rapids are Class IV. We watched a couple of boats running the Double Drop. Water rushes from the Upper drop to the Lower drop. If a canoe goes sideways in the falls, the boat will flip over. Due to the S-bend shape, the flow here accelerates from the left to right and back to the left. Even skilled paddlers get slammed against the rocks

103

on that right side. Are you comfortable hunkering down, not moving, and enduring a hard bounce? I'd rather you hike downstream than panic as a passenger."

Callie replied. "I trust you and Rorke."

"Trust isn't the issue. If we end up in the water, Crabbe and other kayakers will be at the bottom to help."

Crabbe went first, and Callie felt her stomach lurch with anticipation and worry. Would Crabbe be able to grab the container? Could he run the rapid without getting hurt? She'd watched the kayakers roll. They went underwater and came back up. Every time, she held her breath with concern. Would the person stay upside down and drown? What about head injuries? A helmet didn't seem much protection against the force of the water. A paddler could hit their head and end up with a massive concussion or brain damage.

The beginning spotter listened to the radio and grinned at the team. Crabbe retrieved the box and made the run without incident. Each of their group ran the rapid without mishap or someone going in the water. When they reached Lower Cedar Flats, they turned the canoes, kayaks, and boating gear over to those waiting.

They had to rearrange their seating because Still and Rorke did not drive. The group was being dropped off at an airfield near Lowell to take the large helicopter transport. Each team member used the time to rest, and Callie listened to a short discussion about the helicopter. It was a retired military transport. The state of Idaho had bought the transportation for state agencies to use. Callie had no idea a state could purchase used equipment, but the men were admiring the upgrades. She couldn't relate to the conversation and napped until the car stopped.

Chapter

Rorke gathered the group together after unpacking the vehicles. Before departure, they had to make a decision. As the leader, Rorke had to figure out how tired or worn out each person had become. No one seemed close to being fatigued enough to make a careless misstep. There had been lulls in the exertion with time for cat naps. The men were used to working from dawn to dark. Currently, that would equate to an eighteen-hour day. They'd been on the go for about thirteen hours.

"We must make a choice. We've collected four chests quickly. Fast transportation help cut our travel time. The fifth chest is in Hell's Canyon. The specific location along the canyon walls above the Snake River. Our time zone has shifted from Pacific to Mountain. Sunrise was roughly 530 Pacific time when we started. It is now five in the afternoon Mountain Time. Sunset is at around 9:00 Mountain Time. We've three to four hours of real daylight. There is time to collect the fifth chest, but we have to land, take a vehicle to the trailhead, and hike up."

Tort grinned. "We're not even close to maxing out flight time."

Rorke glanced around to Still, their river guide. "Still, you drove and led the river adventure. How do you feel?"

Still stretched his back and cracked his knuckles. "Today has been a leisurely walk in the park. Let's go."

Rorke smiled and turned to the only woman in the group. "Don't start collecting seeds. The extra pack is full."

Callie didn't agree or disagree. They began to load the helicopter and take turns using the facilities. When Rorke returned from inside the building, Still, Crabbe, and Bash were leaning against the aircraft. Each had stretched his legs to relax and take advantage of not being in a confined space. The three gave Rorke a mischievous look, which made him immediately suspicious.

Rorke walked over. "What did I miss?"

Crabbe's face split into a smile. "Callie's going to be a handful. She waited for you to go inside and consolidated the food. The additional seeds that she gathered are in the empty cooler. I don't think any of us mind because her actions aren't dangerous. The girl is kindhearted and cares. My opinion: Solomon's concern for her safety is justified."

Still added, "We pretended not to notice her rearranging the gear. Figured we'd let you be the fearless leader."

Rorke went to where Callie was pruning the flowers by the office and said, "Walk with me."

Rorke made sure that no one could overhear. "Why are you deliberately wandering?"

"How do you know my actions are deliberate?"

"Remember? No games. You are too well versed in outdoor safety protocols to be wandering."

Callie admitted, "We are being watched and monitored by more than Solomon and his crew. Perception, inferences on behavior, unpredictability, and element of surprise might help. We might be able to flush them out or add some pieces to the puzzle. I'm gauging reactions from the team players. Still is correct. I won't do anything to endanger anyone."

"You heard? How? We aren't carrying phones to piggyback conversations."

"Solomon gave me a phone in case of an emergency. The phone is linked to our communications. I'm taking advantage of turning the table on his little experiment."

Rorke praised but warned, "Nice problem solving with the seeds. I don't care about hauling additional weight in transports, but I will have to say something, as the group leader later."

"All right. You won't hurt my feelings."

The fifth treasure chest was located around Hell's Canyon. The canyon was one of the deepest in North America. The drop was about 8000 feet from the rim to the lowest part of the Snake River. The gorge was almost 2000 feet deeper than the Grand Canyon to the East. Snake River was the division between Idaho and Oregon. Idaho's mountain range along the east side of the river was the Seven Devils Mountains. Oregon's west side of the river was the Blue Mountains. Ancient glacier movement and the Snake River flowing north from the south helped carve out the deep walls of basalt rock. Salmon River joined the Snake River to the north.

Beautiful scenery, wildlife, flora, and history were abundant in the region. Archaeological sites were scattered throughout the area. The name originated from those trying to tame the river and land. Try being the operative word. Taming the land on economic, political, and environmental levels was challenging. Protecting and preserving had to balance with developing resources.

Time zones were slightly deceptive. Oregon's side of the canyon was Pacific time, and most of Idaho's side was Mountain. Callie's group ignored the clock time and hiked to their coordinates. The terrain was steep and rocky.

During a water and snack break on an outcropping of rocks, Callie asked softly, "Would anyone mind if I backtrack and meet you at the vehicles? You don't need me to secure the fifth box."

Rorke studied her to see if there was an injury or physical reason to abandon the scavenger hunt. "Why?"

Callie used a soothing, comforting voice. "Rorke, you're not in danger, but don't make any sudden movements. Slowly pick up your compass. Leave the sandwich on the rock. Everyone continue up the trail."

Still spoke in a soft, deep drawl. "We'll trade partners. I'll stay and go back to the vehicles with Callie."

Rorke picked up the compass without sudden movement. "What sort of new friend is eyeing my snack?"

"American Bald Eagle. If anyone even mentions the word shoot, I'll not be happy."

While securing the straps on the pack, Rorke said, "Eagles are protected. Even to save one from slowly dying, we'd be breaking the law. The Bird of Prey Sanctuary is too far, and they don't have the personnel to make a trip. We don't have the resources to help. As hard as the decision is, we must let nature take its course and leave the bird alone."

Callie countered stubbornly. "I have resources and time to see that a vet treats my new feathered friend. The juvenile eagle is injured and in desperate need of care. He or she will die if we don't help. The leg wound looks severe enough that life in the wild won't be an option."

Rorke tried to talk Callie out of her course of action. "A panicked bird of prey is liable to hurt you or anyone trying to help. How do you plan on tranquilizing and transporting?"

"I have tranquilizers, an animal first aid kit, and a sling. Solomon arranged for my alternate birthday wish when I turned twenty-one. I had my degree in botany and wanted to secure my permits in wildlife rehabilitation. Most jobs in the field require a degree in biology, but I fulfilled the rest of the requirements for permits."

Bash looked at Callie curiously, "Why did you decide wildlife rescue and rehabilitation?"

Callie shrugged. "Story for another time."

Still remained while the others headed up the trail. Callie slowly took out a small basin to fill with water. Alongside the basin, she placed what looked like a meatball. The round orb was made of food with a measured amount of tranquilizer.

The noise of hikers moved away, and the clearing turned silent. The eagle slowly dragged itself over to the turkey sandwich, water, and meatball. Quickly drinking and eating, the eagle studied his new friend.

Callie softly coaxed. "I'd give you more, but it's not a good idea. We'll take you to a man who will help. Beautiful, brave bird."

When the bird fell asleep, Still helped her immobilize the leg in a splint.

Still used the walkie-talkie. "Rorke, do you copy?"

"Yes."

"The bird is asleep. If I take the eagle, would you bring my pack?"

Callie started to say that she would take the eagle or extra pack, but Still silenced her with a single look. Rorke agreed to pick up the backpack, and he told Still to take the radio. Still placed the radio in an easily accessed pocket. They carefully wrapped the bird, and Callie helped tie the sling in place.

Downhill was faster, but it was easier to fall with the increased momentum. Surefooted, Still slid twice but kept on his feet. Several times, Callie tried to take a turn carrying the bird. Still told her to keep eyes on the trail. If she got them lost on the trail, he'd let her drown in the river next time. Callie knew Still wasn't serious but took the hint to remain quiet.

An outfitted vet truck was at the trailhead. A vet with a portable examination table waited for the patient.

Callie hugged the gentleman and smiled. "Dr. Lintel, meet Still."

Dr. Lintel nodded and chastised. "Girl, you realize…."

Still carefully set the large bird on the table. Dr. Lintel lectured Callie in a soft tone while studying the bird's injury.

Dr. Lintel turned his attention to Callie. "Your new friend is going to need surgery. Girl?"

"Yes, sir."

"I am not going to lie. If it survives surgery, living may depend on how adaptable it is to life in captivity."

Callie asked, "What about rehabilitation?"

"Doubtful. Someone shot the bird. I think the leg was broken and mangled on impact. If he lives, we are not going down that road again."

Callie's expression remained neutral, but her eyes glittered with stubborn defiance. "The barn owl is doing well."

Dr. Lintel shook his head. "End of discussion, girl. Don't make me regret letting the owl stay in the BE greenhouse."

"The owl's name is Tufty, and she found an owl friend."

"What have I told you about naming the wildlife?"

Callie's expression was only mildly guilty. "I refuse to use a species with a number for identification. The method is too impersonal."

Still took his walkie-talkie and updated Rorke. Their six companions were about twenty minutes behind. Still found out that Dr. Lintel had a private practice but worked closely with state and federal personnel.

The group returned to the lodge well after dark. Ms. Lion had hot food waiting. After a blessing for the food and thanks for a safe return, Rorke confronted Callie about how she contacted Dr. Lintel.

"Where did you acquire a phone to contact Dr. Lintel? We agreed to use provided gear and not take personal equipment."

Callie answered, "The phone is not mine. Years ago, Solomon gave me a number to memorize. When we landed this morning, I called to ask for a phone with the direct lines to rangers, state agency contacts, and other individuals that know me. I promised not to use the line unless the reason was urgent."

Rorke asked, "May I see the phone?"

Callie retrieved the device, and Rorke scrolled through the contact list as well as history. "Why did you contact Solomon before dinner?"

"Could I answer after Solomon decides to reply?"

The men had gained a good understanding of how Callie's mind worked after one day of working together.

Crabbe grinned at the others. "What did you ask Solomon?"

Callie weighed her answer. "Um, I wanted to know if I could split off from the group for a little bit? Tomorrow, one of our box's location is up in the Lost River Range. You don't need me or my expertise. The straightest path to retrieve the box goes near Jedidiah's place. I try to look in on him four times a year and bring him a few items from the outside world."

Whipper quipped. "Is there anywhere in Idaho you don't know someone?"

Callie knew Whipper was teasing. "How well do you know state history?"

"Most of my information is what we learned in school. Idaho became a territory when the US signed the Oregon Treaty. I think the state entered statehood as the 43rd state on July 3, 1890. The month and day I remember because the day and month is my mom's birthday."

Callie confirmed the information. "Yes. The treaty was in 1846, but Idaho was included in the Oregon and Washington Territories until it became a territory in 1863. I am not trivializing because history is important. Idaho went through growing pains: trappers, Native

109

Americans, miners, westward trails, religious topics, Oregon Trail, and the Railroad are each of great significance.

"Jedidiah was born in 1952 and served in the military during the Vietnam Conflict at eighteen. When he returned, he made a home in the mountains and now lives a solitary existence.

"Laws have changed since he made a home, but he's adapted. A part of him is always concerned that some clueless lawman who won't listen will try to arrest him. Honestly, I'd feel sorry for anyone who tried. Jedidiah is not an uneducated, lawless mountain man. The man has the mind of an engineer and has set traps around the area. Each will injure but not kill.

"Over time, he took college classes remotely. First, the courses were correspondence credits. Then, he took classes on the computer. Earned a degree to work for the weather service."

Still the river expert interjected, "There are many who live a solitary life in the woods. Jedidiah is different but similar to Buckskin Billy, or Sylvan Ambrose Hart."

Bash looked intrigued. "Who?"

Still explained, "Billy was a hermit who bought land on Five Mile Bar on Salmon River. The man loved his solitude but liked to socialize with those that came to visit. The man built a house, forge, garden, and a bomb shelter."

Bash asked, "Why a bomb shelter?"

"Nuclear war was a huge concern in his lifetime. Billy was born in 1906 and volunteered for service in World War II. He couldn't serve in the military due to a heart condition, so he went to work at the Boeing plant in Kansas. He wasn't the only person. Many families prepared for nuclear war by building fallout shelters. After the Wilderness Act, the government had the legal power to evict him."

Bash looked scandalized. "That isn't right. He bought the land."

"Billy lived there until he died of natural causes."

Callie changed the subject back to her friend. "Jedidiah works for the national weather service and is a vegetarian. He designed and built a greenhouse that blends into the rocks to grow vegetables and herbs year-round. Goes into town twice a year for tea, coffee, flour, seeds, clothing, or any other necessities."

Tort asked, "What does he do for the weather service?"

"I think a type of monitoring stations. My disconnect is the solitary mountaintop place with multiple computers. Due to Jedidiah's work, the man has cell service and internet. The man has more computers than some companies. He is well connected with world events though he

110

lives in isolation. Jedidiah loves to watch game shows and share tidbits of trivia."

Rorke sighed and addressed the weakness of the expedition team. "I am not comfortable with you splitting off, which could lead to problems."

Callie disagreed. "I knew everyone's position each second. I have the best climbing skills and agility. The waterfall wasn't a problem, but treetops are different. I offered my opinion and stayed out of the way. Everyone but Crabbe and Thicke stood watching. Well, Tort gave directions. I couldn't watch someone fall and break his neck."

Rorke tried to explain in a different way. "We didn't have you in the line of sight. Each time we stopped, you disappeared to take pictures or collect seeds. The same thing happened when we began to discuss the best way to retrieve the boxes. You cannot roam and leave the group."

"I never left."

Ms. Lion entered the debate and tried a third tactic. "I'm not an outdoor person, but I do understand group dynamics. Callie, my words are not a criticism, but you are the only girl and the weakest link. You are the smallest, shortest, and have the least amount of physical strength. The flip side is that you are in shape, knowledgeable, and careful. I think the concern is that something will happen. Say you took a picture and fell off a ledge without a sound. You become unconscious, and the others wouldn't know there was even a problem or how to find you."

Callie giggled in amusement. "Ah, Solomon didn't tell you, did he?"

Rorke looked around the table at the blank faces before hesitantly asking, "About?"

"After my father died, the man took his promise to keep an eye on me way too seriously. My hiking group didn't make camp at the named site but further south. Nothing wrong or dangerous. We were enjoying the outdoors. Solomon phoned and asked why we were at Moose Ridge instead of our camp. I must say the exactness freaked me out until Solomon admitted to having a tracker on me. Solomon bought us new clothes. I am sure he put a GPS in a shoe, jacket, belt, or pack."

Bash asked, "Doesn't that bother you?"

"I am used to Solomon being nosey and bossy from afar. A part of me is thankful. He cares, and I never have to worry about anyone not finding my body."

Lion snapped. "Not funny, young lady!"

Callie was a little taken aback at Lion's tone but didn't comment.

111

Rorke decided to put on his leader hat and gave an order. "No wandering! Am I clear?"

"I'll try, but…."

"No conditions. Yes or no."

"I will try not to wander while we are on the trail."

During dessert, Callie asked, "Lion, do you play cribbage? There is a cribbage board and cards on the shelf. My grandfather taught me, and I wouldn't mind playing. We need directions to review the rules."

Lion admitted that she played and offered. "Why don't you take a shower while I clean up? Then, we'll play a few hands."

Lion and Callie played cards, and the others regrouped in the map room. After the third game, Lion shuffled the cards but didn't deal. The young woman made a mental note not to trust Lion with tea. A sleeping agent had been added to the drug to help her sleep. Callie sent Lion a reproachful look and wrapped herself up in a blanket.

Chapter

When Callie was asleep, Lion called Solomon. "Hello."

Rorke started the conversation. "Are we about to find out that our scavenger hunt has a hidden agenda?"

"Yes, but I would not say the agenda is a secret. Callie is my concern. If Nigel's research relates to the present, there is a certain amount of danger moving forward."

Still asked, "Is there any evidence that Mr. Rivera's accident is more than a hit and run?"

"No. Yet, the timing of filing a report and his accident is coincidental and too convenient. My only request is to attempt to keep an eye on her as much as possible. Callie is stubborn but tenderhearted under the thick skin. She tends to plow ahead with her agenda instead of worrying about safety."

Rorke looked around at the others. "Would you answer a couple of questions?"

"If possible, yes."

"Do you have a tracker on Callie?"

Solomon didn't deny the fact. "Yes. The trackers have a revolving frequency, and I am the only person with the codes to access the location. I've always known who was with her on the trail."

Rorke continued to speak on the group's behalf. "I'm not judging, but you have made enemies on both sides of the law. You protected Callie with anonymity over the years, and she has no clue as to your role in the overall picture. How concerned should we be about an enemy using Callie to flush you out of the shadows?"

The team heard Solomon sigh. "I'd rather not find out. As to the next logical inquiry, I would not bend the rules for Callie's life. I would not deal with blackmail, ransom, trading, or negotiating if someone held her hostage.

"Nothing has happened in ten years. The odds are low that there is a connection between the past and present. There are similarities but enough differences to believe the cases are unrelated. My biggest concern is that Callie is liable to do something foolish."

Tort asked, "Would the girl go off by herself to find whatever her father hid away?"

"I'm hoping and praying that she has the common sense not to do such a thing, but she might."

Rorke asked, "Why was Callie acting strangely at The Kootani Refuge?"

Solomon chuckled. "Don't let Callie know you picked up on her discomfort. The girl is paranoid about showing emotion, and the knowledge would make her clam up. Callie would tell the story very differently, but her fear is why I asked for any pet dogs to stay home."

"Callie's version is that a pack of wolves hunted her and a friend during a hike. Two hunting dogs were lost. The puppies equated people with food and home. They started following the two hikers and baying. Callie's partner was faster on the ground and had her climb a tree while he went for help. No idea if the puppies saw Callie as help or a treed critter, but they sat at the bottom and howled until help arrived. The person went and found food to lure the dogs away. Used a flare to scare them toward the other people and food."

Crabbe guessed correctly. "She was treed in a Ponderosa Pine."

"Yes. Ever since, Callie has been terrified of big dogs. I marked the Kootenai Refuse as the last retrieval so that she'd trust the group before facing her fear. When the team decided to start at the reserve, I wasn't going to interfere. I was curious to see how she controlled anxiety on the trail without coddling."

Rorke asked, "Would you please do us a favor? Fill out the forms for Callie that she was supposed to complete on the airplane. She never wrote in having wildlife training or possessing other types of certifications. If we are a team and protective detail, knowing specifics would be helpful to us."

Bash shifted uncomfortably in his seat. "I have two questions but don't wish to offend anyone."

Solomon said, "I'd rather you ask than wonder. Go ahead."

"How will you react if Callie is hurt on the trail?"

"If the concern is retaliation, my anger will not be directed at the team. I'm grateful that each of you agreed to join the expedition. The pay for each field trip isn't much, but there will be work for a while. If you decided to send her over a cliff on purpose, then we have a problem. Second concern?"

Bash verbized his second inquiry. "Each of us had to provide a weapon's permit, sign out a firearm, and attend a class. The instructor went through the rules and such. Callie isn't wearing one. Does that mean she isn't certified?"

Solomon chuckled. "The young woman has certifications and permits for a concealed weapon. Callie's proficient with handguns, rifles, and knives, but she's never fired a weapon in the wild. No one knows how another person, or themselves, will behave under fire for the first time. If a situation goes sideways, I don't want her shooting someone on the same team."

Rorke asked, "We compared notes. The provided weapons were checked out from a generic homeland office. Who's keeping the firearms between field trips?"

Solomon praised their attention to detail and research. "Agent Isley's office will have a locked safe. Callie has a handgun, has carry permits, and usually carries the piece on the trail. The make is small enough to fit in her hands but not effective for long-range."

Still asked, "What is the story on Jedidiah? If she asked to visit, why not say yes or no right away?"

"Callie made Jedidiah promise to check in each day with her or Rosa. The hermit will not be happy with a surprise visit because he is not at home. Jedidiah is recovering from a heart attack and has not told Callie. The man will be fine but had to have four stents. Doctors want to put in a pacemaker, but the man is refusing."

Lion spoke from where she sat knitting. "When was the surgery?"

"Six weeks ago."

"If Jedidiah is strong enough to travel, have someone drive him out. Flying might be too hard on his system. Doubt anyone will be able to drag her anywhere until the girl sees for herself."

Solomon commented. "That puts you on medical duty."

"Here? There? Everywhere? I am a medical technician but able to dial emergency numbers if needed. Ask Jedidiah if he plays cribbage. I need to practice. Callie beat me three games in a row, and she was half asleep from the tea."

Solomon asked, "How is Callie reacting to the tea?"

"The substance is mild, and I had to lower the dose. The girl's system isn't used to sedation or taking pain medication. She was out before game four."

The young woman found herself in her room the following morning. Someone moved her from the chair to bed. The fact annoyed her, but there wasn't much she could do. Showering and dressing, she shook off the early morning groggy feeling. Gentle, deep laughter came from the common area.

Callie knew the laughter came from Jedidiah. Her friend reminded her of a very thin Santa Claus with wild, long hair. The silver-white hair and beard were full. The man kept the thick hair braided when she and her father visited. A few times, he'd had the lush, beautiful silver hair down. Callie begged several times to brush the hair, but the man ensured the girl kept away from his head. He wasn't keen on physical touch and refused to let Callie greet him with a hug. Regardless of these feelings, Jedidiah had an easy smile and radiated an open, friendly spirit.

Callie padded into the main lodge. "Jedidiah! What in the world?"

"Here for my daily check-in. No one's stuffed me in the attic."

Callie laughed. "I was nine, and you are still teasing me."

Jedidiah turned to Callie's curious friends. "I see everyone is too polite to ask. One of Callie's classmates told her an urban legend. The story goes a man starts looking into the illegal behavior of his in-laws. Two of the in-laws drew straws to see who would kill him. They murdered him and stuffed his body in the attic because the ground was frozen.

"Fifteen years ago, cellular phones didn't have as much range or coverage. Callie insisted that her father drop everything and bring her up to check on me. Two years ago, the weather created a communication blackout, and the girl couldn't contact me. Afterward, she decided to make me check in each day."

Jedidiah prompted Callie. "Go fix a plate of breakfast. You're too thin."

Callie returned in kind. "You look like a boulder the size of Idaho fell on you."

Lion figured Callie was more interested in her friend than food and brought a plate to her.

Callie smiled her thanks and started asking Jedidiah questions. "What if you had been in trouble instead of the weather causing problems? How come you are here?"

Jedidiah didn't seem upset in the least at Callie's interrogation. "The world does not revolve around your whims. You didn't need to trek up the mountain and visit. I'm down in the lowlands for another week or so. Had a minor procedure on my heart."

Callie chastised her friend with a parental tone. "You didn't tell me! Who is taking care of you? What sort of surgery? Prognosis?"

Jedidiah laughed with his gentle, good-natured voice. "The fact that you are such a mother hen is why I didn't share. My heart didn't suffer long-term damage, and I'll be fine. The doctors put in a couple of stents. Stop talking and eat."

"How did you check in with me and still have surgery?"

Jedidiah chuckled, "Called and left a message before a nurse poked me with needles. I phoned from my room the following day." Callie's face showed that she wasn't happy at being duped.

Callie announced. "You're coming home with me to finish recovering. I have a television with cable and lots of game shows."

116

"We are not arguing. I'll rest better at home. I like peace and quiet. Noise and confusion tend to surround you. We'll compromise. I'll stay for the day and have supper. We go our separate ways and chat each day on the computer.

Rorke offered. "Our plans have altered. Two treasure chests are arriving later, and we are only collecting one more."

Callie shifted her gaze to Rorke and asked, "Is the modification why Bash is outside staring at the sky?"

"Yes. We're going to a shooting range, attending a team-building workshop, and listening to a hostage negotiation lecture. Lion and Jedidiah are coming along."

Rorke diverted the conversation from Bash. "Has Callie always gone off on her own?"

"No. The girl was a proper young lady, but Nigel's death changed her entire demeanor and behavior. Callie has a heart of gold, but the girl wants to save the world."

Callie finished eating, and they loaded up to head to Hailey.

Chapter

The journey to Hailey, Idaho, was much shorter than their travels the day before. They stopped at a shooting range and quizzed on their knowledge of weapons. Each showed the instructors his or her skills with handguns and rifles. Jedidiah and Lion did not participate. The evaluators assessed the team members as proficient in firearms.

Solomon had not been entirely upfront about the team exercises. Ten groups gathered to participate in challenges had would build trust and communication. Matching shirts identified each team. Solomon sent a box of shirts for the expedition team. Callie knew to print and expedite a last-minute order would have cost a ton of money. A part of her worried about the money Solomon was spending. She wondered if her guardian had robbed a bank to finance the team.

Bash shook out a shirt and read it before saying, "Really, Callie?"

Callie went over to see what Bash was talking about and smiled. The name of their team was Wildflowers. Their names were printed on the back with a picture. The same picture was on the front but without the name. Bash's image was Rabbitbrush, or Ericameria Nauseosa.

Bash handed out the shirts. Crabbe had Ponderosa Pines. Still's flower was a Mimulus Lewisii, or Purple Monkey Flower. The plant liked to live near stream banks or moist soil. Rorke had an Ash Tree, and Tort had Horsetail or Equisetum Hyemale.

Tort sighed. "I do miss ranching and horses. Remind me to phone my horse on Sunday and tell him not to eat the Horsetails. They're poisonous."

Callie began to laugh spying Whipper's shirt, and apologized. "I am sorry, but the plant is a Nodding Onion. The flowers look like someone napping, and you like to nap."

Whipper grinned in delight at his shirt.

Thicke held his up and sent an inquiring look to Callie. "It's called a Bird of Paradise because the flower appears to be a bird in flight."

Rorke rolled his eyes. "Glad that none of us have doubts about our self-confidence or manliness. Remind me to share an opinion on Solomon's choice of shirts."

Callie piped up. "Remind the man to consult me about plants next time. He lumped trees, weeds, shrubs, and flowers together as wildflowers."

Bash held up the last piece of clothing. "Callie, what is your flower?"

"Wood Nymph."

The first event was a fire building task. Each participant would build a small fire to burn through a piece of twine. The twine was strung between two metal stakes. Everyone received twigs, sticks, lint or cotton, flint, and a c-shaped metal striker. Their workspace was the size of a folding tray. Since each person had to complete the task, the teams were divided up and sent to different stations. Each person drew a number from a bag, and Callie pulled a four. Callie walked with the other fours to their fire building station. No one would be able to see how quickly his or her teammates completed the fire-building task.

Callie set up twigs and sticks into a teepee shape. Taking the flint, she used the rock and her knife to send sparks into the moss. Callie's twine burned in less than six minutes. A judge or supervisor wrote in her time and told her that she could walk back to the main clearing.

One of the ladies looked around and started protesting that Callie had a knife to use. A knife was easier to use than a metal striker. Frustration at the situation rather than Callie was the problem. The woman was having a hard time starting a flame.

Callie looked around the clearing and figured only two others had experience with making fires. Their strings were almost gone with flames underneath. The other seven didn't know basic methods to build a fire. Callie went over and showed the woman how to complete the task. No one told Callie she couldn't help, and their proctor didn't stop her. She spoke so that the others who needed guidance could follow along.

The cotton and dryer lint went into the center. The next step was to build the sticks into a teepee shape with the smaller twigs on the bottom. While building, the trick was to interlock any pieces to keep the structure from falling during lighting. The second hint was not to be timid making sparks. Callie explained that making sparks was not easy and had to be practiced. You had to hold the steel and strike the rock toward the wad of cotton and dryer lint.

One of the older women tried hard, but her hands were not strong enough to strike a spark into the center of her creation. Callie waited for everyone else to finish. When the judge's back was turned, Callie guided the lady's hands to strike the rock with her knife.

Callie hid the knife and backed away as the woman exclaimed with delight. "It worked! The flame is spreading!"

The judge wrote down the time and spoke. "We won't wait for the string to burn. Our staff will put out the flames and secure the area."

Callie had the group talking and laughing as they took the short walk back to the main area. Each contestant returned to their respective

119

teams. The proctors met in the middle of the circle to confer and report times. Before the judge for Callie's group shared times, he spoke at some length.

Tort asked, "Ah, Callie, why is the judge of your fire building contest providing a detailed explanation? Every one of the proctors keeps looking over here."

Callie shrugged and asked, "Did we win?"

Rorke answered, "Winning or losing is not the goal. Our times are added for a total. Each team returns and repeats the tasks in October. The objective is to have a better time during the second run."

Callie scanned the other teams milling around. "That stinks. A stopwatch won't be faster or slower for me. Rorke, where is the list of rules?"

Still spoke quietly. "Callie, if there is a commotion, why do you always seem to be in the middle of it? I'm sure whatever the topic of discussion is due to you. Would you take a gift card for food in exchange for not talking or creating more confusion?"

"I don't take bribes."

"Fine. Here is a challenge. Do not talk for a ten-minutes and earn a prize."

The judges stopped deliberating and announced. "We'll log these times for fire building to use in October."

Callie turned to Rorke. "Are we coming back?"

Rorke hedged his answer without commitment. "I don't know. We were a last-minute addition, and the proctors were kind enough to allow us to participate. Consider today a friendly competition. Winners earn bragging rights."

"Oh, well, why did you not say so in the first place?"

Whipper nudged Still. "I think your money is safe."

"Why do you think I told the girl ten minutes?"

Callie pouted. "Ha! Ha! I was quiet for longer than ten minutes yesterday while I made notes for class."

Still disagreed, "You were not. We had to answer queries about our knowledge of plants."

The second team-building exercise was guessing animals. Taking turns, the person acted how their animal behaved without sounds. The others of the group had to deduce the animal. Each member received one guess. If no one could name the correct animal, the game moved onto the next creature.

Callie mimed a long nose, pointed to an ant, and pretended to snort up the ant. Bash and Whipper both shouted Anteater at the same time.

A gentleman from a different group turned around and inquired. "What did Callie do? I have no idea how an anteater behaves."

The speaker's face went scarlet. The question gave away the animal on his paper. Callie's team guessed their animals in less than two minutes. Rorke's group went down the line from where they sat. Each stood up, mimicked their animal, and the others guessed. The group who took the longest was having trouble with individuals going up to mime their animal.

Rorke watched Callie squirm in discomfort at the team still trying to finish the task. Callie couldn't sit and watch.

Callie stood, and Rorke whispered in an authoritative tone. "Callie! Learning takes trial and error!"

"Learning also requires someone to guide. They need help!"

Callie crossed the area, plopped down in front of the eight individuals, and softly provided directions. Proceeding down their line, Callie directed each person to take their turn. Looking over the group, the oldest was probably twenty-one.

Callie asked, "May I ask who your leader is today?"

A young man about Bash's age looked ready to cry but remained composed. "McLeod had a heart attack and is in the hospital. His wife called earlier. The doctors say that he'll be fine."

Callie inquired. "Family run business?"

"Yes. We are from a small town of about three thousand. McLeod hires a bunch of us to help restock and clean out cabins after the tourists leave but before school starts."

Callie praised. "You are doing well. I have three quick questions. Who has been working with McLeod the longest?"

The young man who answered raised his hand.

"How many of you know how to drive a tractor?"

Half raised their hand.

"How many ever ate a worm?"

A few of the girl's giggled, but three of the boys hesitantly raised their hands.

Callie said, "The gentleman who mimed the elephant and answered yes to each question won the title of Mr. McLeod for the day. My team finished first, and we have the best communication without words. We'll help you fill in the gaps."

Rorke locked eyes with the person in charge. "As the leader of our group, I apologize to the staff members for Callie taking over and giving orders. My apologies to the other teams for her boastful announcement."

Callie glared at Rorke. "I wasn't boasting. We did the best during the first two tests. I saw the clipboard. Our team had the lowest, combined time in fire building."

Suppressed laughter sounded from various places.

The proctor smiled. "We're aware of the extenuating circumstances surrounding Wildflowers and McLeod's teams. The choice to help is up to you after your task is completed."

McLeod's party traded places with the Purple Dots to sit in beside Rorke's group.

Plank walking was the next challenge. Two long boards lay on the ground. Each board had eight loops where the members could secure their shoes. One long rope went from the front to the back of the board. The long piece of rope was used as a handle and for balance. Walkers had to line up and work together to walk and move the planks a certain distance. Callie thought the activity was interesting. It would require the group to line up as if all eight were skiing on the same ski.

Crabbe grinned at his companions and drew them into a huddle. "We did a similar exercise in the Boy Scouts. Line up from shortest to tallest. The person in the rear calls cadence. River Walk and Rare Gems work well together, and they have a chance of winning." Crabbe paused. "If we were racing, we had an advantage because of our outdoor experience. Animal charades aren't a challenge."

Callie glanced around the circle and caught the gleam of challenge in her friends' eyes. "Um, what happened to a friendly competition? I thought that we were going to help McLeod."

A flicker of emotion appeared in Bash's eyes, and a smile lit the young man's face for the first time that day. "We should win without any problems."

Callie looked at Rorke, who answered with a note of suppressed excitement at a challenge. "We do both. Win and then help."

The only female on the team sighed. "I guess the attitude is a guy thing."

Wildflowers won the Plank Walk. They also won the tower building with boxes and making a rope square while blindfolded. A pretend minefield exercise ended up being a tie between their team, Purple Dots, and River Walk.

The next to the last contest was called an electric fence. Two ropes were strung across a pair of trees. One was above the other in parallel lines. The aim was for each member of the team to cross a pretend electric field. Every person had to stay connected to their team figuring while the group went over or under the electric fence. The participates could not run, dive, or perform gymnastics to cross the pretend fence. Anyone who did so would disqualify their team.

Crossing an electric, pretend fence was a tame exercise after retrieving treasure chests. McLeod's young group was looking lost and kept glancing towards the Wildflowers for guidance.

Callie's team huddled up to discuss the challenge, and Callie asked, "There is one more contest after this one. Does anyone care about the current event?"

Rorke scanned the faces around the circle. "No. Why?"

Callie grinned. "I am getting hungry. The old buzzards are looking a little concerned about the strength needed. McLeod's kids are waiting to see what we do, and Huckleberries will take forever listening to their ideas. I'll disqualify us so we may hurry up the process and help the others."

Bash eyed Callie. "How are you planning to disqualify us?"

Callie asked Tort if she might borrow the gloves that he kept in his cargo pant's pocket. "I'm going to vault over."

Crabbe quipped. "I suppose we have plenty of qualified medical people in the area if she breaks a bone or her fool neck."

The event started, and Callie took off running. Cries of protest and noises of concern filled the air. Referee whistles blew. She continued, jumped up, and used a tree branch to swing over the fence.

Once ineligible, Rorke split the Wildflowers into pairs. Thicke and Tort helped the Huckleberries because Tort could direct without being bossy. Bash and Still had an advantage of strength with height, so they helped the Old Buzzards. Callie and Rorke explained various methods to complete the task to the McLeod crew. Crabbe and Whipper moved around the Putters, Purple Dots, Brew Beer, and Hot Air to see if anyone had questions.

The proctors who could have provided advice or directions decided to stand back and not interfere.

A spider web was the last event. Each team had to pass members through a rope web without touching the lines. There were two problems to solve. One was each opening could only be used once. The second was touching the ropes. If ropes moved, the team had to start over.

Wildflowers came in second because Whipper was a lot heavier than he looked, and they dropped his legs. They had to start over.

When finished for the day, McLeod's team asked Callie for her contact information. Rorke sighed as Callie gave out his new email and phone number as well. The young adults also wanted to know if the Wildflowers would be back in October. Callie explained that she

123

couldn't predict their schedules. Six of their team members were volunteers for search and rescue. They never knew when their group would be deployed to help someone.

The hostage negotiation lecture was not as Solomon advertised. Callie discovered River Walk and Rare Gems were part of law enforcement branches and participating in a training exercise. The two groups merged to play hostage-takers. The Wildflowers were the hostages as well as rescuers. Proctors asked her team to hand over knives, weapons, and phones. A pair of uniformed men double-checked that there were no hidden items.

Callie went to Rorke. "Why are Lion and Jedidiah playing? Jedidiah had heart surgery."

"He's going to be a hostage and only sitting. No one will let him overexert or do anything to jeopardize his health."

Callie heard a voice over an intercom. "Those with Mr. Asher will be the blue team and consists of five rescuers and five hostages. The blue team's goal is to rescue the hostages. The red team has ten guards, and their objective is to take out the rescuers before a recuse occurs. If a paintball hits you, you are out."

Lion, Callie, Jedidiah, Bash, and Thicke followed a staff member to a concrete room.

Three men in camouflage clothes, military boots, and safety gear entered. "Have a seat. We are tying you up. The door will be open but guarded. Jedidiah, we are not binding you, but you may not help the others."

Lion's Irish Brogue was back, and she smiled sweetly. "Would you be kind and bind my hand in front instead of the back? My circulation is not the best in my old age."

Lion caught Callie's eye and made a slight motion to watch. Lion moved her palms and fingers to provide some slack in the ties. Callie carefully observed and repeated Lion's movements. As soon as the guards took a position in the doorway, Bash and Thicke moved. Bash caught Callie's attention and waved for her to talk to Jedidiah.

Callie started a conversation. "While we are waiting, what else have I missed in your life?"

Jedidiah's form was relaxed and unaffected by what was going on around him. "I am getting a puppy. Certified St. Bernard. A man on the Texas coast bought a puppy, but it's too hot for the dog there. Poor puppy overheated, and the owner became angry at the vet bill. He abandoned the puppy at the vet. A friend is collecting and bringing the puppy to me. Will you hike out and visit me if I have a dog?"

124

"My fear is of wolves and coyotes. They are not domestic pets."

Callie found that Bash and Thicke cut their zip ties with a hidden knife. The guards had not thoroughly searched their hostages and paid for the oversight. Before the guard facing the inside could move, Bash pelted the sentry with paintballs. The second guard entered to take out the threat, and Bash tossed another round of paint at the lookout. Lion had used the play in the rope and was free of her bindings.

Bash shook his head to be quiet as Callie went to speak. Bash Callie's bindings. Thicke and Bash picked up the guards' paint guns. Each took a position on either side of the door.

Lion whispered to Callie. "How upset will you become if the men don't follow conventional methods?"

"Uh, I don't know what constitutes conventional. I didn't see how you got out of the ropes. Will you teach me?"

Lion smiled and nodded.

Thicke took the paintball guns from the downed guards. he withdrew paintballs from the gun's ammo holder. "Red team knows that we are loose. Who has the best throwing arm?"

Callie reached out a hand to stop her friend, and she whispered into Thicke's ear. "Not able to throw but able to sneak up without a sound."

Thicke grinned. "Worst that happens is a couple of bruises from paintballs."

Bash went over and motioned to the guards. He didn't want to hurt the guards their removing the gear. One of the guards rolled his eyes behind his safety glasses, but both handed over the communication battery packs and earpieces.

Smiling as if her birthday came early, Callie took five orbs from Thicke's hand and pointed up. Thicke understood and went to the window. He stood on a chair and inserted his knife blade between the frame and window. Using the handle as a crowbar, he pried the window out. Callie helped place the glass quietly on the ground.

Thicke gave Callie a leg up to sit on the window ledge. Quickly, Callie climbed onto the roof. The air was still, and she moved to a sheltered corner to survey the surroundings.

Two guards were on the roof, and she could hear the voices on the radio. "Hostages are out of their bindings. Backup is moving to cover the main floor, and hostages are contained. No one will be able to leave without us intercepting. Any word on the five hostiles? They slipped into the trees without communication gear."

A red team member asked, "Could we start an offense instead of being defense? Usually, we're the ones rescuing."

125

The first voice returned. "If you have a clue on their plan and whereabouts to finish the game, I am open to suggestions. We're not able to see them on our equipment, and no one has a visual."

Red team probably had rules to follow, but no one from the rival team seemed focused on the inside. Everyone was intent on the surroundings. They were more focused on trying to figure out what the rescuers were doing. Callie used the angled roof to keep out of sight. When she was close enough, Callie tossed paintballs and hit the Red team sentries. Over the radio, she heard the supervisors tell the red team that the two roof guards were out. The communications went silent with surprise. Then, questions started. No one had a line of sight on how or why the team members were out of commission.

Tort and Whipper obtained a truck, roared up next to the building, and pelted the door guards. Still, Crabbe, and Rorke entered the rear of the building using the tree line as cover. They tagged the rest of the opposing team.

A voice sounded over the radio. "The game is over. Blue team has immobilized the Red team and rescued their hostages."

Chapter

Everyone regrouped in a conference room. Lion and Jedidiah didn't stay for the meeting. Lion wanted to start dinner, and Jedidiah needed to rest. The teams discovered that the red and blue flags had been in the rooms with the hostages.

A supervisor started the meeting. "Blue team, thank you for participating in the drill. We realize that a missing element is realism, but every practice is a learning opportunity. Bash and Thicke, where did you acquire the knives? We searched you with metal detectors, and we secured belts, shoelaces, and electronics."

Thicke smiled. "Trade secret."

The supervisor wasn't upset. "I tried. Red team, what was the biggest mistake?"

Captain answered without embarrassment. "We are usually the rescue team and underestimated the hostages. The group acted quickly and unexpectedly. Callie, nice play with the window."

Callie blushed. "Thicke is the person who deserves the credit. I would have had to break the window, which would make a noise."

The emergency phone that Rorke wore chirped for attention. He went outside to answer and returned. The look was concerned rather than alarmed.

Rorke handed over the phone. "Solomon wants to talk to you privately. I'm to reassure you that everyone, as in your family and friends, is fine. It's about BE. Take the call outside but stay close. I'll stand in the doorway to keep an eye on you."

Callie grinned. "I promise not to wander and remain in sight."

Solomon sounded more tired than the previous day. "Callie, I need the truth. Did you know Thessa is alive and did not die of an overdose?"

"Yes."

"A situation has occurred. Tell me exactly what you know."

Every muscle in her body tightened, and she closed her eyes. Breathe. No crack in the stone. No emotion. No outward sign that could be used against her.

"Short version. Thessa and Pica had broken up permanently after you interfered with their relationship. Thessa and a new boyfriend witnessed a murder. They went to the police, and her boyfriend died under mysterious circumstances a short time later. Thessa had no idea who to trust, and she went to Dusty for help. Dusty had the sense to go to my father. You and Dad helped Thessa disappear by having her

127

arrested for trespassing. Supposedly, she started using drugs and died of an overdose."

Solomon asked, "What else?"

"Not much. I'm not aware of Dusty's involvement after you became involved. No one ever told Rosa and Pica the truth. Pica was never quite the same. Pica blames you because you broke them up the last time. Granted, I think he holds you accountable for every negative thing in his life."

Solomon didn't mince words. "Thessa's identity became Bree Candle, and she married a man named Orlin Brody. I'm dealing with a lot and will have to explain the rest later."

Callie asked, "You told Rorke it was about BE business. What reason do I provide for our discussion?"

"The matter could wait, but Nod and Mer gave Isley access to BE's finances. The three looked at your checking account, and your uncle decided to pay a couple of your bills."

Callie blurted, "What?! I am going to wring my uncle's scrawny neck!"

Solomon waited for her to finish. "Nod is supervising Isley and Mer. Wither and Sumo will arrive shortly with paperwork to explain Bree's circumstances. Do not be angry at Sumo or Wither as the messengers. The two have no idea of the connection from past to present. I would ask that you not share as well."

Rorke waited for Callie. He could tell the conversation rattled her, but he didn't pry. They went back inside to where a debate about strategies was occurring. Oddly, Bash was offering several ways to improve their tactics. One was making a detailed search of the hostage's holding cell. There were many items in the room to help a hostage escape.

Twenty minutes later, Wither and Sumo entered the conference room. Callie secretly thought that Sumo should be a movie star. Whenever they went out in public, she caught ladies taking sideways glances at him. The man was handsome with piercing eyes and dark hair. Sumo had a calm, comforting, and reassuring aura. The man's stature helped as well. He was tall, muscular, and moved with grace. Callie greeted her friend delightedly and went to hug him.

Sumo returned the hug. "Nice to see you, Starry Eyes. I brought your plant back in person."

Callie asked with a sly grin. "So, City Dude. Are you here to tackle the big outdoors? See my cabin? Go camping? Rock climbing?"

"Nope. The best my schedule allows is dinner with you and Rosa when I come to town for business."

Sumo's smile extended to everyone in the room. "I apologize for interrupting, but we need to borrow Ms. Rivera for a few minutes. Before she and I speak together, four witnesses need to sign a form that I handed her a sealed package."

Callie took the package hesitantly. "Is everyone all right?"

Wither reassured her. "Family and friends are fine. Ms. Nod would have accompanied Mr. Sumo, but she's supervising the home front activities. Isley is going over BE's paperwork with her and Mer."

Callie made a disapproving face. "Solomon called a short while ago to alert me. Isley and Mer are becoming a bit too chummy for my liking."

Sumo recalled fondly, "Says the girl who has never met a stranger. You ran off to the Hot Air Festival in Boise with Brine Pickle without a worry in the world. If I remember, you were twelve, and Ms. Brine was sixteen. Never realized two girls could consume so much junk food in one hour and not get sick."

Callie made a yum noise. "I was so happy that Dad asked you to babysit until he and Gran arrived. You bought us cotton candy, funnel cakes, soda, caramel popcorn, and corn dogs."

Crabbe teased. "Guess her eating habits haven't changed. Did she eat that much food?"

Sumo answered. "Yes. Well, not the cotton candy, but I took the container home. Callie warned me that she'd never tasted the spindly mess. If we bought the treat and she didn't like it, I was not to waste the food."

Callie explained. "Gran is strict on eating out and treats. She ensures there is no food waste. Scraps or peels go into a compost pile. Why are you and Wither wearing business suits? You both look ready to attend a formal event."

Sumo answered with a question. "Do you remember Bree Candle? She stayed with Rosa and Nigel as a foster child for a brief time. A wonderful couple adopted Bree. She grew up and married."

Callie pretended not to recognize the name and waited for Sumo to continue without confirming or denying memories.

Sumo continued. "My concentration is family law. There was a car accident, and her husband died. Bree was severely injured and not expected to live. She listed you as the estate executor and medical proxy. The hospital needs official answers from the person listed on the living wills. You are to open the sealed package, read the enclosed

129

information, and make decisions. Is there a private place you may read the documents?"

Callie looked lost while attempting to take in the situation. "Ladies' restroom or a perched in a tree, but you had better stay. If these documents are like what Nod hands me for BE, you're going to have to translate. How much do you charge?"

Smiling and half teasing, Sumo answered. "More than a struggling college student can afford, and the estate will pay for the travel, weekend work, and any fees."

Callie used her knife to carefully open the package, which had been wrapped in a layer tape with sayings and signatures.

The top item was a beautiful picture of fairies in a garden having a tea party. Seventeen fairy men and women were dressed bright colors, but individual tastes brought out personalities. Some wore ribbons, bows, a business suit, or feathers. Teapots and cups made of flowers covered the table. Only four fairies were at the table. The rest were arriving by various means. The fairy at the head of the table was dressed in a rainbow motif. Details of the tea party were beautiful images to a casual onlooker, but each part held great importance to Callie.

When Callie was younger, Thessa, her aunt, would play Fairy tea party with her. Each member of her family had a fairy name. Feather Fairy was Thessa because she loved to dress up in feather boas. Rainbow was Callie. Invisible was Solomon. Nigel was Dandelion as king of the garden. Dusty was the Banished Fairy. Nigel had banned Dusty from tea parties after she stared to teach the Thessa and Callie how to play poker. Dusty wasn't allowed back until she promised not to teach gambling. Dusty had been stubborn and absent from tea parties for a year or so. The woman found out her fairy's name changed to Banished and loved the inventive replacement. She wanted to remain Banished.

Thessa, as Bree, had reached out to Callie via an organization that helped women and children in need. Fittingly, Bree had invited Callie to have coffee and cake around teatime. They had met and visited through social media.

Callie praised the painting. "Wow! Such a beautiful, colorful, and detailed picture. The picture isn't signed. Dr. Wither, could you put that on my chair?"

An envelope slid out of the packet and had "Open Me First" scrawled across the front. The note inside was handwritten and covered about half the page. Callie found her composure thrown as she read the words.

'Dear Best Fairy Sister in the Garden,

    Feather Fairy loved her family and friends. Tea parties with her sister Rainbow were a highlight of the day. Feather witnessed alien invaders in the garden. They were stealing from the earth, destroying, and murdering. Feather was almost caught but escaped. Feather didn't feel safe going home and went to see the Banished Fairy. Banished advised and accompanied her to visit Dandelion for guidance. Dandelion reached out to Invisible.

    Invisible, as garden protector, and Dandelion helped Feather relocate with new powers. They set up Feather's demise, so there was no trace. Feather's one regret was having to lie to the other fairies. Later, Feather reestablished air communications with the garden fairies as a stranger from the Wind Fairy Clan. Rainbow, heir to the garden, will take excellent care of the fairies who live or pass through the realm.'

Callie folded and put the paper aside. A second letter was dated several months prior.

    The story did not end. As a Wind fairy, Feather had to be silent as alien invaders continued their destructive ways. She thought that none of the other fairies, like Invisible or Dandelion, were defending against the danger. Word came that Dandelion had been silently watching, but he was caught and murdered. Invisible explained that acting in haste would endanger all fairies, especially young fairies.

    Years passed, and alien invaders finally made a mistake. Fairies and humans found the invader's lost possessions. Feather rejoiced but grew frustrated as the threat grew closer to the garden. Invisible tried to make Feather be patient, but she refused to listen anymore. Feather had already lost everything and had nothing more to lose. Unfortunately, Feather discovered more could be lost after poking around.

    The discovery would add to the garden heir's duties, but new flowers always need a place to grow. Understandably, Rainbow Fairy may not be ready to raise brand new flowers in the garden. If Rainbow is not, there are many gardens where the seedling may grow in hope, faith, and love.

Callie peered at Sumo with an unreadable expression. Drumming her fingers on the paper attached to Sumo's clipboard, Callie used the code taught to her by her father's friends.

Callie asked, "Did you know Bree as a child or a young adult?"

Sumo returned in the code. "No."

Callie pulled the rest of the paperwork out, scanned the first page, and groaned. "Here, lawyer. Read and translate for me. Solomon's replacement phone only has certain numbers. My phone is with Isley, and I don't have anyone's contact information. Wither has most of the same names. My bag with paper and pen is in the car. Wither, could you come with me to the car? I'll copy the numbers that I might need. Sumo, I'm assuming you have the hospital information. Would you help me?"

Sumo nodded that he would. Callie walked with Wither to the vehicle.

When Callie was sure no one could hear, she asked, "What is your connection to Bash?"

Her friend stopped and turned to the young woman in complete shock at the question.

Collecting himself, Wither sighed. "Geez, Callie. How did you figure out a connection?"

"During our adventures, Bash never grew impatient at my supposed wandering or stopping to help the Creek family. The young man went with the flow. I was standing beside Bash when he spied you and Sumo. His entire body stiffened, but I doubt anyone else noticed. Everyone was focused on the door. His eyes flickered with recognition and concern. He knows you and Sumo.

"Bash is proficient with weapons, and you are a sharpshooter. You keep in practice by teaching gun safety and coach for various shooting contests. Why did Solomon have you and Sumo interact with Bash?"

Wither rubbed his eyes tiredly. "We need him as much as he needs us. We are getting older, and Bash needs a purpose and human connection. Bash's family lived in the mountains until he was fourteen or so. They moved to the city, but the move was stressful. The father became abusive. One day, Bash protected a younger sibling by beating the father up. His father retaliated by throwing him out of the house at fifteen. The young man finished high school and joined the military. There was an incident, and Solomon discovered the circumstances surrounding Bash's decisions. Solomon had Bash turned over to his supervision."

"Was Bash justified in the decision?"

Wither answered. "That is the core of the problem. Bash disobeyed a direct order based on his life's experiences and observations. The call saved fifteen hostages, but the people giving the orders were not happy. Pride and politics became more important than the lives saved. Solomon asked us to spend some time assessing his skills."

Callie thought and said, "The explanation provides the reason Bash sleeps on the roof. Lion wanted windows closed, so the wildlife stayed outside. Bash closed the window and slept on the roof. Uncle Mer came to the farm after a rough situation, and he never closed the window except for really bad weather. Thank you for being honest, and I won't tell anyone."

Rorke approached the couple before they returned inside. "Sumo gave us what information he could without violating privacy laws. Bree and her husband have no living relatives. Bree would have chosen Rosa as executor, but you are younger. We'll start back to the Lodge. You and Sumo can ride in the same car until we have to go separate ways."

Callie asked Sumo. "Objections?"

"A whole bunch regarding several other choices in your life but not about the plan. As long as you don't put on the speaker function, you adhere to the privacy laws."

Callie started to say that the everyone could hear what was going on in the car, but Rorke stepped between her and Sumo.

Rorke whispered. "Don't muddy the water. We'd find out anyway due to the circumstances."

Rorke drove Sumo, Callie, and Wither. Tort drove Wither's car, and Still drove the rest of the team. Callie reviewed the medical decisions with the doctors. When the time came to separate, Sumo and Wither continued toward home. Solomon made contact after the team took a northern route by themselves.

Callie spoke to Solomon about traveling to be with Bree. "The doctors don't want to move Bree until they are sure that she is stable. If I am supposed to make more decisions, I need to be with her."

Solomon explained. "A security team is at the hospital, and Bree will have a twenty-four-hour guard. Once she's stable, we'll medivac her to a local hospital near you."

Callie grew annoyed. "Look, bossy! I am supposed to oversee medical care! Bree is alone!"

Solomon tried to soften his tone. "Callie, there is nothing to be done except wait. Any change in her condition will be relayed."

"What are you not telling me? Why do you sound so worried?"

"Let's say that I am not one for coincidences. Until I know more, you aren't going near the hospital!"

Callie clarified Solomon's concern about a connection. "Meaning Bree's accident might be intentional because the timing is near the anniversary of my father's death."

"I do not know there is a connection other than when Bree was a foster child at the farm."

Callie felt a surge of frustration toward Solomon. She'd loved her aunt and thought that she'd been safe. Whatever happened, Aunt Thessa was facing her real death alone.

Callie's pitch rose, and a small hint of hysteria invaded her tone. "You aren't the boss of me!"

Solomon's tone became that of a commander. "Don't cross me! You'll find yourself in a world of trouble!"

133

Callie recognized her state and needed to find a sense of calm. She decided to end the call rather than say something that she'd regret later. Her feelings bordered on overwhelming grief and hopelessness. Mixed into the emotional wash was anger at the situation. She should be at the bedside of a beloved family member going through a health crisis. If Solomon didn't give permission, she'd not be able to go, and the subject was closed. Yet, trying to squash being overwhelmed and angry was not easy.

Rorke turned onto the private road so they wouldn't have to worry about traffic. He continued about a mile before stopping and putting the gearshift into park.

Rorke helped Callie as she stumbled out of the vehicle. He walked with her a bit and waited until she stopped shaking. "The problem is deeper than Bree and her husband's accident. What's wrong?"

"Solomon may not have the connection, but I do. Bree's letter was a confession. She started snooping when the shipping containers surfaced eight months ago. Bree believed the only liability was to herself and her husband, but she found out that she is pregnant. She's in surgery but was conscious when medical help arrived. The staff knows Bree's instructions, and the directions were crystal clear. If we must choose between mother or child, the baby's life is the priority.

"Sumo specifically wrote on his notepad to not discuss the baby. If Bree dies, I become the child's guardian. Why does Sumo not want me to discuss the baby?"

Rorke paused to digest the news. "My guess: Sumo was probably trying to protect you, Bree, and the baby. Adoption, especially babies, is a huge business. If word spread that Bree does not have family, she'll become a target. You are dealing with a lot of stress but trying hard to be the strong, immovable mountain. Remember, you are not alone."

Callie felt some of the tension leave her shoulders until Rorke asked, "What are we having, a boy or girl?"

Callie's face flushed and hissed. "We?

Rorke gazed into Callie's eyes. "I love you and refuse to let go. Vance is correct in that you will be a great mom."

"I'm not in the mood to be teased! We have no idea if we'd survive a week of dating, much less a month, or long-term."

Still whistled from the second car. "Pick up the conversation later. Lion wants us at the lodge immediately. A security team is here to escort Callie and Jedidiah off-site!"

Callie thought Rorke muttered a couple of curses under his breath but wasn't sure. They hurried back to the car and would have to discuss their relationship later.

Chapter

As soon as they pulled into a garage in the back, the expedition team disembarked. Callie walked through the house. An unfamiliar vehicle pulled up to the porch. Jedidiah and Callie were ushered into the backseat of the car. Callie studied the transport but couldn't see much in the dark interior.

Jedidiah buckled his seat belt. "Will there be a day when life swirls around you in a gentle breeze instead of a tornado?"

"There are many, many days where my life is calm and orderly. Blame Rorke. The man has been in my life for a week, and chaos followed him through the door."

Jedidiah was not one to make physical contact, but he patted Callie's arm. "I approve of the relationship. He's a good man. Solomon called about your friend, and I am sorry."

"Thank you."

The driver halted along a tree line. "Ms. Rivera, climb out. Lion is waiting."

Callie hesitated and spoke to the driver. "How do I know Jedidiah will be safe? Who is directing this so-called rescue, escape, or whatever is happening?"

The driver answered up. "Solomon hired us, and we know about Bree Candle and her husband, Orlin Brody. If Jedidiah agrees, we'll transport him to the hospital. Jedidiah may stay with Bree until she is able to be transferred. We could even check him in as a patient."

Callie found her composure destroyed as tears slid down her face. "Thank you! Thank you! Call once you arrive safely."

Jedidiah sighed. "I haven't agreed."

Callie offered with great effort. "I'll puppy sit while you are in the hospital. Please! I need someone that I trust to stay with Bree because Solomon won't let me near the hospital. Bree may not live through surgery, but she has to live. She's having a baby, and I am not in a position to raise a child."

Jedidiah took in Callie's pleading face in the dim light of the open car door. "Baby?"

"Yes. Bree wants me to raise the child if she dies."

"Darn. Rorke needs to move faster. I want to be an honorary grandfather."

After Rorke's comment, Callie flushed a bright red. "Jedidiah! Oh, my goodness!"

The driver's amusement was apparent and gently told Callie. "Ma'am, we need to continue to our destination. Be careful. A gentleman named Mr. Notice is about to arrive, and he may have divided loyalties."

Lion waited in the shadows and led Callie to a bunker in the forest. Lion had no problem navigating through the trees and was sure-footed. The two women entered an underground bunker. Inside, monitors showed the images from the security cameras mounted around the perimeter and inside the lodge. They could watch and listen as events unfolded.

Callie quipped, "You are built for outdoor adventures."

Lion disagreed. "No. Necessity is the mother of forced adaptation. Journeys into the wild are not a part of my personality."

Three helicopters landed. Callie lost count of the individuals with weapons climbing out. Talk about overkill. Her seven friends wandered to the porch without any visible weapons. Rorke's team was not engaging the invaders but making a play for time. Time for Callie and Jedidiah to go as far as possible without pursuit.

An official-looking man, who Callie assumed was Mr. Notice, walked up the steps with purpose and greeted the men. Callie's only thought was that the man looked like a weasel. "Hello. I'd like to speak to Miss Callie Rivera."

Rorke offered to shake hands. "Rorke Asher."

Notice nodded without extending his hand to return the gesture of greeting. "I'll be blunt. Our schedule is tight, and we are to escort Ms. Rivera to the hospital."

Rorke didn't take affront at the intended insult. "Are you Mr. Notice?"

"I am."

"You supervise a team with private security service. The company has contracts with a government agency, but Callie hasn't hired you. Hence, we have no obligation to allow Callie to accompany you. She is fine with us and has coordinated care for Mrs. Candle."

"We are contracted at the federal level and have better security clearances. Mr. Asher and your friends have clean records and good reputations. Cooperate, or we change that fact."

Rorke leaned on the porch post and spoke in a neutral tone. "Let me guess. Bree Candle's husband, Orlin Brody, worked for the federal court system. Your security was surprised and failed in their task. A car accident is a cover story. The problem being is a far more sinister plot.

Orlin Brody died protecting his wife in an assault, and Bree is in critical condition. Complicating the matter is that she is expecting a child."

Mr. Notice did not hide his dislike of Bree. "Orlin wasn't the target, and he was a respected, good man. Bree wanted to play detective! Never had much use for her. She was sneaking around, hiding disposable phones, and had little regard for protocol. We lost six team members! My people, and Orlin, did not deserve to be collateral damage in some Hatfield and McCoy's conflict."

Rorke's voice never changed tone or pitch. "How do you know Bree was the cause?"

Mr. Notice answered. "The woman made no pretense of trying to be discreet. Damn woman! She started digging and asking questions about an investigation into poaching or counterfeiting. Someone stealing illegal moonshine from a neighbor in the mountains is more likely. Bree heard about a report Nigel Rivera filed ten years ago about plant stealing. She was concerned that someone would try to murder Ms. Rivera. Bree's meddling brought attention to the Rivera family. We don't want unnecessary violence to an innocent party."

Still leaned against a window frame. "You don't sound as if you care about Bree, who is fighting for her life."

Notice's voice radiated with authority. "Bring Ms. Callie Rivera outside! The woman became a high-profile asset, and my supervisors want her in protective custody."

Rorke stated empirically rather than emotionally, "Ah, the core of the problem. Superiors don't like when people die on their watch. You don't care about my friend's health or safety. You care about covering your ass. Callie's not here. Even if she were present, we wouldn't allow her to leave."

Notice went ridged with anger but controlled his temper. "You don't have much choice, Mountain Man!"

Still raised an eyebrow. "Asher, I might take offense, but the city dude just showered you with high praise."

A woman brought Notice a computer and whispered to him.

Notice flipped through a couple of screens and demanded. "Ms. Rivera arrived at the lodge and left with an older gentleman. The vehicle went to the local airstrip, and four helicopters took off. Their airstrip doesn't have monitors outside. We are not able to confirm if Callie boarded a transport. Where is Ms. Rivera?"

Rorke asked incredulously. "You verified that Callie accompanied us back and didn't stay? Wow! We're on private property. Guess we had better be careful running around naked with such accurate surveillance. Bash, make sure to wear clothes while sleeping on the roof."

Bash didn't have a problem with shyness in backing Rorke's play for time. "Oh, man! I planned on performing a rain dance tonight in the buff. If I have an audience, does that mean we earn more prayers for the rain?"

Notice wasn't amused. "Here are my numbers. As soon as Ms. Rivera makes contact, have her phone immediately!"

When the helicopters were gone, Lion led the way to a truck parked in the trees. Callie climbed into the bed and placed a blanket over herself. No one would be able to spy her returning. Parking in a closed garage that had a door into the main building, the two entered through the kitchen.

Lion immediately went to the stove to check dinner. "Stupid man! He'd better not have messed up my bread and pumpkin pie. They look all right. Callie, grab the potholders and take out the bread. The rest of the food is on the table."

Dinner smelled delicious. Callie did as Lion requested, and they sat down to eat. After the blessing, Callie found her appetite was gone.

Callie turned to Lion. "You have a background in the medical field. Would you consider staying with Bree until Solomon stops being unreasonable?"

"Child, I understand that you're in a difficult position. My answer is not to hurt your feelings or create more distress. Bree has a good medical team. We'd only be in the way, and there is not much to do but wait."

"I've read that an unconscious person or people in a coma still hear. Bree will know that she is not alone."

"Jedidiah will be there, and you trust him. I know the security detail, and they have an excellent reputation. They'll make sure everyone, including the puppy, are safe."

Crabbe remarked. "Security is going to be busy babysitting and dog sitting."

The phone rang, and Solomon was calling with an update. "I do not have more news on Bree's status. We're working to authenticate whatever data possible. Orlin Brody worked for the court system, so we must try to separate assumption from fact. We had no idea that Bree was poking around an active investigation or found out about Nigel's report. Callie?"

Callie repeated. "Yes."

Solomon heard much in that one word. Callie was trying to be strong, but there was a slight crack in her voice.

Her unofficial guardian repeated himself to ease Callie's mind. "We're gathering information. Notice has more information about the attack, but I haven't spoken to him. I'm waiting until my temper cools. His attitude makes me want to kick him into next year. We'll try to arrange a visit with Bree, but there are many eyes, friend and foe, on the case. Let's continue the conversation on a happier subject. Your goal for the weekend was to work as a team in a scavenger hunt."

Lion smiled and took a handful of keys from her pocket. "Last two containers arrived while we were gone. Name tags are attached to keyrings."

Each person found the chest with the corresponding key and opened their prize. Callie opened hers to find two handmade books. Nigel had writing his name across the bottom. Pressed flowers with detailed descriptions were inside. The second notebook had beautiful, colorful, and sketches. Flowers and plants were cataloged by alphabet.

Bash cleared his throat. "Ah, Solomon?"

"Yes."

"What am I supposed to do with a computer? Taking a new piece of electronics to my residence is not an option. There is no place to lock up valuables."

Solomon explained the reason. "Bash is the only person that I may officially order to back up Rorke to protect Callie. Each of you was willing to accompany Callie and Rorke on field trips. Due to the change in circumstances, I would feel better having each team member within reach of Callie's location.

"We secured the funds to pay for the field trips. Crabbe and Still, if you agree, you will receive official transfer letters Monday. Thicke and Tort work for their family businesses. We reached out, and the families are willing to find someone to fill your shoes until the Christmas break. I'll figure out a way to compensate the family businesses. Thicke, we found an airplane pilot willing to substitute and take your flights through November. If agreeable, we'll arrange for the team members to attend the classes. Callie, please don't argue with me on the matter."

Callie ate a small nibble of cornbread with chili on top. "I am not arguing."

Solomon announced. "You may discuss the options with family. No one needs to provide an answer until tomorrow night."

The line disconnected, and Callie decided to take a shower instead of eating or having dessert.

139

When Callie was in her room, Rorke asked Lion to call Solomon back. Solomon answered and was slightly surprised. He expected Callie. The presumed subjects being the team's presence in her life or going to stay with Bree. Rorke didn't invite anyone to join him and took the phone outside.

Rorke asked, "How bad is Bree's condition?"

"She's in God's hands, and we can only pray. I release you from any feelings of a debt to me, and I'll understand if you want to bow out. You'd stay because of your personality: a strong sense of honor, a protective nature, and a promise made to me. I planned on discussing the matter privately when Callie was asleep."

Rorke had walked away from the lodge, leaned against a tree, and gazed up into the stars. "I'm rather insulted you think I'd leave at the first sign of trouble."

"I had to ask. I suppose that I could put up with you in Callie's life. You're good for one another. Are you aware she loves you?"

Rorke chose his words carefully. "Yes, but she needs time to adjust and accept the feelings."

Solomon returned in a half teasing tone. "The good news is that she hasn't kicked you out of the house or her life. Regardless of my words to the team, Callie is my one weakness. I've spent my life upholding the law, but I'll break every law on earth to protect her. Before you return to civilization, did Callie share anything about Blake and Beau?"

"Yes. Blake caught Beau's father's attention, and Beau tried to protect Blake from his father. Blake was hurt, and Beau took her to the hospital. Beau called Callie because he didn't know who else to contact. Callie and Beau met to make plans during their supposed dates. When they've met, the meetings are a ruse to trade information. She has not told me her end game."

Solomon sighed. "The girl is smart and resourceful, but she has no idea how to think like a criminal. I'd relocate Beau far, far away, but Callie won't let me interfere. I briefed Isley on the Dew family. He and I have agreed not to interfere unless the situation escalates. There are more pressing matters to settle."

Still and Crabbe joined Rorke after he hung up the phone. Crabbe took out his knife and twirled the handle through his fingers.

Still watched the motion of Crabbe's fingers with fascination. "Rorke, how bad is Bree?"

"Time will tell. I consider you both best friends. I'd never ask you to follow me down this dangerous road."

Still smiled in his lazy way. "Been a while since we worked together. Looking forward to not doing much."

Crabbe and Rorke had not discussed their past. Crabbe's family was Rorke's last foster home before he turned eighteen and aged out. Crabbe's parents offered him a place to stay as long as he needed. Rorke knew that they didn't have much but would share what they had. Rorke had stayed in touch over the years.

Crabbe's four brothers worked with their father in logging and salvage. Mrs. Crabbe was kind, caring, and didn't complain. There were very few women around to socialize with or do girl stuff. Her sons figured that was the reason their mother loved to play matchmaker.

Crabbe couldn't resist needling Rorke about a girlfriend. "Mom wants to meet Callie. I bet is that she'll use me as an excuse to visit. Mom will probably introduce herself to Callie as well as Callie's entire family."

Rorke sighed. "Great! You told your family. I love your mom, but she tends to be a little too enthusiastic about matchmaking."

Crabbe put his knife away and commented. "I'm sure it's hard for her to be the only female in a logging family. Dad finally got over me going into law enforcement instead of taking over. My brothers are doing fine without me. Finally, my father admitted that he was more worried about my dangerous career choice. Logging is a lot more dangerous."

Rorke had his answer. "Thank you for having my back. Floor space is available at my place until we have sorted details."

Chapter

After breakfast and cleaning up, Lion hugged Callie and whispered, "I am sorry about your father."

Callie asked, "Will we see you again?"

"Yes."

"Would you not tamper with the tea next time? I appreciate the attempt to help me sleep, but nightmares are normal. The dreams will be over by next week."

Lion did not deny her actions. "You have done well. The burden you have carried is more than a child, or young adult, should carry alone. Your father's friends had one another. Callie do not do something unwise. The best way to protect those you love is make a lot of noise with what information you discover."

Callie asked Lion's opinion. "What if we only find old, diseased seeds? Names, dates, routes, and transportation methods could have been in the car or cabin and destroyed."

Lion reassured her that Solomon's plan was sound. "Hopefully, the authorities will have a chance to collect information. Friend and foe will be watching. If the current case is linked to the past, Isley and Solomon are investigating. Detecting one crack in the wall could lead to more dangerous fissures if one looks closely enough."

Rorke waved to Callie that it was time to go.

Callie said, "Thank you for the company and food."

"Next visit, we'll have to play cribbage. We are sending you back to the Cherry Outpost. You usually leave from there to go to the cabin, and the place is a meeting ground for various groups. The men left their vehicles at the parking lot and took a charter to a nearby airport."

Each expedition member climbed aboard the helicopter, and they started back to civilization.

The scenery from the Sawtooth area to Moreland was breathtaking. Fall had begun so a few trees had leaves turning to gold, brown, red, and orange. The flight had to head north before cutting back to the south. If they flew in the straightest line possible, the path would be over the Crater of the Moon.

Callie asked into the headset. "Rorke? I've hiked around the Lava Beds, Snake River Plains, and preserve area, but it's been years. What do you remember?"

Rorke rattled off what he retained without a review. "The official name is Craters of the Moon National Monument and Preserve, and the area is the Great Rift of Idaho. The region has open rifts or cracks and three lava fields. There are fields of vents, spatter cones, hardened lava rivers, and cinder cones. Cinder cones were left when molten would shoot up out of the vents. Lava would cool and harden into the cones. There is a drive that is about seven miles long that goes past main points of interest. Big Cinder is one of the world's largest basaltic cinder cones and is about 700 feet high. Astronauts trained for the moon landing in the park."

Crabbe asked, "Isn't there something about a Devil or Inferno in the area?"

Rorke smiled at the question. "Yes, but we'd have to make a stop at the Robert Limbert Center for details."

Callie's eyes went bright with glinted excitement. "We made a school trip in high school. My favorite part of the tour was the tree molds. The trees were incinerated or fossilized and formed a mold."

Rorke was sitting next to her and shook his head in a negative manner. "We are not stopping. Part of the park is the Devil's Orchard. Fragments or monoliths broke off during an eruption. The Inferno Cone is a steep trail, but the end is a beautiful view of the Spatter Cones and Pioneer Mountains."

Bash added shyly, "I liked the caves when my family camped out. We explored the lava tubes and caves. We stayed for two weeks, but I could have spent much longer exploring."

The fact that the young man mentioned his family was a huge leap of trust. Bash was the only one who had not spoken about family.

Callie reached out, put a hand on Bash's sleeve, and smiled encouragement. "Let's look at the schedule. We could plan a field trip to the area before the cold weather. The Loop is closed to traffic during the winter months. Cross country skiing is considered too dangerous due to the sharp lava and holes hidden by the ice or snow."

The team completed the rest of the trip in silence. Once the helicopter landed on the pad and the passengers climbed out, Callie walked to the main building, which acted as General Store, outpost, mailing office, cabin rental center, supply place, marina, and fishing license station. There was an emergency medical clinic if campers, hikers, or others needed to wait for a medical evacuation. Several tour groups arranged to have their groups meet at the outpost for a day of hiking or day trips.

The proprietors, Mr. and Mrs. Cherry, were a couple in their mid-fifties. Mr. Cherry was a quiet, balding man who rarely spoke or smiled, but he was friendly enough and helpful. Mrs. Cherry wore glasses and her hair up in a bun. Callie always thought of the grandmother in Little

Red Riding Hood. The pair were strict about making sure tourists and locals had the required licenses for fishing and knew basic water rules before renting equipment. Their base had expanded over the years to include water sports. Originally, the outpost offered canoes and small fishing boats. Now they leased paddleboards, jet skis, kayaks, and larger watercraft.

Callie was surprised to find Isley waiting.

Mrs. Cherry met the travelers with a clipboard. "Hey, flower girl. Collect lots of seeds?"

"Yes, ma'am. Bagged, tagged, and ready for inspection. I'm heading up to the cabin for a couple of hours. Could I leave the collection and pick up my treasures later?"

Mrs. Cherry answered. "Sure. Ranger Cattail is on duty, and I am certain she'll appreciate the extra time. We've had several lost tourists today."

Her companions had started to unpack Callie's bags and looked pointedly at Rorke.

"We'd like to come with you to the cabin."

Callie understood the reason for Isley's presence. He appeared to make sure she let the group tag along. "Ah, the sentiment is much appreciated, but there isn't enough room."

Isley eyed the young woman and asked in a slightly quarrelsome tone. "How many acres of land and water do you see?"

Callie shook her head. "I mean, there isn't enough room. Maximum weight means only three or four would fit on my boat."

"Boat?"

Mrs. Cherry grinned with conspiracy at Callie. "Our mid-size is ready to sail. We know Callie has the required licenses and knowledge. You could lease the boat for the day."

Callie shook her head. "Thanks, but school starts tomorrow. I spent my shekels on tuition and supplics."

Isley made a face of resignation. "How much for the day?"

Mrs. Cherry answered while checking that everyone had signed the forms for their helicopter trip. "$3000, but we'll give you a ten percent discount."

Isley blinked a couple of times to make sure that he'd heard correctly. "The amount is indecent and borders on highway robbery! I'll pay the fees because there doesn't seem to be another choice. Fair warning, Callie. If a Loch Ness monster eats me, I will haunt you."

"A sense of humor. Who knew? I also suggest you change clothes. Those shoes won't work for boating or hiking."

144

Callie took her camera and matched the pictures with the labeled, sealed bags. Then she marked each one off on a list.

Still asked, "Why the paranoia and double-checking?"

"I trust the team, but the general public is a different story. The box will be sitting in the open be while waiting for inspection. Anyone could walk off with a bag. Once, we had a tourist try to buy the entire inventory. My father refused, and the guy tried to take everything later."

The eight expedition members stowed their gear and met at the dock. Isley reappeared and walked down to the boat rental in a pair of different shoes. He had not changed from his suit pants, dress shirt, or jacket.

Tort stated his disapproval. "How attached to the business suit are you?"

Isley ignored the question and tone. "Let's go before I wring the owner's neck. Highway robbers! Plus, I'll yell at the next person who asks to come with us. Ten or more curious individuals asked if we had room for additional passengers. You never, ever have guests. Ranger Cattail arrived at the main building, listened to the conversations, and grinned like she had the best secret in the world."

Callie explained, "I've known Ranger Cattail for a long time. She was one of the rangers Gran asked to keep an eye on me. Gran had to run the rentals and didn't want me wandering in the woods alone. I rode along with various rangers until I was able to go on my own. In return, the rangers have a place on private land to use. Locals know that trespassing is liable to annoy me or the rangers. Neither of which is a good idea."

The air on the river was colder, and the wind picked up. Forty-five minutes later, Callie pulled into a tributary and tied up at a dock marked private property.

During their hike to the cabin, the team kept an eye on Isley. The man kept pace, which slightly surprised them. The only noises were the breezes through the trees, birdcalls, and squirrels scolding the humans for interrupting their food searches.

Their twenty-minute hike took them uphill and well above the flood plain. A cabin appeared, and it was nestled in the lee of the rocks. Upon further inspection, the place was more of a house than a cabin. Callie checked the perimeter before going inside. Isley followed and inspected the area. The others had filed in as well and looked around.

Isley commented. "A bit unsecured for a paranoid owner."

Callie smiled. "The place is open for anyone who needs shelter or help. I'd rather not have anyone breaking down the door to use the radio or get food. Sensors on the windows and doors will send out an alert if

145

opened. There is electricity with two backup generators: one water and one gas. Keys and crucial components to run the equipment are biometrically locked up. I am the only person with access. There is a solar generator with a gas backup. Fuel and flammables are stored in a rock nook for safety."

Rorke scanned the area. "I love the place. What do you do for sunlight?"

Callie flushed at the praise and unlocked several latches on the west wall. Instead of using the hand crank, she activated a mechanical crank. They wouldn't be there long, and hand cranking took time.

The wall receded to expose a wall of hurricane proof glass. Sunlight spilled into the room. Callie smiled at Rorke's longing glance to explore the area beyond the closed doors. "Go ahead, but make sure to keep an eye out for wildlife that found their way inside. Every so often, we have a snake or other wildlife that needs eviction. I have a climb to the garden, which will take a few minutes. We shouldn't linger. I want to be back in time for evening church services."

A small flower sat on the kitchen counter. Callie took the clay container and started the rest of the way up the bluff. Still walked with her. She wondered if the men had drawn straws to see who accompanied her. There was not a path, but she knew the way by heart. Still followed her into the wilderness. The terrain was rocky and steep in a couple of places. Callie halted in a grove of trees beside an outcropping of boulders. She took the young seedling and added it to a small clump of flowers. The flower for her father was in its new home. It was one of her father's favorite spots because of the river view.

The hike down was much faster. She secured the cabin and found out why Still joined her. The self-proclaimed river man asked for the boat keys. He had been scouting the water and wanted to drive. Callie didn't argue and was impressed that Still navigated to Cherry's orchard without needing directions.

A forest ranger was waiting at the dock as they pulled into the original slip. The ranger was a beautiful woman a little older than Callie. She had the classic features of her Native American heritage: high cheekbones, jet black hair, and dark eyes. Her hair was cut short but hidden under a ranger's hat.

Her friends tied up the lines, and Callie hopped out to hug her friend. "Hey! Ranger Cattail! Did you send another tourist into the crater?"

Cattail nodded to Callie's crew but spoke to her friend. "Ha! Ha! Isley! Rorke! If you put my flower girl in danger, I'll drop you into the

146

forest without a knife or provisions. We'll let the wolves have you for dinner."

Isley replied in kind. "She's not my problem anymore. I have recused myself from the Plant Project."

Cattail appeared utterly shocked. "What!? Really? Why?! It's your first case in charge of the local office, and you pass. Are you dying?"

"No."

Callie decided to harass Isley because he'd been a thorn in her side. "Rorke is Isley's son who is working on the book project with me. Thanks for the taking my class. It will be nice to have a friendly face in the audience."

Cattail looked from Rorke to Isley. "Wow! Talk about the apple falling far from the tree, as on a different continent. Rorke and Isley are about as different as day and night. Outside of the mountain men or women and forest service, Rorke's the best guide in the state, and he's way above some of them. I'm ready to drop-kick a couple of newbies into next week. Pair of juniors let campers stay in a gulch instead of moving them. The juniors followed procedure and alerted the station to the presence of the campsite. We relocated the group before the rain."

Callie backtracked the conversation. "Why are you concerned about Isley getting me into danger? We're researching."

Cattail was delighted to share the news. "The project has stirred up interest across the state. Lots of places, local and statewide, want their names mentioned. Groups involved want to send you out with representatives to document and photograph. Do a show and tell with plants in their natural habitat. The homeopathic company wants to add lectures with props at various offices. Wineries, juice manufactures, and farmers are sending letters to offices to be included. Legal finally had to be involved. Isley's agency was tasked with oversight and making sure everyone plays nice."

Callie whispered, "When was anyone planning on telling me?"

Isley grumped. "We weren't saying anything. You have other responsibilities, and I am also aware that you are concerned about Dusty interrupting the flow of life. I've taken care of the woman, and she will not arrive until after the meeting."

Rorke asked half-seriously, "Stuff her in a trunk until tomorrow afternoon?"

Isley had every person's undivided attention, including Callie. "No. I bribed and blackmailed. We had a chat on Friday. She doesn't make an appearance until after the meeting is over. If the lady declines, I'll arrest her for trespassing. She may explain to her husband why she decided to interrupt a private event and is being hauled in by the authorities to answer questions about a charity account."

Rorke arched an eyebrow at the lengthy explanation. Isley wasn't usually so chatty about his actions. "I am not sure whether to be impressed or disturbed."

Still asked, "Who exactly is Dusty?"

Callie explained. "Dusty will charm, fascinate, and lure her way through one's defenses. Once inside the walls, she'll take whatever her desire happens to be at that second. If you are lucky, her only goal is sex."

Still observed, "I guess there is bad blood between the two of you. Did Dusty sleep with a boyfriend?"

"Dusty found out that I was dating a nice guy named Linus. We did talk of a future or maybe getting married. The woman appeared out of thin air and made friends with the gentleman. Dusty lured him to Boise to fulfill his life's dreams. He left with my blessings because we'd already figured out that we were not right for one another."

Cattail put a comforting, protective arm around her friend's shoulders and blurted. "Callie! Unless you are talking about plants, that is the most words I've ever heard from you at one time. You've never mentioned the woman, and I've known you since grade school. I don't think I've heard the family talk about her. What's the story?"

Callie sighed. "Dusty dated my father while they were in college, and the two remained friends afterward. The two had a very odd relationship. Her behavior toward my father was strange, and she did not try to manipulate his emotions. Granted, she did try to pull him into a few of her ideas. As far as I am aware, he never gave her money. She's not bad, just flighty, and it takes a lot of energy to keep up. Learned early to ignore her quirks and not buy into any of her wild ideas. Isley, you said Dusty had a husband. She never said a word about a husband. Wow."

Isley decided to tell Callie the rest of the news. "Good news is that Dusty's husband is independently wealthy and doesn't care about her indiscretions. Sexual liaisons are discrete, and a causal onlooker would have no idea of their marital choices."

Cattail raised an eyebrow at Isley, "Open marriage?"

"No idea. I didn't ask for details."

Chapter

Callie moved everyone along, after glancing at her watch. "We need to go. I want to be back for evening church services."

Rorke stated. "Callie, you're riding with me. Isley's following us in my truck."

Callie started to comment until she glanced over at Bash. The young man shook his head and mimed to listen to Rorke. Walking back to the cars, Callie fell in step beside Bash.

The young man glanced at her before explaining. "The team is splitting up and regrouping tomorrow. Solomon's orders. Isley and Rorke are staying with you until the rest of us make arrangements to be nearby."

Callie wasn't happy at the explanation. She remained silent on the drive home. They didn't arrive in time for church, and she blamed Isley. The man drove the speed limit and insisted on a sit-down restaurant to eat. She wanted fast food.

Rorke parked by the back door, but Callie left her belongings. She walked to where Isley was parking at Rorke's rental unit. Her stony expression spoke volumes to Isley, and he knew the young woman was not pleased about something.

Isley tried to joke with Callie to break the serious mood. "Should I be ready to draw my weapon?"

Callie asked, "Did you have permission to tell me about the discovery eight months ago?"

Isley answered with authority and a clipped tone. "I was in charge and didn't need permission. As to the file your father left, my superiors have the case. Connecting the dots and approaching you is the next logical step. No one else is aware Nigel told anyone about the report or your presence at the accident."

Callie nodded to Isley, but her tone was equally firm. "Thank you for your honesty. I agreed to be bait, but I am adding two conditions. One, Rorke is to take the role of public affairs or spokesman. I cannot do anything about what has already circulated, but I'm concerned about the impact to my father's garden as a business. Two, you become the liaison between the agencies and the project. Any relationship which might create a conflict of interest has been voiced and reported."

Isley's mouth made a thin line of disapproval. "I appreciate the fact you think that I have that much power, but I don't. Plans have been made and set in motion."

"Then make sure you are present when the authorities approach me. Comply with the requests, or I bow completely out."

"You can't back out."

"Call my bluff and watch me."

Callie returned to the house and checked her messages. There was no change in Bree's condition. Jedidiah and Rosa left short texts that all was well. Wither left a voice mail. She needed to wear business attire in the morning. A contingency of supervisors was meeting with them at nine. The conference with everyone would be at ten.

Nod called to clarify a couple of points about the project documents. Callie needed to be prepared to specify her position without damaging anyone's reputation or participation in the project.

Pica knocked and wanted to provide an update on Blake. Callie listened as she was rearranging bouquets.

Pica asked, "Why do you have two baskets of flowers?"

Callie looked down and sighed. She didn't want to hear Pica rant about Solomon if she mentioned Thessa. Part of the lecture usually dealt with Nigel and his friends. They should have kept Thessa out of jail where she died. Pica wasn't as vocal about Nigel and his friend's share of the fault. The fact that Thessa resurfaced as Bree Candle and might be dying made the loss harder. Yet, she wasn't going to lie. Every year, Callie sent flowers and a monetary donation to two charities.

"After Aunt Thessa died, my father started a tradition that I continued. Thessa loved to volunteer at the animal shelter, so BE sends a bouquet and money donation. The second is for my father, which goes to child services. The anniversary of their deaths are three days apart, and I miss both very much."

Oddly, Pica didn't say anything about Nigel or Thessa. Instead, they spoke about Blake and BE. Pica returned to his house when Isely knocked. Isley made a bed on the couch, and Rorke slept in the spare room.

Monday morning, Callie dressed in dark navy-blue pants and forest green blouse. She felt like her body was made of lead and had trouble moving. Sleep had not come easily, and the lack of rest had nothing to do with her father's death.

Isley made breakfast. Callie found Bash and Rorke at the table.

Bash smiled in greeting. "Thank you for inviting me for breakfast."

Callie had no idea about the invitation but responded, "You're welcome. Isley, is breakfast the only type of food you make?"

"Yes, and I'm not in a mood to hear complaining. It's too early for snide remarks about dinner out and missing church."

Callie was still upset about the fact, but she didn't realize Isley had noticed.

Rorke diverted the conversation. "Mer stopped by after you went to bed. He asked if you'd drive Rosa's car to work. Yours needs gas, and there wasn't enough time to fill up both. Rosa and your car are registered under the same parking pass. Follow me today, and Isley will trail behind you until we park. Hal is meeting us to walk you to the meeting area. Isley and I will then park in different areas of the campus."

Callie took a deep breath to center herself. Today, she had to portray a sense of calm and balance. There were bigger issues in life to worry over than parking fees. Callie managed her money and bank accounts like a miser. Her father worked hard to make sure she could go to college and be financially stable. A fund set up for her education made tuition payments directly to the college. Disbursements for books and living expenses went to her checking account the week classes began. Callie knew registering multiple vehicles under one student meant additional paperwork and cost. If she took a BE truck, she obtained a visitor's tag for the day. A part of her felt irritated that everyone wanted to be in her business.

Rorke dropped her at the lab building where Hal met her. They used a golf cart to drive over to the student center. Hal parked and made sure Callie went into the conference room and glanced around the room. She'd had memorized the short biographies after Dean Wither's warning text the night before. She recognized the people behind the titles because the pictures and biographies were in university publications. The university's president, vice president, and several upper administrative staff were gathered. Dean Wither and Dean Lite stood on either side of Ms. Nod. The lawyer's attendance was a pleasant surprise, but her concern heightened. If Nod rearranged her schedule, there was a good reason. Callie had learned from the best. She might as well turn on the charm and play along.

Smiling warmly and making a wide pageant, dramatic wave, Callie said, "Dr. Wither's asked me to see him, and I am sorry to interrupt a prestigious meeting of the university's top executives."

The young woman went around the room and greeted each person with their name. There were two individuals whom Callie did not recognize.

Moving silently with what she hoped was grace, Callie went to stand beside the two. "I haven't seen you around the university, but I am Callie Rivera."

A tall, distinguished gentleman with graying hair and wearing an expensive suit shook her hand. The man looked like he belonged on a golf course conversing with retirees about his grandchildren. Granted, Callie had no idea if the man was married, had children, or grandchildren.

"Agent Moss. I supervise the state's offices of the FBI."

Moss introduced his assistant, Agent Moss, and Callie shook hands. The man had the build of the wrestler's viewers watched on television, but Monarch wore more clothes. A pink long-sleeved dress shirt contrasted nicely with the pink shirt. His black hair was tied and tucked back. If you weren't looking, you'd miss the long hair.

Callie smiled and said with a slight lift to her voice. "Now, I may say that I've met three very nice federal agents in one week."

Agent Moss asked, "Three?"

"Oh, yes! Mr. Rorke Asher's guardian, Agent Isley, was so supportive during Rorke's move. He helped sort flowers after we had a small mishap at my father's garden. We had such a nice time that I forgot to ask why the FBI cared about a book project."

Rorke's amused but inquisitive voice came from the doorway. "I was very curious, asked, and Isley clammed up. Hello."

Dr. Lite introduced Rorke to the men and women in the room. Callie watched Rorke work his own brand of charm on those in the room.

The agents were the last to be presented, and Agent Moss took the floor as the speaker. "Organizing one large group is challenging. Put four together, and someone must led. Since our agency is not directly involved in the project, we are able to supervise with impartiality. The decision has been beneficial to all those involved because of the interest in the project. Isley had the idea to narrow down the applicants with tests, and he immediately recused himself, when Rorke was identified as the best qualified."

Callie would not break Wither or Isley's confidence and made a confused face. "I don't remember taking a test."

"A committee sent representatives plant pictures and incentive prizes to various botanists. The higher the score, the bigger the prize."

Callie grinned. "Oh, the picture test. I won a six-hundred-dollar gift card. Easiest money I ever earned."

"The only two to make a perfect score on the test were you and Dr. Wither. Full disclosure, he did ask to check three of the plants. The proctors allowed the measure because he'd written in the answers. Each response was correct, so he didn't change the responses."

Well-done expressions were sent to Callie and Dr. Wither.

Agent Moss continued. "As to state's geography with knowledge of writing, the challenge was slightly harder. We needed a person knowledgeable about written language and Idaho's landscape. Rorke had a perfect score on location and area, and he did the best on the written exam. Luckily, Rorke had applied to the university, and Dr. Lite is an excellent candidate for supervising. The dean has numerous publications to his credit. He also has outstanding student and faculty recommendations."

Dr. Lite nodded as others sent him equally praising looks.

Agent Moss said, "Both deans worked extra hard to pull together a workable outline with the last-minute changes. We appreciate their hard work, and Dr. Lite will share the details."

Dr. Lite expounded. "Thursday, Ms. Nod, the family's lawyer, contacted us after Ms. Rivera shared concerns about the project and a conflict of interest. Ms. Rivera runs a business, and accusations of biases could ruin her reputation. Academic record and exam results create an added layer of protection. We decided that if an individual or group wishes to participate, they may. Interest from individuals or groups, who wish to be included, is starting. Anyone providing input may submit their name for credit on the book. Verification is not hard given the nature of the material. Ms. Nod's passed along a second legality issue. Ms. Rivera officially inherits her father's business next month."

Agent Moss asked Dr. Lite, "May I break into the conversation?"

"Certainly."

"We are aware of the circumstances and have ensured every transaction is transparent. We will ensure paperwork on candidates' selection and course material is accessible for any inquiries. Ma'am, I am sorry for your loss."

The words and gestures naturally flowed. Callie'd practiced tone inflection, facial expression, hands, and sentences until the output satisfied her.

Callie nodded slightly. "Thank you for the condolence. My father died ten years ago, so the family has had time to adjust."

Dr. Lite continued, "A donor set up a six-million-dollar grant. Specific amounts earmarked for certain expenses. One million will cover classroom costs. The items included are office supplies, computers, guest teachers to instruct Rorke and Callie's other assigned classes, and graduate assistants. The only class Callie will teach is biology, and Rorke will be instructing the literature course."

Rorke asked politely, "What is the catch?"

"The donor, who wishes to remain anonymous, is willing to supply the grant with several non-negotiable conditions. The basis of the book was to use plants native to Idaho as the book's core material. Our new sponsor wants to use recent pictures or drawings of plants in their natural environment. We discussed a budget for taking field trips for taking pictures. The donor will back publishing in return for a percentage of the profit."

Rorke chuckled in amusement. "Sorry, but profit? Publishing on any level is a gamble."

"Think about the potential of the subject. Grapes are one example that we discussed. Idaho has many orchards that grow grapes, and grapes used for wine. The subject is discussed in many historical writings. We have emails and counted requests for 20,000 books."

Tourism and winery popped into Callie's mind after their conversation with Cattail.

Rorke glanced around the room. "Seriously? We haven't even started." The slight, polite smiles of those gathered indicated the sincerity.

Dr. Lite was delighted at Rorke's surprise and disbelief.

Callie brought the conversation back to the donor's requests. "How are we to collect pictures?"

"You will be taking lots of field trips. We'll put together a team of qualified volunteers. Part of the budget consists of a stipend for travel, equipment, and lodging. A number of places sent offers for a free night's stay in exchange for a listing in the book."

Callie turned to Nod, who spoke for the first time. "The answer is yes. Offers are legitimate and above reproach. As to businesses offering amenities, they may use the offer as a tax write off or part of advertising expense. We'll dissect details later."

Lite said, "You will teach Tuesday, Wednesday, and Thursday morning. Botany will start at eight, and Intro to Lit at nine-thirty. We moved you to a larger classroom, which has the capability to support distance learning. As of last night, we had 200 students registered to be in the classroom and 40 remote stations."

Callie could feel her control beginning to slip. "Why are you discussing remote stations instead of distance learning?"

"Several places, like a ranger station in the northern region, wish to join us, but the distance is a factor. Our donor is supplying laptops which the IT department formatted and set up over the weekend. A delivery service transported the computers to places around the state this morning. Everyone with a computer will log in at three-thirty today for a test run."

Rorke asked, "What about grades?"

"Only students physically present are eligible for grades. Most students are auditing the class. Representatives from the organizations sent individuals who were interested in the project. Again, if anyone wants to help for a moment in the spotlight, they are more than welcome. We'll be glad for the input or thoughts, but you two are the leads. If there are any problems, direct the situation to Dr. Wither or me. Have I forgotten anything? Does anyone have questions?"

Callie had several, but she wasn't about to air her thoughts in the room. "I would like to say thank you. The only reason that I could participate in such a wonderful project is with your support. The opportunity is very much appreciated."

Rorke chimed in behind Callie. "There is not much for me to add, except my gratitude. Thank you."

Agent Moss smiled. "Representatives are waiting in the banquet hall for the meet and greet, but there are a couple of housekeeping issues. Even I have superiors, which require a few signatures from Mr. Asher and Ms. Rivera. Dr. Wither and Dr. Lite have signed their forms. Most of the paperwork says that you'll follow state and federal guidelines collecting photographs, not plagiarize, and your licenses are up to date. Ms. Nod has a copy of everything. Leave Callie and Rorke with us, and we'll join you in a few minutes."

Callie thought of a receiving line as the gathering filed out. The men and women filed out. Each shook her and Rorke's hand and wished them well. The individuals offered to help in any way possible. The room emptied of everyone but the two federal agents, Dr. Wither, and Ms. Nod.

Chapter

Agent Moss invited Callie and Rorke to have a seat. Nod went over the paperwork. Once the needed signatures were on the documents, Moss secured them in a locked briefcase.

Then, Moss sprang his surprise. "Dr. Wither has provided one assessment of a photograph. Ms. Rivera, I'd like you to look at the picture and offer your observations. The subject might be emotional, especially after our earlier conversation. Your father took the photo."

Callie took the paper passed to her and verbalized. "The foliage is subalpine and doesn't usually grow below 7000 feet or so. Yet, some plants defy the odds, such as those in the picture. The plants and flowers in the background are growing naturally and thrive in lower elevations. The environment indicates that no one doctored the image. If you look closely enough, the roots, stems, and leaves of each plant are alive and in their natural setting."

Wither visibly relaxed because Callie had corroborated his observations.

Moss made notes and continued. "Dr. Wither shared that Nigel used developed shorthand notations which could only be interpreted by your father. What could you tell us about the notations on the back?"

Callie flipped over the page. "The writing is my father's script. Before answering, may I ask what is going on? My father died ten years ago."

"Nigel Rivera sent the authorities a box with pictures the day before his car accident. Recently, a case surfaced that has similarities to a few of the pictures."

Callie pointedly stated, "If the next words out of your mouth are that my father was under investigation, we're finished with our conversation. I don't care if my family's lawyer is present or not."

Moss studied the younger woman. "I swear that his good name and spotless reputation is not in question. Your father was supplying evidence to the authorities. The problem is no one has been able to figure out what he was trying to say in the pictures."

"How do you know the materials were evidence?"

"Whatever you see or hear may not be shared outside these four walls."

Rorke entered the conversation. "Don't be coy, Agent Moss. You had us sign nondisclosure statements. If we shared with anyone, you could charge us with treason."

Callie wasn't surprised but used a reproachful tone. "How sneaky!

So, to be clear, something happened, and my father's box found its way out of a mothball closet. You hope that something in the pictures will help shed light on a current problem."

"Yes."

Callie turned back to the paper and expounded on the notes. "These notations are my father's shorthand. Think of what, where, when, and characteristics of the featured plant. Look at the pink clump of blossoms. The plant is an Elephantella. The name derives from the flower looking like a tiny elephant head with ears and trunk. The scientific name is *Pedicularis Groenlandica,* and the plant belongs to the Snapdragon family."

Callie frowned, and Moss prompted. "Yes?"

"The date is labeled three years after he died. Look at the latitude and longitude. Land and coordinates don't match. I'd have to check maps, but the geography appears further north than these numbers."

"Would you have any idea why the discrepancy?"

"No, but my father was careful with notations. He didn't want any doubt about licenses and collecting samples."

Moss took a different picture from his case. "What do you make of this?"

Callie flipped the page over, but her father's handwriting did not appear on the reverse side.

"The bag's size available at almost every store and can be used for practically every outdoor activity. The bags are lightweight, watertight, and have a durable construction. Each container allows for a good amount of storage but is easy to carry. Boaters keep dry towels or clothes inside. Campers haul food to keep eatable. The handle is great to use as a bear bag."

Moss asked, "Bear bag?"

Callie studied the contents inside the bags and answered. "Tie the bag up in the air and out of reach of the bears. Poor seeds! They might be old, but there are great uses for seeds. My father….."

The young woman stopped to peer at the agent again. "Are we back to veiled accusations?"

"No, ma'am. An investigator snapped the photo less than a year ago. Please continue about uses for old seeds."

"My father was a huge believer in not wasting. Old seeds still have a protective coating and have a degree of nutritional value for soil or roots of other plants. Also, a seed contains an embryo inside which has research value."

Moss asked, "Would you or any family members have kept Mr. Rivera's research?"

Callie hoped her crestfallen, disappointed, and teary look was believable. "No. All my father's notes, photos, research, and journals were at the cabin. The place burned to the ground a week after the car accident. Investigators ruled arson, and the rangers filed a report. Gran and the rangers refused to let me read the actual documents. I've tried to look through public records but never found one."

Nod made a humph sound. "Nice try, young lady, but I will not share my copy. The place was a total loss. The temperature was hot enough that any metal in the cabin melted. That place was special to you and your father, and we agreed to bury the report."

Moss looked at Rorke. "Mr. Asher, would you have reservations, doubts, or concerns about working with Agent Isley?"

"No, but we have a relationship outside of work. Isley has always been careful not to cross personal and professional lines."

"The others are probably wondering what is taking so long. We'll blame explaining the amount of red tape. The truth but not everything or details."

Callie asked nervously, "If possible, I mean, could I have a copy of a few flower pictures? They would be nice to have, especially if the box has been sitting around for almost ten years."

"I'll see what we could do."

Callie brightened, put lots of feeling into her voice, and hugged the senior agent. "Thank you! That would be so wonderful!"

Agent Monarch led Callie and Rorke to the door.

Callie turned around to ask as an afterthought, "What meet and greet? The memo about the meeting stated a conference with the interested parties."

Wither smiled. "Welcome to politics. The gross income for the project is now roughly six and a half million dollars. That means each of you is worth roughly three and a quarter million in new funds."

Callie felt the control of her emotions finally slipping. "Rorke, I'll meet you there. I need to use the restroom."

"I'll be a gentleman and wait. Do you think I am walking into a room full of human-eating vultures alone? I don't know who's who, but you do. I listened at the door before entering and called them by name. I think a few of those individuals were drooling in anticipation of the additional budget."

"Great! Thank you so much for that image! I will envision people in the meeting as vultures, and some of the student names on my meager list are friends. There were thirty names on the attendance roster. Pile of poop! Cattail is one of the students and will be here with lots of people. I don't wish my friends to see me nervous."

Rorke had a better understanding of Callie's nature. He was able to separate when she was pretending to be anxious, and she was on the verge of a panic attack or meltdown. Rorke tried humor to help calm her stress. "Geez, panic much?"

"No, and you know it! Next time, I'll let the bird of prey have your shiny compass and turkey lunch."

Callie closed her eyes and found a center until Hal Bear walked down the hall. "Hey, Flower Girl! Agent Isley sent me to deliver a message. Dusty arrived and made a grand entrance. You were not kidding. She's aged beautifully and knows how to work a crowd."

Callie knocked on the conference door that was still ajar and reentered. "Ms. Nod, Dusty's here. When do I receive my five dollars back and the five dollars that I won?"

Confused, Wither asked, "What are you talking about?"

The young woman explained her view. "Nod's office started a pool to guess when Dusty would appear. I placed a five-dollar wager. I win money since I matched the time. It's like the lottery ticket Uncle Mer bought me for my twenty-first birthday. It cost six dollars. I matched numbers and received twelve dollars."

Wither advised, "Let's talk about the bet later. Ms. Nod needs a chance to collect herself."

Callie noticed that Monarch and Wither were blocking her view of the lawyer. "What's wrong?"

Wither figured Callie wasn't leaving, sighed, and explained. "Seeing Nigel's pictures was a little emotional, and Ms. Nod is concerned that you will break off contact after your birthday."

Nod sat as quietly as she could and sobbed into her arms. Callie went to comfort and hug the woman.

Softly, the young woman comforted. "I wanted to talk later, but you may have me bugging you way longer than you wish."

Nod wiped the tears away and blew her nose. "Why?"

"You are not off the hook after my birthday. I studied various business options. You've been overseeing accounts. Someone at the law firm has been handling the part-time employees and tax forms. I'm sure there are items that you've handled, but we've never discussed. I will need a lot of help from someone that I trust to be available. Guess who gets to answer my questions and offer advice?"

"Callie, I am a family lawyer and haven't done much corporate work."

"Then, make sure to find me a cheap, trustworthy business lawyer and a resource firm with whom you are able to work. I am not signing ownership documents until I am positive about every detail."

Hal knocked and opened the door. "Ms. Rivera, they need you and Mr. Asher in the ballroom."

Callie stood, sighed, and straighten her back. "Rorke, don't say that I didn't warn you about Dusty."

Two hours later, Callie's face was sore from smiling. Dusty loved to crash social events or parties so she'd have an audience. A positive about Dusty's presence was that she took center stage, and Callie blended into the background.

Ranger Cattail joined Callie near the window with a glass of ice water. "You were not kidding about Dusty. I'm jealous. The woman is twice my age and looks amazing. Her naturally wavy hair is professionally maintained. Her smooth, soft skin makes guessing her age difficult. That outfit probably costs more than I make in a month."

Callie was used to the reaction and didn't blame her friend for being enamored. "Remember, the beauty you describe comes at a cost. You forgot the ruby red lips and long, black eyelashes. Those lashes aren't cheap fakes. The deep blue eyes will grab your soul in seconds."

Cattail was seeing a new side of her friend. "Why did Dusty come today?"

"I'm sure part of the reason was Isley told her to stay away. Officially, Dusty invited me to join her and her husband for dinner. Rorke agreed to come as well. They do not have a financial stake in the project, and I couldn't decline due to a conflict of interest. Publically, rejecting declining a dinner invitation in front of the gathering would not reflect well."

Cattail laughed and inquired about Isley. "How is Isley taking Dusty calling his bluff?"

"Let's say that Isley is having a horrible morning. Isley's boss is here and invited Isley to a surprise meeting."

Hal Bear entered the ballroom and motioned to Callie.

Cattail said, "A man in a security uniform is waving at you for attention. That does not bode well."

Callie explained. "Hal is an old friend who happens to be head of campus security, and he oversees security at the greenhouse when I am gone."

160

Cattail tagged along as Callie went to talk to Hal. Isley came in behind Hal and looked very grumpy.

Hal handed Callie his phone. "Blake needs to talk to you. She asked if I could check and see if you could talk."

"Do you know what is wrong?"

Hal shared what he knew. "No, but she's yelling about keeping away from the ducklings."

Callie took in that Hal, Isley, and Cattail were hovering and answered, "Hello."

Blake didn't bother with an introduction. "A mama duck and her babies are sitting on the pond island and squawking up a storm at a turtle. I think the turtle is stalking the duck family."

"Turtles will eat a duckling if they can catch one."

The answer distressed Blake. "What do I do? I don't know how to swim, and Mr. Pica told me not to throw rocks in the pond."

"Nothing. The ducks are wild and made a nest on the island. Nature is to be respected, and there are times we shouldn't interfere. The most you can do is shoo the turtle onto the bank and see if he'll stay until the ducks swim away."

"Could I toss pinecones near the turtle to scare him away until you arrive?"

"Yes. Pinecones float and easily gathered later. It will take me about forty-five minutes to wind my way to the greenhouse."

Callie sat down in a chair, took a pair of walking shoes from her oversized bag, and quickly changed her footwear. The place had quieted and heard her side of the conversation. Callie pretended to concentrate on holding the phone and tying shoelaces. She disconnected and returned Hal's phone.

Isley looked happy at having a reason to leave and started giving orders. "I'll drive! We'll deal with collecting your car tonight. Rorke, come with us!"

Callie figured that Isley was unhappy with his conversation with his boss, Agent Moss.

The young lady didn't argue but used a sweet, honeyed tone. "If you take us, we have to be back by three for a computer test. You are certainly cranky. Are you all right?"

Callie ignored Isely's answering glare as Cattail caught her attention.

Cattail asked, "May I drive over and see the place? It has been forever since I've been able to visit. We could grab lunch. Don't worry. I am on audit status and will make you buy your food. You are so sensitive about appearances as well as making everyone follow the rules."

Her friend's teasing didn't ruffle Callie, who returned, "Says the inspector ranger who told me that I counted the seeds in the sample bag incorrectly."

"Oh, please! I wasn't a ranger yet. You were fourteen, and I was nineteen."

Isley's jaw clenched, and his patience was wearing thin. "Ladies, may we continue the discussion after rescuing the ducks? Who grows up in Idaho and doesn't know how to swim?"

Rorke asked, "Swimming is not the problem. That pond is only a little over a foot deep."

Callie smiled slyly. "Would you like to bet on that?"

"No, ma'am. You have a home-field advantage, but I'd like to know what I missed."

Cattail smiled her impish grin and didn't enlighten Rorke. "Good idea on not betting." As children, the girls had used the pond as a pool and playground. The water was at least 12 feet deep in places.

Outside, Rorke held the car door for Callie and directed her to sit in the front passenger seat. He was taking the back seat.

Isley hadn't even pulled out of his parking spot before asking with an annoyed tone, "What on God's Green Earth?"

Callie replied primly. "I warned you that Dusty might call your bluff."

Rorke explained. "I think Isley is referring to you!"

"Me?"

Callie understood why Rorke took the backseat. Isley drove, talked, and waved his right hand. Luckily, he was a safe driver. His focus remained on the traffic and road. The problem was that he had no idea where his hand was in the air. A couple of times, his fingers came close to touching her nose. Nevertheless, Callie found the motions fascinating. He could direct a symphony one-handed.

Isley ranted while he changed lanes. "My boss! The man is the head of the entire state agency. The man defines a political dream or nightmare depending on whose side you are on. I have never seen Agent Moss ready to fall off a cliff for anyone. Take a bullet, yes. Threatening another agent, no. One conversation! One! I have been reassigned to the case and with protecting you. A tiny scratch, I'll lose my job and badge."

Callie tried to soothe the man's outrage. "I learned from the best. If I receive a booboo, we won't tell. If Agent Moss does find out, I'll make sure that he doesn't fire you."

Rorke asked curiously, "Why are you concerned about me doing the talking? You did well by yourself."

Callie admitted. "My composure is only controlled for so long. I was serious about not liking center stage. Self-preservation means going toe to toe with Dusty, but one must practice. I've been burned on multiple occasions trying to keep up with the woman or put out fires she made and left. You held your own."

Rorke said, "I developed reading people and using words as survival skills."

Callie noticed that Rorke did not offer an opinion about Dusty. Linus was a good friend, and he held a special place in her heart. She'd told the team the truth about Linus. They had figured out their goals in life were different, and a romantic relationship would not endure. It still stung that Dusty inserted herself into the relationship and meddled. Linus had no problem with Dusty using her influence to expedite his rise in the political world. Rational or not, she was slightly afraid. Callie feared that Rorke would meet Dusty, and he'd depart her life as well.

Callie broached the subject and tried to gauge Rorke's feelings about Dusty. "My advice is to work through dinner. Don't feel obligated to spend the evening with us."

Rorke spoke from his position behind Callie. "We'll have your back. Isley, drop me off so that I can change clothes. Rumblings started about Ranger Cattail's idea. Several people mentioned coming to see BE and find some lunch."

"Great! I better send out a call out for reinforcements. Nod's accountant is going to go crazy with the payroll this month."

Callie sent a text to the part-time workers to help if extra people were coming to visit.

Chapter

When they reached their destination, Callie asked to be dropped off by the loading dock. She walked to the pond from the back. Blake didn't see Callie, who studied the young woman.

Blake was a small woman whose athletic build came from hard work. Intelligent blue eyes peered out from under sandy, blond hair. Callie thought she remembered the style being a pixie cut. Blake had laugh lines around her eyes, but Callie had not seen her smile much.

Blake looked around and was relieved to see Callie. "Thank you for coming. Sorry for calling and interrupting your meeting."

Callie reassured her new employee. "We finished, and I was glad to have a good excuse to leave. How was the first day of class?"

"Good! Thank you for the job. Mr. Bear, Mr. Pica, and Ms. Nod have been great. Mr. Pica is a little intense, but he doesn't mind explaining more than once. Ah, what are you going to do about the turtle?"

"Bribery. My dad wouldn't let me have a dog or cat, and Mr. Turtle was a rescue turtle. He broke his leg and wasn't going to survive in the wild. I didn't want to tell you on the phone. Believe it or not, these ducks and Mr. Turtle are friends. They nest near one another, and the mother is teaching the ducklings not to trust a turtle in the water."

Callie called, shook a can, and waved a shiny fish on a stick. "Here, turtle, turtle."

The turtle saw, heard, and swam to Callie. Blake watched the mother duck lead her ducklings to an opening in the wall to the outside.

Blake eyed the turtle. "Bribing a turtle is weird."

"Have you spoken to your family lately?" Callie changed the subject.

"Yes, but short conversations. They don't seem to want to hear from me. One brother talks to me but mainly when he is on the bus to or from school."

"Don't give up. Different views on life do not define their love for you."

Blake gazed into the water and shared, "I understand. A part of me realizes that no one else has dreams outside the ranch, but I needed to try."

Callie heard the front doorbell ringing for attention and shared. "We may have lots of visitors this afternoon. I must be back to test a computer system, but I'll be around for the rest of the time. The guests may wander. If anyone makes inquiries about buying plants, refer the person to me."

164

Callie and Blake walked to the front, and Callie unlocked the door so that Rorke could enter.

Rorke reached out to shake the young woman's hand. "You must be Blake."

Blake smiled shyly. "You must be Rorke."

"I hope you're hungry. Isley sent over a huge basket of food."

Blake looked uncomfortable at the mention of Isley's name and started to cry. "I am sorry. Mr. Isley confronted me about the Dew family and the truth. He wanted me to file a report."

Callie kept a packet of tissues in her pocket, gave Blake a couple, and tried to provide a measure of comfort. "Isley has his faults, but his nature is to protect. The man's core being is to defend anyone that he believes needs help. His problem is people skills. The agent expects everyone to follow his orders without pause. Do what you think is best for your well-being. Let's eat before my friends show up. Ranger Cattail wants to visit, and she tells great stories."

Rorke tried to help Callie divert the topic. "I'm crushed. Didn't you like my stories while hiking?"

"A man who almost lets an eagle take his sandwich is suspect."

Blake managed to stop her tears and asked curiously, "What happened?"

Rorke shared, and Callie gave him a grateful look for understanding. The story would change the subject and distract Blake. Less than two minutes later, Rorke had Blake sharing her entire life's story, apart from her run-in with Beau Dew's family.

Ranger Cattail wandered in and introduced herself to the new assistant. Callie asked Blake to provide a tour as the parking lot grew full. Rorke directed traffic and sent guests to the side entry. Isley stood at the door, and Callie suspected the man was taking pictures of anyone who entered.

Callie's phone chirped, and Wither texted that she and Rorke did not need to return to campus. The computer department and graduate assistants were taking care of the testing.

Around three-thirty, Lilac and her father walked into the greenhouse. Lilac's mother provided permission for her daughter to keep in touch. The girl had been texting Callie about school and the renovation progress on her room. Lilac sprinted to Callie. Happy to see Callie, Lilac gave her the five dollars and change. Lilac's father told the girl to go back to the car to her mother. They had to go to practice. Lilac wanted to stay but stomped back to the car.

165

Lilac's father ordered Callie, "If my daughter contacts you, don't answer! You are not to have any further dealings with Lilac! Forget she exists!"

Callie knew the reason but feigned ignorance. "Is everything all right?"

"My daughter is not to associate with likes of you!"

Cattail came around the corner with Rorke, took in the scene, and repeated Callie's question. "Is everything all right?"

Lilac's father spat out. "Keep your Indian nose out of my business!"

Cattail raised an eyebrow. "What did Ms. Rivera do? She's your kind."

Callie stepped between the pair to play peacemaker. "Lilac's father discovered that my grandmother's family immigrated from Spain in the early 1800s."

Cattail sympathized. "I'm sorry. Sailing across that huge Atlantic Ocean on a small ship for weeks is a difficult journey."

Lilac's father disappeared with a huff, and Cattail's eyes glittered with distaste. "Hate never vanishes from some hearts. Callie, the next time you step between me and an argument, I'll send you sprawling. Granted, I'll wait until we are alone and without witnesses."

Callie shrugged to dismiss her friend's warning. Bash entered the greenhouse and looked uneasy. The young man was not one to be easily upset, and he was glad to see Rorke.

Bash handed an envelope to Rorke. "I received a call to pick up a letter and check. The letter is confusing, and I've never seen that much money at one time."

Callie read the letter over Rorke's shoulder.

Rorke clarified for Bash. "You and five are to be assistants for the project's field trips. The job is to accompany us, provide help, and take pictures. Assistants will stay in a six-bedroom rental that Gran owns. The check is a stipend to cover two months of travel and living expenses."

Bash did not react as Blake brought visitors over to see Callie.

Blake said, "Ms. Rivera, there are questions about buying flowers. Would you mind if I sign out? The last bus to the university will be at the stop shortly."

Callie introduced Blake and Bash. Then, she asked the two for a favor. "Blake, Bash is a trusted friend and arrived today. He'll be staying at the end of the street in rental Number Seven. Could you show him? Bash, afterward, would you mind driving Blake back to campus?"

Callie sent the two on their way and turned to the customers. She named the prices and told the guests to bring whatever plants they wanted to the office. A clerk would take care of the rest. If a person carpooled, Callie could transport the flowers to class in the morning. The visitors wandered back down the paths.

Wither had appeared and waited until Callie finished with the customers. "Callie, I saw Bash leaving with Blake. Don't start playing matchmaker."

The young woman grinned innocently at his chastising. "I'm not. They are starting school in a new place and don't know many people. I had a message from Nod that the new renters were coming today but did not provide details. The details were in Bash's letter. How did you swing the rental?"

Wither sighed. "I'm merely the messenger. Nod handed me the paperwork after the meeting. Solomon recommended individuals who would be good assistants, and the donor figured in the amounts for a field trip team."

*****

After dinner with Dusty and Baker, Rorke guided Callie to the passenger seat of his truck. Dusty's husband was not what Callie had imagined. Baker was low-key and spoke clearly but softly. Gray peppered his naturally brown, and brown eyes didn't miss much in his surroundings. His pale skin indicated that he worked inside. The gentleman moved slowly but with purpose. Baker held his own in the conversation, and Dusty's mannerisms for remaining in the spotlight did not bother or unsettle him. Callie found she liked Dusty's husband very much. Oddly, Dusty and Baker fit well together as a couple.

Rorke waited to say anything until after he merged onto the interstate. "Baker seems like a friendly person, and he handles Dusty's quirks beautifully."

"Nicely put. Baker's accepted Dusty as she is and hasn't tried to change her core nature. The fact that they care for one another is apparent."

Rorke asked, "May I ask why you have kept in contact with Dusty if you are uncomfortable in her presence?"

Callie provided a reply but didn't answer the question. "Dusty was well-behaved tonight, and she doesn't see you as a challenge."

Rorke glanced at Callie as he checked the blind spot and changed lanes. "I would never become romantically involved or have sex with another man's wife."

Callie was still looking out the window but picked up on his concern. "Stop worrying about my emotional state. I am fine."

Rorke asked, "Would you mind if I stopped by Isley's house and collect a couple more books?"

Callie didn't mind and texted Rosa about the dinner. Dusty's surprise was a five-year-old marriage, and she brought her husband to town for Callie to meet.

The phone rang seconds later, and Callie said, "It's Gran."

"Go ahead and answer if you don't mind my presence."

Callie put the phone on speaker. "Hey, Gran. I have you on speaker. Rorke's driving."

Gran's outraged tone wafted through the cab. "Mija, don't send such a message on the phone! Are you all right?"

"I am fine. Remember I told you about Isley? He's the agent that is Rorke's guardian. The agent found out that Dusty was married and told her to stay away from today's meeting. If not, he'd tell the husband about her being questioned by authorities for past financial dealings. Isley's misguided attempt backfired."

Her grandmother chuckled. "I assume Dusty took up the challenge and made a grand entrance?"

"Yes. Dusty invited Rorke and me to dinner in front of an audience. Declining would have created a political nightmare. Baker, her husband, and Dusty are heading back home in the morning. Blake is doing well at the greenhouse, despite Mr. Turtle creating a scene. Blake isn't ready to forgive my pet yet."

"Did that monster reptile bite her?" Gran understood the matter of Dusty was closed as far as Callie was concerned.

Callie had relaxed enough to tease. "Gran, you and Mr. Turtle need to have a cup of tea together and mend the relationship."

"Ha. Menacing reptile stays in the pond."

Rosa spoke about her family and reconnecting. She was bringing lots of pictures so Callie could put faces to the names.

Rorke pulled up alongside the curb and turned off the motor. Callie waved for him to go ahead, but Gran heard the car door close.

"You are home, so I'll let you go. Are you sure you are all right?"

"Truly, I am fine."

The two sent air hugs, kisses, and goodbyes. Rorke wasn't back, which meant he had to find whatever he needed. Callie studied Isley's yard. The lawn was maintained and edged. A few of the shrubs were shaped but needed some care as well as fertilizer.

Callie took off her shoes. Wandering to the far end of the house, Callie spread out a light, rain jacket that Rorke kept in the back seat. She took care not to rip the material or ruin the coat. Using the jacket as padding, she knelt on the combination of grass, dirt, and mulch. Her fingers were strong and sure as she started to prune. Quickly, she used her nails to snip the stems.

Isley pulled into the driveway and asked what she was doing to his bushes.

Callie explained. "Rorke went inside to find some books, and I am giving haircuts. Thank you for warning me about Dusty's marriage. That was an enormous shock to the system."

"Would you like a cup of coffee?"

"No, thanks. I have a few more hours of work, and caffeine will keep me up the rest of the night."

Isley tried to coax her away from the bushes. "Come inside before my neighbors see a young woman wearing evening clothes in the yard. "

Callie smiled. "Afraid that they will tell the lady love?"

"No. I have a decent relationship with those living on the street. Idle gossip and answering questions is not my idea of a productive conversation."

Callie laughed as Isley helped her to stand.

Isley picked up Rorke's jacket. "You are barefoot. Stay here!"

Callie kept pruning, and Isley returned with a pair of pink bunny slippers.

Isley sighed. "Please leave the plants alone. Here. The bottoms are regular soles."

Callie took the slippers. "Isley, you never cease to amaze. Pink and bunnies."

"Don't be cheeky! I bought an entire box for presents to give to the sisters, nieces, or other girls in the family. I had a few extra."

Rorke was waiting at the end of the sidewalk on the driveway. Even in the fading light, Callie could see his tight jaw.

Callie looked at the men. "Should I worry about the work environment? You look ready to take a swing at one another."

Rorke looked startled, and Isley used a superior tone. "Rorke did something stupid, and I told him to be careful. He didn't need additional problems."

Callie asked bluntly, "If you are arguing about Dusty's invitation, please don't. I have no desire to go to a key party with Dusty. If Rorke wishes to go back, his choice."

Isley asked, "Key party?"

Callie sighed dramatically. "I am sure her invitation had a double meaning. She could send Baker and me to a party while she seduces Rorke. No idea what sort of presents we needed to bring, but Dusty has expensive tastes. I guess is that the minimum requirement would be something akin to a bottle of wine worth about two hundred."

Rorke's mouth opened to speak, but Isley interrupted. "Probably a wise choice to decline."

Callie admitted. "When Dusty joined me in the restroom, she indicated that they would only attend if we went. I don't have the time to shop or extra money to spend on an outrageous present."

Isley's mouth developed a twitch as he tried not to smile. "I think you should head home."

Callie knew the true definition of a key party, but she wasn't about to discuss the matter with Isley or Rorke. Key parties were an adult version of spin the bottle, and she wasn't about to participate. Dusty slyly offered to make sure that Rorke would be Callie's partner. If Callie didn't want Rorke, she'd take him. Dusty's sole reason for the subject was to manipulate Callie into revealing her feelings about Rorke. Dusty meeting Rorke made Callie nervous, but she refused to allow the older woman access to her emotions.

Rorke pulled into the driveway of Callie's house and parked. "I've been listening to opinions about Dusty. Meeting her, I understand the views about her behavior. She appears to have matured, and the lady cares about you and Baker."

"Don't try to fix or intervene in my relationships. Positive or negative change is relative. As to Dusty and Baker, the subject is closed."

Callie's phone chirped with a text, and she sighed. "Be aware. There is a gathering in my office."

Rorke watched Callie open the back door, and Mer's voice floated from inside the house. "Callie? We're in the office."

They walked back and found Mer, Pica, Hal, Nod, Wither, Blake, and Bash working. Hal and Wither had taken the two permeant desks. Extra folding tables and chairs gave the others a place to complete his or her task.

Wither looked up from his computer and complimented her. "You look nice. Tell me that the dirt on your leg is from burying Dusty."

Nod made a disagreeing noise but winked with a grin. "Don't say a word if you decided to take her out. Bailing you out of jail will stress me out. My list is long enough, and there is not enough time in the day."

Mer told the lawyer, "My niece knows better. Untraceable poison would be the best play."

Callie laughed but reassured Blake and Bash. "They're kidding."

Blake looked up from her book. "We discussed your family's history. I thought my family was dysfunctional. Did your father's ex-girlfriend seduce your fiancé, Linus?"

Callie reproached Mer. "Really? Today of all days. Is everyone gossiping about my life?"

Mer continued read, typed, and answered. "We are indulging in idle gossip, but you may blame Ranger Cattail for sharing."

Blake smiled shyly at Rorke. "Did you pass the test?"

Rorke asked, "What test?"

"Resist having sex with Dusty."

Callie said sarcastically, "Is that the rumor? For crying out loud! Dusty did not seduce Linus with sex. My friend had political ambitions and moved to the capital for fame and fortune.

Pica relaxed and chatty. He chimed in while repainting a flower on the wall. "You put up with Dusty out of respect for your father, but I never approved. Dusty finally did us a favor, regardless of the method. We didn't think that Linus, as a fiancé, was your best choice."

Callie dramatically returned, "I doubt my family has approved of anyone that I dated. I may never find another boyfriend because my family won't mind their own business or their manners."

Uncle Mer laughed and continued to type on his computer. "You catch on very slowly." Mer made sure to smile at Rorke and then Callie.

Pica changed the subject while dipping the paintbrush into a swirl of color on his pallet. "Blake helped me make baskets for those who could not take the plants today. The purchases are on the back porch. Blake and Bash are studying here. The internet won't be up at their respective abodes until tomorrow. Nod is finishing the bills and other accounts from the weekend. Wither has your new computers for class, syllabi printed, and other school-related material. Mer is doing his usual computer security stuff, and Hal is sorting applications for security personnel for BE."

Callie turned to Hal. "Your granddaughter had a dance recital tonight. Please tell me you went."

"I did, and there will be no arguments about extra security measures."

Callie spoke to those in the room. "I never argue about safety, and I appreciate everyone's help today. Thank you. I need to take a shower. The makeup and can of hairspray that I used to hold my hair in place needs washing off."

Chapter

Callie moved down the hall to take a shower, and she heard Blake confront Rorke a second time. "You didn't answer my question. Are you planning to have sex with Dusty?"

"I'm not. Baker and Dusty love and respect one another, and the relationship shows that feeling."

The conversation faded into the background as Callie retreated and closed her bedroom door. She'd made it through the meal. Baker was a nice gentleman and loved Dusty. Rorke and Dusty had met, and Rorke didn't seem upset or flustered by Dusty's personality. Rorke had professed his love, and he was willing to take on the responsibility for a family if Bree died. Half of her felt safe for the first time since her father's death. The opposite half stood alone among family and friends. She fought and ignored her feelings because the danger was too great. Secrets about the past could reach out to kill.

Callie tried to fall asleep, but thoughts and feelings kept swirling around in her mind. Pent-up emotions that Callie had been suppressing bubbled to the surface. Her thoughts shifted from Rorke to Solomon.

Solomon had enough of the secret puzzle to be dangerous to her overall scheme. Her annoying protector was right to be concerned, but he only thought he knew the scope of the problem. He had reached out to Rorke because her self-proclaimed guardian was worried enough to call for reinforcements.

Callie doubted Rorke remembered meeting her many years ago, but she recognized him instantly.

Eight years prior, Callie was driving back from collecting plants. Traffic was having to turn around and divert to a secondary route. A rockslide had occurred up the road, and a forest ranger was directing traffic to turn around and use an alternate route. Rolling down the window, she waved to gain the ranger's attention.

Callie knew the forest ranger. "Hey, Ranger Arc. The detour is two hours out of my way, and I need to use the rocks. May I park on the other side and use the outdoor facilities?"

"Sure. Don't worry about oncoming traffic. The road is completely blocked further up."

Callie saw the worry in Arc's eyes as he kept looking down the slope. "What else is going on?"

"A driver went off the road right after the rockslide occurred. They were lucky and had a cell signal. I'm able to communicate with them, and reinforcements are on the way. Both the family and the car are stable. My concern is someone going into shock, but the four are conscious and talking."

There was an hour or two of daylight. Callie studied the terrain. Night rescues were significantly more dangerous. Callie sent a quick text to her grandmother. The road was closed, and a detour meant an extra four hours of driving. She'd decided to go to the cabin which was closer and stay the night. She'd be home in time for church and to finish her homework for school on Monday. Gran returned the text and agreed with the decision. Callie returned to her car and opened the rear hatch.

A stranger's voice asked, "Are you planning on going down?"

Callie didn't turn around and continued to pull out ropes and a harness. "Yes. There isn't much daylight left, and the vehicle isn't as stable as it looks. I'm repelling down to see if anchoring or evacuation is an option."

Ranger Arc took a deep breath to launch into a lecture, but the second person motioned for the ranger to be quiet. Callie looked around to see why Arc stopped talking.

Rorke spoke again. "Name's Rorke Asher. You are?"

Callie recognized the name. She knew the man was a respected expert mountaineer and could navigate tricky terrain in dangerous situations. He was also a volunteer for Search and Rescue.

"I'm Callie, and the answer to your next question is yes. I'd bet my life and those in the car that we can't wait. Ranger Arc needs to be free to move around up here. I am rigging a pulley system between my car and the ranger's vehicle."

Rorke understood Callie's design to counteract the weight on the ropes. "My transportation is heavier. We'll use Ranger Arc's and my truck instead."

Ranger Arc was not happy. "There hasn't been a shift in the rocks. Rescue crews will be here soon. I can't let you do this."

Callie continued knotting the lines. "Objection and concern noted. I need whatever harnesses you have and a belt radio. I'll keep in touch on the radio. Westbound traffic is blocked, so we don't have to worry about oncoming traffic. While Rorke backs up, I'll park my car in the other lane. Please write me a ticket for stealing your equipment or illegal parking later. Registration, licenses, permits, and insurance are in the glove box."

Once over the ledge, Callie made her way nimbly down the cliff. She was slightly surprised to find Rorke followed her down. The man's movements told her that he was an experienced climber, and she continued her descent.

173

When the two were able to study the situation up close, they agreed. The car wasn't going to stay on the ledge long. They anchored the vehicle long enough to bring the family up safely.

As soon as the family was safe and on the main road, Callie handed Ranger Arc his radio and belongings. She disappeared quickly and quietly.

Back on the highway, Callie stayed the night in a motel instead of making the journey to the cabin. Using cash, she was glad the clerk was busy and didn't bother checking for identification. A person had to be over eighteen to stay in a room alone. Luckily, Callie never had trouble looking older.

Solomon called within an hour of her checking into the room. "I heard about the rockslide. Are you all right?"

Sleepily, Callie answered a bit snippy. "Of course, you found out! I'm fine but tired. I stopped at a place to stay, showered, and sleeping. I'll be home in time for church and homework."

"Do you need money?"

"No. I am tired and going back to sleep. Goodnight."

Callie's thoughts shifted ahead to the night her father died. Time offered perspective and understanding. Callie understood Nigel's position regarding his secrets. She'd made promises to her father and been standing alongside his shadow to protect innocents and those he loved for ten years.

The night of her father's accident, Nigel had used a back road to drive to the cabin. Callie stowed away in her father's car. When she emerged, Nigel not angry.

Nigel asked in a tired, concerned tone, "Why?"

Callie admitted. "I heard you talking about the investigation and refuse to let you die."

Tears trickled down her father's face, and they scared Callie far more than words. "Come inside. You'll die if anyone discovers you. Unacceptable! Swear to stay away from the ambush and live! Swear to me!"

Hesitant but resolved, Callie promised and listened.

Her father said, "The story started a long time ago with my brother and me."

"Solomon?"

"Yes. God knows how you made that leap, but I kept my promise. I never told anyone our secret. Solomon, my brother, met a girl and lied about his name. He gave the woman my name. He fell in love but feared telling her the truth. Solomon accepted her without conditions or

174

expectations. Dusty wanted to give Solomon his one unattainable wish: a family. Dusty understood, accepted her limitations, and had no intention of raising a child. Solomon is your biological father, and Dusty is your mother."

Callie asked, "Why did Solomon lie?"

"Our parents were murdered by poachers. Solomon has been playing cat and mouse with the organization for years. When Solomon found out Dusty was pregnant, he came to me. Dusty couldn't raise a child, and he refused to put you in foster care or place you up for adoption. His profession is dangerous. My brother wanted a safe, stable, and loving family for his child. I agreed to be your parent and never once regretted or doubted my decision."

Callie hugged her father. "I know you love the rest of the family and me. Did you collect evidence about poaching and counterfeit plants because poachers murdered your parents? Is that why you didn't share the entire truth?"

Her father confirmed and wrapped his daughter up in a bear hug. "Yes. I was vague about the proof on purpose. Most individual's word association with poaching is wild animals, but the definition is theft or stealing. Growing, manufacturing, and distribution could be anything. We are talking about millions of dollars of profit. They'll murder without hesitation to protect the product and supply lines. The pictures that I sent to the authorities are partial clues and a large puzzle. I'm betting that the box will be stored on a shelf without much thought. One day someone might investigate, but I doubt it.

"The goal is to protect you and everyone else. Our family is more than the Rivera clan, but I am not explaining the dynamics. My death will weigh heavily on Solomon. He'll behave irrationally and get himself killed. Then, there would be no one to protect our family or innocents caught in the middle."

Callie didn't believe her father was going to die. He was dependable, smart, and was larger than life to her. "How is filing a report protecting us?"

"The person who revealed the research had no idea broaching the subject would be fatal. The individual was trying to help and does not have any specific knowledge. A report adds layers of shielding. The threat will be neutralized, if the enemy believes the evidence ignored or filed away."

"Who is the person that blabbed to the criminals?"

Nigel studied his daughter before answering. "The person truly did not understand the consequences of one conversation. Common

175

knowledge is that I keep everything in the cabin. The data is a misdirect, but the poachers will destroy everything. When the time comes, you'll figure out where my journals, maps, and research are hidden."

Callie guessed, "Another layer of protection?"

"Yes. One day, if the past becomes a problem, you will be able to solve the puzzle. Solomon is currently the closest person to the cabin. I'm calling him to take you home. I suspect that he will conceal his face. I'm younger, but we look enough like that we could be twins. If my brother discovers you learned the entire truth, he'll run instead of lurking in the shadows. Responsibility for you and Rosa might be the difference between him seeking justice outside the law or disappearing. He'll need you more than ever, especially later. Do you remember the scar on my chest?"

His daughter nodded that she remembered.

"The circle is a tattoo that reveals a picture in black light. If you see that scar, the person is trustworthy. Currently, eight children are alive, who have that tattoo. We made a pact to protect one another and any innocents caught in circumstance beyond their understanding."

Somehow, her father telling her the secret brought home the seriousness of the situation. Nigel reminded her of her promise to remain, and she pleaded for him to stay. Her father also reminded her that his garden would now become her responsibility.

Her bossy guardian made his arrangements, and she made hers. Callie decided to try to work since she couldn't sleep. The house had quieted as everyone else had finished their respective projects and left. Her office light was still on. Rorke was the only one working in the office.

Callie read through the documents that lay on her desk. She braided her hair while working. She reached back and ran her fingers down the French Braid. Annoyed at the sideways line, the braid would wait. Reading and braiding were not activities to attempt at the same time.

Rorke walked over and undid the work. "You are driving me nuts."

"Thanks. Gran usually braids for me."

"You're lucky."

Callie agreed with his opinion. "Yes. Most men would not volunteer to braid and appear unmanly or weak."

"I meant that you are lucky to have a large family who cares about you."

Callie handed Rorke the hairbrush, which he put back on the desk. "I recognize how wonderful but exasperating my family is. I am grateful,

176

appreciative, and thankful. I pretend to complain because they expect to be teased or harassed."

Rorke asked, "Do you believe in love at first sight?"

Callie did not want to continue the conversation that they started at the lodge. "What happened to uncomplicated? Mutual attraction is not the best foundation for romance. Add in the amount of stress we're about to experience. The mix is not a good idea."

Rorke continued to stroke her hair. "You made a conscious decision to distance yourself, but I decided on a different course."

Callie couldn't concentrate on an answer as Rorke gently turned her around. He kissed way any words of disagreement she might have uttered.

Chapter

Three days later, Callie heaved a sigh of relief. The first week of classes went smoothly. A few glitches with the distance learning portion were easy fixes for the technical department or teaching assistants.

Rorke dismissed the literature class for the day, and Callie packed her notes. She saw Blake waving from a rear door in the auditorium. The young woman's face read panic, and her motions radiated fear.

Callie left her stuff, walked up the stairs to the back of the auditorium, and Blake whispered tensely. "The grocery store wouldn't deposit my last check electronically. I had to pick up the pay in person. Beau's father sent his top henchman and crew to make me sign papers. I had no idea what the documents were. When I refused, Beau tried to diffuse the situation and gave me a chance to slip out. They followed me back to campus."

Agent Moss and Monarch entered with Wither, but Callie decided to pretend not to notice. Rorke could deal with whatever the group needed.

Callie took a gentle but firm grip on Blake's arm so she couldn't bolt. "We'll go to the greenhouse where security is in place. When we arrive, you go to the computer room and call Isley for backup."

Callie went to gather her belongings and pulled Blake along with her. She hoped to slip away without calling attention to their departure. Rorke stayed behind, but the rest of the team follow. Great. Hopefully, the men would only watch and stay away.

Her phone rang as she started down the main highway. Caller identification read Rorke, and Callie answered using the wireless device in the vehicle.

Callie answered as if she didn't have a care in the world. "I have you on the hands-free speaker device because I am driving."

"You left in a hurry. Is Mr. Turtle causing a ruckus again?"

"No. Mr. Dew and his buddies are creating a problem. I'm taking Blake to work and then having a chat with them. I may have underestimated the situation because we have a convoy behind us. That doesn't include, um. What do we call your friends?"

Rorke understood that Callie knew the other team members were following and advised. "Drive around for a little while. My friends are attempting to run interference without calling attention to themselves."

"We'll meet you at BE. Blake and I will be safe there. I rather not involve anyone else or be trapped on a narrow street. Traffic is picking up. Bye."

Blake shouted. "Look out!"

178

Calmly and without a trace of unease, Callie replied, "I see."

Callie and sped up. The driver tried to pass and force her off the road. She made sure that the traffic was clear and could swerve without causing an accident.

Blake looked as if Callie had gone crazy. "How are you so calm? Aren't you scared?"

"A little. I drove Gran's car. If she returns and the vehicle is scratched up, she'll ground me. It doesn't matter how old I am."

Rorke's voice came from the dashboard. "You aren't going to have to worry about Rosa's reaction."

Reaching the back road to the property, Callie turned onto the gravel without warning. The trees were thick enough for only one vehicle to pass.

Callie grinned. "Rest easy. My father taught me never to gamble with safety. There is a log jam up ahead. I know the secret around the roadblock, but the other drivers will have to turn around and use the main entrance. We have plenty of time to reach a safe place."

"How come you didn't tell Rorke to call the police or bring Isley?"

"Don't worry. There is a plan, and we're not alone. Blake, the birdhouses on the right are the markers for a side road."

Callie slowed down. She had the advantage of being the rabbit in the hunt, and there were multiple rabbit holes for escape. Beau and buddies wouldn't know how to navigate the barricade or route through the trees. She'd outrun Beau and his friends with plenty of time to prepare.

The road disappeared as Callie slowed and turned to the left. She navigated through the underbrush and around a pile of long poles. Callie stepped on the gas as soon as she returned to the road.

When they were inside the greenhouse, Callie ushered Blake into the computer office. Callie opened a wall safe. She withdrew a handgun and checked the firearm.

Blake called Isley, who picked up on the first ring. "Hello."

"Mr. Isley, it's Blake."

"We are on the way. What's Plant Princess planning?"

Blake answered, "That's funny! I am not sure. Uh, are you aware Callie has a gun at work?"

Isley ordered, "Yes. Do not leave the greenhouse until I clear you! Leave, and I swear to high heaven to find something to arrest you for later!"

Callie made sure each door locked behind her. She scaled a ladder to the roof. The main beam over the locker room was solid and would hold her weight along with at least one elephant. She could walk the path by heart.

She sat on the main brace, and her vantage point gave her a bird's eye view of the entire area. Callie carefully secured the holster to a metal clip along the beam. Beau and twelve of his buddies parked, exited their vehicles, and gathered in a group below.

Callie whistled. "Hello! I am up here! How may I help you?"

Beau asked with hesitation. "Were you the one driving like a bat out of hell? That wasn't your vehicle."

"I have a critter problem that needed checking out. What's wrong?"

Beau answered, "We're looking for Blake."

"Isn't she a little young to be taking to a strip club?"

Beau flushed and stated without much feeling. "My business with Blake."

Callie arched an eyebrow. "You realize that you are standing on private property, and there is a security system in place."

Beau's expression told her that he was more concerned about the group than Callie. "Please, cooperate. They'll start tearing the place apart."

"That sounds rather ominous! Tell everyone to put away their weapons. Then we will have a nice discussion like mature adults."

Callie's perch allowed her to watch two police cars block off the property's rear and front exits. Isley's vehicle and a similar looking one came from the northwest. Beau and his cronies would not see the other guests arrive.

Callie scanned the trees and surrounding landscape. The expedition team had followed and would insist on helping, but they were not law enforcement. Gun permits and outdoor knowledge did not mean that they could legally help. She should probably ask Isley about the rules. How much could the men help in such a situation?

Rorke's truck appeared at the driveway. He waited, and Callie figured that he was waiting for some signal. Rorke wound his way to the greenhouse and parked away from other vehicles.

Rorke closed his door and relaxed against the metal frame before talking. "Don't you think the firepower is a little overkill for hunting a tiny, defenseless fox?"

A voice in the crowd yelled, and Callie figured that the owner must be the henchmen's leader. "Half breed! Mind your own business! This doesn't concern you!"

Rorke disagreed in the same genteel manner. "Oh, but Callie is my concern."

180

The leader's grating voice informed Rorke. "Take my advice. Find another bitch to warm your bed. This one is as frigid as an icicle and not worth the effort."

Callie asked sweetly, "I would lecture you on being kind, but the words would fall on deaf ears. Are you upset because I didn't drink the drugged wine? Feeling hurt that I didn't fall into bed after the first dinner?"

The unidentified and faceless leader commanded. "Boys, find the other bitch and take care of the half-breed!"

Isley's voice ordered from the walkway between buildings. "Federal agent! Everyone put your weapons on the ground!"

Several things happened at once, and Callie couldn't keep track of who moved where. Part of the crowd turned to intercept Rorke. Blake bolted out of the greenhouse. A steel door separated Blake from Isley and his partner. A section of the mob surged toward the open door spying their quarry.

Callie only saw the danger to the girl. She jumped from the roof to protect Blake. Sounds of fighting broke. Unfortunately, or fortunately, Beau moved directly below her as Callie moved.

Callie landed on Beau, and the momentum sent him to the ground. Beau righted himself and defended against a physical threat. Callie clung to his back as the man stood and refused to release her hold. Two of the men tried to pry Callie away, but she held on like glue. She figured that Beau made a good shield. Letting go would leave her at the mercy of the men. Beau used a new tactic. He ran backward and slammed into a truck. The impact freed Beau, and Callie found herself having trouble breathing.

Beau turned to confront his assailant and stilled in shock. "Callie? What? Why? If I'd known, I would not have rammed you into the side of a truck. Are you all right?"

Callie could only nod as her system absorbed its shock.

Beau helped her to sit on the ground amid the chaos. "Have a seat and catch your breath."

A new car pulled alongside Rorke's truck. Seconds later, a gunshot rang. The sound acted as a pause button. Motions froze, and silence settled over the crowd. Callie was slightly surprised that none of the other guns had gone off with the number of rifles waved around.

Agent Moss's authoritative, deep voice rang through the parking lot. "Who would like to tell me why a parking lot turned into a bar brawl?"

Callie gave Beau credit for stepping up and taking responsibility. "Honestly, I am not sure what happened, but we have had a huge

181

misunderstanding. I thought that someone attacked me from behind, but Ms. Rivera jumped from the roof. Who does that?"

Agent Moss asked, "Ms. Rivera, are you all right?"

"I am fine, sir."

"Medics are on the way. Here is what we are going to do!"

Blake and Callie were escorted inside the greenhouse and didn't hear what the rest were going to do. Agent Valley and another female agent stayed with the two. Blake needed a distraction because she was upset and scared.

Filling the space with idle conversation, Callie spoke in a soothing, calm voice. "Have you wondered why there four office spaces for the greenhouse? I suppose that the titles are misleading. Each was the main office at some point in the history of BE. The first was also a maintenance shed. Today, we use the outbuilding to store landscaping equipment such as lawnmowers. Ms. Pickle, who managed the place for years, used the cottage as her office. It's now our sample flowers are displayed and reception area.

"I begged for my own office. My father designed, built more of a playground and called it my Fairy Garden. I played or studied while he worked. Aunt Thessa and I had regular tea parties. She never declined an invitation to have fairy garden tea. Other family or friends would join us as their schedule allowed. We currently use the room for the computer and security servers. Mer renovated for the computer systems, but I wanted to save my childhood toys. Various tea sets wait on the shelf for the next tea party."

Callie watched Blake's body language as she spoke. The girl's facial expression began to relax, and her eyes focused on Callie.

Blake started to pay attention to the words rather than tone. "Awesome! I guess you use the flower bedroom at the house."

"Yes. Thank goodness for laptops. I'm able to work remotely."

Blake explained the reason she left the computer room. "Mer is the reason I came out. There was an additional breach in security, and Mer wanted to let Isley or you know."

"Ah, good. We weren't sure how the system would react with the dense foliage. The information means the remote radars on the forest trail are working but slow."

"Did you trip the sensors on purpose?"

Callie answered. "Yes. The fact that we were chased with weapons was captured on an official security system. If the gang wants to change the story, anything but the truth doesn't fit the evidence."

Moss entered the greenhouse and walked over.

Callie asked, "Sir, you won't fire Isley, will you? He had nothing to do with my actions."

Moss's face took on a parental, stern expression. "Don't concern yourself about Agent Isley's occupational status. Unless he broke the law, I would never fire him for helping a young lady in distress. You, on the other hand, put lives in danger."

Callie took offense. "I disagree! Blake was safe, and I was out of reach on the roof."

Moss remained calm and unruffled. "We are not arguing the matter. Agents and police personnel responded to a call about a high-speed chase and discharged weapons within city limits. We found loaded weapons. Callie, protecting someone is admirable, but the methods are unacceptable. Let me be clear to both of you! Neither of you will go anywhere without someone along for protection. Am I clear?"

Blake looked ready to cry. "We didn't do anything wrong. Why are we being punished?"

Moss waved the others to depart, had a seat on the bench, and waited until they were alone to answer. "You haven't, and the caution is not a punishment. Beau's father, Mr. Dew, and I have crossed paths in the past. I am not a fan of how he dictates his family or his business dealings. When we must meet for a purpose, we are usually on opposite sides of the subject, topic, or opinion. I don't trust him. Mr. Dew could apply pressure to sweep today's events quietly under the rug.

"I have a selfish reason. Ms. Rivera has started a project that has created a lot of attention and scrutiny. Many eyes are watching us because of the amount of money involved as well as interest. My organization is to be supervising or acting as a referee. If I am in charge, I want a positive, glowing, and smooth operation. It makes me and the organization look much better. Negative attention is never good in my line of work. We have to keep Callie's focus on the project."

Callie sighed. "Why does life boil down to politics? Power resides with who is holding the biggest stick at the top of the mountain. I never liked playing King of the Mountain. My experience with the Dew family says that they will try threats or bribery first. Blake is a student and lives in the dorm. How exactly is Blake supposed to make sure there is someone nearby?"

Moss answered with slight amusement. "Ms. Blake will be moving from the dorm to one of Rosa's rental units within the hour. Isley will be supervising carpools to the campus for both of you. If anyone approaches you to talk about the Dew family or Beau, you refer them to Agent Isley or Ms. Nod."

183

Moss sent a couple of agents with Blake to pack and act as guards.

Callie gazed with curiosity at Moss and took advantage of his undivided attention. "Thank you for protecting Blake. You could cut her loose and let her fend for herself. Politics is a nice, neat answer, but I understand the undertones. Mr. Dew rubbed you the wrong way."

Moss studied the room's layout while speaking. "Nicely played, but you're out of luck fishing for information. Where is your handgun?"

"It is on the roof."

"Please, collect the piece so we may check that you did not fire the weapon today."

Callie wasn't in the mood to be cooperative. "My computer and handgun are clipped to a latch on the roof. Let one of the others climb up and retrieve the equipment."

"We could, but there would be additional paperwork. I could not guarantee when the firearm would be returned. You may retrain possession, if the gun was not fired. Agent Valley will accompany you."

Agent Valley swabbed Callie's hands for gunshot residue before they climbed the ladder to the roof. Valley checked the weapon, took more pictures, recorded the results, and went back to the ground. Callie remained on the beam and looked around. An ambulance had arrived, and Isley sat on the back bumper. The man looked grumpy while a medic took his blood pressure. Adrenaline had been pumping through her system, and she suddenly realized her body was tired and sore.

Rorke called her name, and Callie answered, "I'm up here."

"Come down so we may finish and find something to eat."

"My body needs a few minutes to settle. I don't feel so well."

Rorke immediately moved up the ladder and was beside her in seconds. "Callie, there is blood seeping through your jacket. Does your back hurt?"

"A little, but I'm dirty and covered with sweat from the tussle. When Beau backed up, my sleeve caught on the truck and tore. I grabbed a long-sleeved shirt from a hook to cover up the damage."

"How about I support you to the ground? Let me feel useful."

"Isley used you as bait earlier."

Rorke teased, "I have been reduced to expensive bait."

Callie found that she couldn't verbalize a reply. Rorke's image faded before going black.

Chapter

Rorke made sure the woman didn't tumble off the roof as she collapsed. "Does anyone know if Callie hit her head on the truck?"

No one had a clue, and Isley swore. "Rorke, have these nice paramedics get the woman down to the ground! If she has more than a scratch, I'm having a field day adding charges to anyone we arrested. We're taking her to the hospital for a full battery of tests. Do you still have the waivers and forms that Callie filled out for the trip last weekend? Her medical information was included in the packet of papers."

Rorke sighed to himself. Dealing with Isley was going to be more of a hassle than Callie's injury.

Assessing the wound, Rorke explained, "Copies of the paperwork is in my computer bag on the truck's back seat. No offense to the police or fire personnel here, but they need to stay away. Competency is not the issue. If emergency responders help, they'll have to radio in the station. News about Callie's injury will spread. Valley, bring up the medical kit from my truck. Isley, Solomon gave you a contact number. Call and find out if Solomon cares where we take Callie. A doctor will need to stitch up her shoulder."

The reasoning upset Isley because he should have thought about that angle. Isley didn't have to call because Solomon had been watching and listening. Callie's guardian named a hospital and shared that the staff would be waiting.

They put the seats down and placed blankets in the back of Isley's Sport Utility Vehicle. Rorke climbed in beside Callie after she lay the padded surface.

Callie's weak voice asked, "What happened?"

"You blacked out after standing up too fast. There is a cut that needs stitches, and we're taking you to the hospital."

Callie pleaded. "Take me home! We'll stick a butterfly bandage on it, and I'll be fine."

When no one agreed, Callie tried to wiggle out of the car. Rorke held onto her so the others could close the rear hatch, but he found himself trapped between a panicked woman and the front seats.

Isley started the car and turned on the sirens. The sound terrified Callie, and she thrashed around trying to escape. Isley powered down the siren but put on the lights. They had no idea if she had hit her head or had internal bleeding. Her panicked movements would make the situation worse. Rorke struggled to reach into his bag and pull out a

185

syringe. The serum wasn't strong enough to knock her out but relax her. Rorke felt her muscles loosen and settle in his arms. He continued to speak in a reassuring, soothing voice.

Looking up at Rorke, Callie found herself asking, "Do you remember meeting me at rockslide eight years ago?"

"Yes. I'm glad that you stopped to help."

Callie found herself saying much more than she meant. "Me too, but I was afraid Ranger Arc would give me a ticket. I think that I developed a slight crush on you that day."

Isley joked from the front seat. "Any other secrets that you wish to share?"

Callie had forgotten Isley's presence but didn't care that he heard. "Omission is not lying. Whether I fell in love with Rorke at first or second sight is none of your business. If you want secrets, ask Gran. She was stuffing ducks with condoms and never told me. Isley, don't tell Moss about my scratch. He'll fire you!"

Isley's attention never strayed from the road. "I was venting my frustration. I suppose those words are going to come back to haunt me for a long time. You sound sleepy. Take a nap. Moss took charge tonight. Rorke, take off my windbreaker. The material is not made to withstand her tugging and pulling. You helped yourself to my extra jacket to cover the guy's blood that stained the shirt."

"How do you know the blood is not mine?"

"I checked to make sure you were all right and saw you give the guy a bloody nose. I'm glad you acted as such because your attacker reached behind his back for a hidden pistol."

Rorke decided to ignore the observation and glanced at the GPS. "She's drifted off to sleep. Where are we going? I don't recognize the address. We're traveling a long way for a doctor to put in stitches."

"Place is not on the mainstream list of hospitals. It's normally used by those who have connections or want care without filing insurance. The unwritten meaning is that you must have connections, be willing to afford discretion, and have money to cover medical expenses."

Isley could see Rorke gazing at Callie with love and concern in the rear-view mirror. "When's the wedding?"

Rorke shifted to look out the window. "Callie needs time to be comfortable with a relationship. She'll want to make sure her friends and family approve."

"I have spent enough time with the group. You're approved."

Rorke brushed a lock of hair out of Callie's face and warned. "Don't meddle. I wondered if she remembered me from the rockslide but was afraid to ask. A part of me would have been disappointed."

Isley's grinned in the rear-view mirror. "Should we discuss safe sex?"

Rorke teased right back. "Sure. What methods are you and the girlfriend using? Granted, are you able to have children at your age?"

Isley's phone rang, and he answered in his serious, business tone. "You're on speaker with Rorke and me. Callie's asleep."

Solomon's voice sounded tense from juggling many responsibilities at one time. "The hospital is a private facility, but they agreed to file our medical insurance. Rosa and Callie are my dependents for tax purposes and on my medical policies."

Isley asked, "Is that legal?"

"Yes. I provide a percentage of income, pay certain bills, and deposit money into a shared account for their use. Callie can stay on the medical policy until she turns twenty-five."

Isley was slightly impressed. "What about your secret identity? We, or Callie, could compromise the connection."

Solomon didn't laugh or chuckle at Isley's attempt at a joke. "My law enforcement name is used for deposits and payments."

Rorke broke into the conversation. "I guess that you and Nigel set up multiple identities to protect the family."

"Nice supposition. Continue."

Rorke knew that Solomon wouldn't confirm the information and made a second deduction. "Rosa spoke to me a little about Callie's father. She shared that Nigel and his brother refused to give anyone their real names, and they went to a children's home. The brother ran away before the adoption. Are you Nigel's brother?"

Solomon didn't answer the specific question. "Interesting hypothesis. How deep did you poke into Nigel's background?"

Isley looked intrigued and impressed at the same time, but he didn't interrupt. Rorke started to smooth Callie's hair as she slept. The motion helped calm him as well as the fact he loved touching her hair.

Rorke answered. "Enough to figure out that there is an interesting family history. Nigel's biological parents lived off the grid and managed a lake property with several cabins. A group of poachers arrived and had no idea people were in residence. Poachers murdered the adults and had no idea that children hid nearby.

"The attack left three of the fifteen children orphans. One challenge the authorities faced was that two of the boys refused to cooperate. Their parents were never found or identified. No one ever discovered papers, birth certificates, or tax information. The property owners turned over their documents, but the provided information proved to be false. If my research is correct, you have more at stake than being Nigel's friend. You would be Callie's biological uncle. I'd like to know how you passed background screenings and psychological tests to be in law enforcement."

Again, Solomon didn't confirm or deny the theory. "Good luck figuring that out. Also, Dusty and Baker are at the hospital. Baker was there visiting a friend, and Dusty heard a nurse taking Callie's information. Dusty immediately interrupted to find out what happened."

Isley muttered something unintelligible and asked, "How big of a problem is Dusty going to create for me?"

"I have no idea. Dusty is an enigma, and her attention span on long term projects is not the best. Callie's never been to the doctor except for yearly school physicals. I think she went once for the flu, which turned out to be bronchitis. My turn to switch the topic of conversation. How much information have you gathered on Beau and Blake?"

Isley made a rude remark about Callie and Blake being stubborn. "Enough to know that Beau, Blake, and Callie are in way over their heads. When Beau went fishing at the river on Saturday, he was alone. Since Rorke's team was busy with Callie, I decided to interrupt his fly casting to have a friendly chat. Explained our conversation would stay private and wasn't out to create problems.

"He figured out that I was not a threat or working for his father. I think that he was relieved to have someone listen. Blake crossed Beau's father, and Beau tried to protect her. Blake needed medical attention, and Callie was the only person he could think to call. Beau was disciplined for helping Blake but declined to provide details. He and Callie pretended to date so they could try and figure out an escape plan for Beau. The son has tried to leave the family fold several times, but his father finds his son and brings him back. Mrs. Dew attempted to help by sending Beau out of state for college, but the boy had to come back after graduating."

Several phones rang in the background, and Solomon said, "I have to go, but that matches the information on my end. Isley, I am contacting Agent Moss and a lawyer that deals with federal crimes. A federal angle might give us a few legal loopholes for use to our advantage. I'll be in touch later."

Isley disconnected and praised Rorke. "Good job on the research. Solomon's overprotective attitude makes a lot more sense. Callie is his only living relative. Given the family history, he'd go to great lengths to protect her."

Rorke kept an eye on Callie's pulse. "I hope that Agent Moss is willing to go out on a limb for Beau."

"Doesn't matter. If Solomon explains Callie's involvement, Moss will cooperate. Moss's mission is to make the project run smoothly and be a resounding success."

Isley made the turn into the hospital. Dusty and Baker were waiting with two staff members. Callie came semi-awake as Rorke untangled himself and climbed out.

Callie saw the waiting gurney when the hatchback opened. "Nope! I was born in a hospital and stayed out of one until Grandpa died."

Dusty came to stand beside Rorke and made her presence known. "Girl, I taught you proper etiquette and manners. You're lucky Baker was visiting a friend, and we were here. What were you thinking? Ladies do not leap off a roof for any reason."

Callie stilled as the realization that Dusty was present. "I had an excellent reason."

Dusty arched a very nicely lined eyebrow. "I don't care! You are to show polite grace to these orderlies. Be a good patient and let these nice, excellent medical specialists do their job."

Callie responded automatically, "Yes, ma'am."

A nurse walked outside with a laptop. "Mr. Asher, we were informed you provided medical care on the scene. Come with us so that I can input the additional data. The rest of you may wait in the lounge."

Isley told Dusty and Baker. "If you want to leave, I'm staying and will be glad to update you."

Dusty took Baker's hand. "Baker agreed to move his afternoon meeting. We'll remain until I know Callie only needs stitches." Dusty's voice began to crack as she listed possible injuries. "The girl could have hit her head, have broken ribs, or blood clots to the brain."

Baker hugged Dusty to comfort her and whispered reassurance. Isley found the whole interaction very strange. Solomon must have called Lion because she parked and joined them. Isley made introductions before moving his car out of the driveway. Entering the lobby, they heard a commotion on the other side of the double doors. Sound easily traveled through a set of locked, swinging panels. Callie's voice echoed in the quiet area, and she was not happy.

Isley looked at Dusty and tried to ease the worry. "I don't think she cares about minding her manners. Fighting mad is good. It means that

Callie will be fine. That is quite the outburst and interesting word choice."

Rorke emerged from a side corridor in a clean shirt and shared with the concerned gathering. "Don't worry about the yelling. It was not due to pain. A staff member voiced a concern that I may have caused the injury, and a nurse asked me to step out. Callie took great offense at the insinuation. She's making sure everyone knows her outrage and that I would never hurt her on purpose."

A couple of hours later, a doctor came to talk to the group. "Ms. Rivera is fine other than needing stitches. We ran diagnostic tests, which is why it took so long. The gash in her shoulder was the only injury. As soon as she's dressed and ready, you're welcome to take her home. I've sent a prescription for antibiotics and a pain killer."

Isley handed Rorke a backpack and started giving directions. "Lion has a little medical experience as a lab technician and agreed to stay at Callie's house. Dusty and Baker, we have your contact information. We'll keep you updated."

Dusty watched as Rorke take his equipment from the bag and clip several holders to his belt. Isley then handed over a weapon, and Dusty approached the two men.

"Mr. Asher, why are you wearing a gun?"

Rorke looked around surprised. "Oh, sorry, ma'am. I forget that not everyone knows my background. I lead a search and rescue team and never leave home without certain gear. I automatically started putting the equipment on my belt."

Dusty asked, "Why do you carry a gun to help people?"

"Uh, my certified to have the gun if that is the worry. The other, honest answer is not for the faint of heart."

"Go ahead. I rather hear the truth."

Rorke's jaw tightened. "One never knows what will happen when we are deployed to wilderness location. We went to help a driver who hit a deer and went down a ravine. The driver survived but had to be airlifted to a hospital. Deer had a broken back and lay suffering on the embankment. Once, we found a hiker with two broken legs and a rattlesnake. The rattler wanted to defend its territory instead of slithering off."

Dusty didn't seem bothered by the answer, and everyone went home.

Callie slept soundly and awoke to the smell of pies cooking in the oven. She began to stretch but stopped as the pain in her shoulder increased. Noting the surroundings, she was in bed, and night had fallen.

190

Rorke sat on the bed to gain her attention. "It's still Thursday. How are you feeling?"

"My body feels like I was run over by a speeding train. What happened? We were talking about expensive bait. Wait! I didn't embarrass myself by falling off the roof, did I?"

"No, but we need to talk."

"Oh, boy. That sounds like you are breaking up with me, and we haven't even been on an official date."

Rorke studied his hands. "Isley drove us to the hospital. There wasn't anyone else present, but you admitted to liking me after meeting at the rockslide. You remember me?"

Callie tried to scoot away, but the bed was too small. "Yes. Your voice made me look up from tying a knot. I glanced up, caught you staring, and forgot how to tie a line. Those deep brown eyes made my knees wobble. We worked well together."

"That family was lucky that you insisted the car wasn't stable. They would have died when the rocks shifted."

Callie disagreed with his opinion. "You wouldn't have let the family slide down the ravine."

Callie doubted that discussing the accident made him nervous. "You're fidgeting. What are you afraid to tell me? Are we getting kicked off the project?"

"No, but Isley is going to be a real pain. He's ready to set a wedding date for us."

Callie turned the tables on Rorke and tried to relieve Rorke's uneasiness with humor. "Well, if he approves of the relationship, the man won't try to sleep with me."

"Not laughing. I think that Isley is serious."

"Rorke, we are both adults and do not owe anyone an explanation. I was serious. My secrets could drive a wedge into the relationship or put you in danger. Trust is not the problem, but there are promises that I've made."

"There are secrets that I keep, as well. How about we agree to let Isley sweat until Rosa comes home? We'll wait to discuss an official date and marriage when she's here to talk."

Callie was not agreeing. "No promises. We have several months of hard work and pictures to take. Love, serious dating, or a long-term romantic relationship is not on the table. Plus, I have no idea what will happen with Bree."

Rorke kissed her cheek and whispered in her ear. "Bree is continuing to heal. If something does happen, I have no problem raising a child with

191

you. There is a secret that you need to know. The information cannot be hinted at or revealed. Isley, Solomon, and a select few people know about my job. There are reasons that we don't disclose my association to the sheriff's department."

Carefully, he took out a badge and identification card. Callie folded up the case up and slid it back.

Callie reached up, hugged him around the neck, and whispered back. "The sheriff's badge and Mountain Rescue Association Id were clipped to your belt the day we met in the clearing. I was close enough to read the inscriptions."

"You mean the day you almost shot me? I didn't think you noticed."

Callie released her hold and teased. "I didn't almost shoot. I'm starving."

"Isley's here with Lion and the expedition team. We're having a late dinner. Agent Valley and another lady are staying with Blake tonight. Solomon shared that you've never been in a fight. There is going to be an emotional and physical toll. If you want to talk, I'm here."

Callie smoothed the blanket and picked at the binding. "I smell Lion's pie cooking, and that wonderful smell makes my mouth water. Let's go eat."

Rorke made sure that Callie stood and supported her to the kitchen.

Chapter

Callie let Rorke fuss until they neared the kitchen. "I am fine and perfectly able to walk on my own."

"After that stunt, suck it up."

"Oh, please! I am aware of my limits. I've been jumping off that roof since I realized that I could."

Isley called from the kitchen. "Stop arguing and come eat."

Callie breezed in, nodded to Bash, Still, Crabbe, Whipper, Thicke, and Tort. She gently hugged Isley.

"Thank you for helping Blake."

Isley lectured, "Do you understand how fortunate you were that Rorke was up on that roof? You're lucky a few stitches are the only consequence. Solomon is ready to declare war on the Dew clan."

"Speaking of overreacting, why in Heaven's name did you drag me to the hospital?"

Isley shrugged. "As you so eloquently put it, I was protecting extremely expensive bait."

Callie sat down at the table. "I didn't start the rumor about bait. The university is looking at over six million dollars in grant money."

The front doorbell rang, and Still went to answer the hail. Wither and Lite looked around the crowded kitchen.

Lion asked in her strong Irish brogue. "Would you like to join us?"

Wither accepted the invitation, and Dr. Lite answered. "I appreciate the offer but ate earlier. I'm on my way home. We stopped to talk to Isley."

Isley asked, "Dr. Lite, I know that tone. Who is causing trouble?"

"We are receiving emails of protest. Several parties are not happy with the program details. University officials asked us to reach out to the liaison on how you'd like us to handle the communications."

Isley turned to Rorke, "Time to earn your stipend. Draw up a nice letter and tell any protestor to go to hell nicely. I'd send a one-line response, but words are your department. I'll read the draft and forward the letter for anyone important to distribute."

Lite asked, "Would you rather have me put a statement together as a supervisor?"

"I appreciate the offer, but we need to put distance between direct parties and anyone creating dissension. Dr. Lite, I'm going to be blunt. You are my one hope of supervising Rorke's part in the project. My strengths do not extend to reading and words. I fall asleep within five minutes as interesting as Rorke makes stories sound."

Lite praised Rorke's teaching skills. "We've had nothing but positive statements about the class. Glad we found a great teacher. If you need anything, call me."

Lite went on his way, and Callie teased Isley. "I am proud of you. That little speech almost sounded sincere."

"Almost?"

The group offered thanks for the food and started to pass dishes around the table. Rorke sat next to Callie and handed the plate or bowl around her to Isely. Isley put the food on the table. Callie was not to hold any weight. They didn't even let her take the loaf of bread, which was only a few ounces.

Wither turned to Callie. "I wanted to discuss a different matter. Do you mind talking business at the dinner table?"

Callie answered. "No."

"You were assigned one class, the book project, and a work-study group at the lab. We're reassigning the work-study to another supervisor. Moss politely informed me that you are to concentrate on the book and picture set."

Callie sighed dramatically. "If Moss thinks that I am changing my mind about his proposal, the answer is and will always be no."

Wither asked, "What proposal?"

"Moss's office listened in on classes and like the content. The man wants me to spend part of next semester touring government offices and giving an introductory botany seminar. I received an email asking my opinion on a guest lecture series. Moss wants me to talk about plants to various groups. He inferred that I'd have more time in winter because trees and plants sleep in the winter. It's the reverse. Holidays mean more work. I cited that my responsibilities to stop any talk of more teaching. I'm a graduate student, doing research, beginning a doctorate, putting together a book, traveling for pictures, and running a business. Oh, pile of poop! My answer was to hedge."

Rorke pretended to be hurt at being left out. "No one asked my opinion."

Callie ignored Rorke and told Wither. "I apologize for not thinking about forwarding the correspondence. The subject seemed to be unimportant."

Wither turned his attention back to Isley. "Um, not to be selfish or paranoid. I realize we spoke about the subject, but could you restate how the candidates were selected in your communication? A colleague at a different university contacted me. We know one another from the universities' trap team. She has no stake in the project, but a mutual

194

acquaintance is crying foul. They're filing a protest. Two of their university's gifted students didn't score as well on the tests, but no one knew the reasons for the exam."

Isley muttered unintelligibly about adults acting like children. He placed his dishes by the sink and decided to take a walk. His excuse was to check the perimeter.

Lion wrapped up a piece of pie and poured a cup of coffee for Wither to take with him. Lion had made a separate meal for the girl and the two ladies staying with her. Still and Bash helped Lion take food over to Blake. The rest of the group filed out. Callie and Rorke were left alone in the kitchen.

Callie was grateful that the soreness was on her left side. She was right-handed. Writing and light work would not be a problem. She went to take the plate to the sink, but Isley returned and stopped her.

"Stay seated. I want to talk without an audience. Callie, never, ever jump into the middle of a fight. You were trying to help, but patience would have been the better option. We had the problem handled. No one was close enough to hurt Blake. Valley and I shoved her inside before anything happened. Why did you not tell anyone you were injured?"

Callie answered honestly. "I thought the scratch was not a big deal and was afraid that Moss would fire you."

"Worry about yourself! Doctors put five stitches in your shoulder. I uttered many prayers of thanks that Rorke was up on the roof when you keeled over. Is there anything that either of you would like to share?"

Callie sat back and told Isely very seriously. "Yes. I'm very tired of being tranquilized or sedated. I understand that you wanted to transport me out to the lodge without an argument, but the tea was overkill. The substance made my head hurt, and I don't need to become a drug addict. Someone gave me strong painkillers today, and I feel miserable."

Isley smiled at her. "We needed you to rest. Lack of sleep causes carelessness. The last thing that we needed was an accident during the treasure hunt. Lion's tea is mild, and the substance isn't addictive. I promise that we're taking your health seriously, and we didn't continue the tea after you got home. As to the shoulder, you were panicked about going to the hospital. We didn't need additional injuries to occur. I'm not apologizing. If I feel the situation warrants it, I'll not hesitate to use either again. As to sharing, I had a specific topic. When's the wedding?"

Callie's mouth twitched. "Um, I think you and your lady friend should set the date around your schedules. Although, I'd like to meet and check her out before walking down the aisle. Someone should complete a background check for you. Ensure that you aren't rushing

195

into a quick decision with lasting consequences. Think about the choices while I take a shower. We'll talk later."

Isley sat with his mouth ajar.

Rorke followed her to the bedroom and whispered, "That was well done, but no shower. I need to look at the dressing."

Callie had trouble falling asleep between the pain and hearing noises that her visitors made. It wasn't that anyone was loud, but the sounds were not normal for her to hear at night. Lion padded softly down the hall in slippers to the guest room. Rorke and Isley whispered in the living room. Rorke checked on her several times, and he tried to do quietly. Once Callie fell asleep, she slept the entire night.

******

Callie woke when the alarm went off and felt less foggy. Her shoulder and back ached more than hurt. Rorke helped her cover the stitches so she could take a shower.

Trix arrived on time but stopped short climbing out of the cab. His usual greeting died on his lips. "Girl, you look like I ran you over with the rig a couple of times and backed up for good measure. Are you all right?"

Callie smiled. "I am fine."

Isley didn't comment but made Callie go back to the reception center. She sat organizing orders, balancing accounts, and checking purchase orders. Several hours later, she grew annoyed with Isley limiting her activities. The agent gave her a choice. Stay put or go back to the house and rest.

An expensive-looking vehicle pulled up and parked. Callie recognized the driver and looked at Isley. She could see he was wondering if the guest was someone he could arrest.

"Isley, the visitor is a friend, and his mother's birthday is Sunday. Please, don't be rude."

Callie greeted the visitor warmly and with a hug. "Hey, stranger. I hear wonderful things about you making strides in saving the world."

The gentleman smiled. "Thanks. I heard about the book project and you creating chaos at every opportunity."

"Linus, life needs a little chaos every so often."

Her friend nodded hello to everyone. "Do you have time to take a short walk for a private conversation?"

"Sure."

Isley piped up and ordered, "Ms. Rivera, stay in my sight and do not wander far."

196

Callie took Linus's arm and walked to the fence on the opposite side of the parking lot. Linus made sure Callie settled on the top rail and leaned on the post facing the pasture.

Linus said, "It feels like a lifetime ago that we used to sit here and talk about the future."

"It was a lifetime ago. You're as nervous as a chicken cornered by a fox. Let me save you some time and stress. We were each other's first love and will always have a special place in each other's hearts. We've remained friends after our formal breakup because we recognized the reality. You're a city boy, and I work outdoors. We went camping twice. You didn't whine or complain but were miserable. I'm not interested in mediation, politics, and making people play nice. You're a brilliant tactician and try to make the world a better place. I hear Ginger is nice and compliments your goals. Are you proposing marriage?"

Linus's soppy, lopsided grin provided the answer. "I forget how perceptive you. We're hosting a birthday lunch for my mother on Sunday at one o'clock. Consider coming?"

"Of course! Would bringing a date help?"

Linus grabbed Callie's hands, pulled her off the fence, and hugged her with enthused relief. "Yes! I had no idea how to ask without making me sound like an insecure nutcase." Linus didn't notice her wince of discomfort. "Thank you! You are the best! Love you!"

Callie thought that Linus turned into a kangaroo as he hopped and down.

Rorke's amused voice came from behind them. "I hope that declaration doesn't mean I have competition for Callie's affection."

Linus released Callie and shook Rorke's hand. "Nope. You must be Rorke. Linus."

Rorke asked, "How is the salmon conservation project? I heard rumors that the negotiations stalled."

Linus never let debate or work issues bother him once he left a room and told Rorke as if amused, "I doubt anyone involved ever heard of the word compromise. If so, the term was deleted from their vocabulary. A solution must be their idea and completed by their rules. The parties want to argue about who is right instead of finding a workable solution."

Callie patted Linus's arm. "If anyone can find a resolution, you will."

Linus asked, "Callie, may I have a private word with Rorke?"

"No, you may not."

Rorke raised his eyebrow. "Linus wants to make sure that I don't abandon you when the going gets tough."

197

Linus grinned at Rorke. "If the man is serious about a relationship, I have a few tips that could save him some trouble."

Linus had Callie's full attention. "Like?"

"If you miss curfew by fifteen minutes, Pica's weakness is watercolor art by a specific painter."

Callie shook her head. "I'd forgotten about the flat tire."

Lion pulled into a nearby parking spot and waved. She and Blake unloaded food.

"Lunch is here! I hope Lion brought pie. You're more than welcome to stay and eat. Both of you come inside. I don't want or need the only two men I've liked romantically to compare notes or tell stories."

Callie went inside and pretended not to notice the stunned expressions on Linus and Rorke's faces.

Linus sputtered. "Damn! That means serious trouble. Callie is too controlled to slip. What's going on?"

Rorke provided a short, sharable version of events. Linus took the flowers and left to meet his mother. After dishing up, Blake took her food to eat by the pond. There was a spot where she liked to sit, eat, and study. Bash, Thicke, Tort, and Whipper joined Blake. Crabbe, Still, and Rorke found places to eat among flowers.

Callie finished her sandwich and started to work on the computer in the front office. A vehicle pulled up, parked, and a couple disembarked. Callie identified the pair immediately as Beau's parents: Mr. and Mrs. Dew.

Callie asked, "Still, I'm going to let you into the greenhouse. Would you find Blake and make sure she stays put until these visitors depart?"

Still slipped out the back.

The couple entered, and Callie smiled brightly. "Hello, Mr. Dew. Mrs. Dew. How may I help you?"

Dew demanded. "Turn off the cameras. We want a word."

"My apologies, but security is contracted out. As to privacy, the restroom would be our only space. I doubt three of us would fit."

Dew looked around as if he'd forgotten his wife's presence. He ordered her to go to the car, and the woman obeyed without question. Callie felt very sorry for Mrs. Dew.

Mr. Dew leaned over the counter to where he could stare down at Callie. "This nonsense is to end right now! I want the charges dropped against my son. Damaging a good family's name is not in anyone's best interest. Beau stays out of trouble with the law. We don't want Beau's name dragged through the mud because some bitch accused him of unwanted advances."

198

Callie had no trouble putting Dusty's acting lessons to use and teared slightly. "Beau and I only had dinner a couple of times, and I've never accused him of anything. We apologized to each other after the misunderstanding."

"Oh, stop with the tears! Beau took responsibility for the confusion, and he would never purposely hurt a woman. You're not the problem or pressing charges, but state and federal authorities want to prosecute him. We pay extortion prices for the lawyers, but they are being stonewalled. Damn court system wants two million in bail. You are going to resolve the issue. Contact your family lawyer to get the mess cleared up quickly and quietly."

Callie answered softly but firmly. "I am sorry that you are having trouble, but my priority is managing my father's garden, Botanic Enchantment. My recommendation is to let the lawyers earn their money. If Beau is a good citizen, I doubt much will happen."

Mr. Dew's eyes were full of hate. "You could lose a lot if you don't help. Your grandmother could find herself facing problems. She is a citizen, but Mexicans and blacks have no business raising white kids. You're over eighteen but still living with her. A young woman managing a large company by herself faces many hurdles in today's world."

Callie's own eyes went as hard as stone. She knew better than to say the words running through her head aloud, but she leaned forward, with her nose almost to Mr. Dew's face.

"Are you threatening me?"

"Offering friendly advice."

Callie's voice went icy as a glacier. "I, also, have some friendly advice. If a family member or a drinking crony comes near me, or anyone I care about, make sure to have additional bail money available. Dealing with paperwork for trespassing, stalking, or extortion would be such a nuisance and waste of resources."

Callie watched the blood creep up Mr. Dew's face. It was like watching mercury rising in a thermometer that had been thrust into boiling water. As the man started to turn from red to purple, he pushed Callie back.

"Don't threaten me girl! I'll…."

Rorke moved to the front of the counter. "Sir, I think you had better not finish that statement."

Dew turned his venom toward Rorke. "Don't interfere, half-breed. Stay out of my business! Touch me, and I'll send you to the reservation in a box."

Rorke opened the door. "Sir, I think you had better leave."

Dew realized that there were others in the room. "Getting in a customer's face is not a good business practice, young lady. Make the phone calls."

Lion had her phone out with Solomon on the line in seconds of the door closing. "Be useful. Find and rent a six-bedroom place for me. Then, locate four other girls who need a new residence. Blake's relocating as of ten minutes ago."

They could hear Solomon ask, "What happened?"

Lion spoke to Solomon and everyone else at once. "I decided to become a house mother until further notice. Stop wasting time! Rorke, take Callie home to rest. Crabbe and Isley, help me clean up and collect the others."

Callie decided that she did not want to ever be on Lion's bad side. Rorke and Callie walked back to the house. Rorke carried her backpack and let her set the pace. She stopped ever so often to snip off a small branch or pack soil around a bush or flower.

Chapter

Rorke settled Callie in bed, and his phone rang. Reading the caller's name, he frowned in concern. Rorke answered, and Callie listened to the conversation and figured out the problem. A group of kayakers who were rock climbing in northern Idaho needed help. The location was in the Sawtooth National Forest area. Even air rescue had to have special permits to fly into or over the dense foliage. One of the climbers had a broken leg. A second person was injured. Their companions couldn't get to the pair safely to assess the seriousness of the injuries. Rorke was to gather a rescue team and be at the airport in 30 minutes.

Callie spoke after Rorke hung up the phone. "Gets cold at night. Exposure will be a problem."

Rorke led Callie into the house. "You aren't invited for several reasons-with or without an injury. I may or may not be back Sunday to show off my new girlfriend."

"A public announcement is not a wise idea."

Rorke smiled, leaned down, and kissed her. "Deferring the subject will not change my mind about coming along on the rescue. You are going to take a nap and skip this adventure. End of discussion."

"I wish my knees would stop turning to mush when you do that."

"Mush? Good."

Callie set her alarm, and Rorke sent texts while she snuggled into the covers. She had time to wake up and dress for girls' night. Callie found several messages had come in while she slept. Bree continued to be stable. Her grandmother called to say that she was going to a ballgame. There wasn't a signal at the stadium, so they'd talk tomorrow. She had hoped that Rorke had sent a text or left a voice mail, but he hadn't. She changed into casual attire, styled her hair, and did her makeup.

Agent Valley sat at the kitchen table with Isley. "I hope you don't mind if I crash the party."

Callie smiled. "No problem. Are you babysitting?"

"Yes. Isley wants a nap and would stick out as the only guy."

Isley departed, and Callie explained Girls' Night. "We usually go to Happy Hour at a local sport's bar to catch up on the gossip. We visit, share our concerns, or seek advice. Sometimes, we'll go to a movie or bowling. You've met Cattail. She found out her husband of ten years is having an affair. Pickle went on a few dates with a new boyfriend, and things went weird. Another friend is hoping her guy asks her to marry. Tonight, we are meeting at Pickle's house. I don't drink and usually end up being the designated driver."

The security chimes sounded, and Callie checked the monitor. Ranger Cattail arrived and looked miserable. Callie met her friend at the door and drew her into the kitchen.

Cattail nodded to Valley and asked Callie, "May I use the couch while you go out? I brought liquor and need a place to drown in my sorrows. Oh, Callie! It's worse than I ever imagined."

Callie told her friend that she was always welcome. The circumstances didn't matter. Callie's phone rang, and Cattail told her to answer while she could unload the car.

Nod spoke when Callie answered. "Hey! Head's up. Cattail may be coming your way. She contacted me after you gave her my information. I ordered dinner for fifteen people, and the delivery will come to your house for girl's night. Give the leftovers to the college boys down the street. I'm sure that they'll eat anything. Isley phoned to inform me about Mr. Dew's visit. Are you all right?"

Callie didn't share that Cattail had arrived. "I'm fine other than hopping mad. My concern is Blake. Lion decided to take the young woman under her wing and made noises about being a dorm mother. I don't know the outcome because I took a nap."

Nod made a distinctive groan. "The outcome was more work for me. I have never had to deal with Solomon on a legal level, but the man is extremely pushy and demanding. He wanted a six-bedroom rental immediately-like today. We found one in an apartment complex on the top floor. He also asked for the names of four girls who needed a place."

Callie shared her opinion. "Sounds about right for him. In fairness, Lion called him to make the arrangements. I understand you must be careful about client and attorney confidentiality. Could you provide a rough estimate of how bad the situation is for Cattail and her boys?"

"Cattail has a steady job with benefits. The biggest hurdle is emotional, but she has a strong support system. Her parents are close by, and the boys are with them for the night. The rest is up to her to share."

"Thank you for being an awesome lawyer and great friend."

Nod verbalized her thoughts about Callie's compliment. "Don't butter me up. I'm not happy about the stunt you pulled with Mr. Dew. Callie, you're playing with a fire that is liable to burn home and forest down around you. I'm going to Mer's office to download a copy of the video of today's event."

Callie wasn't upset or shamed in the least. "Watch the recording before you lecture. I have a few aces up my sleeve."

"Now, I am very concerned. What are you planning?"

Callie disconnected and sent a text to the other ladies to tell them about a change in plans. Anyone who wanted to have a free meal was welcome. She and Cattail were staying home.

After the food was delivered, someone organized a buffet in the dining room. Callie called everyone to eat.

Cattail was distressed when she entered to find the buffet set up. "Oh, Callie. Rosa uses the dining room for family gatherings."

"You are family. The table is the only place large enough for all of us without holding plates in our lap."

Callie offered a general blessing. The rest of the evening went by in a blur, but she made sure to converse with Valley. Reasons varied to make her feel welcome and discreetly listen to office gossip. Other agents were good sources of information about other people involved in the operation.

***

Callie awoke the next morning to Isley calling her name. "Stop shouting! I am on the couch. Please bring me some water if you are going parental. I promise everyone was of legal drinking age, and no one drove home after drinking."

Isley could guess her definition of parental by looking around the living room. "The place looks more like the morning after at a college party. Are those darts sticking in the wall?"

"Yes. Hold on. Let me check my messages."

Callie felt around for her phone. Bree's condition hadn't changed, and Ranger Cattail had told her family.

Isley handed Callie a bottle of water, and she explained why the change in plans. "Cattail married her high school sweetheart, but the guy is not a great example of fidelity for the male species. I met him when I was fourteen and could view the relationship objectively. He was charming and would sleep with anyone who caught his eye. During one of my college trips home, he propositioned me while Cattail was in the kitchen. I only visited when he was on a business trip after that. Cattail was going to check her work email and discovered her husband's second phone. During our break on Tuesday, she asked me for Nod's information to seek advice."

While Isley made eggs, turkey bacon, and pancakes, Callie continued with the story. "Thank goodness Cattail followed Nod's directions. Cattail drove home, talked to her husband in general terms, and broached the subject of counseling. She followed up with texts and emails about therapy. Wednesday, Cattail was supposed to stay in town, but Nod sent her home with an investigator to collect documents. They found the husband in the bedroom with another woman. The low life gave up everything. Signed over the house. Refuses to pay child support, alimony, or have any more contact."

"Did you tell Cattail about her husband's behavior?"

Callie decided her head hurt enough to lay it in her crossed arms on the table. "Yes and no."

"Meaning, you remained friends without bringing up the subject. Don't you become tired of meddling in other people's lives?"

Callie ignored Isley and started eating the eggs and pancakes in front of her.

He sat across from her. "What's on your agenda for the day, Plant Princess?"

"Please, find a different nickname. One that doesn't sound so pretentious."

"I am delighted that you are annoyed. You have created enough trouble and paperwork for me. What are you doing today?"

"Trix is scheduled to pick up a load of Chrysanthemums on Monday morning." Callie smiled at Isley's frown at the flower and explained. "Chrysanthemums are a type of mum. I also need to set aside flats of Pansies, Aster, and Dianthus. Should take a couple of hours at the most."

"We will start on pictures today. I have roughly 3000 pictures for you to sort. Where do you want to set up a sorting area?"

Callie poured syrup on her stack of hotcakes. "Does it matter who views the photos?"

"No. The pictures are not classified information. If the entire box disappears, copies are floating all over the state."

"Then, let's use the home office. I'll have space to spread out and computer access. Do I have time for a shower?"

Isley nodded. "Yes. I'll clean up the kitchen and bring in the boxes."

After a shower and changing, Callie felt refreshed and ready to tackle sorting photographs.

Isley greeted and updated her on the pictures. "Techs did the leg work. After your conversation with Agent Moss, the pictures are tagged with three tabs. The top has the flower names. Longitude and latitude are on the second. Last label has the date. The back material matches the information in the front."

"Cool! Did anyone check to make sure the subject matter matched the scientific names?"

"Um, yes, if those are the long, alien-looking words. Each photo has a location code in the upper right-hand corner. The number corresponds to the latitude and longitude shown on the wall map."

Callie studied pictures and worked for a couple of hours. She took a break when her stomach growled for lunch. Wandering through the living room, she found Burnly fixing the wallboard.

Burnly spied her. "Received your text asking to repair the damage of the dartboard. Isley let me start to work but told me to stay out of your hair. Guess it was a wild girls' night."

"We stayed home. Before you accuse me of having a horrible aim, I did not touch the darts. There are a couple of things I have to do at BE. Text me when you are finished."

"Sure."

Callie found Lion in the kitchen. "Wow! The place looks cleaner than when Gran left. Thank you so much."

Lion dried off her hands and commented, "Don't get used to the idea of free help. I shall be exacting interest from you in the form of translating. Five teenage girls are driving me crazy in less than 24 hours. Every ten seconds, one is asking if the internet is up. They would have a person believing the world was ending every minute that they aren't connected. Coming over here was the saner option."

Callie laughed. "You volunteered."

"No one told me that the age group might as well be aliens speaking an unintelligible language. What is BFF?"

"Best friends forever."

Lion looked confused at the notion. "How does one know a person will be a BFF a month from now? I think Nonce broke up and reconciled with her boyfriend in a matter of an hour. What sort of name is Nonce? Blake is in the reception center downloading homework. Mer is working in the computer office. Callie, be careful. Facing Dew was a brave but dangerous move."

Callie shrugged as she finished making a sandwich. "I figured a confrontation was imminent. Research, quick learning, and paranoia come in handy every so often. His business and the Greenhouse intersect in one area, and I took care of the problem last month. Yes, I am young, single, and a woman, but I am not a mimosa pubica that will fold up at a touch. There is only so much pressure that Dew will be able to apply.

"Humans tend to dwell on the negative, and there is so much hate in the world. Conversely, there are many good people of every age. If we aren't willing to reach out to others and take a chance, humanity will wither and die."

Lion peered at Callie with an unreadable expression. "Nice sentiment but naïve. Overconfidence, inexperience, and taking on the system is for dreamy-eyed youth. The reality is that Dew has connections, power, and money. He may buy his way out of a lot of trouble. If money doesn't work, he'll threaten or find a way to make you remain silent."

Callie smiled, packed a snack for later, and continued to sound unconcerned. "What happened to make as much noise as possible?"

"We were discussing exploration and discoveries. Our conversation didn't include poking a hornet's nest for fun. Are you always so sassy and smart lipped?

"I have to go to work and make sure Dew hasn't burned the greenhouse and my father's garden down."

"Not funny!"

"Wouldn't be the first time. Last one out locks the doors! Bye!"

Lion called after her. "Callie! What do you mean wouldn't be the first time?"

Burnly commented from the living room, "Don't waste your breath. The girl won't listen or answer. Callie's lost loved ones and beloved places a total of three times in her life. Each time fire took them: her grandfather, her father, and the cabin. Grandfather's stroke was induced by a fire, started by arson, which burned down the barn. Thank God, it was summer, and the stock was in the pasture. Her father's car exploded into a ball of fire after the accident, and the cabin ended up as ashes."

"Crap! I didn't make the connection."

Callie kept walking and pretended not to hear. She composed her face. Deep breath. No tears. No emotion. Cracks led to gaps. Protect. If nothing else, Dusty had helped Callie develop acting skills to disguise her feelings. She wasn't a great role model following through or finishing a major project. She had taught Callie a great many life lessons. The woman flew into town with hurricane wind strength and flattened anyone in her wake. Then, she moved onto the next place to wreak havoc. Her father had always provided balance and explanations in the aftermath of Dusty's visits.

What could she do to protect Rorke? How could a crush turn into love in less than two weeks? Callie wondered if she had the courage to start a long-term relationship. Rorke commented on waiting for Rosa to return before talking about marriage. Doubts began to creep into the mind. Was he serious or trying to distract her? Where did Rorke's loyalty lie? The authorities? Isley? Other law enforcement? Solomon? Callie decided that Rorke cared and might be in love with her.

The book project would only take so long. Was letting Rorke close a good idea? After they finished the project, would he vanish into the trees like a deer slipping away before a predator caught its scent or movement? A part of her recognized she felt incomplete now that he was gone.

Isley's voice invaded her thoughts. "Halt! Stop! Pay attention! Do not go anywhere by yourself!"

"I was walking on a path with lots of people in calling distance. Isley, please calm down."

Isley turned a shade of volcano lava red. "Calm down!? You did not just tell me to calm down!"

"I have one order to put together, but there are many items on my list to complete. Either walk or move aside."

Isley walked beside Callie to the greenhouse. She could hear the man's teeth grinding in frustration.

Before going inside the greenhouse, Blake bounded out of the reception office. "You're here! Guess what?! Ms. Nod found a program for me and four girls. Each of us received a grant to stay in an apartment with an RA. Ms. Lion agreed to be our supervisor. The apartment has a kitchen, washer, dryer, and dishwasher."

Blake went from ecstatic to unsure in a blink of an eye. She shifted from foot to foot.

"Could I ask? Ms. Nod called my parents about needing a guardian even though I'm over eighteen. I am not exactly clear on the reasons. Um. Mr. Isley, did you adopt Rorke when he was 18?"

Isley muttered, "Yes. I hate teenage hormones and mood swings. Please, say that Nod did not volunteer me. I did my time with Rorke."

Blake and Callie both knew that Isley would help, but they didn't share the opinion aloud.

"Ms. Nod called them yesterday to ask if they'd allow me to have a legal guardian. My parents look at eighteen as being old enough to be on my own. I walked out, and my life isn't their concern. They agreed to sign the papers. Their only condition was that they weren't wasting time or gas. We had to send the documents to them."

Callie tried to ease Blake's uncertainty. "Look at the situation as a gesture of love from your parents. It's not been easy to trust their child's safety to someone else."

Blake pushed her toe into the hard floor and rotated her foot back and forth. If the ground had been dirt, she'd have a huge hole. "Cows, chickens, horses, and such are fine, but I want to be around people. My dream is to finish college and not live on a farm for the rest of my life. I want a degree in hospitality and a minor in art. My day job could be working in a hotel, reception area, or greeting people at the door. Art is more of a hobby, but I love drawing sketches. Do you think that's dumb?"

"No. Have you spoken to Mr. Pica? He has worked in art sales and teaches a few classes at the university every so often."

Blake glanced up to see if Callie was serious. "Absolutely not! The man is talented. Did you see what he did to your house? WOW! The detail and lines of composition. Um, Callie, I have another question. If Beau's lawyers offered you a million dollars to transfer schools and be quiet, would you?"

"No. A million dollars might seem like enough to make problems go away, but there would be other consequences. If the Dew family is behind the bribing, I doubt they'd leave you alone. The next time, the price would be to look the other way while someone else was hurt. If the situation escalates, the Dew family will threaten friends or family. May I ask what happened?"

Blake showed Callie an email on her computer.

Callie read remained quiet for a long time but kept her face from showing her thoughts. "Blake, do you trust me?"

Callie typed a response. "I do not know whose idea of a joke this is, but I'm not interested. I have no idea why someone would think that I would blackmail the Dew family over Beau. We never spoke on the phone, through the computer, or by text. I would never blackmail anyone about a liaison that never started. Take me off your contact list as I am blocking you from mine."

Blake asked Isley, "If they come after my family, does this count as evidence?"

Bluntly, and perhaps not as gently as he could have, Isley answered, "The Dew family is smart, and they have never been caught doing anything illegal. Look at the format. The email is from a generic account without a specific lawyer named, and the firm is huge. A defense attorney would say that anyone could send such a letter from any computer in the building. Even having a warrant for a specific IP address wouldn't help. The public has easy access to a computer."

Blake started to cry, and Callie glared at Isley to be quiet. "Blake, don't let Beau and his family make you feel worthless or insignificant. You are a good human being with a bright future."

"How do I repay everyone? Ms. Lion bought me clothes and a bag yesterday. I saw Ms. Nod's prices. She only made me pay one dollar. It's Saturday, but I am supposed to go see her with Ms. Lion at three."

Callie understood that Blake needed to feel like she mattered and not a charity case. "One way is to help me keep an eye on Rosa. My grandmother is awesome, but she will not admit to getting older. Her bones ache sometimes. Cleaning out a rental can be physically taxing, and I try to do the heavy work. You could help by making sure Rosa doesn't strain or lift anything heavy."

Blake perked up at hearing the task. "I don't mind cleaning, painting walls, or washing. One of my former jobs was as a hotel maid. I gave my two weeks' notice on Friday. One of the perks was the food. If a guest did not claim food in 24 hours, we could take and eat it. Some guests left unopened milk or unopened sandwiches. May I use the printer in your home office?"

"Yes. Bash is waving at the door. Humor me and see if he'll drive or walk you over to the house."

Blake went to the door to let Bash inside. Bash listened to Callie's request and nodded that he would walk Blake to the house. Blake turned and waved goodbye before disappearing.

Isley asked, "Do you ever cease and desist?"

Callie answered, "No idea. Before I start pulling trays and call Gran, I want to stay hi to Mer."

Chapter

Isley walked with Callie to the computer office where her uncle was working. After greeting Mer, Callie asked if he minded finishing later because she wanted to talk to Gran.

Mer agreed but sighed, "Fine, but no more than an hour. I have time to relax and chill. It's Saturday. I'll wait in the shade outside. Isley, hit the green button on the wall to your right."

Isley heard a mechanical whirl and the entire north wall of the office started to move. "Should I worry about strange noises?"

Mer answered, "No. Nigel loved hidden passages, camouflaged doors, and hidey holes. If you want a beer, I brought a cooler. Folding chairs are by the door. Help yourself."

Sunlight flooded the room, and Isley asked, "Did you run out of makeup or leather? You appear almost human today."

"Old enough to separate professional and personal. Employers and clients are only so enlightened. I had to go to work before coming here. Callie, how are you doing?"

Callie reassured her uncle. "I am fine. More concerned about Blake. Lawyers offered Blake a million dollars to shut up and go away. Dew made veiled threats against Gran and the rest of the family during his visit. Should I tell them to be careful or wait and see what Dew does?"

Mer hesitated before admitting, "I called everyone last night and spoke to the siblings with spouses present. We agreed to let you tell Rosa. I doubt Dew would exert pressure on family that lives out of state, but they have an idea of what's happening. They understand that you feel the need to rescue every person from their problems. Callie, there is only so much you can do to help. Saving the world from itself is an impossible task. At some point, a person must fail or succeed on their own. Be careful and don't do anything stupid."

"Thanks, Uncle Mer. I'll be fine. I have no desire for you to move back home and paint my bedroom in shades of black. If I die, I will haunt you until you add other colors."

Mer did not think her words were funny. "Leave the jokes to me. If you go to war with the Dew family, the consequences could be financial collapse or a ruined reputation. Lower the shatterproof defenses and take the advice of the experts."

"I'll take my chances."

Mer did grin and wink at Isley when he said, "Change of topic. Who's walking you down the aisle? I see the way you look at Rorke, and he loves you."

Callie glanced sideways at her uncle. "What are you talking about?"

"That's right. You were too busy stirring up trouble. I have the scene cued up on the computer. Watch Rorke, and not your stupid, reckless behavior."

Mer started a video. When Dew made rude comments about Rosa, Rorke moved. Before he could go around the counter, Crabbe grabbed Rorke's arm. Crabbe motioned for the firearm that Rorke had secured at his waist. Callie had seen Rorke's expression, but she wasn't about to admit her feelings.

When the video ended, and Callie turned the swivel chair to face Isley and Mer. "That is my handgun. Why does Rorke have my firearm?"

Isley shook his head in disbelief at her takeaway. "Rorke was returning the weapon to the safe. Mer locked the piece in the safe this morning."

Mer refrained from comment and rolled a chair outside. Isley took a second chair and followed.

Callie placed a corded phone that was at least twenty years old in front of her. Then she used the cell phone to ask Gran to call the greenhouse landline. The bill would not accumulate a long-distance charge, and her uncle couldn't use the wireless or greenhouse surveillance to listen to the conversation. Callie purposely waved, smiled at her uncle, and shut down a couple of computers. Between the corded phone and power turned off, the conversation would stay private. Mer made faces and rude gestures through the window, which made Callie laugh.

Outside Mer, took a sip from his bottle. "Man! We taught her too well. I wanted to eavesdrop."

Gran rang back. Callie shared a condensed version of events regarding Blake, Beau, and Beau's father. Callie pointedly asked if Nod had contacted Gran about being Blake's guardian. Rosa wanted to talk to Callie before committing. They agreed that Rosa should be Blake's guardian on record. Gran was more interested in Lion's plan about becoming an instant dorm mother. Gran wanted to know if Lion had a clue to the challenge.

After a short discussion on supervising teens, Callie shared what happened at girls' night and why. Gran was more concerned about Cattail than the holes in the wall. The last issue Callie broached was Rorke.

Callie asked, "Gran, what should I do about Rorke? I may not be able to protect him if Dew makes trouble."

"Mija, you've tried to be the strong, responsible one. Don't throw away a chance at true love because of responsibility, fear, or guilt."

Callie hung up after a few more updates on family, flipped the computers back on, and went outside to join Mer and Isley. The two were sipping beer like old friends.

Callie asked her uncle, "Do either of you know why Solomon wants to make changes to my contract with Trix? Solomon left a message while I was talking to Gran. I'm to see Nod and sign his version of an agreement that I drafted to hire Trix as an independent hauler."

Mer closed his eyes and counted to ten before saying, "Callie, start over. Remember, we aren't able to download thoughts to read on a screen." Isley grinned at Mer's words because he found someone who could get through to Callie. Well, maybe.

Callie explained. "My research concluded Dad's garden, Botanic Enchantment, and Dew's family had one intersecting business associate. We use the same trucking company. Dew Enterprises does several millions of dollars of business a year with hauling groceries, produce, and frozen goods. Our contract is for roughly a million dollars. Good business sense is to keep Dew happy."

Mer sat up a little straighter. "How the hell do you sell a million dollars of plants in one year?"

"Hey! Language. I'll tell Gran you used the "h" word. Don't you pay attention to the paperwork? Each time Trix loads up, the cargo is roughly eighty thousand dollars' worth of plants."

"Please tell me that's a joke."

Callie led Isely and Mer to pallets of red flowers. "Popular name is Impatiens, and people like to plant to attract songbirds to the garden. Each container holds six. My cost is relatively low because I take the seeds to germinate and bloom. Let's hypothesize. Let's say my cost is two dollars for pot, dirt, time, and seeds. I sell the flowers to the distributor for six, and the store sells for ten to twelve. The more flowers, the larger the profit margin.

"The truckload that Isley was trying to hurry had roughly four hundred thousand dollars of flowers on board. We divided the load this month because the plant containers are larger. The first had 200 mums in three-gallon containers. Each resells for about thirty dollars, which equals about 6000 dollars. There were 100 flats of succulent flowers, which sell about 80 dollars, and the value would be about 8000. Fall is busy because people begin to plant and decorate for Labor Day and Halloween. Sunflowers, Mums, Pansies, and such. Should I continue?"

212

Isley said, "Stop! Oh, dear sweet, Lord in Heaven. Is there anything in that cooler stronger than beer? Shit! When I looked at the taxes, I looked at the bottom-line numbers. Debit versus credit. I am beginning to understand why various agencies are so upset about a few dead plants. Who pays 30 dollars for a plant that will die in a few weeks?"

Callie smiled sadly. "Mums are a Chrysanthemum and a perennial. They have beautiful red, yellow, orange, light purple, or white blooms. Some growers use hybrids to change or vary the color, but the plant is popular for fall decoration. Buy, display, and don't need long term care."

Mer rubbed his chin. "Solomon and Nod would never steer you wrong. Sign the papers. Damn! Isley, I'm joining you for a strong drink."

Callie chastised. "Why are you so upset? I am the one who should be distressed. My babies go off to wilt and die on a stranger's porch."

Isley's phone buzzed for attention. After listening, the man ordered. "I'll be back. Do not leave without phoning me! Do you understand?"

"Yes, Mr. Dictator." Callie resisted the urge to stick her tongue out or make a childish face.

Callie separated and moved flats, trays, and pots. Then, she started pricking out several species of flowers. Seeds had matured into seedlings, and the baby plants required growing room. Each seedling had to be loosened from the rest, transplanted, and positioned into a new, larger home. Then, Callie moistened the soil with a mist and placed the plants in the shade. The seedlings needed to recover from the stress of moving. She made place cards for each area with dates planted and when to add fertilizer.

Her phone played a symphony while she was writing the cards. "Hello."

Nod was on the phone. "I'm meeting you at the house to sign papers about transporting plants. Solomon wanted a few alterations in the wording. Hopefully, the documents help protect the trucking company and you from reprisals. I wouldn't be surprised if Dew tried to strong-arm the company to lose, divert, or delay shipments out of pure spite. I reached out to Trix and his crew, and they aren't concerned about the changes or Dew. Trix owns his rig, and most of his business is through third parties."

Callie asked while she washed her hands, "Did you have to consult with another firm? I know you mainly deal with family law rather than corporate. Have them bill me next month after my birthday."

"You are generous with money that hasn't been deposited. Is that the third or fourth time you told me to use that money?"

213

"I am keeping track of amounts. See you in a few."

Callie changed shoes and met Isley at the main door. Her body ached, and she was ready for a break. Pricking plants was delicate work. The process needed undivided attention and patience, but Callie had been grateful for a period of uninterrupted time.

While the pair walked back to the house, Callie asked Isley about the pictures. "Would one of the offices have the capability of printing out an updated image of the latitude and longitude? I could check each one with a map internet program, but the ink alone would be a small fortune. An option is to save the image from the internet and send the pictures to a local printshop. I have no idea what the legality or rules are governing such a large amount of data."

"I'll look into the matter. What are you doing for dinner?"

"I saved a plate of food from last night. I hid it in the oven so Bash, Still, or Crabbe didn't scoop up every crumb."

Isley shared. "Lion gave the food to Blake for lunch. Plan B. We order take out. Don't worry about the bill. My treat since I know you have fifteen dollars in your checking account."

Callie's eyes flashed in anger. "Stop snooping into my checkbook!"

Isley ignored the accusation and switched the subject to Rorke. "I hope you will give Rorke a chance. You are the best thing to cross Rorke's path in a long time."

"That is a nice thing to say, but I may not be a good, safe bet."

Isley's eyes continued to scan the surroundings. "Eight years ago, I received a call from Rorke asking for a favor. My first thought was that he was in a car accident or needed bail money. The boy never admitted to needing anything. I had to play guessing games on clothes or school supplies. Rosa's expertise and advice would have been a gold mine to me. I had no idea what I was doing.

"Rorke wanted to make sure that Ranger Arc didn't write a young lady a ticket. The girl was a minor and had saved a family from certain death. He had a name, age, license plate number, and car information."

Callie rolled her eyes and made a noise. "That's a slightly dramatic version. Rorke followed me down the cliff and anchored the car. I figured that Ranger Arc would write a ticket. Wasn't sure if it was for stealing his radio, harnesses, or the very least, a traffic violation."

Isley continued without arguing the point. "The conversation is the first time Rorke talked to me openly and without weighing every word or being defensive. He didn't view me as a prison guard or warden. Rorke was concerned that you were sixteen. If he asked too many questions, trying to help could backfire. Looking into the matter was a small price to pay for a turn in our relationship."

"Thank you for your help. I never did receive a ticket."

Isley informed her as they entered the house, "Ranger Arc would have been a fool if he had. A petite girl who weighed the same as a wet rag took over his accident scene. She correctly detected the vehicle's unstable position on the cliff. Rorke did not mention you again until the night of the incident with his girlfriend. He disappeared after the confrontation and went drinking. I followed and joined him as a designated driver. Sometime during the drinking binge, he wondered if you would remember him. You would be in college and over eighteen."

Callie hoped her face remained neutral. "Isley, why are we having this particular discussion?"

"Your uncle knows that you and Rorke previously met. Mer asked me for details, and I shared."

"How? Did you blab?"

"No, but Mer admitted to hacking into the hospital's security system. He watched events unfold on the greenhouse cameras and wanted to make sure you were all right. He assured me that no one would ever suspect, and I made discreet inquiries. There isn't evidence of an extra pair of eyes. A nurse asked Rorke to step away. They wanted to make sure that Rorke had not caused the wound. Mer was quite impressed with the eloquent Spanish and English pouring forth from your mouth. You stood up for Rorke and informed the accuser about Rorke having your back and support for years. Mer wanted the details."

Callie was not happy at her life being the center of gossip. "Remind me to fire my uncle as head of security when I see him at church tomorrow."

Chapter

Callie signed the papers that Nod brought. The rest of the evening was spent identifying, sorting, and cataloging. Isley made her take a break and eat. He ordered cuisine from four different restaurants. Bash, Crabbe, and Still joined them at the table. The men did not have talkative natures, and Callie didn't feel the need to fill the quiet with words.

Toward the end of the meal, Bash suddenly had a revelation. "Callie, you are a girl."

Callie kicked Crabbe under the table as he opened his mouth to make a snide remark. She waited for Bash to finish his question.

Bash asked, "How did you know you'd fallen in love with Rorke and didn't just have a crush on him?"

Callie ignored the insinuation about her feelings and tried to answer the best she could. "I may not be the best person to offer advice. You need time to distinguish the two in your mind. A crush is where the love will dissolve with disillusionment. Love will grow and withstand the test of time. Even in a strong relationship, emotions will bounce around. Did you hear about my friend Linus visiting yesterday?"

"Yes. Pica uttered a few choice words about you attending his mother's birthday party."

Callie continued without an opinion about Pica's viewpoint. "Linus and I were in love for about a year. Time showed us that a lifetime together would be disastrous. Our goals in life were not remotely conducive to years together. Linus is a city boy. Outdoors is a big part of my life, and he tried to fit in. We went camping twice. Both trips were disasters, but he never complained. During the second campout, he developed a case of Poison Oak.

"Linus's world is meetings, politics, socials, and brokering deals. His way of saving the planet is to attempt a compromise between groups. The goal is to act instead of getting bogged down in laws or legislation. I did not and do not have the patience to deal with constant spotlights on me. We could have tried to make the relationship work, but we had vastly different dreams and goals in life. Our feelings changed to a comfortable friendship, and we'd never cross a line to interfere with the other's love life."

Bash restated for his clarification. "Then, the real reason for going tomorrow is to show everyone you're not in love."

Callie laughed. "I suppose, but I would like to meet Ginger. Linus plans on asking her hand in marriage next weekend. There is a big

216

public event where he is going to pop the question. I'm sticking my nose into your business because I care about you and Blake. She's had a rough summer. Blake stood up to Dew's bullying, but he is as mean as a riled-up cobra and as venomous as a Komodo dragon. Try not to push a relationship or make her talk about the incident."

Bash took the advice without comment. "Does anyone else want the rest of the eggrolls or sweet and sour chicken?"

Isley said, "Take whatever is left. Leftovers never taste right."

Bash took a container from the counter and filled it. "Thanks. I must study for the quiz on Wednesday. Callie, do you have to give a test so soon?"

"Yes. Let me look and see if I still have vocabulary flashcards in a file."

Callie told Bash to wait, and she disappeared into her office. She returned with a recipe box of index cards. Inside were 3x5 notecards.

Bash asked, "How do you use these?"

Callie didn't react with surprise or exasperation. "These are a study aid."

Removing a rubber band, Callie showed Bash the front of the card. The word read botany, and she told him to think of the definition.

Bash stated. "That one is easy: the study of plants."

"Yes. Flip the card over and check yourself. Take the box. I don't need these back until the end of the semester."

"Cool. Why hasn't anyone ever thought of these before."

Bash collected the food, box, and went to study.

Isley heard the door close. "What are the school systems teaching these days?"

Still and Crabbe stored the food in containers, rinsed the dishes, and loaded the dishwasher. Callie returned to the office, continued dividing photos, and fell asleep with the pictures as a pillow. The next thing Callie felt was someone gently touching her arm and calling her name. Rorke was home.

Callie woke up, greeted him with a cry of joy, and reached up to hug him. "Are you all right? The others?"

"A few bumps and bruises, but everyone's fine."

Rorke refused to release her and buried his face in Callie's thick hair. "I wanted to let you know that I was back and in the house. Are you planning on attending church services at ten?"

"Yes. If you want to cuddle, my shoes and belt have to go."

Callie snuggled against Rorke but could feel his entire body tense. She tried to move to see his face in the dark.

217

"I am fine."

Rorke had their belts off before she moved.

Yawning, Callie said, "I am not sure whether to be impressed, jealous, or disturbed."

Rorke wrapped the woman he loved in his arms. He felt her relaxing back into a deep sleep and went to take a shower. Then, he slept deeply for the first time since he had departed.

***

Sunday morning, Callie took a seat on the pew beside her uncle. Mer was decked out in his goth persona. Rorke sat on her other side.

Mer whispered, "You're almost late."

She responded in similar hushed tones. "The key word is almost. Overslept, and we have to hurry out for the birthday party."

"Great. Leave me to answer the nosey questions about the man you brought to church services."

Callie smiled and patted his arm. "You receive great 'uncle pay.' Free hugs and a yearly birthday present."

Mer negotiated on top of the free pay and hugs. "My salary needs to be more than a hug. A ride to the airport in the morning? I should leave the house at seven."

"Done. Geez, the whispers are loud, and volunteer ushers are looking around. If anyone asks, please don't tell some wild story. Mer, remember, we're in church. Tell the truth. The gentleman is new in town, and we are working together at the university."

"So skip the shacking up part."

Callie's eyes grew wide, and music started, which drowned out any reply.

Rorke drove out to a retreat house near American Falls, but he parked instead of driving up to where valets waited. "Do you mind walking? I am not letting a stranger in my driver's seat."

Callic had been very quiet on the ride over. "Walk slowly. I'm in heels. Rather not mess up my hair and makeup with sweat. I should look my best for meeting Ginger."

"You are much prettier than Ginger."

"Thank you, kind sir. Showering you with praises would be shallow accolades. Are you jealous about my friendship with Linus?"

Rorke admitted. "No. Linus doesn't threaten or concern me, and we friended one another on social media. I've skimmed through everyone's posts and mutual correspondences."

Callie pulled out her phone. "Great. No signal. I wish I had known earlier so that I could review."

218

Rorke grinned slyly. "Let's make an appearance so we may head home. Isley told me that I am way behind on studying for a test and verifying locations in photos."

An hour later, Callie climbed back in the passenger's seat with a sigh of relief. She kicked off the dress shoes that were killing her feet.

Rorke closed his door, started the engine, and carefully maneuvered back to the main road. "I thought Linus was going to have heart failure discovering you and Ginger chatting by yourselves."

Callie looked out the window and remained silent. She didn't offer a defense, opinion, or observations. She deliberately avoided talking.

Rorke decided to confront Callie on her mood. "What's wrong?"

"I'm concerned about the situation with the Dew family. Anyone around me, might be caught in the middle. My stomach knotted up when you confronted that mob. I couldn't protect you and Blake. Firing a weapon would have escalated the situation, and my clip only holds ten with one in the chamber. Plus, I would have aimed for the heart and not a limb."

Rorke was still drained from the rescue and didn't want to argue or debate. "Did you ever consider that you were in danger?"

"I was out of reach on the roof. Could we stop about a mile ahead? I have my backpack, and there were some Baptisia, or False Indigo, growing on the hillside. We're not on federal land, and I would like to collect a couple of the seeds."

They were back on the road within a few minutes, but Callie asked to stop four more places before they reached city limits. They arrived at the house, and Callie did not recognize the vehicle parked at the curb.

Callie watched Rorke's jaw tightened. "Do you know the guest?"

"Yes, and the man does not usually visit with good news."

Rorke parked behind a large station wagon. Callie slipped on her good shoes with heels and climbed out. She almost didn't recognize the man who climbed out of the vehicle.

Callie went and greeted the man. "Ranger Arc, it has been a long time."

The man smiled despite looking tired and worn. "Why, if it isn't Miss Sassy? I am not a ranger anymore and have a desk position. More paperwork but fewer bugs."

"Thanks for never writing me a ticket regarding the rockslide."

Mr. Arc smiled, but the grin was weary. "My coworkers would have never let me live it down if I had. Luckily, I knew you were a certified climber, and Rorke was there for backup. If not, I'd have handcuffed you in the back of my car to keep you off that site. Ms. Rivera, not to be rude, but I have papers to go over that are confidential. You may leave the backpack. I'll sign off on what you collected. Goodbye."

Callie refrained from telling Arc that she didn't need signatures, but she couldn't resist while leaving. "I see part of your life changes include a wedding band, station wagon, and two car seats. Give the family my regards."

Isely waited for her at the back door and advised, "Don't press Rorke into talking."

"I won't, but may I ask why?"

"Familiar with River of No Return?"

"It's a protected wilderness area. Named so because boaters couldn't return upriver after navigating the water downstream."

Isley nodded and told her what he knew of the situation. "The kayakers and climbers did everything correctly. They were a safe, experienced, and cautious team. The preparedness saved at least two lives, but there was still a cost. Rumor is one of the four that Rorke's group rescued died at the hospital. A second is in critical condition."

Callie's eyes filled with sorrow and compassion. "Tort, Whipper, and Thicke went with Rorke. Are they all right?"

"Yes, Plant Princess. I'll bribe you to give them some space and not mother them."

"Didn't we establish, I don't take bribes?"

Isley tried a different tactic. "I have updated satellite images you requested of the locations."

Callie skipped over, gave Isley a huge hug, and kiss on the cheek. "Thanks. I love you. Tell Rorke I'll be in my office."

Isley called down the hall. "What are you doing for supper?"

"I hid a plate of food from Bash last night and stuck the leftovers in the fridge."

"I hate warming up food the day after."

Callie yelled back. "Not my problem."

Rorke entered the kitchen and placed Callie's bag on the counter. "Should I be concerned the lady that I love is kissing you?"

Isley took the playful comment as intended. "I hope so. The girl is a firecracker waiting to go off, and you are holding her. How are you doing?"

"Honestly, terrified. Isley, Callie jumped off the roof without a second thought to the danger. I tried to talk to her about putting herself at risk, and the warning was like spitting into the wind. My mind kept wandering while we were on the trail. The only reason I managed to stay slightly focused was that I knew you were here.

"Even with planning and preparation, people die. The kayakers were experienced, prepared, and reacted as each should. One still died. We did what we could, but help was too late. Isley, if something happens…."

Rorke stopped, sat at the table, and put his head down in his arms. Isley didn't care what people thought about him hugging Rorke. The man put a comforting arm around his friend's shoulders.

"I suppose while you are in a mood, we should talk about what you missed. Callie expressed that her one concern about the Dew family: a mutual transportation company. She didn't voice a worry about retaliation toward herself. Mer and I spent last night revisiting the finances, and he is beyond upset. Her uncle is worried enough that he was ready to resign from his day job and not travel. Mer wants Nod to draw up prenup documents for you to sign without Callie's knowledge."

Rorke picked his head up, and Isley moved to make a pot of coffee. "I wondered why her uncle was giving me murderous glares at church. Isley, I have no problem signing whatever will make the family happy. Not telling Callie is probably wise. She would argue against the idea and create a family rift."

Isley almost spilled the coffee he was spooning into the maker. "Do you think so little of yourself?"

"Has nothing to do with self-confidence. I have my own assets, don't spend beyond my salary, and debt-free except for a car payment. My only problem is controlling my temper, so you're not bailing me out of jail. I was ready to kill Beau's father."

"Jail is the least of your problems. I haven't even touched the other events like girls' night."

Callie continued to work until dinner. Rorke and Isley came in with plates of food. Isley placed her food on the only clear place he could find.

Callie looked and realized the meal was homecooked. "Did Lion make dinner again? Isn't she supervising the girls at the apartment?"

Isley laughed. "Lion refused to eat pizza four nights in a row. She wished to cook a proper meal and doesn't have the kitchen equipment on hand."

Callie would walk over, take a bite, and go back to work. Isley kept reminding her to eat.

Tort wandered in a little while later. "Hey, Teach. Do you have any more flashcards? Bash won't share."

Callie glanced up. "Yes, but aren't you auditing the class?"

"I am not failing a test just because it doesn't count as a credit."

Callie went to the wall behind the desk, pushed a flower, and a drawer popped open.

Tort made a surprised noise but praised, "Love it!"

Callie touched two other flowers, and drawers appeared. "My father didn't want to clutter up space with a dresser. He asked Mr. Burnly to build three drawers in the wall. Isley, the closet is behind you. Slide the faded Blazing Star, or the fluffy purple plant with a tuft on top, toward you."

Callie handed over him the small bundles. "I think there are five sets, and you may share. It's my entire stash."

Tort took the cards and asked, "Any other cool stuff?"

"I wish. The bathroom pipes run beside the closet. Windows run the entire north wall. The South wall is the hall, and the other bathroom pipes with air ducts run next to the dresser drawers. Believe me! If I could renovate and add, I'd have done so years ago. Go ahead and call the others to show them the storage spaces. You are chomping at the bit."

Tort took the cards and went down the hall.

Rorke complained. "Did you think of saving flashcards for me? Do you know how long it has been since I had to take a school exam?"

"Look under the laptop."

"I love you. Thanks."

Callie remained quiet but took a sideways glance at Isley before going back to her stack of photos. If Isley was paying attention to the word exchange, he didn't react. Work ground to a halt as the expedition team, Lion, and Blake crowded into the office.

Slipping away, Callie whispered to Isley that she had to be up at six to take Mer to the airport. Isley nodded, and Callie went to organize her belongings. Monday would be busy, and no one could predict what would happen. She packed two extra sets of clothes in the bag. Checking orders and emails, she tried to braid her hair. Feeling the result, she made a disgusted noise.

Rorke chuckled from the door. "Having trouble?"

"Yes. Rorke, Isley doesn't want me going anywhere alone. Would you be able or willing to work at the cabin after Trix picks up the load tomorrow?"

Rorke walked over, started undoing her braided work, and stared into her eyes through the mirror's reflection. "Yes. Everyone else has gone for the night. Where are you sleeping?"

Callie tilted her head and asked hesitantly. "Is that an invitation or flirting?"

"Inquiry. I have decided not to let you go."

"Rorke, how many times do I need to remind you? There are secrets and things about me that will change those feelings."

"Like?"

"If I explained, the issues would no longer be a secret. I promise no games, but you could drown without even knowing you are in trouble."

Rorke leaned down and kissed her.

Callie came up for a breath of air and whispered, "You are doing it again."

"Knees mushy?"

Callie tried to look cross, but Rorke smiled. "Your tiny bed, a sleeping bag in the efficiency, or down the hall? The guest bed is the best choice of the three."

"I suppose the guest room. You realize Gran is coming home soon."

"Yes. I promise, no sneaking around or in and out of windows. Rosa and I discussed me asking you out for an official date."

Callie pretended not to know that Solomon previously shared everything with Rosa. "I am too tired to be angry or outraged. Next, you are going to tell me you talked to Gran about proposing. Your funeral and not mine. Then you deal with the long list like Mer, Pica, Nod, and Solomon."

Rorke brushed and played with Callie's hair. "Would you be willing to go on a real date? Dinner? Movie?"

"I'd go out on a date with you, but we haven't discussed important topics such as former love interests. The tale of Isley and ex-girlfriend doesn't count."

Rorke had no problem discussing his past. "I've had a few girlfriends, but I've never asked anyone to marry me. Skip ahead a year. Your promises are no longer an issue."

"Would you be tired of stopping to collect seeds?"

"No, but I won't stop and be late a shindig."

Callie asked, "Do you even know the definition of shindig?"

"Party, celebration, dance, or get-together. Would you like to know the origins as well?"

Callie's turned around to smile at Rorke mischievously. "The word derives from shindy or dance."

"My turn to be slightly impressed."

Callie went to move her left side and flinched slightly.

Rorke asked, "When's the last time you took anything for the pain?"

"None of your business."

Rorke didn't argue, led her down the hall, and tucked her under the covers. "I'll be right back."

He returned a few minutes later and undressed.

Callie muttered. "Sorry for not whistling at the free show."

"Here. Take the antibiotic that you didn't take at dinner, and here is ibuprofen and acetaminophen. Each is over the counter."

"Fine, but only because I am too tired to argue."

Callie drifted off nestled in Rorke's warmth.

Chapter

A phone ringing in the house woke Callie the next morning. The sun was up, so she made herself get up and go to the restroom. Coming back, she glanced at the bedside clock and double-checked the time. 10:00 AM. She had slept through taking Mer to the airport and meeting Trix to pick up the load.

Rorke's voice came from the doorway. "Don't panic. I took Mer to the airport and met Trix so he could load the plants."

"What sort of pain killer did you give me?"

"One is for aches. The other is for pain or fever. The combination helps the pain so you may sleep. What else do you need to do before heading out to the cabin?"

Callie sulked about Rorke tricking her and taking over her responsibilities. "You are uninvited."

"Then, you stay home. No driving a car or operating a boat until identifying side-effects of any medication."

Callie pouted while she dressed.

Lion sat in the kitchen making lists. "I hope you don't mind if I borrow the kitchen."

"Guess the college diet did not agree with your system."

Lion made a gagging noise. "If I see or smell pizza in the next week, I may vomit. I'm trying to devise a supply list for groceries and other items. Blake was taking a shower without a curtain, and one of the girls was using a shirt to dry herself after bathing. Someone did a load of laundry without detergent. Lists about packing for college from the internet are only slightly helpful."

Callie placed a hand on Lion's arm in comfort or support. "I'm not trying to pry or interfere. My words are unsolicited counsel. I do not know the other four girls, your financial stability, or job situation. You could go broke supporting five young ladies. Providing four walls, a roof, and having a person who cares is the most important part.

"Before you spend an entire paycheck, Gran put together several moving boxes of basic supplies for an unprepared renter. The equipment is used but clean and sturdy. When you are able, bring back the reusable items. The supplies, like toilet paper, talk to Gran about replacing when she returns."

Lion commented, "Child, you realize the advice is the opposite of everything you have advised, said, or done in the past week."

Callie disagreed. "I have not spent a cent of my paycheck and only been a friend. Let me show you the storage closet. Gran will have better guidance on being in charge after adopting six children."

Lion said, "Show me the closet, and I'll round up the rest of the troops to help. You're not doing anything with those stitches."

Callie wrote Rosa's number on a piece of paper. "Selfishly, I won't argue. Rorke agreed to take me to the cabin. Ask Isley to reset the house alarm when you're finished. He talked my uncle out of a set of keys and security codes. Fair warning, the kitchen, living room, and my office are under surveillance. Any of the expedition team is welcome to anything they might need as well."

Callie led the way to a room off the garage. The closet was more bedroom size. There were containers labeled kitchen, bedroom, bathroom, or electronics.

"We save gently used and unwanted furniture or items the renters leave."

Lion beamed as if Midas had turned her car into gold.

Callie asked, "Are you sure about being a resident assistant? Wait until the stress of midterms or finals comes around."

Lion patted her hair with a sigh. "Go before I change my mind and take you shopping with me."

***

Rorke drove and parked at the Cherry outpost. Ranger Cattail waved to Callie, who went to talk while Rorke checked in with Mr. Cherry.

Cattail looked tired and stressed but greeted Callie with a warm, slight smile. "Thanks for being a friend."

"How are you holding up?"

"A part of me is still in shock. Callie, my husband didn't even try to save the marriage. Divorce is one thing, but the man does not want anything to do with the boys. There will be no contact, visitation, or phone calls. They love him. A lawyer representing him brought the papers back with revisions about the boys. He'll pay a portion of child support but gave up the rest without even saying goodbye."

Rorke finished in the lodge and came over. "Ma'am, if the boys ever want to talk, I'll be glad to listen. Been on my own since I was a boy."

Cattail looked startled. "I thought Isley was your father."

"My birth mother was from the reservation, but my biological father wasn't. We moved a lot. One day, my parents decided that they didn't wish to be responsible for a child. I went to school one daya , and the two vanished. Isley became my guardian later."

"You and Isley should be proud of how you turned out."

226

"Thanks, but I am not telling him. The man has a big enough ego."

The ranger warned the couple. "Be careful. Winds have picked up, and the water is choppy. We've retrieved three boats with seasick pilots and passengers this morning."

Mrs. Cherry joined them. "Callie, could I talk to you?"

Rorke continued to converse with Cattail while Mrs. Cherry brought Callie out of their earshot. "Have you considered renting out the cabin?"

"No."

Mrs. Cherry asked, "Would you think about leasing the property to vacationers? We are looking for additional rentals. Our cabins for the outpost and the forest service places are booked solid for a year out. We would work around your schedule. Let us know the days you be there, and we won't book. I'll admit we have a few mix-ups but not often. We use a certified company for third party contracts. Computers have helped keep errors to a minimum, and the extra money for the owner is worth a few hiccups."

"I'd have to think hard about the offer. My schedule is tight sometimes. I had not planned on a trip today, but the opportunity presented itself. Send me a copy of the contracts and have Ms. Nod take a gander as well."

Mrs. Cherry frowned and tried to keep the disapproval out of her tone. "You start overseeing your affairs next month. Keep in mind that your grandmother and Ms. Nod are not inclined to rent the place. They were honoring the bond between you and your father."

"Thank you for the candid honesty. Any decision will be mine and mine alone."

Mrs. Cherry patted Callie's shoulder. "We'll be able to work something out. Do you feel well? You're a little peaked."

Callie went a few steps, knelt on the ground, and threw up in a clump of shrubs as an answer.

When the heaving stopped, Callie told Rorke. "One word or look that resembles 'told you so'...."

The threat remained unfinished as Callie finished emptying her stomach contents.

Cattail and Mrs. Cherry looked at Rorke for an explanation. "Callie had a slight mishap which required stitches. She ignored the pain meds, but she must take antibiotics. I advised her that eating a greasy breakfast was not a good idea with the antibiotic and generic pain medication."

Cattail laughed. "Good call not letting Callie drive or operate a boat. I wondered how you talked Callie into taking you to the cabin. She usually refuses to let anyone accompany her."

Mrs. Cherry directed Rorke. "Help Callie back to the main building. We'll send someone with a deodorizer for the smell and find a ginger ale. The drink helps settle the stomach."

Cattail's radio beeped for attention, and she left to help the next person. Rorke helped Callie to her feet. She knew the problem wasn't the medication but a shock. The last pieces of the puzzle were in place with Mrs. Cherry's offer. Rentals would be a perfect cover for knowing dates and locations of vacant property. Finding the evidence was easy, once she had the who. Problems would be any spies hiding in plain sight.

Inside, she sat back in a chair, leaned her head back against the wall, and closed her eyes. When Callie felt better, Rorke started the drive back home. He glanced at her worriedly when she asked him to turn off on the main road. The gravel driveway was overgrown but passable. A cabin appeared further down the dirt road.

Callie explained. "Uncle Mer's place. My uncle travels so much that he rarely comes out. Mer rents a room from Wither, so he doesn't have to deal with upkeep on two places. Park inside after I open the garage door."

Rorke parked on the left side and studied the all-terrain vehicles stored on the right. Two motorbikes caught his attention. One had Callie painted on the frame.

Rorke commented. "You are certainly full of surprises. Didn't take you for a motocross girl."

Callie didn't tell Rorke whether she was or wasn't. "Solomon calls each year and asks what I want for my birthday. When I was little, I'd request stuff that my dad wouldn't buy me. One year I asked for a real pony because I was going through a horse phase. Solomon never told me yes or no, but he sent a huge barn playset with four ponies.

"When I could legally drive, he gave me the bikes with lessons. The last couple of years, I told him the best present is taking me out for a birthday dinner and talking to me in person. He sends a gift card for a restaurant instead along with his present. We can take the bikes out to the cabin from here."

Callie took a phone off a small workbench and pushed the one number on speed dial.

Solomon picked up on the first ring. "Hello."

"Hey! You are on speaker with Rorke and me. Water travel was going to be too rough. Is it all right if Rorke takes your bike?

Solomon didn't answer the question immediately. "Glad you are using a birthday present. What would you like this year?"

Callie laughed. "We were discussing your birthday presents. Dinner with the mysterious stranger who has known me since I was born. No loopholes or gift cards, and Gran will have a fit if you pull that Paris stunt."

Solomon joined her laughter, but his chuckle was still unpracticed and sounded strange. "Birthdays come around once a year, and you have never been unreasonable. Nigel and I were both aware that a few of your wishes were an attempt to manipulate your father. We always conferred about my gift. You asked for a meal in Paris knowing full well that I wouldn't take you to France. I thought my solution was quite creative: a French restaurant with a miniature Eifel Tower and reproductions of Louvre art."

"I think that I am slightly disappointed at the confession."

Solomon went back to the subject of the bikes. "I have no problem with Rorke taking my bike, but you're not operating one with the shoulder injury. Ride with him."

Callie made a gargoyle face at Rorke and the phone. "Before we head home, I'm going inside to see if there is anything edible."

Callie returned with a lemon and lime drink, and she nibbled on some crackers.

Rorke grinned. "Let's take a test drive with you as a passenger. I saw a hill about a mile from the here."

"When I drive the bike, the only person on the vehicle is me. I've only ridden double once, and it's a memory that I don't wish to re-live."

Rorke understood her fear and confirmed. "The only time was after your father's accident."

Rorke waited while Callie controlled her fear. When her eyes finally settled from looking everywhere but the bike, Rorke put out a gloved hand.

Callie finally said, "You kill us, I'll haunt you."

"I'll love you in this life and the afterlife."

Callie put on the helmet while Rorke took a seat. After Callie settled, Rorke drove with confidence and expertise. The hill was rocky with about a 45-degree incline. Rorke didn't halt until they reached the top.

The young woman did not climb off with the sexy movements of a model in television commercials. The actress on-screen would stand and remove the helmet with perfectly falling hair as it swished around a dazzling smile. Callie's reaction was to claw her way off while trying to unstrap the helmet. She was twirling and wiggling like an animal with its head caught in a trap. Rorke physically held her and removed the helmet. Free, Callie gasped for air. Then, she threw up the crackers and soda.

Callie crawled upwind and away from the contents of her stomach. She flopped on the ground to let her heart rate and the adrenaline dissipate.

Rorke sat down beside her and let her rest.

Callie's voice sounded tiny and afraid as she asked, "Solomon didn't take me home the night of the accident, did he?"

Pure shock at the question provided Callie the answer, and she whispered, "Why? Why did you let me think?"

Completely thrown by the turn in the conversation, Rorke blurted. "Do not tell Solomon you figured that out! Solomon trusted me."

"Explain, please."

Rorke gathered his thoughts. "Solomon found me at the treehouse and was driving me to the station. We parked, and his cell phone rang. After answering and hanging up, the man was angry, frustrated, but scared. Solomon studied me, which was slightly unnerving. I don't intimidate easily. He asked me if I could ride a motorcycle. When I nodded yes, Solomon made me a deal. He'd make sure I went to juvenile court. My records could be sealed. My part of the bargain was to take someone home and return to the station. There had to be a tremendous amount of trust in the deal. I could have run and disappeared at any time.

"We reached a cabin out in the woods and started looking for someone. Then we heard the explosion. He immediately radioed for help. He panicked until we found you, but you were in shock. Solomon stayed at the scene, and I took you home. How in the world did you identify me as the driver?"

Callie tried to clarify her thinking process. "Every person has a unique of riding and driving. I suppose the mannerism is much like writing. There are details about the night I don't remember. Other things are burned in my memory. I recall the odd way you change gears on the motorbike."

Both stopped talking and became lost in their thoughts. One of the things Rorke loved about Callie was her empathy for others. She reached out to help others while wrestling with her grief and fear. He found trying to understand Callie's mindset was a work in progress. Her next question reinforced the idea because the subject was a complete surprise.

Callie asked, "Were you ever curious about what happened to your parents?"

"No. I'm past the point of angry, grief, or reasons. My biggest issue was survival. I did question what I did or didn't do to warrant their

230

actions. As an adult, there was finally a realization that the problem had nothing to do with me. Isley and I needle one another, but he tried. We managed to muddle through a couple of tough years. I think that he needed me as much as I needed him. Thanksgiving and Christmas were comfortable but disastrous at the same time."

Callie shifted to where she could study Rorke's expression. "Cattail is correct. You and Isley did well. I feared he didn't date because of Dusty or myself. When I asked, my father never answered with a tone of irritation or disappointment. He told me that we were not the issue. Dusty was not wired to be a part of a large family. Her commitment staying with a long project needed work. I am thankful for the wonderful family and people in my life."

The two sat and relaxed in the sunshine on the hill. Neither spoke nor moved for a long while.

Chapter

Tuesday started off normally. They went home after class, and Callie changed clothes before eating lunch. Rorke offered to take and drop her off before running some errands. He wanted to go and return before dinner. Rorke rounded a corner in the driveway but swerved. The driver's side now faced the main road. He was on his phone immediately while telling her to get down.

Callie remained upright in her seat and looked around. Rorke unbuckled her seat belt and pushed her to the floor. Whatever he said was lost in a hail of pings against metal. It took a few seconds for the idea that someone was shooting at them to register. Rorke ordered her to move out of the cab and crouch down by the tire on the passenger side. Callie obeyed, and Rorke followed her.

Callie asked incredulously, "Is someone shooting at us?"

"Yes. The shooter must wish to scare us and stayed off the property."

"Why didn't you keep driving into the trees for cover?"

Rorke answered while scanning the tree line behind them. "The shooter used a quieter weapon to out the engine and front tires. I didn't hear an echo of a discharge. Isley is on his way with reinforcements. When he arrives, you go with him. No argument."

Callie's eyes and jaw hardened. "I am not leaving you."

Isley's car appeared a short time later. He pulled up beside the pair sheltered behind the wheel and rolled down the window. "Appears the immediate area is secure, but we're checking. Callie, crawl into the backseat when Rorke opens the door."

Rorke smiled reassurance when Callie peered at him with a look of defiance.

Callie relented. "Fine, but one of these days, your smile is not going to work."

Rorke opened the rear door. Callie went to stand and climb in, but he put a hand on her head to make her stay low.

Callie asked as Isley backed up and drove toward the house. "Will I be able to collect my bag? It has my gear to check security at BE."

"No. Mer added me onto the system as a guest."

"I'd be annoyed at Mer's actions, but I'm currently too upset to lecture."

Callie retrieved her phone from a pocket and dialed Rorke, who answered on the first ring. "Don't wait up. Love you. Bye."

Callie huffed at being dismissed without being able to talk. "Turn the car around!"

"Sit there and be quiet. Argue, and we go to my office. You'll sit handcuffed to a chair in a cubical and do nothing until I say otherwise!"

Callie crossed her arms and sulked.

Isley decided Callie was already in a mood. "Mer gave me the house codes as well. You were in class, so I let Lion in to take a break from the girls."

"I don't mind. I would ask that you send me a text and reset the alarm. If anyone tried to break-in while Lion's alone, the system would alert us."

Lion was waiting at the back with a worried frown. When they arrived at the house, she found that she couldn't open the door.

Isley turned around in his seat and used a parental voice. "My car has childproof locks. I release the door, and you march into the house. If you try to bolt or leave out a bedroom window, we'll adjourn to wait in my office. Am I clear?"

Mulish, Callie nodded in agreement, and Isley unlocked the door.

Lion opened the screened door and welcomed her into the kitchen. "I've been reading and heated water if you'd like tea."

Callie tried to find a reason to return to see Rorke. "My laptop is in the backseat of the truck. I need it to organize for work and class in the morning."

Isley gave her directions. "Take a shower and let Lion make sure the stitches haven't broken open."

Callie showered, changed into clean clothes, and reentered the kitchen. Isley was on the phone. Seeing Callie, he waved to the counter. He'd brought her backpack with laptop and garden bag.

Lion asked, "Pie?"

"Yes, please."

Isley handed his phone to Callie so Rorke could talk to her. "I'll be filling out reports and talking to the insurance representatives until late."

"I'd rather be there. Is everyone on the expedition team all right? I am aware that they have been taking turns following us."

Rorke reassured her that everyone was fine and ended the call. Callie handed Isley back his phone. The agent went back to pacing and continually checked out the house.

Lion tried to distract Callie. "The items from storage are much appreciated. I spoke to Rosa, and we talked for a couple of hours. Tell me about her. Here is a cup of fresh tea."

Callie peered into the mug. "Did you add anything to the drink?"

"Me? No. I promise."

Callie sipped, and the brew tasted normal. The two talked about family, and Lion stood to rinse out her mug.

Callie leaned over to whisper conspiratorially. "Love the pink bunny slippers. Isley let me borrow a set from a box he bought for presents. I approve of your relationship and won't tell. If Rorke notices, he may figure out the secret. There is an identical pair at Isley's house."

Lion almost dropped her mug in surprise, but Isley wasn't paying attention to Lion as he entered.

The agent asked, "How are you feeling?"

Callie found herself sleepy. "You did something to the tea instead of Lion! I'm not happy."

Isley was quite pleased with himself. "The last thing I need is for you to sneak out of the house. Come on. I'll help you to bed."

***

Wednesday, Callie slept until her alarm clock went off the next morning. Rorke had propped a note against the lamp. He came in late and was heading out to class early. Someone had put something in the tea to help her sleep. Her dry mouth and headache told her that she'd been tricked. Again. That was the last time she was taking a drink from anyone.

Isley was relaxed at the kitchen table and reading the paper with a cup of coffee. "There are eggs, pancakes, turkey sausage, and juice. We leave in fifteen minutes for the university."

Callie dished up and squelched her wish to lash out in anger about Isley's tea. "Thank you for breakfast. I would not have snuck out the window."

Isley put the paper down. "Do you know why I rather investigate instead of babysit?"

"No."

"People are unpredictable and do not follow directions. Complicating the matter is human nature: flight or fight response; protector verse protected; leader or follower. Every situation has variables, and one carefully weighs what action to take. There are times for defense. Other times, playing offense is the best choice. You are the worst type of person to protect because you feel the need to protect and allow emotions to rule that need. The combination makes my life suck. The only reason you are not in a safe house or under guard is the fact that you are bait."

Callie grinned. "Glad to help make your life complicated. What else?"

"Rorke believes, wrongly, that he can control and counter your actions in a dangerous situation. I am walking a fine line with my role and level of interference already. Overplaying or underplaying could be disastrous."

Isley escorted her to his vehicle, and Callie asked politely. "May I sit in front?"

"Yes."

While they were going to the university, Callie decided to ask Rorke's parents. "What do you know about Rorke's biological parents? He told me a little, and you would have researched their whereabouts. I don't care about their lives or making amends. My concern is his mother or father coming back in his life and hurting him."

"They won't. Rorke's biological mother died of a heart attack fifteen years ago. Father has a new family and refuses to admit to a first marriage, much less a child. I don't think Rorke's parents are why you are wearing a worried expression. What's wrong?"

Callie answered. "My warning bells are ringing about a member or members of the expedition team. Each man went through a rigorous screening process. I am the child Solomon promised to protect, and my opinion does not count. Solomon is not taking me seriously, secretive, and feels a huge responsibility. I'll use your descriptions. He is a leader, fighter, and protector. The problem is Solomon decides, and the choice is ironclad. There is no gray area. Trust or untrustworthy. Reliable or unreliable. My intent on sharing is not to create discord with you and Solomon."

Isley asked without judgment. "What is your intention?"

"If, and I preface with if, a member is compromised, Solomon's plan is worthless. He didn't tell anyone, even Rorke, that he provided me a set of false coordinates. If the team is compromised or forced to find evidence, he wants me to lead them to the location."

Isley understood where Callie's concern and restated, "Solomon's trap would turn into an armed confrontation with hostages."

"Yes. Rorke does not know, and I wanted someone else to be aware of the problem. I appreciate you not telling me that I'm overly paranoid and an untrusting person."

Isley asked candidly. "Let's say that my nature is to be suspicious of friend and foe. Do you have an alternate plan?"

"Honestly, too many variables are in play. There are roughly eighty-four thousand square miles of Idaho. Granted, less than thousand is water, but we're dealing with mountain ranges, lakes, rivers, plateaus, and a crater. As we cull through data, an opportunity may present itself."

235

"Don't seize that opportunity if on the defensive. We don't know who is involved and at what level. Let me see what I am able to find out without raising flags."

Isley made the turn onto the campus and bypassed the parking garage.

Callie reminded Isley. "Uh, you missed the turn. Vehicles are not allowed on side streets of the campus."

"I have a special permit to drive on campus, and we're using a side door. Agent Monarch, Moss's assistant, is going to meet you at the door and escort you to class."

Callie felt trapped, but the trap was her own making. She had agreed to be the bait.

Chapter

Agent Monarch opened the door to the building and greeted Callie. "Hello, ma'am."

"Hello, Agent Monarch."

"You remember me."

"Of course. I never forget a handsome, chiseled face."

Monarch blushed. "May I ask a personal question: are you seeing anyone?"

Monarch just made his critical error, and Callie prayed she didn't slip. She'd learned early to research and study every player on the field. Monarch had fallen into an unknown category. There was underlying friction between Moss and Monarch. Their differences could be chalked up an age gap. An older generation paired with an assistant who could be his grandchild's age. Yet, Dusty's training provided additional insight. Monarch's jaw tensed when Moss introduced his assistant. There had been keen interest in Callie's words about the photos. Monarch had been in the classroom, but he found a way not to accompany the group to BE when trouble brewed. Lastly, the man's reputation preceded him. Politically inclined, he used his connections to work the system. He dated ladies whom he could manipulate or acquire information. Valley called his method 'wining and dining for a payoff'."

Callie asked shyly, "Did you travel all this way to ask me out?"

"Agent Moss asked me to make a visit in person and make sure that you are all right. I'm using the opportunity to inquire. I would not interfere with your friendship with Rorke. I know he took the case because he is the best qualified and an old friend."

Monarch's words made Callie's blood turn ice cold, but she smiled sweetly and remained controlled. "I didn't realize that you had worked together."

"We have only crossed paths. Law enforcement asks when a case needs an outdoor guide or source, and he is the best. When Isley found out Rorke was helping because of you, Isley was angry and went straight to Moss. The meeting was closed, but Rorke is still involved, so Isley lost the battle."

Callie chuckled at the image of Isley losing the battle. "Isley certainly had his Karma messed up. The agent ended up babysitting me and being the referee on the book project."

"Moss about had a heart attack reading the daily update, and he doesn't ruffle easy. Did Isley tell someone to send a message about going to hell if they had complaints?"

"Basically. Isley changed his mind and decided to devise a politically correct response. Could we continue our conversation in a moment? I need the restroom before standing in front of a class for an hour and a half."

"Sure."

Callie slipped into a stall for privacy. She put her head against the cool metal and closed her eyes. Rorke accomplished what very few had ever done. He'd wound his way through her defenses and then betrayed that trust. The man she loved would protect her with his life, but he told her that Solomon volunteered him. Then there was the conversation about Rorke owing Solomon. At least, Linus was truthful about his direction in life and never purposely misled her. The truth was Rorke volunteered with Moss.

Solomon's vetting process required an update. Control. No emotional outburst. No drama. No tears. Deep breath. Smile. Friendly. Pleasant. Interested in others. She'd expected the action from Dusty.

Hearing the flushing of the toilets, she retucked her shirt. It would appear to anyone outside the stall that she'd used the restroom. Back straight, she washed her hands and exited the bathroom. Callie asked to revisit a dinner invitation once her part with Nigel's pictures ended. Agent Monarch walked with her into the auditorium and waved to Rorke, who returned the hand motion.

Rorke was sitting at the main desk and scanning several pages of notes.

Callie put her bag down and asked, "Are you all right?"

"I am fine. What are your plans for lunch?"

"Brought a sandwich to eat. I am way behind on unpacking seeds that I gathered on our field trip. They need to be stored and cataloged. When you have time, I wanted to show you a couple of pictures. Satellite images and the photo don't exactly match, but my experience with the type of maps is limited."

"How about we swing by the house? I'll take the images with us to BE. I'll study while you poke holes in the dirt. When Isley is done at the office and can stay with you, I should go shopping."

Callie nodded as students filed in and took their seats. After the quiz started, a woman took out her phone and began texting. Callie quietly went over, picked up the test paper, and whispered to take the call in the hall. The woman argued that the test just started, and she wasn't looking up answers.

Callie smiled with a detached expression. "Take the phone outside. Ms. Heist, you're auditing, and the grade doesn't count. Others are taking the test for college credit."

The woman sounded like she was hissing. "The text is important."

Callie handed Ms. Heist her backpack, walked to the rear door, and ushered the woman out to the hall. The door closed and locked automatically behind them. During class, security dictated that the doors remain locked. A person had to have a key or be let inside.

The computer tech had worked with Callie in the past. He handed Callie a note that he'd sent an Email to the deans. The teacher nodded appreciatively and made a thumb's up sign for a good job. Once the test was over, Callie told the class that they would take a ten-minute break before the lecture portion.

Ms. Heist reentered and approached Callie. "Ms. Rivera, I apologize for texting and interrupting the test."

"My understanding is that students auditing the class are volunteering. If there is a conflict with schedules, we could work out a solution."

Ms. Heist took a step into Callie's face and spoke with the venom of a viper attacking. "The ice queen's holier than thou attitude may fool the men overseeing the project. They see a courageous, wide-eyed little orphan who needs a strong, male figure. The men are watching every move and hanging on every word hoping for a piece of ass. I know better."

Callie's expression never wavered. "Let me save some time. I guess a supervisor chewed you out and ordered you to apologize. My passion is playing in the dirt and nurturing seeds. Plants are less judgmental and much quieter.

"I'll be more than happy to turn everything over to you for the lecture. Please teach in my place for the male species' attention. Here are my notes. The teaching assistant, also a computer tech, will work the presentation for you."

Callie picked up her bag and left out the rear door. Rorke met her in the hall with a questioning look, and Callie noticed he was limping.

"We're not in a typical learning environment, and Ms. Heist is teaching the rest of my class. I have the tests, and we're ahead of official lesson plans. Homework is on the board."

Rorke wasn't sure how to respond except to say. "You're not leaving alone. Hold on."

Still and Crabbe joined her. They headed outside, and Callie sent a text to Wither. Rorke altered Solomon and Isley. The two agreed that

239

Still and Crabbe go back to class after she locked herself in the greenhouse. Many people were monitoring her father's garden. The surveillance probably including every angle, including upside down. Three hours was probably the maximum time she had before anyone knocked.

After the ambush yesterday, she had mulled over whether to put her scheme into motion. Agent Monarch's appearance and the knowledge of Rorke agreeing to help months ago made her choice easy. Time to gather the final fragments of the puzzle. There were a few last pieces to collect. Hopefully, she could have the overall picture in the next day or two. Each passing hour, the danger grew exponentially, and her fears increased at the same rate.

If the data confirmed her suspicions, she'd launch the snowball down the mountain and wait for the tiny orb to gather speed and mass. There would be no stopping the resulting avalanche of consequences that followed.

Callie walked straight to the computer office. She went to the back and uncovered an old computer. The computer relied on a disk operating system and connected to the outside world using a landline. The computer term was using the intranet. When started, the machine whirred, and a fan kicked on.

She pulled out a folder with a command cheat sheet and prompted the query. "Are you still receiving messages here?"

While she waited to see if an answer popped up, she used a modern laptop to update spreadsheets.

A beep broke the silence, and words scrolled across the screen. "Whoa! Welcome to the dark side of the universe. Are you dying?"

Callie made sure the command signs were correct for the programming. "Physically fine, but over my head in another area. Need a fairy godmother's advice. Problem is that the assistance could lead to clipped wings or the death of a fairy."

"That is serious. What advice?"

Callie answered. "Need everything on nine individuals to include any nasty skeletons in the closet. Untraced info and ASAP. Tomorrow night at the latest."

A reply came back. "When you go dark, you go all the way. Hit me. Owe you."

Callie tried to make sure that the person on the other end understood the danger. "No. Beyond favors. Entire Fairyland will fall and burn if anyone found remotely poking."

"Hit me."

240

Callie sent the list. "Pend Isley, Rorke Asher, Till Still, Rab Crabbe, Nash Bash, Rap Whipper, Mort Tort, Pike Thicke, and Agent Monarch at FBI state office. DO NOT take chances."

A part of her was glad that Ms. Heist made a scene. Monarch had dropped a ton of bricks on her about Rorke. Distance from Rorke would help her focus and bury emotions. The man had deceived her, but she was more upset at herself. She'd lowered the defenses, and the walls had been breached. Granted, she allowed the flaming arrows through the barriers to burn the center of her heart.

Old fashioned gardening and a good cry would help. There was one area where surveillance had a blind spot. Going to the most fragrant part of the greenhouse, she entered a plastic partition that sectioned off clematis, oriental lilies, irises, and heliotrope. A person who entered the area would immediately need tissues for running noses and eyes. Anyone joining her would never know that she was crying.

Her estimated time of three hours was on target as the doorbell buzzed. Using the computer pad, Callie answered without moving from the Sweet Alyssum she was pruning.

"Hello?"

Rorke's voice asked, "Would you let me inside? Somehow, Isley has access but not me."

"I will allow you access if you tell me why you are limping?"

"I'm fine."

Callie refused to accept the statement. "No answer. No entry. Goodbye."

Rorke was a bit surprised and pushed the buzzer again.

Callie asked, "Truth?"

"Stop being a spoiled brat and unlock the door."

Callie listened as Rorke took out his phone and called Isley. Callie gave Rorke credit for telling Isley the truth. Callie couldn't hear Isley's response, but the reply wasn't what Rorke wanted to hear. Rorke left, and he was clearly irritated. A part of her was glad to see him in pain, but the other side of her shattered into pieces.

Her phone rang, and Callie heard Isley's annoyance at having to play referee. "What is going on?"

Callie sniffled. "I provided Rorke a choice. Tell me why he is limping, or I'd see him at the house later."

"Are you crying?"

"You clip Alyssum without eyes watering, and I'll grant you three wishes."

241

Callie disconnected and found herself starting to cry all over again. Isley arrived and used his guest code to enter.

Isley phoned Callie from the lobby area. "Where are you?"

Callie replied sweetly. "Working."

"Direct me to your location!"

Callie had left the cart up by the locker room, provided directions, and watched the cart's progress. They'd have to enter the next area on foot and walk. Isley took about four steps through the plastic and retreated.

Isley called. "I know you are watching. Point made. Come out."

Callie came from the loading dock area, and Isley stated. "You are done for today."

"Am I?"

Isley was not amused. "Don't test my patience, young lady! Are you quite pleased with the commotion you created?"

"Was there a disturbance?"

Callie climbed into the driver's seat and listened to Isley's lecture. The topic for their entire ride was her behavior. He was thankful that he had the foresight to stream the classes to his office and knew what happened.

After Callie parked, she interrupted Isley and locked eyes with him. "Finished ranting?"

"Why?"

Callie handed Isley a small binder. "I make no pretense that the class is recorded and clearly state the rules. Students sign a form saying that they have read and understood the policies. The university has a no-tolerance policy on bullying and threats. Another word of lecturing, you may find yourself needing a remedy for stinging nettles."

Isley stared opened mouthed at Callie as she turned off the lights and went outside. Callie started to walk to the house, and Isley silently fell in step with her after setting the alarm system.

Isley finally spoke. "I apologize. Part of me wanted to strangle the woman for how she treated you. If the knowledge helps, I backed your play."

"Jealousy and self-entitlement are not new. Step in and interfere in an argument, the next contest will escalate. I do not need help fighting a battle of wills with a student."

Callie didn't care whether she had Isley's support on the matter. "Is Rorke all right other than being stubborn?"

"Yes. He's limping because his shoes were too small. He was going shopping yesterday, but the shooting took place. He's out shopping."

"I'm not going to let him off the hook, and he'll have to share. You are lucky. I should be giving you both the silent treatment after the temper tantrum."

"Understood. You realize that Rorke is liable to be obstinate."

Callie wondered at her feelings of stubbornness on the matter. Was she making Rorke tell her out of spite because she hurt? Then, again, why care? The man lied to her. She wanted to trust him and have Rorke trust her. "I am very good at the silent treatment."

Chapter

Callie went from the quiet greenhouse to mass confusion at her house. Everyone had BE and her under guard, but no one seemed to care about her home. Surveillance was off, and an invasion had taken place. The expedition team was lounging throughout the kitchen, living room, and dining room. Lion and her five charges were in the office. Blake was showing them the dresser drawers and closet.

The noise was loud enough that Callie never heard the doorbell ring, but Isley brought Pickle to the office. Pickle was shy, especially around new people. Blake made introductions using Pickle's first name, Brine. Brine was sensitive to her name. If Pickle was comfortable imparting her full name to Blake, the two worked well together. Brine socialized for a short period and motioned to Callie.

Brine asked softly, "Would you mind if we spoke outside? I'd rather talk where our conversation is private."

"Let me tell Isley we're having a girl chat. I rather not create panic over a last-minute vacation."

Brine smiled at the memory. Callie was referring to the same trip that Sumo had spoken about at the team building complex. Callie and Brine had wanted to go to the Boise Balloon Festival. Brine was five years older and had a car. They left notes for Nigel and Gran about their trip but took off without asking permission. Her father and grandmother did not find the messages until Callie texted five hours later. The girls announced that they had arrived safely and checked into the hotel. Callie and Brine headed to the festival to eat and check out the balloons.

Callie thought her father's rules about her movements were strict, stupid, and too authoritative. The only reason she thought he might be lenient was that she was with Brine.

Gran called Brine a short time later, and she had to stick a finger in her ear to hear. Gran spoke to her for several minutes, and Brine hung up with a grin.

"Guess what? Your dad and grandmother are joining us. Gran asked if we had enough money, gave me the stranger danger lecture, and made me promise not to leave your side until an adult arrived. A friend of your father, Sumo, is meeting us with extra cash and has the code word."

Callie made an annoyed face but didn't complain. A gentleman in a suit appeared at the appointed place and time. The man was tall, handsome, and graceful.

Sumo introduced himself and tried to say. "Omphalodes Cappadocica."

Callie laughed. "Close enough for an amateur. It is also a flower called Starry Eyes. Are you a movie star?"

"No. Is this your first time at the festival?"

"Yes. The colors are as bright as the garden flowers."

Sumo gave a tour of the festival. He told them about hot air balloons and ballooning history. Gran and Nigel arrived less than three hours later. Sumo joined the family for dinner and the activities for the weekend. Nigel and Sumo went out after the girls were in bed to spend some time catching up.

Later, Callie shared with Brine that her father did not reprimand her until they were home. He threatened to take a switch to her backside if she ever pulled such a stunt again. Nigel had never threatened her with a spanking, and Callie was angry at the scolding. Callie had done the right thing, left notes, and called. The episode was the beginning of Nigel and Callie arguing about rules and restrictions surrounding her activities. A part of Brine felt guilty, but Nigel and Rosa never brought the subject up with her.

Callie walked outside and saw Brine's face filled with a look of reminiscing.

Brine asked, "Did you send Sumo a Starry-Eyed flower on his birthday?"

"I did. Are you thinking about the Balloon Festival?"

"Yes. Sumo always returns the flower on his next visit, which is usually your birthday. Do you know if he is going to be able to have dinner with you this year?"

"No idea."

Brine started sobbing, and Callie went around to the driver's door and hugged her friend. While she comforted, Callie scrunched herself next Brine, turned on the engine and radio. Then she reached into her pocket and hit a button on her phone. A revolving jamming signal would ensure that the conversation remained private.

Callie stated. "No one will be able to overhear us. What's wrong?"

"Nigel took those pictures all over the walls."

Callie explained. "The authorities found a report and a box of prints that my father filed before he died. How do you know he took the photos?"

Brine answered with gulps of air. "I recognized a couple of the images. Callie, before he died, he started to investigate counterfeit seeds. When I discovered the maps, he promised that he had arranged to hand over the evidence. Two days later, he died in a car accident. Then, the fire destroyed the cabin. I thought research, books, camera, and everything burned."

Callie felt lightheaded and nauseous. No wonder her father never told anyone. An unexpected fragment of the puzzle turned into a dagger that pierced her heart. Callie's world came crashing down for a second time in twelve hours. Deep Breath. No emotion. Smile. Reassure.

Gently, Callie's soothed and comforted. "Walking into the office must have been a shock."

"Shock and surprise. I'd forgotten how good Nigel was at composition and design. Dear Lord, I feel ill. I owe my entire life to your family. Why do you have the box?"

"Someone in law enforcement discovered the box in storage and wanted to follow up. My father labeled each sheet and asked if I'd translate his notes. Who else knew about the investigation at the time?"

"No one. Nigel was pretty upset that I found him studying the maps. The only thing that he shared was that he thought dangerous people were into illegal dealings."

Callie sorted and compartmentalized her research inside her mind. "Did you tell anyone?"

Brine looked horrified. "No. I would never endanger Nigel, Rosa, or you."

"How about a conversation on counterfeit merchandise?"

"One of Nigel's friends from college, who worked for the state at the time, came to pick up a huge order for an event. I knew that Nigel trusted him and asked what he knew about the subject. Callie, is looking into Nigel's research dangerous?"

"No. The report and pictures are ten years old. Currently, our biggest problem is the Dew family."

Brine had been eighteen when Nigel died and taken on the responsibility of managing BE. Callie comforted Brine and found she couldn't be angry or hateful toward her friend.

Crabbe exited the house, came over to the car, and eyed the two trying to sit in the same seat. "Is the man you went on those dates with last month, Mr. Teton, causing more drama?"

Brine's head came up and gazed accusatory at Callie.

Callie defended herself. "I swear that I never said a word."

Crabbe's deep voice was coaxing and soothing. "The girls from Lion's place wanted to know why Pickle was so upset, and Blake told them about Teton's antics. If Blake has the story correct, the man broke up on the phone. The reason being that you weren't sexy enough. Men like Teton are fools and give the rest of us a bad name."

Brine slid down in the seat and would have crawled under the car if possible.

Crabbe explained. "I thought men could be vicious, but girls are a nest of vipers when riled. Isley and Lion want Callie to try and talk some sense into the girls. They collected phones before they go hunting."

Brine groaned. "Callie, I'm so sorry."

Crabbe asked, "If I am not intruding, may I ask why the tears? If I were you, I'd be glad to see Teton in the rear-view mirror."

Brine was too embarrassed to share aloud, so she took out her phone. After clicking a couple of buttons, she handed Crabbe the phone. Teton had sent Brine scathing advice on improving her looks and losing weight. The good part was that the texts were private and not public.

Crabbe didn't comment. "Ah, that explains why Isley and Lion are taking phones and locked themselves in the kitchen. The girls were looking up castration and discussing who didn't mind a little blood."

Callie sighed. "Isley may have to put Mr. Teton in protective custody until their tempers have cooled. I am surprised Rorke hasn't used his honey words to talk them down."

"He's trying but without success."

Callie took the laptop that Crabbe handed her and logged into the security system. It wasn't on, but she could see what was going on inside via the cameras. Isley and Lion sat at the kitchen table and discussed what to do next.

Switching the image, Callie blurted. "Oh, thank you, dear angels! Gran won't be home for a few days."

Crabbe's image of stirred up vipers was accurate. The dining and living room had turned into a war zone. The girls had dragged buckets of party supplies to the main hall from a storage closet. The men had given up trying to talk sense, but the girls were loud and angry. Lion's girls filled the water balloons and threw them from one side of the room. The boys used the movable furniture to shield and barricade the hall to the kitchen side. When a balloon sailed through the air, the intended victim would try to catch the missile. Then, if one of the girls tried to run across the room, a water balloon would be tossed at the runner.

Brine wasn't sure whether to laugh or cry.

Callie turned to Crabbe. "Please, don't let Brine drive home until she feels a little better."

Brine protested. "I'll stay and help clean up."

"No. If you say anything, it might poke the nest again. Crabbe, I'd feel better if you made sure Brine gets home all right."

247

Crabbe agreed to the plan. "Fine by me. I rather not be pelted with more cold water. Managed to escape with only one balloon burst on my shirt."

Brine offered a compromise. "I want to make sure things settle before I leave. The curtains are open. Callie?"

"All right."

Crabbe peered uneasily at the two ladies. "You want to spy into a house that has water dripping down the inside of the windowpanes."

Callie called Isley's phone. "Could you hand me my car keys out the kitchen window? Crabbe and Brine are sneaking up to the bay window to make sure I don't wring anyone's neck."

"Hurry up. I have to be up early for work, and my bedtime is soon."

Isley opened the window and screen to toss the keys to Callie. The agent had at least three wet spots from water bombs. Callie grabbed an air horn from an emergency bag in her trunk. Entering her bedroom from the window, she came up behind the girls.

Pressing the button to set off a shrill siren, the girls immediately stopped talking or shouting and covered their ears.

Callie commanded. "Ladies! That is quite enough!"

When movement halted, Callie shared, "I appreciate the outrage on behalf of my friend, but we have taken care of Mr. Teton. If you seek retribution, you will have wasted justice previously exacted. The only person that would be hurt by more interference would be Brine."

Blake was the first to stand and demand. "How?"

"A friend of ours is, um, an expert at handling bad dates. She friended Teton on a dating site and went out with him for drinks. Later, she took down her profile but left a scathing review that did not attack his manhood. The assessment spoke about his lack of manners and boring conversation. Men get vindictive if their his physical assets or sexual experience are judged. Teton also developed a severe case of hives. The type that makes you miserable and requires a doctor's visit."

Blake started to cry. "I hope he is still suffering."

Callie ordered from her position in the hall doorway. "Retrieve your phones and collect your stuff so that I may finish grading tests."

Bash's voice came from behind Gran's dining room table. "Man! I hoped to find out how I did tomorrow." Callie knew that the table was heavy, but the men had turned it on its side to use.

Callie took the empty bucket and collected the unused water balloons as the girls marched past. Everyone cleared the area until Callie and Rorke were alone.

Rorke smiled. "Thank you for ending the silent treatment."

Callie returned the smile, but her eyes were as hard as diamonds. Before Rorke could react or move, Callie threw four missiles with accurate aim. Each balloon burst on impact as it hit Rorke's forehead, face, chest, and stomach. Callie had forgotten Crabbe and Brine at the window, and she heard a quick scurry from the window and battle zone. She took the container to her office without a word.

Chapter

Isley entered half an hour later and shared the cleanup progress. "The children have returned the furniture to its rightful place and mopped up. Nothing was broken or dented, but Mr. Burnly should check a few wet spots to make sure water did not compromise the wallboard."

"Thank you for supervising the not so fun chore of cleaning up and making everyone help out."

Isley grinned. "Don't mind at all. I like directing."

Callie could imagine that he enjoyed giving directions and told Isley. "The graduate assistant, Ms. Roach, texted me and is on her way with the rest of the tests. I'll scan, check the grading, and input the grades. I need to find the sample contract we used. I'll be in Gran's office. If I don't hear the doorbell, please, don't scare Ms. Roach. She'll want to hand the tests directly to me and not a third party."

Isley pretended to be hurt. "I shall greet the young lady with a bright, sunny smile. You'll be happy to know that Rorke bought new shoes and clothes for teaching."

Callie nodded and went to Gran's office, where records of BE were stored in a closet vault. She scanned dates on the filing cabinets, pulled open a drawer, and quickly flipped through several ledgers until she found the correct book. She looked at the receipts and pickup orders for two days before her father died.

A woman who looked to be about sixteen knocked and entered Gran's office. Roach, the teaching assistant, had short, auburn hair with bright green eyes. Lion hair was bright red, but Roach's was a much darker shade. Her naturally curly hair bounced as she walked. Ms. Roach was more than an assistant. She was a computer hacker and a good one. The woman stayed low profile and had never be caught. Callie had helped her with a life issue, and Roach told her if she ever needed anything to make contact. Callie had not wanted to involve anyone else, but she needed help.

Roach handed over a bunch of folders and slipped a burner phone in Callie's pocket. "Hey, teach! I heard about the commotion when I picked up the tests from the office."

"I suppose the rumor mill is spilling over with gossip."

Roach shared with a mixture of awe and envy in the tone. "Do you realize the hero worship and jealousy attached to the story? How many professors would love to say the same thing to a student but are worried about getting fired? The student's actions were recorded, and you handled the situation with grace. Many teachers end up on the news in a bad way because of some negative comment or standing up for themselves."

Callie made a sad face. "Wither warned me that the student filed a formal complaint. I must report to the dean's office for a scolding before class. I'll receive a formal reprimand as well."

The phone dropped in Callie's pocket was untraceable and prepaid. She typed in a number from memory and then a message. "A journey's end with promises to keep. My father's garden is in danger, and his defenses breached. Death is creeping close to all the flowers, but one Anemone sees the threat. The flower will face and embrace death by the next sunset to save the rest. Starry Eyed." She saved the message as a draft.

Roach continued the conversation about the test in case anyone decided to interrupt. "No! That is wrong!"

"So much for truth, right, and the American Way. I appreciate your help in grading. The number is a ridiculous amount to grade in one day."

Frowning at the coded timeframe in Callie's statement, Roach confirmed the one day. "A project's due date sneak up quickly. You are more than welcome to help me with a project tomorrow instead of being unfairly lectured."

Callie sighed wistfully. "I wish, but my fate is sealed. It'll take me two hours to input grades. I want to finish tonight. Then, after class, I'll escape and care for my beautiful, blooming, babies."

Ms. Roach nodded in understanding but with tears in her eyes. Callie wanted her message sent in two hours. The rest of Roach's assignment would take place tomorrow on Callie's signal.

Roach whispered, "The world is a much better place with your colorful life in it. Good luck. If I...."

Callie stopped her friend from saying anything further. "Thank you for going above and beyond."

Callie took the papers back to the office and entered the grades. While working, she flipped through the files that Roach gave her.

Callie's mind raced with the last pieces of the puzzle: her conversation with Mrs. Cherry, Brine's admission, and the team's information. Ten years of watching, waiting, designing, revising, and forming plans. A decade of standing in her father's shadow, attempting to protect family and friends.

After her father's funeral, Callie waited until she thought no one would care about her movements. She found the research within two weeks and continued his work.

Gran gave her a lot of freedom to travel because of Solomon's influence. The man promised to make sure Callie always had a companion that he trusted. Gran would drop her off at Cherry's orchard, and Callie could accompany forest rangers or join various activities. She knew that Solomon had someone follow her on hikes or trails. It took her a little while to figure out a way to discover and surprise the person. Callie was shocked to find out her fellow traveler was Sumo.

Once Callie had a driver's license and car, she spent every possible moment investigating on her own. Collecting seeds and flowers was an excellent reason to travel. Well, almost alone. She knew that Solomon always had someone following her, and Callie decided to find out their identity. The surprise on Sumo's face when Callie snuck up on him was worth the pain of his reaction. She found herself on the ground and a gun trained on her.

Sumo identified Callie and immediately relaxed. Then, he realized Callie's leg was bleeding and took his shirt off to stop the blood flow.

Callie recognized the symbol and reached up to touch Sumo's chest. She admitted to her role the night of the accident and shared her father's fears about Solomon going off the rails. Sumo understood Solomon's protective nature and agreed with Nigel's assessment.

The two decided the best plan was to be patient. Callie did not tell Sumo everything about Nigel's evidence, and she did not divulge the information that Solomon was her biological father.

Callie asked if Sumo would tell her about the night the poachers raided the camp. Sumo wouldn't tell her much. The adults had hidden the boys and girls to protect them, but they could see and hear.

Sumo taught Callie about the animals, surviving in the woods, and tracking. If Callie went to the cabin, Sumo was nearby in a cave above the house or at Mer's place.

As Callie's trust in the relationship grew, she approached Sumo about setting a trap. Nigel's puzzle would have a solution without compromising safety. The catch was that they might not ever catch the prey. If the time arrived where friends or family were in danger, Callie would have a fallback position. Sumo agreed.

They scouted for the perfect place. The terrain was rough and hard to reach. A photograph Callie possessed showed the ten evidence bags her father had hidden. Callie and Sumo recreated the bags in the photo. Then, they carried the bags, along with supplies, to the hiding place. Additional packs of food, communication equipment, and water were stowed. Sumo took out cameras to camouflage and rigged the area with defensive measures. Every so often, he checked to make sure nothing was disturbed. He flatly refused to take her back out to check.

Callie never disclosed to Sumo, or anyone else, that she possessed every piece of Nigel's research. If Sumo remained in the dark, he never had to lie to anyone. A person couldn't be forced to tell what he didn't know. Sumo became the biggest variable.

Once Sumo received her secret text about midnight, Callie fully expected Sumo to confess to Solomon. Sumo would tell Solomon about their snare to catch the criminals. The problem for Sumo and Solomon was that Callie had devised a contingency measure. She setup up the identical scene at a different location.

Lives hung in the balance, and she wasn't taking chances. The enemy had sophisticated communications and the ability to mobilize quickly. Solomon's network was compromised, and he underestimated the scope of the poachers' power and network. The best she could do now was spring the trap and collect as much evidence as possible.

Rorke knocked and politely asked, "May I come in to apologize?"

"Apology accepted."

Rorke leaned on the door. "Do you need your hair braided?"

"No."

Rorke finally admitted. "My leg is fine. Shutting you out was not my intention. I am used to dealing with problems and forging ahead without a fuss. I was limping because my dress shoes hurt and developed blisters."

Callie grinned good-naturedly but yawned. "Was that so hard?"

Rorke said, "Come on. Let's go to bed."

The hardest thing Callie ever did in her life was to make her body move to embrace Rorke. Solomon omitting information was expected, but Rorke's betrayal about volunteering stung. Lies were difficult for her to forgive. She hid hurt and disappointment because she still trusted Rorke to protect her family. There was not a doubt in her mind or heart that Rorke would give his life to defend those she loved.

Rorke's phone rang at two in the morning. Callie woke up slightly until Rorke swore and started dressing.

Callie came fully awake. "What's wrong?"

Rorke debated and told her. "Dew's cronies started a dust-up, and Isley needs reinforcements. The team is going to camp out here for the rest of the night. Teach my class if I'm late?"

"Not a chance."

Callie let the other six expedition members into the house.

She wasn't sure where to have them sleep, but Crabbe smiled, "We brought sleeping bags. What time do you have to be up?"

"Six-thirty. I have to see Wither before class to sign papers."

The men started rolling out their bags, and Tort said, "When you go back to bed, leave the bedroom door open."

Chapter

Callie entered the kitchen to the smell of bacon, eggs, grits, and waffles. She took a plate and dished up food.

Thicke waved a spatula in the air. "Bash, Crabbe, and Still went to shower." Tort and Whipper sat at the table reading.

Callie ate most of her food before asking, "Is that the reading assignment for Rorke's class?"

"Yes. Did you read the assignment?"

"Went to the internet for a summary and was able to complete the online questionnaire."

Tort arched an eyebrow. "You cheated?"

"No. I used the abridged version instead of long."

Suddenly, Callie's eyes widened. "Abridged instead of long! I know the solution."

Callie dropped her fork and ran into her office. Selecting six of the photos from the wall, she went back to the kitchen. Tort, Whipper, and Thicke were gathering bags to take her to school.

Callie smiled. "I have to be early. You don't."

Tort said, "Our directions are to drive you. What has you so excited?"

She waved a handful of pictures. "Road trip. I know the answer to my father's riddle."

Tort nodded and said, "We'll talk and pack later for a field trip. If not, you'll be late."

The teams climbed into three different vehicles and drove to campus. Still and Crabbe walked with Callie to the administrative offices while the others went ahead to the auditorium.

Wither sat at his desk and smiled when Callie knocked. "Ms. Rivera, please close the door and have a seat."

Callie left the door and had a seat. Wither stood up and shut the door.

"We will make this short and sweet. Signature is not an admittance of wrongdoing. Sign the forms saying we talked. We are done with the subject as far as we're concerned."

Callie read the forms and put her name at the bottom.

The dean asked, "My role as a supervisor is to support the staff and back the program. Regardless of the circumstances, we are not going to tolerate such behavior or threats to instructors. Would you mind if I taught the class today?"

Wither was asking her out of respect and courtesy, so Callie supported the plan. "Ms. Roach is working the computers today, and the lesson is loaded. She's able to follow along and stays on top of changing slides. I use printed notes with the slides so here are my notes and the quizzes from yesterday. Graded and ready to return."

Wither found what he was searching for and continued. "Fortunately, or unfortunately, lectures are recorded. The way you handled the situation yesterday was discussed at length. You have won a discussion with sponsors. Job offers with high salaries and benefits started floating around."

Callie groaned. "I've changed my mind. I'd rather teach. Any chance I could ditch the meeting and work at the greenhouse?"

Wither began shifting papers around again to find a pen. "Here is the room number. Hal is walking you over. Skipping out is political suicide. Remember that you are not the only person impacted by what happens. Smile. Behave and speak as little as possible. Run along so I may lock up and head to the classroom. There are not many chances to teach these days, much less swing my weight around as a supervisor."

Callie stood to leave and had a thought. "Um, how did Dr. Lite react? Is he upset?"

Wither answered while scanning her notes. "No. Dr. Lite is meeting me to attend the class and display a united front. He has battles keeping vultures circling Rorke at bay. Rorke made reading interesting and sexy. A strong, rugged, handsome man with his outdoor experience. The library called because they couldn't keep up with requests for certain books. One of the servers searching short stories crashed. Numerous places want to offer Rorke business proposals."

Callie giggled at Wither's explanation. "Oh, goodness. Well, I don't feel so bad. A part of me felt guilty because Botany seemed to be the focus of the relationship."

"There will be cycles just like any relationship. Once the list and pictures are collected, words will become front and center. Then, we'll find a balance between literature and botany."

Callie gathered her bag and went to walk with Hal.

During their walk, Callie stopped at a bench to tie her shoe. Hal stood beside her and scanned the area.

Callie asked ever so softly. "Hal? Where does your true loyalty lie? Me or the enemy?"

Hal's eyes stopped roaming the area to gaze down at Callie. "So? We have come to an end."

Callie locked her eyes on Hal, and he never looked away.

255

Hal was telling her the truth. "Always you and the Circlet."

Callie confirmed. "Last night, I confirmed that Brine talked to you about my father's research."

"Yes. Nigel approached me about his investigation after Brine's unexpected visit. Nigel was a master at reading people and figuring out effective strategies. His calculations have been frighteningly accurate. He figured that she'd ask someone for help on his behalf. It would be better if Brine talked to someone he trusted. I became a spy and helped write the report to take to the authorities. We outlined various scenarios and what might happen next. We attempted to add layers of protection for every option. I have thanked Heaven many times that Brine did ask me.

"Nigel's only warning that concerns me is Pica. Pica has never hidden his opinion about blaming Solomon about Thessa. Pica has always been upfront with how he feels about us regarding Thessa's jail time and overdose. I haven't heard him say or do anything to warrant suspicion. None of us liked the fact that Nigel asked Pica to meet with us the night he died. I was the only person who understood the reason why. Nigel didn't trust Pica and wanted him in the loop. I could keep an eye on him. Do you think Pica will use the situation to try and hurt or kill Solomon?"

Callie nodded. "Yes, and I'm counting on Pica wishing to exact revenge."

Hal asked. "What do you need from me?"

They continued walking, and Hal listened to Callie's plan. He wasn't pleased with the answer, but he agreed to his part.

Hal escorted her to the appointed place. "I'm to take your phone apart and put the pieces in the bag's front zippered pocket. I will place a second phone on the table in reach. Have a seat and continue facing away from the door until told otherwise."

Hal patted her shoulder. Callie wasn't sure if the gesture was in support or to comfort. Hal exited, and Callie jumped when a voice came from directly behind her. She had not heard anyone enter.

"Hello, Callie."

"Solomon?"

Callie went to stand and turned around, but strong hands clamped her on the shoulder.

"Don't move!"

"Solomon, your hands are shaking. Is everything all right?"

"No! Would you like to explain why one of the strongest, courageous men I know broke into sobs like an old, frail twig? The man began to cry like a baby in a sensitive and secret meeting."

Solomon had to be discussing Sumo, which made the rest of her task easy. Callie rejoiced inside, but she didn't react outwardly.

"No idea who we are discussing. If I do know, I won't lie. Unlike you and Rorke."

"We have not lied."

Callie accused. "The day on the mountain path, you told me Rorke owed you a debt. I found out that he volunteered for this mission, or whatever you call this endeavor, months ago. He claimed not to know about the book project."

Solomon explained the misconception. "Rorke did not lie. Moss approached me for advice when the shipment turned up found eight months ago. We started the groundwork for an entirely different scenario. Then, Isley found that damn box and started digging. Moss and I had to adapt, revise, and start over. Damage control and safety being the top of the priority list. Rorke was not aware or told ahead of time about the university venture.

"If you want to blame someone, Moss and I manipulated Rorke. I trust him to protect you to the best of his ability. I mentioned my concern to Rorke, and he went to Moss to offer any help he could."

Callie felt a huge weight taken off her shoulders, and the world was a little brighter. Rorke had not lied, but she couldn't deal with her feelings until later.

Callie said, "Moss is in a powerful position of authority, and you're awfully trusting of him."

"I do, and trust is not in my nature. Sumo frightened members of an important group last night. He checked his phone, which he has never done in the past. Tears started running down my friend's face. I've known the man for over thirty years, and he does not easily upset. Sumo informed us that he discovered Nigel told you about the symbolic circle. You could trust anyone with the tattoo. Sumo confessed that the pair of you had pictures of Nigel's evidence and laid a trap. None of those men and women rattle easily, but he created chaos in a matter of minutes. Please, tell me that you have not sprung the trap that Sumo helped you build. If you did, we need to stop the reckless plot."

"The play within a play is in motion. The only way to end the game is to finish."

Callie felt the man quivering, and Solomon spoke very softly. "Please, tell me exactly what you have done so that I may undo it."

257

Callie controlled her voice by the merest of threads. "I swore to protect my family, you, and the innocents. You used Sumo to shadow and protect me. I took full advantage of his presence but double-crossed my friend."

Solomon's voice held concern and worry for a loved one. "Why? What have you done?"

Callie reached up and put her tinier, thin fingers on the hands that held her shoulders. She didn't turn around but leaned into the warmth behind her. "I have tried to fulfill my promise to protect my family and friends. My father never gave his reasons but shared that I could trust anyone with the circlet symbol. My father was worried about you, his brother, if he died. He feared that you would disappear and seek justice alone. You would leave the members of the Circlet and other innocents to fend for themselves. Nigel made you promise to watch over us to anchor you to our lives. My guess is the other children within the circle were you, Nigel, Wither, Sumo, Lion, Nod, and Moss.

"I'm aware that Hal's parents died, but he was at his grandparents and not present. The group includes him, but he doesn't have the tattoo. Hal remains on the fringes without total confidence. I haven't figured out the eighth person. You have spent a lifetime protecting friends and family. Thank you for continuing to be a bossy, interfering presence in everyone's lives, but I am afraid that you must sit on the sidelines and trust me."

Solomon stood in silence for a long time. "I'll arrange for a new identity and take you anywhere you want."

Callie knew that the offer was a massive sacrifice for Solomon even to suggest. "Sounds like I am not the only person planning. What sort of scheme did you cook up?"

"Word is spreading that I died on the way to the hospital after an attempt to save a family from a burning car. Family rescued and fine, but sadly the heroic feat cost the rescuer his life. Sumo, as my estate lawyer, has the difficult task of breaking the news. The only immediate family listed is a friend's daughter. A child who I swore to look after and protect upon his death. The truth is only known to you and the Circlet. When the confusion clears, we'll correct the mistaken identity. Be aware, Nod contacted Rosa last night, and your grandmother is coming home."

"Why?"

"Lion was at the meeting last night and asked Isley to babysit. Dew picked the wrong night to round up a few buddies and lay siege to the apartment. Rosa's presence will be required as Blake's guardian at a court appearance. Your grandmother booked the next flight home."

Callie asked, "Is everyone all right? Isley called Rorke, who told me there was a dust-up. Guess the situation turned into more."

"No one was seriously hurt. The girls were more shaken than anything else. Isley is angry but slightly impressed at the defenses Lion put around and taught the girls."

Callie asked, "Are you aware?"

"Yes. I know Lion and Isley are dating. The clock is ticking, and you are stalling. Child, please let me stop this madness."

"You had your chance and didn't listen."

"What are you talking about?"

Callie had spoken to Hal about what she would tell Solomon. Granted, she thought a conversation with Solomon would be later. "You underestimated the problem and scope of the bigger picture. The criminal network has grown in power and resources in the last ten years. A trusted person is compromised. Two of Moss's coworkers are untrustworthy. Lastly, I came right and told you that your vetting process needed an overhaul. I don't trust everyone on the expedition team.

"Live or die. My life is here in the rugged landscape of Idaho. We have come full circle. I understand why one man, my father, was willing to die to protect his loved ones. Every life is precious. It doesn't matter if that being lived in the past, present, or has a future life. Land. Water. Air. People. Each is etched in the blood of our very being. If, and I say if, the choice is one for many, I will make that sacrifice."

Solomon's grip slightly relaxed, and Callie moved. Swiftly, quietly, and ignoring the shoulder pain, she stood, turned, and faced an older version of Nigel.

The young woman wrapped the man in a firm embrace and whispered. "I love you! Come out of the shadows and have dinner in person for my birthday. Regardless of what happens, the secret of my parentage is safe with me. I know you are my biological father, and Dusty is my biological mother."

Solomon studied the intelligent, intense eyes searching his own and asked, "Where do we go from here?"

"I will respect and support whatever choice you make regarding our relationship. If you stopped lurking in the shadows, my father, your brother, directed me to give you my necklace. Perhaps his reason for leaving a message will offer a direction for you. Professionally, you will have a busy, heavy workload ahead. I identified the lower and middle

259

tiers of the poacher's ring. I have at least one upper management. Maybe one thread will unravel the entire web."

Callie took off her chain to hand Solomon. The man ignored the necklace, and he hesitantly reached out to touch her face.

The young woman leaned into his fingers and stretched out her arms to hug him. "I love you. Any girl would be lucky to have my wonderful family and two such fathers in one lifetime."

Then, Callie grabbed her backpack and vanished before she could change her mind.

Chapter

Callie glanced at her watch and discovered more time had passed than she thought. Botany class had twenty minutes left. She used her key card to unlock the auditorium's back door and slipped inside. A partition sectioned off the computers. A smoky glass started about halfway up and went to the ceiling. Anyone seated or lecturing would not know that anyone sat behind the wall.

A commotion erupted in the front. Hal Bear escorted Nod and Lion. Blake and her four suite mates followed them into the classroom. Moss and Monarch followed not far behind with Mer.

Mer looked around, saw Wither, and spat angrily, "I have been dragged out of my hotel room twice and flown back at an ungodly hour in the morning. I'm sure that Callie is the reason. Where on God's creation is my niece?"

Wither arched an eyebrow. "If you are referring to Ms. Rivera, she's meeting with a high-profile visitor sponsoring the project. The young woman is fine and surrounded by high, priced security people of the sponsor."

Mer relaxed hearing his niece was safe. "I'd love to meet the person who could bribe Callie away from her precious garden! We'll be prying her cold, dead hands from those flowers before she agreed to work elsewhere."

Lion paled. "Stop that nonsense! That is not a nice thing to say about your niece."

Mer turned and shrugged. "Haven't met, and don't care about your opinion. Am I wrong?"

Lion glared without an answer. Wither wasn't sure the reason for the interruption, but he asked the front row to shift. Their guests could have a seat.

Mer smiled gratefully, took a seat, and closed his eyes to wait. Her uncle kept his eyes shut as Nod sat down and whispered a brief synopsis of the last couple of days. Lion and her charges on Nod's other side. The girls did not sit long.

Lion and the five teenagers immediately surrounded Isley when he entered. The teens pulled on his sleeves or shirt to gain his attention. Lion tried to speak, but her voice was drowned out by the girls. Isley attempted to make them back away and have a seat without yelling in front of his boss.

Roach made sure that Callie was in a blind spot and whispered. "How do you want me to proceed?"

"If possible, I need fifteen or twenty minutes without anyone being able to track me. We are about to have a visitor, Mr. Sumo, who is sharing that Solomon has died. I am not supposed to know yet. Sumo will want to tell me in a private setting. If you clear me on the campus camera, I've taken care of external security. Once the door closes, jam everything and anything electronic. That will lock everyone inside. I'll slip away as soon as I tranquilize Sumo. He'll wake up around the time the locks open."

"You are extremely calm about a friend's death. Unless the person didn't die."

Callie smiled sadly. "Solomon appears to like playing gambit after gambit with people's lives. I won't presently confirm or deny. Is bringing down the electronics in the room a problem?"

Roach smiled widely. "Please! Child's play! Good luck. Here's a disposable phone. Send your messages when you are ready. Turn on the power, and everything will send automatically."

"Yes. There are no words to express how much I appreciate you helping to protect those that I love. Thank you."

Roach went back to a monitor and relayed. "Are you leaving your bag in front of the room?"

Callie nodded yes, and Rorke continued. "I'll take and hold onto the backpack for you. Rorke and a friendly, handsome gentleman are about to enter."

"That's Sumo. I thought for sure the girls would have stopped pestering Isley by now. The noise has increased as he tries to ignore or direct them to seats."

Callie watched Rorke enter and take in the scene. He placed his computer bag on the desk.

Rorke's expressive voice demanded instant obedience. "Be quiet and have a seat!"

Roach took a side glance at Callie and whispered breathlessly. "Oh, my! How handsome and commanding! Rorke makes quite a picture with mussed hair, a strong profile, and a concerned frown. He's also wearing his weapon and a windbreaker with police on the back."

Callie rolled her eyes and wasn't about to agree with the opinion out loud. The teens sat, but Lion and Isley stood without moving.

Rorke looked toward the back because he had not forgotten the teaching assistant. "Ms. Roach, please turn off any recordings devices and join us."

Roach did as Rorke instructed, and Rorke gestured to Isley and Lion. "Both of you take a seat as well!"

Isley reddened slightly and took a breath to say something, but Rorke didn't let the agent speak. "Now!

Blake raised her hand and asked without being recognized. "Is that blood on your shirt?"

Rorke looked down but didn't outwardly react. "Not mine! I gave a guy a bloody nose to keep him from discharging a weapon. I suggest you remain quiet for a little while."

Blake started to cry even though Rorke had not yelled or reacted in anger. "Why are you mad at us? We didn't do anything wrong."

Lion handed Blake a couple of tissues, but the tears did not bother Rorke in the least.

"You were ordered by a person responsible for your safety to go into the restrooms and barricade yourselves inside. Instead, you confronted armed men in an area where families are living."

Lion started to defend the girls. "See here!"

Rorke turned a steely, unyielding gaze to Lion. "I suggest that you be very quiet if you want to continue supervising these young ladies. Teaching self-defense is one thing, but we are not in the wilds stalking prey. You are lucky those booby traps didn't seriously hurt anyone. We had to deal with multiple problems instead of containing the situation and making arrests. All six of you will have to stand in front of a judge and explain your actions.

"Ms. Lion, don't look toward Isley to save you. I saw you wearing pink bunny slippers at the lodge and at Callie's house. Isley ordered a huge box to give out as presents last Christmas. I suggest collecting the bunnies from Callie's kitchen. Rosa is coming home today, and those slippers are a dead giveaway about your relationship."

Mer opened his eyes and sat up. Rorke now had Mer's undivided attention. "Why is Rosa coming home early?"

"Rosa agreed to be Blake's guardian. I apologize for bringing a family matter to class. We have a situation that will impact everyone here. Most of you have some connection to law enforcement, so you will hear more later. I apologize for the lengthy family history to those who know about Callie's past. When Callie was a girl, her father died in a car accident. Mr. Sumo, do you want to take over from here?"

Sumo cleared his throat several times. "I'll try. Please, pardon my rambling. I am a family lawyer in Boise and don't usually mind public speaking. But. I. There were three of us in foster care and bonded. Our personalities were different, but we became best friends. The Rivera family adopted Nigel. He and I kept in touch over the years.

"When Callie was twelve, I was in court, and a firm's paralegal interrupted. I had a call, and the man insisted on talking to me immediately. He was going to murder anyone who hurt his daughter. The judge allowed a recess but made me put the phone on speaker. I informed Nigel he was on speaker inside a courtroom, and he didn't care. The only intelligible words were Callie and gone. I asked if anyone was there, and he said, Mom. I had never heard him call Rosa any derivative of mother."

Sumo stopped, chocked slightly, and couldn't continue.

Rorke had heard the story and continued. "Callie and a friend, who was over sixteen, had taken a road trip without permission. They left notes. They drove across the state to Boise for the Hot Air Balloon Festival. The two called upon arriving safely. Their trip without an adult chaperon sent a single father into a panic.

"Rosa had raised six children and remained the voice of reason. She talked to Sumo while reassuring Nigel. Rosa kept repeating to Nigel that the girls were fine and followed the rules. The girls had a room at a hotel within walking distance of the festivities. Sumo met and stayed with the girls until Rosa and Nigel arrived.

"The third friend is the reason for our meeting. Callie has never met the man in person but has spoken to him every week since Nigel died. Each year, the hermit asks what she wants for her birthday. Callie asks for a creative present to try and coax the recluse out of the backwoods or river country."

Sumo leaned on the whiteboard with tears running down his face and interrupted. "I always wondered why I received messages to arrange strange, elaborate reservations for Callie's birthdays. One year, it was a dinner in France by the Eiffel Tower. We found a restaurant with French food. That dinner was almost a thousand dollars with travel, food, overnight lodging, and decorations. Rosa had a fit when she found out, and I received the lecture about expensive presents. Granted, I felt better knowing Rosa scolded everyone involved."

Sumo couldn't continue, and Rorke closed his eyes a moment before opening them and explained. "This morning, a car skidded off a mountain road. A mother and three children were pulled out of a burning car by a person in the vicinity. The family is fine, but the rescuer died on the way to the hospital from smoke inhalation and burns. He is well-known in law enforcement and outdoor circles as Solomon."

Callie slipped out as a swell of noise erupted. Deep breath. Back straight. Smile. Friendly. Bright. Lives of those she loved and innocents hinged on the next few minutes. She walked down the empty hall, turned the corner, and went into the restroom.

As the bathroom door swung shut, a woman knocked on the window of the classroom. The sound was a warning to the occupants that Callie was on her way. Callie turned on an untraceable phone while washing her hands. She put the phone into her pocket so the person on the other end could silently listen as events unfolded. As soon as the door closed behind Callie, the person would make sure she escaped with the time that Roach provided.

Callie exited, approached the woman standing guard, and smiled before using her keycard to enter. "May I help you?"

"No, ma'am. I am here with Agent Moss."

Callie unlocked and opened the door with her keycard. "Agent Moss does not have to worry. I didn't take any of the nice job offers dangled in front of my nose."

Callie entered the classroom and spied Rorke. "I'm glad you are here. I was serious about not teaching your class. Is that blood on your shirt?"

"Yes, but not mine."

Callie spied Sumo and started to skip over delightedly. "Hey City Dude! Did you decide to take me up on the offer to visit the great outdoors?"

Callie took four steps and stilled. "What's wrong?"

Sumo pulled himself together. "Let's take a walk."

"Sumo? Did something happen to Gran? Bree?"

Rorke repeated his statement while ushering the pair outside. "Rosa, Bree, and Mer are fine. Step into the hall with Mr. Sumo."

The door clicked closed behind Callie and Sumo. Roach did her part, and the unknown person that Callie called acted as well. A van came barreling through the outside wall and windows. Callie didn't tell Roach that a vehicle would breach the classroom windows to offer a distraction.

The driver had planned the stunt very carefully and made all the preparations himself. Callie trusted the driver's arrangements and had visited the training site. The building itself was easy. Replace the windows with breakaway glass. Replace bricks or wood with material that was light but create noise. He trained the pets to unlock the travel carries upon impact and flee the van dramatically. The driver would make sure everyone inside was clear, and no one would be hurt.

Birds, cats, dogs, and several wildlife creatures spilled into the classroom from the broken doors. Commotion helped delay anyone coming to look for Callie and Sumo. Solomon was less than happy finding Sumo unconscious in an empty classroom. Then, the breach in security was discovered. Callie's movements were deleted, and she's vanished.

Chapter

Passing a self-appointed mark, Callie activated a burner phone. A general message of love to her friends and family list. Three additional communications went out as well.

Callie's text to Sumo expressed her sorrow for the double-cross, hoped he would forgive her, and that she loved him. Callie asked Solomon to take care of Rosa if her scheme went sideways. She shared documents to honor Bree's wishes were left on her desk. Care would pass to Rorke or Isley with Lion. Rorke's message was less emotional. Expressing her feelings would weaken her resolve. She asked him to trust her. Her request was to protect those she loved and provided a set of coordinates. Rorke needed to tell Sumo that Callie reset the trap with his cameras at that latitude and longitude.

Either Rorke or Solomon would have plenty of time to send reinforcements before her arrival with the poachers. Callie turned into Cherry's Outpost and parked. Taking the pictures, she entered the lodge. Mr. and Mrs. Cherry were sitting down for a cup of coffee in a quiet office.

Mrs. Cherry smiled and asked, "Going to the cabin for the weekend?"

"No, and I need the fastest transportation available to Center Mountain or the Medicine Lodge area by the Targhee National Forest."

"Why? What is going on?"

Callie took the pictures, put them together like a puzzle, and showed the couple. "I will be frank and don't have time to explain in entirety. My father hid a group of items that I need to retrieve. The location is remote, difficult to reach, and probably booby-trapped. You know that I do not run off unprepared or on a whim. My abilities are professional level. I am the only person who can retrieve the articles safely. If anyone figures out where I've gone, the cost could be a severe or fatal injury."

Mr. Cherry studied the pictures. "Let's see what we can find out. Organizing may take a few minutes."

"I'll be in my normal spot doing homework while I wait."

Callie learned that she had a lot of time on her hands waiting on ranger, groups, or weather changes. She'd found a sheltered spot to wait. The view was beautiful. Best of all, the vantage point allowed her to watch the entire area. Anyone who was looking would know where to find her.

Mr. Arc joined her at the sheltered picnic table. "Hey, Miss Sassy."

Callie smiled in greeting. "Hey, former ranger. I've never seen you here."

"We come out occasionally for incident reports. I don't want to have to return and fill one out for a stubborn young lady. You appear. Mr. and Mrs. Cherry show visible worry and looking at helicopter routes. Word travels fast. People are discussing Solomon and the accident. Such news makes those in our business jittery. I'm sorry about Solomon's death."

Callie picked at the pages of her book. "Thank you, but the words are wasted on me."

"That doesn't sound like you. How about a trade? Tell me what is going on, and I'll go with you."

"No! You have a wife and children."

Arc sat down without invitation and countered. "I'm divorced without children. I drove to your house in a friend's car. He asked to borrow my vehicle to take his wife on a date."

Callie smiled and asked, "A sport's car convertible?"

Arc grinned sheepishly. "Good memory. I kept a picture of my dream car in the work vehicle. After the divorce, I bought and restored one. Much cheaper. Would you mind if my work partner joins us?"

"Do you trust the partner?"

"We have to investigate when accidents happen in some pretty remote places."

Callie agreed and watched Arc talk to his partner while she read. One of two faces that haunted her nightmares appeared in front of her. If she slipped in the conversation or made an incorrect gesture, she would not make the trip home alive.

Callie knew Mr. and Mrs. Cherry were involved. When Mrs. Cherry approached her about renting the cabin, she figured out the connection. The couple would know about remote places and vacant times.

She had to figure out if Arc was involved or a clueless innocent? Deep breath. Back straight. Smile. Friendly. Bright but with slight trepidation. Mr. and Mrs. Cherry walked over with Arc and introduced Pitter. Callie remained seated but shook hands.

Arc started, "We understand time is important, and you're probably trying to keep ahead of Rorke. You realize that he is going to be beyond angry."

Callie returned defensively, "I may work with Rorke at the university and let him lead field trips. The man is not my supervisor, regardless of his need for control and order, but you are correct. He and the expedition team will not be happy that I ditched them."

267

Pitter nodded. "I like you. We heard about Solomon. My condolences on the loss."

Callie explained again, "Thank you, but I have never met the man. My father and Solomon were friends. Solomon calls, or called, once a week since my father died to see how we are doing. He sends me a birthday present every year.

"As to the trip today, Agent Isley brought me a box of pictures taken by my father. The pictures of seeds and plants were a puzzle to a location. No one would tell me the details, but my father wasn't the trusting sort. He loved to invent puzzles with twists. As I got older, he made the game a little more, uh, risky. Nothing ever dangerous to me, but I did get a face full of ink once."

Arc shook his head and restated the situation. "You think that you discovered the location and didn't want to tell Rorke, Isley, or Solomon. They'd ignore warnings."

"Correct. I know old seeds and plants do not mean much, but I am curious. My father went to a lot of trouble, which means he had a good reason."

Mr. Cherry looked at the others. "We'll help on one condition. Someone goes with you. That area is treacherous for experienced climbers even with optimum weather conditions and equipment. We'll sort permits and give you as much lead time as possible."

Callie went to change and grab her climbing gear. The four others sat and conversed before leaving the table. While changing clothes, she activated the cameras on site and made sure the system was recording. The signals may or may not send from the remote location, but Sumo could retrieve the footage later. Callie locked the computer in a hidden compartment. She didn't like leaving valuables in a parked car for long periods. There were additional electronics and equipment hidden in the rocks at the site.

Pitter inquired if he could recheck Callie's bag. Trust wasn't the issue, but they had not worked together. He wanted to make sure she was competent with the correct gear. Callie agreed, letting him unpack and repack the bag.

Pitter, Arc, and Callie climbed aboard a helicopter. No one talked during the trip. The pilot landed and turned off the engine.

Callie asked, "Is the transport staying?"

Pitter turned the conversation to Callie and her safety. She insisted that three people at the top of the ridge was enough.

Arc made sure Callie's helmet, harness, descender pieces, and ropes were secure. Then, Arc attached a short-wave radio at her waist. He explained the mic on her shoulder was always on and handed her an earpiece. Pitter and he would be in constant contact.

Callie had gone to great lengths and extreme care to recreate Sumo's booby traps. The man was a genius at using the environment to set traps that were theatrical and not dangerous. Each mechanism needed four releases. If climbers happened upon the spot, they could go right over the rock face and never know or find the hidden crevice.

The first trap was about a quarter of the way down the slope. She activated three releases on the way.

Callie stopped and used the radio. "I am shifting way to the left to find and retrieve a long branch."

Finding a twelve-foot branch that had fallen from a tree, she said, "I have to cut a couple of smaller twigs off. If I swing back, could the two of you hold my weight? Make sure I don't slip as I go around."

Arc sighed. "Remember, we don't have any visual capability. Talk to us. What are you about to do?"

"I am descending about three feet, then veering back to my original position and triggering the mechanism. Be prepared for anything. Repelling down."

Callie stopped and swung. It took three tries, but she activated the trigger. Ping! Ping! Snap! Snap! Snap!

Instinct would be to repel down or stay put. Instead, Callie climbed as quickly as possible.

A rolling rumble disturbed the silence of the entire valley. Five boulders, each the size of a van, catapulted down the rock face. The sound of a rockslide started, and Callie followed the boulders down to where they had started their descent.

Arc's stressed voice sounded over the noise. "Callie?!"

"I am good. Loose rocks filled with punji sticks are rolling on down the hill."

"Punji sticks?"

"Yes. Sharpened sticks are used in booby traps to injure someone. The wood is attached to the rolling stones."

Arc did not like the conditions of the climb or the danger. "You're done! Come back up."

Callie disagreed. "We're too close, and Dad always used sets of three. If I feel the task is beyond me, I'll come up."

Arc looked at Pitter and asked, "You or me?"

"You're better in free fall than I'm if a problem occurs."

"Ah, a compliment. Scared?"

Pitter made a grunting sound. "Damn right! I was thinking of a swat over the head with a tree truck or falling in a pit. These traps are serious!"

Callie ordered. "Be quiet! I need to focus. Ah, found it. A cable of reinforced steel leads to a box. I pulled the cable, heard a mechanical whirring, and a hiss like a gas grill lighting. Cover your ears, gents!"

An implosion happened instead of an explosion. A trapdoor caved in, and Callie waited for the dirt to settle. Inside the crevice were ten storage bags like Agent Moss had shown her in the picture.

Callie whooped in triumph. "They're here! Oh, my! We found them! Send down a rope!"

Slowly, she tied nine bags by the handles and sent each up the cliff. Arc and Pitter had not placed a camera for visual on her. They could not see the additional packages Callie opened.

Carefully, Callie reorganized the gear. She took off her jacket and placed two handguns within easy reach. She replaced four of the cams at her waist. Each had a delayed tracker attached. One of her items was a small case with cash and identification cards. She zipped the wallet in an inside pocket.

Pitter and the pilot matched numbers on the bags to a list on a clipboard. Arc dealt with the ropes. A line was sent down for the last bag, and Pitter secured Arc's weapons.

Arc eyed his partner. "What's going on, Pitter?"

"I have orders to take the bags and leave you with Callie. Behave, or I'll kill you before we leave."

Arc, now a hostage, had no idea what was going on, but he didn't like the conversation's direction. While they waited, he looked around to figure out a way to warn and protect Callie.

Callie had been quiet too long, and Pitter took the radio. "What is happening? The last bag should be coming up."

"I found the last trap and need to figure out the details. There are wires buried underneath and heard clicks. An additional bag is attached to the last one. I am not able to see the exact contents, but it appears to be a potpourri mixture."

Pitter said, "Switch the ropes. We'll use the manual belay lines for the bag and bring you up with the winch. Be aware, your friends are about ten minutes out, and Rorke is on a warpath."

Callie made a dramatic sigh of relief. "We were able to locate and retrieve the bags. You may lose audio while I go into the rock and trace the ends. If you want to leave me with the last one, I'll make my way up and wait."

Pitter snorted. "Rorke is not a threat or my concern."

Callie moved inside the rock cave and turned off the radio to Pitter and Arc. Using stored electronic equipment, she asked, "Sumo? Isley? Rorke?"

Solomon's voice answered. "We are online. Sumo and I are in the ridge covering your back. Bash and Wither are in a long-range position. Rorke is also on the comm line, but the others are not in our loop. That may not be the case shortly. Mer and the teaching assistant, uh, Roach, complained about the wasted time, red tape, and incompetence. They went straight to BE. The two picked up your camera signals in minutes. BE has become Command Central. Mer, Roach, and Moss are the only three inside the office. They are relaying video and audio to everyone else."

Callie asked, "Did you tell the expedition team of your presence on the ridge or that you are alive?"

"No. News of the mistake hasn't been made public. The Circlet, Bash, and Rorke are the only ones looped into the situation. Sumo is supposed to be on his way to the hospital for a check after being found unconscious. Publically, Rorke asked Bash to stay behind to help Isley watch Lion and the girls. Wither, Sumo, and Bash came with me. Rorke is leading the rest to the summit."

Callie stated specifically to Solomon, "I fully anticipate the mole or moles on the team to show their hands. The leaders of the poachers may have changed their orders from abandonment to kidnapping. If that is the case, don't interfere. We have a chance to end the game. I have ten remote, delayed trackers hidden on me. Each tracker will remain dormant until I activate the mechanism."

Solomon was not about to let Callie go with Pitter. "You're not leaving the area without one of us! If we aren't careful, the enemy will cut loose ends. Ranks will close. You'll be dead, and we will be back to square one."

Callie sighed. "Not exactly, but we'll talk about that later."

Sumo's voice groaned. "What else have you done, Starry Eyes? I am beyond angry but also proud. Even though you moved locations, you stayed to the script without killing yourself in the process."

The young woman's voice caught. "You taught and prepared me. I am sorry for going behind your back, and until today, you were always there to catch me. You are the sole reason for me being able to come this far. My biggest fear was that you would discover the switch before the trap was sprung. The last thing I want is someone hurt attempting to help or protect me."

271

Solomon's voice interrupted the heartfelt exchange. "We will discuss past actions later! Callie, what have you done?"

"I made a promise not to interfere the night of the crash. My oath was to survive and protect those we love. I am asking you to let me finish the game playing by my rules. Not yours. Not theirs."

Solomon whispered, "We can't lose you. I can't lose you."

"Trust the training of your friends who taught me. Even if I leave with Pitter, I'll not become a hostage."

Bash's voice broke over the radio with confidence and reassurance. "Callie, we'll find you. No matter what happens, Rorke and I will bring you home."

Callie signed off the frequency. "I love each of you."

Walking back to the edge, Callie made sure Arc's radio was active. "Hello? I'm coming up first because I have no idea what will happen when the bag comes loose."

Relieved, Arc answered, "Roger."

Callie made sure weapons and other gear would not bang around. Ascending, she envied spiders with eight legs. Her arms and legs went every which way to keep her away from the rock face. Each time she could, she swung away and used the ropes to keep herself from twisting around. The hours of practicing with an electronic winch paid off. She was glad that she didn't have to cling to the rock face. If the ropes suddenly released or were cut, she'd have to find a quick hold or go plunging downward.

Arc grasped her hand as she popped up at the ridgeline. A second explosion went off. The effect was more for theatrics and would not damage the environment. A blast preceded a giant dust ball that puffed outward.

Chapter

A second helicopter landed on the other side of the clearing. Callie watched the expedition team minus Bash disembark.

Rorke came out last and went directly to Callie. "I was composing a stern lecture on our entire trip. I decided not to say a word. I am just relieved you are safe."

Rorke wrapped Callie in a hug to cover his speaking softly. "Comms are off. Are you sure about your course of action?"

She whispered, where no one could see. "Trust me. When my diversion goes off, get the others to the rocks. Two weapons are secured in shoulder holsters under my jacket."

Rorke used his fingers to squeeze to her shoulder to let her know he understood.

Callie backed away and asked, "Does anyone have a phone with a signal? Gran should have landed by now. I need to talk to Mer so he may let Gran and the rest of the family know that everything is fine."

Tort handed Callie a headset. "Mer cut into our comms and wants to talk to you."

Mer didn't wait for Callie to say hello and hollered, "You are in so much trouble!"

Defensibly, Callie stated back. "I never lied about my movements. I certainly have not acted rashly or illegally. Did Gran come in safely?"

"Yes. Rosa's on her way to meet Nod, Lion, and the girls."

"Uncle Mer, do me a favor?"

Sarcastic and biting, her uncle asked, "Really? What?"

"Open my dollhouse so Agent Moss may see inside?"

Seconds later, Mer said, "It's unlocked and open."

Callie told Moss. "Lean down and peer into the first floor. There is a carpet in the living room. Take out the rug, and there is a note for you on the bottom. Once you open the envelope, you have twenty seconds to read before the letter disintegrates."

Moss opened, read, and paled. "Dear Mary, Joseph, and Jesus. Callie, if Rorke doesn't marry you, I will. The sole reason would be to keep you under watchful eyes. Solomon's vigilant, but you managed to undermine his surveillance. That is quite a feat."

Callie laughed. "As long as you don't mind living in the garden."

The agent cursed as the paper crumbled in his hands.

"I warned about the twenty seconds."

"Rorke! Change of plans! Take Callie directly to the lodge! Keep her there until I send someone to collect you. Mer cut all transmissions to everyone, including law enforcement."

The line went silent. Pitter eyed Callie with a wicked smirk.

Pitter pointed his weapon at Callie. "A change of plans is a great idea! Callie! Come and stand by me! Tort, secure the others. Destroy their communication gear. Whipper and Spivy, join us. Thicke, help Tort tie everyone up."

Callie obeyed but stayed several steps away. Whipper had been the pilot, so Spivy had to be the copilot. Everyone did as Pitter ordered.

Thicke gathered weapons and told the others to lie down on the ground. Thicke tied the hostages' hands behind their backs, and Tort destroyed the radios and disabled the team's chopper.

Pitter asked, "Where's the kid?"

Rorke offered. "If you are talking about Bash, I asked him to stay behind. We needed someone to keep an eye on Lion and the girls until we returned. Lion might be able to manipulate Isley into changing his orders, but Bash won't listen to Lion."

Tort confirmed the answer.

The helicopter's engine started, and Callie looked at her former teammates. "Why?"

Tort's eyes shone with malice. "Solomon's dead, and the payday is more money than you will see in a lifetime."

Callie tried to warn Pitter. "Those bags we brought up are dangerous. If one expands, explodes, or comes open in the air, the consequences could be disastrous."

"Shut it! Your friends are fortunate. Instead of killing anyone, we are leaving them. You may or may not be so lucky."

Thicke protested. "Kidnapping was not part of the deal. We were to collect the bags and leave."

A gunshot echoed, and Thicke crumpled to the ground.

"Objection noted." Pitter waved to Callie. "Climb aboard."

Callie paused. "I'm very tired of people ignoring me regarding advice or warnings. If I climb aboard, you sign your own death certificate."

"Please! Nice try! We destroyed every piece of communication gear on your friends. Help is far, far away."

Callie stood her ground and very sweetly threw out the bait. "I am aware my value dropped to zero when Solomon died. If I die, sensitive information will find its way to the authorities. One important item is regarding Orlin Brody. Orlin died, and Bree is not expected to live. The

274

catch: I know why the couple was a target. Someone discovered Orlin wanted out and was working for Solomon."

Tort looked stunned. "What the hell are you talking about, Callie?"

Pitter wasn't surprised and told Tort. "Bree started being nosy, and Orlin became a liability. Notice failed to keep the couple under control as Orlin's handler."

Tort sighed. "Pitter, why do you have to be so chatty? Every connection to Orlin had better be erased."

Callie felt a knot in her stomach for the first time since she set the plan in motion. "Was Bree involved?"

Pitter laughed. "Notice blamed Bree because he never liked her. Bree was a clueless, uneducated street urchin who never finished high school. The woman used Orlin's money to help disadvantaged women and children. She'd drop everything if one of her pets needed help. Orlin's blind spot was the woman, and he loved her. There weren't any problems until that damn shipment went missing. Any other stupid questions?"

Callie asked in a honeyed voice. "Heard of Ockham's Razor?"

Pitter answered. "Nope, and don't care."

Tort snapped. "Pitter! Be quiet! Callie, continue!"

"Why don't you share my observation with the boss and see if my value has increased from zero?"

Pitter and Tort listened to a voice in their ear, and Tort snapped. "Employer wants a little more than a conspiracy theory. Pitter's babbling was more informative than your hypothesis."

Callie sighed dramatically. "Agent Moss showed me a picture taken eight months ago. The picture was items found in a shipment of counterfeit goods. The bags we hoisted up today went missing over ten years ago. Humans are creatures of habit. I sent up two bags packed like evidence found eight months ago. My father's ten-year-old bags and eight-month-old bags are connected. Past and present have collided. Once the authorities know where to look, connections are easy to make."

Tort heard a voice in his ear again. "Looks like your life became worth more than zero."

Callie's tone changed from sweet honey to sticky, sugary syrup. "I hope that you have reinforcements. Your transport is smoking, and you disabled the other transport."

Pitter's pilot coughed as he opened the windows and doors. Pitter and Tort went to find out why there was smoke. Rorke's team took full advantage of the distraction. Whipper cut Spivy, the copilot free. Callie found herself crouched beside Spivy, who looked terrified but in control of her emotions. She couldn't have been more than twenty or so.

The woman spoke hesitantly. "Ms. Rivera, I doubt you remember, but eight years ago, you and Rorke pulled my family out of a car."

"Oh, my goodness. Look at you. All grown up! Why in Heaven's name did Rorke let you come?"

"Cattail refused to let Mr. Cherry be the copilot. I was the only other person around with qualifications."

Callie took one of the weapons from the holster under her jacket. "Do you know how to shoot?"

"What Idaho girl doesn't?"

"Quite a few, but here's a handgun. Easier than the rifles laid out among the rocks. The clip holds ten. One in the chamber. Here are two extra clips with twelve rounds."

Ms. Spivey stared in awe at Callie. "You don't mess around! You are my hero. Again. What did you do to make the smoke?"

"I had ten years to investigate, research, learn, plan, revise, and plan again. Certain plant oils make a very smelly type of smoke. Lucky for us, we are upwind and won't gag on the smell."

Callie took out a modified computer tablet. She'd retrieved the device from the niche and hidden it in the padding of her jacket. The harness, jacket, and hard outer case should be enough to keep the components from breaking. She'd tested to ensure the precautions would hold. She'd added hardware to boost the signal. The tablet could log into the greenhouse security system and activate the intercom system.

A computerized message echoed over the BE speakers. "Apologies for my next move. Those of you set up in the field are about to lose cell phone signals and electric power. I respect Mr. Asher and Ms. Roach's computer skills too much to allow interference."

Then she shut down the main power and disabled the backup generators. Callie triggered a cell phone jammer and sent an electromagnetic pulse through the property. She turned off the tablet and secured it back in her jacket.

Rorke approached the two women kneeling against the boulders. "Ms. Spivey, do you have any doubts about shooting a person if they come past us?"

Spivey set her jaw and checked the gun. "No, sir."

Callie told Rorke. "I'll place trackers on any equipment that I drop out of the helicopter. Collect the items and try to keep Solomon from starting a fire he won't be able to control."

Rorke responded, "Come home in one piece, or I'll help Solomon build the bonfire. I'm trying to figure out a way out of the mess without your stepping foot off this rock. Reinforcements are too far out, and we have no idea who to trust. No matter what. Survive. We'll find you."

Solomon appeared from behind an outcropping of boulders. His voice sounded as if his life was being squeezed out second by second. "Rorke, help me reset the team's comm channel. Sumo says that these cameras are recording, but BE went dark."

Callie didn't share, and Spivy didn't tattle.

Rorke followed Solomon, and Still came over. "Crabbe, Whipper, and I have a general understanding of what's happening. Callie, we'll back you. Spivy, I'll ask you to stay right beside me. If we must retreat down the rock face, I'll provide direction."

Callie patted Still's arm in thanks. The air was thinner and colder at this elevation. A brisk wind came from the north and blew through the boulders. They listened as the sound of helicopters became more distinct.

Waiting, Callie studied Solomon. She could understand why Solomon was concerned if Rosa or Callie saw him. There were striking similarities between Solomon and Nigel. Blond to Strawberry blond hair. Tall but not thin. Solid came to mind. Solomon sported a little facial hair along his jaw and mustache line. Blue eyes peered from a long face. Callie noticed that Solomon had his hair cropped short, but Nigel wore his long. There were times that he'd tie it back or tuck the stands under his collar. Callie hadn't thought about her father's hairstyle in years.

She'd inherited Solomon and Nigel's golden skin tone, but her eyes were green like Dusty's. A part of her was jealous that she hadn't inherited the men's height. Nigel and Solomon were about six feet. Rorke was slightly shorter than Solomon.

Dusty, Nigel, and Solomon had led vastly different lives, but each loved Callie. Dusty's methods might be focused in selfish or self-centered behavior, but the woman cared enough to teach Callie what skills she thought were important. Dusty was always spouting about proper etiquette and manners. Callie knew that she would not have been able to face or interact with the enemy without Dusty's training. In a way, Dusty had taught her skills to survive and face the enemy in everyday circumstances.

Nigel, Solomon, and their friends taught her to survive in the wilderness. Skills and the methods that she used today. She soaked up

277

every tiny bit of knowledge and training to ensure her friends and family's protection.

The last two parts of her plan hinged on Hal and Tort. Hal had succeeded in the first of two assignments at the campus. They would have to be patient to see how his role of spy played out. Tort's behavior was the second condition. The only way she'd escape the helicopter safely was using the poacher's habits. Tort needed to use the network's established air routes.

Callie would watch and wait as the poachers' network closed their ranks. It didn't matter how tight the foe made the space between those defenses. Nigel's shadow had already slipped behind their lines. She'd used his research as a starting point and collected the information. Live or Die. Her fate did not matter. Instructions would be relayed on how to access the research and take down the enemy.

Sumo reestablished the communications as two helicopters approached.

Callie spoke into the headset. "Bash and Wither, do you see the Amanita Muscaria, uh toadstools with the red caps, scattered on the plateau?"

"Yes."

"The ones with the purple spots on top will explode like a flashbang if you shoot them. If Pitter's reinforcements try to take out the others after I leave, the distraction will offer time to act. I hesitate to share, but the Toadstools with the yellow spots on top have a stronger charge. The force is enough to disable the helicopters but could hurt someone."

Bash and Wither confirmed their understanding.

The helicopters landed, and Tort shouted. "Surrender Callie, and we'll leave without harming anyone."

The only outcome of an armed confrontation was sorrow and grief, and Solomon's voice whispered, "Callie, resurface by dawn and relatively unscathed. If not, I swear by Heaven and Hell to break every oath I uttered to Nigel, family, or friends. I love you, child."

Callie surrendered and climbed aboard the smoky helicopter. They'd opened the windows, which gave her an advantage. The more noise the better. Tort tied her wrists together, but she could move her arms and fingers. He used a second cord to bind her ankles and closed the door. No one else joined her in the rear which relieved Callie. The position of her bindings and seclusion made getting out easy.

Luckily, her backpack lay on the floor by her feet. She looped a rope through the ten evidence bags and attached them about a foot apart. She wrapped a second rope around bars used to secure the seats. The line would be her anchor. Odd. Tort and Pitter murdered her father. If her plan didn't work, she might die a decade later by the same hands.

Chapter

Hours later, Solomon started a pot of coffee in Rosa's kitchen. Solomon had made sure his presence went unnoticed. His apparent demise wasn't corrected because there were too many loose ends. The biggest being Callie's absence. He waited for the others who were taking showers. Sumo was the first to join him.

Sumo rubbed his face. "I'm trying to be angry and upset but find myself only worried. My only consolation is that we know she escaped from Tort and Pitter, and no one has found her body."

"I owe you. That was one hell of a design on the traps."

Pouring a cup of coffee, Sumo spoke candidly. "You may revise that statement. Whatever Callie put in that note, Moss went straight to the courthouse and talked to Judge Walrus. A private security team took Lion, her five girls, Pica, Nod, Mer, Roach, Rosa, and Pickle out to the lodge. Isley's orders were to tag along as an armed escort. The group was unhappy about the evacuation. Then, they found out that phones and the internet wouldn't be available. Is BE still in lockdown mode?"

Solomon made a sour, disgusted face and tapped his foot in annoyance. "Yes. When the place started its lockdown process, Mer got Roach outside. The greenhouse is locked up like Fort Knox. He thought they'd be able to bypass the system and return inside. No one has been able to undo Callie's new controls. I helped build the system and tried. No luck. Did Moss say why Hal didn't go to the Lodge?"

Sumo added three heaping spoons of sugar to the cup of coffee. He was going to need the caffeine and sugar. "Moss didn't provide a reason for Hal staying in town. There are nagging questions, but I'm unsure if I want answers."

Solomon agreed with the notion. "Nigel would never have endangered anyone over plants. We know there isn't any knowledge hidden at the cabin because we built the structure. The house, rentals, and greenhouse are clear. We search the places at least once a month for any danger or any new clues. Callie tried to warn me about the vetting process. We still missed key details. How did she know about Bree and Orlin?"

Sumo took a sip of coffee. "No idea. Do you have any idea how Callie knew that Orlin turned to you for help?"

"None, but it explains why she didn't sneak off to find Bree. I expected her to try and had contingencies in place. Thank God! Our team got Bree and Orlin out before the attack. Notice took the word of a medic that Orlin died. Mer started digging into the computers as soon as

279

he arrived at the greenhouse. Has Nod found out how much Mer learned about the Circlet?"

Sumo took a sip of his coffee. "Enough to be hurt and angry. Nod"s had our blessing to tell Mer for a long time. Lion sent a message that Nod was talking to Mer about the past. We'll need to keep an eye on Roach as well. The young woman has been listening, watching, and quickly gathering information."

Solomon's phone rang. Mer wasn't the only person who felt left out. The caller was Arc.

Arc's outrange at the situation was apparent in his tone. "What the hell did Callie drag me into? Head of security is allowing me contact because I'm about to create more problems than help. I've been escorted to an armed camp and ordered to provide backup as well as babysit civilians."

Solomon tried to explain and ease the man's ire. "I appreciate you protecting Callie. We thought it best for you to stay with the group. We didn't want anyone asking about Pitter. There are and will be a lot of questions. I rather not have you under suspicion as his partner. A select few knew you were investigating Pitter. Inquiries and debriefings need to wait until we know Callie is safe."

The explanation did lessen Arc's irritation. "I suppose that I did volunteer. Has anyone heard from Callie?"

"No, and don't tell anyone else about her disappearance. We played for time and lied that she was safe. Currently, the only consultation is that she escaped from Tort and Pitter."

Arc disconnected, and Wither joined his two friends. Wither ignored the coffee and grabbed a bottle of whiskey on the counter. The bottle was from the supply that Cattail had brought.

Sumo eyed his friend and asked Wither, "Are you all right?"

"Yes. Worry about Bash. One of his targets is the person who died. Nothing the boy could do with the wind and sporadic movements. We got lucky on multiple fronts. Sumo, did you teach Callie to make the exploding shrooms?"

"No."

"Callie's planning saved lives. It made the difference between winning and losing a battle without further harm. Taking out the transports by shrooms was safer at long range. We'd have been hard-pressed to extract the team without more critically injured or dead."

Rorke, Whipper, Bash, Crabbe, and Still filed into the kitchen. Bash immediately checked the fridge to see if there was anything to eat. Crabbe filled coffee mugs and refilled the reservoir to start another pot.

Rorke asked, "Solomon, are you aware that an unofficial search started for Callie? Anyone at BE was told to go home after the power went out. As soon as anyone had signals, they began making calls and sending out alerts. Places that I have never heard of in Idaho, which is saying something, are contacting me. Word has spread through states of Montana, Washington, Oregon, Nevada, Utah, and Wyoming. Several of my contacts in Canada reached out as well."

Solomon slumped in his chair. Sumo and Rorke shared a look. They had ever seen Solomon so despondent, worried, or tired.

Sumo tried to bolster his friend's spirits. "I am not surprised. Callie disappeared under unusual circumstances from the university. Those at BE saw the confrontation on the plateau. Mer looped into the cameras quickly. Glad we were able to reach the coordinates before Callie. When Callie cut communications, the home front believed that she's safe."

Rorke's phone rang, and he answered before the first ring finished. "Hello?"

Callie was on the line, so he put her on speaker.

Solomon asked, "Are you all right?"

"A few bumps and bruises but none the worse for wear. I bailed out of the helicopter without breaking my neck. How is everyone there?"

Solomon replied. "We did not suffer any casualties or injuries. I was relieved when you activated a tracker as the helicopter started over the lake. We were able to follow the flight to Lewiston. Tort was smart enough to drop down toward Idaho Falls to follow Interstate 84. After they landed near Boise, the two took a commercial flight to Porthill and headed toward the Canadian border. I feared the worst when they didn't haul you out of the back. Authorities arrested Tort and Pitter as they tried to cross into Canada. Border Patrol agents are escorting the two back. I have my doubts that they will arrive back here alive. I doubt that their employers are happy about your disappearance. The enemy is cutting loose ends, and you're equal a bunch of untied threads."

Emotions bubbled to the surface in her mind. Relief that the end was near. Gratitude for her family. Concern for those left on the ground. Love for Rorke. Hope for a future along with fear of failure. Yet, she made sure not to let any of those feelings take hold.

"I understand, but there is one more item for me to deal with before coming out of the shadows. Thank you for trusting me."

Callie pressed the end button and hoped that she had sounded strong. The reality was that facing the last hurdle terrified her more than everything else that day. Closer than Solomon realized, the young woman had secured the evidence. She put away the climbing gear and only wore a jacket. The buttons on her coat were microphones and cameras. The equipment was connected to a recording device and could record in the dark. There were a few independent systems that didn't rely on primary or backup power.

Callie went to the rocks of the waterfall and retrieved a key. The key opened three locks on a greenhouse door. Slipping into her father's garden and her beloved greenhouse, Callie filled her lungs with the perfume of the many flowers surrounding her. The moon shining through the clear panels of the room provided plenty of light.

A voice stopped Callie as she turned the corner by the main path and turtle pond. "Restrain her gently."

Callie recognized Pica's voice. The fact that Pica was giving the order made her blood run cold. She'd underestimated the man. Pica wasn't only passing along information. He was right in the center and helping to organize. Strong, bright flashlights shone in Callie's face and blinded her. She felt more than saw three people grab her-one on each side. A third person had her shoulders.

A fourth person behind her ordered. "I'm standing out of reach with a gun pointed to your head. Try anything, and I have no problem putting a non-lethal bullet in you."

Callie recognized Hal's voice as the one training the weapon on her. Thank goodness for small favors and Hal's loyalty. She did not doubt that Hal had her back.

Pica started asking questions. "Let's discuss Orlin Brody. How did you know that he was working for Solomon?"

Callie answered honestly. "Bree sent a letter which was delivered in the mail two days ago. Orlin was tired of being caught in the middle of the law and lawlessness. He reached out to the one person both sides respected or feared. Solomon. Orlin arranged for three trucks to go missing eight months ago. The shipments recovered by the authorities, which set current events in motion. If anything happened, I was to turn the letter over to the authorities. They would understand the message that she left. I gave the letter to Agent Monarch, Moss's assistant."

Pica said, "Let's talk about Nigel and his research."

Callie used her father's given name. "Nigel would be so disappointed. He trusted you, Chi Pica."

"Playing detective got the man killed. Nigel was nothing but a man whore who wanted to measure up to Solomon, his childhood friend. I need an honest answer. What do you know about your father's research?"

"I know what you know. My father sent a box to the authorities with a puzzle. I wish that he'd left a note to explain."

Pica continued his questions. "Where are the bags, Callie?"

"Destroyed. We break the cycle of people dying today. Why did you betray my father and work with poachers?"

"Nigel was a means to an end. I had hoped that Nigel would lead me to Solomon. The man destroyed my life and turned Thessa against me. Thessa took her new boyfriend to our place. No one was supposed to be there."

Callie was glad the light was blinding her, but the words escaped before she could stop her mouth from moving. A horrible knot formed in her stomach.

"What have you done?"

"Thessa and her new boyfriend saw things that they were not supposed to witness. Thessa should have gone to Nigel for help, but she didn't. She went to the police. We decided to deal with several problems at once. We figured to send a message by disposing of the boyfriend. Thessa would go to Nigel and insist on Solomon getting involved. Instead, Solomon stayed in hiding and didn't investigate the boyfriend's murder and poaching. I was allowed one visit before she started the jailtime. Thessa was only a shadow of the person I knew. I know Solomon felt his guilt because he had Nod and Sumo threaten me if I attended the visitation or memorial service. Rosa and Nigel had no problem with my presence. Now, Solomon is dead."

Callie tried to be angry at Pica, but she found pity in her heart. "You keep using the pronoun we. How deeply are you involved in this mess? Why are you turning me over to be murdered?"

Pica's voice held no remorse, regret, or sorrow. "Your fate is yet to be determined. Our employers are going to offer you work. Unfortunately, you've caused quite a commotion. I'm burning the greenhouse to the ground."

Callie didn't quite believe what she was hearing. Pica was crazy. The man had to realize that the notion bordered on ridiculous or insane. Her father's garden had a fire suppression system and smoke alarms all over the place. Even with the power out, flames would start, but a fire wouldn't spread.

The young woman gasped out in disbelief. "You expect me to work for someone who is burning down my life?"

Callie felt a push toward the side door as an answer. Hal was here, and she didn't doubt the man would protect her. Trusting others in the overall scheme hadn't come easy. Her prayers were that the situation resolved itself without more violence.

The greenhouse had six secret entrances and three concealed roof entrances. When Pica agreed to supervise, she'd set a trap and shown him a door to use for an emergency. A key for the manual locks was hidden in the rocks of the outside waterfall. There was an independent security camera that was hardwired. No signals went in or out to alert anyone searching that the camera was active. It would record any activity at the entrance or exit.

Rorke was her real test of faith. She shared suspicions about Pica and explained her plan to expose guilt or prove innocence. Now, Rorke had to convince Solomon to listen without proof or hard evidence. They had one opportunity to put a dent or shutdown the poacher's operation. Callie doubted that they could stop the overall illegal dealings. The power and money were too deep. The best option was putting a dent in the structure and bring her father's killers to justice. Rorke had to convince Solomon to listen without proof or hard evidence.

Callie saw three helicopters in the adjacent field as Pica opened the door. Occupied by the conversation, she hadn't paid attention to their landing. The guards let her walk without restraint or holding onto her. That made her movement easier. You'd think someone would have learned from their cohorts, but she was grateful for the mistake.

Hal knew the plan, but she had no idea how fast he could act or react. Pica held the door for Callie. The four guards stepped outside with her in the lead. Pica stood silhouetted in the doorway. Callie turned, darted in reverse, and tossed owl food on Pica.

"Tufty! Fetch!"

The barn owl swooped down from the rafters. The bird dove at Pica, who ran outside to escape. Tufty scooped up her reward and flew back to her roost.

Rorke's voice came from somewhere in the night. "Callie! Down!"

Callie heard pops around her and found herself being dragged back into the greenhouse. Disoriented, she couldn't sort the scene. Lights, noise, confusion, and voices erupted in the dark. A figure helped Hal bring her inside and close the door.

Chapter

Solomon uttered from the dark. "I'm turning on a flashlight! Callie?"

"I'm fine."

Hal spoke to Solomon. "I doubt that Callie's fine. There is a lot of blood here, and I'm not hit."

Solomon grumbled unintelligible words under his breath. "Currently, I'm receiving only. We waited to find you before correcting the misconception of my death. Here's my radio. Get medical in here."

Rorke's voice came over the radio. "We're clear! Hal? Status?"

"I'm good. Callie's bleeding. No details without more light."

"We're bringing a doctor and medical unit. Ask Callie how to cancel the lockdown."

Hal clicked off while Callie explained. "The main power will stay off unless the circuit breakers are reset in a certain sequence. You must start with the alternative power sources such as the solar system. Then, turn on the backup generators. Directions are in the fairy statue standing in the flowers beside the computer room door."

Solomon knew the other couldn't hear, but he spoke softly to Hal and ignored Callie for the moment. "We don't have that sort of time. Have Rorke get the portable lights. Everyone else is safe at the Lodge. Judge Walrus wants to talk as soon as the doctor finishes. I'll disappear but be close. I have one question, Hal. How far in advance did you plot this out?"

Hal admitted. "Callie's doing not mine."

The door started opening, so Solomon faded into the shadows. Callie closed her eyes as her body began to relax.

Rorke entered and shined a light on her. "Callie, open your eyes! Stay awake! We don't need you going into shock."

Rorke had Whipper fly Bash, Sumo, and Wither to the Lodge. The four could reassure the others they were on their way with Callie.

A doctor and his medical team performed a thorough checkup and had a portable X-ray and ultrasound machine inside. Callie had multiple abrasions and contusions. The worst of the injuries were bruised and cracked ribs. She wouldn't be climbing rockfaces for a while.

Everyone but Callie, Hal, Rorke, Crabbe, and Still cleared the area.

A gentleman entered and introduced himself. "Hello, Ms. Rivera. I am Judge Walrus. Agent Moss relayed that you are concerned about certain charges levied crimes committed during the investigation."

Callie found that it hurt to talk. "Yes, sir, but there is a bigger problem in the overall scheme. Um, will it matter if Hal, Crabbe, Rorke, and Still listen?"

"You are the one who is voicing a concern and confessing. I'm also aware that Solomon is here. Come on out!"

Callie explained, "There are true innocents caught in the middle. One example is a landowner with a fishing cabin. He and his family only visit the place from May to August. The man had no idea that poachers camped out other times of the year. Other landowners had or have rental properties leased through a third party. Computer transactions make renting property easier and wouldn't raise undue suspicion.

"My other realization is agency oversight. Three agencies made a huge fuss about supervision of a book project. There will be a huge competition for control of the investigation."

Judge Walrus asked, "Do you understand that my background is family law? My influence only goes so far."

"Yes, but you have an idea of the larger picture. As the eighth surviving Circlet child, you have a vested interest but know trustworthy people. I don't want the innocent mixed up with the powerful, influential people who are guilty. I finally have the missing pieces and identified a few ring leaders."

Solomon let loose a tirade of words. Judge Walrus remained silent as he studied Callie. Then, he went around the makeshift medical gurney and laid a hand on Solomon's shoulder.

When Solomon regained control of his voice, Walrus asked, "What exactly is your crime?"

Callie studied Judge Walrus's face carefully as she answered. "I have written down the confession but want an immunity deal. No charges if I share my criminal activity."

Walrus agreed to her terms. "I'll shield you legally, but you must show us exactly what you and Nigel collected. Having every piece of information is the only way to plan a move forward."

Callie thought about the consequences for too long, and Solomon took his phone, dialed a number, and put it on speaker.

Sumo answered, and Solomon ordered. "Pretend to the Lodge occupants that it is not me. Callie wrote out a confession of alleged criminal activity. The papers are probably in her climbing jacket. The one that she purposely left at the Lodge. Get Nod, take the coat downstairs, and read the documents."

They could hear Sumo retrieve her jacket and ask the living room occupants. "Where is Nod?"

"Restroom."

Sumo spoke through the door. "I have a client on the phone who needs legal advice. Would you mind conferring with his permission? I'll have to rely on my memory because we don't have computers with secure access. I'd feel better with a second opinion."

Nod answered. "Sure. Be out in a second."

"The most private area is in the basement. It's usually cold down there, so I brought Callie's jacket for you."

They waited for Nod and Sumo to retreat downstairs. Sumo explained to Nod what was going on.

Sumo found the hidden letter, read, and exclaimed. "CALLIE! These dates go back to when you were a minor! I was supervising, which makes me an accomplice. Summarizing, the girl has cloned a computer, trespassed on private property, and set up surveillance without permission on said properties."

Solomon sighed. "I'll take the blame, if charges are brought."

Callie chimed in defensively, "I will face the consequence of my actions."

Nod made a distressed noise. "No! No! No! Sumo, turn off the phone. The idiots are going to do what they want regardless of what we say! Crap!"

Sumo asked, "What's wrong? You look like a herd of lions is circling and about to pounce. Ah, Nod?"

Nod bolted up the stairs, and Sumo followed. He didn't disconnect the line in case her distress was an emergency. Nod made a beeline for Mer. Instead of talking, Nod took ahold of Mer's shirt and shook.

Mer finally said, "I am not a salt or pepper shaker. No matter how hard you jiggle me. I will not flavor food."

Nod didn't speak but handed over her phone with a picture.

Mer glanced at the screen. "Ok. I guess we play twenty questions. A picture on the phone is a house a few streets over from Rosa. The sign has a pending contract over 'for sale.' Let's continue the conversation in the other room. It's much more private."

Less than thirty seconds later, Mer hollered. "Someone bring a glass of water, washcloth, and smelling salts. Easy! I'm helping you have a seat. Sit with your head between your knees. Mom!"

Rosa sighed. "That is the tone of unsure panic but without blood, broken bones, or a dead body. Any ideas?"

Roach grinned. "I reached into the coat pocket while Nod was rattling Mer's teeth. Pregnancy test in the pocket is not Callie's, and Nod was carsick and airsick coming out."

287

Rosa started toward the room where Mer and Nod were talking. "I suspected that they were dating. They probably didn't want to reveal a relationship until after Callie's birthday."

Lion brought in a soda and washcloth. "I have a doctor's emergency number. I'll call to see if there is something for nausea."

Solomon clicked the off button. "Why is Roach sure the pregnancy test is not yours?"

Callie rolled her eyes at Solomon. "Roach asked if I had any feminine products. We commiserated with one another about menstrual cycles. Happy?"

Solomon whispered in Callie's ear, and the young woman sighed.

Callie relented. "Fine. The systems are down, so we'll have to go inside through a non-mechanical entrance. There is a separate power source for the lights and computers, but it's not much."

Callie leaned on Rorke to stand, but she was able to walk without aid. She walked into the dark and to where the most fragrant flowers grew. Floodlights didn't provide light past the clearing. The men had flashlights, but she ignored them. She moved to where the most fragrant flowers were kept.

Rorke helped roll a large bed of flowers from the rear wall. Using several mechanical, hidden levels, she opened the door and flipped on a light switch. The men entered and took in the scene.

Callie warned, "Don't touch anything. There are several traps that my father built that will spring."

Judge Walrus asked, "Where is the computer you cloned?"

"Sir, uh, what will you do with the information?"

"As I stated, let us figure out what we are dealing with before making decisions. I'll stand by my word and shield you legally."

Booting up one of the computers, she moved so that the judge could look at the files.

The judge scanned enough data to have an idea of the problem. "We'll deal with the contents later. Solomon, Hal, Rorke, Still, and Crabbe, this room does not exist until I say the place exists. Hal, I'll ask that you go home to keep your cover as a double agent intact. The rest of us will regroup at the Lodge. I'll call the airport and have two helicopters waiting for us. Callie, go ahead and lock up the place."

After landing near the lodge, they switched to vehicles. Callie wondered why Sumo told Nod that they would go downstairs. She had not seen a staircase to indicate that a lower level existed. Rorke led Callie to a broom closet in the garage and opened the right wall. The wall was a pocket door that slid and revealed a stairwell.

Rorke helped Callie down the stairs. Instead of finding a damp, dark, and musty basement, bright lights illuminated a cozy lounge. There was seating enough for everyone to spread out, but a few were sitting together.

Nod was sitting and leaning against Mer. Isley and Lion were relaxing on a sofa with glasses of iced tea. Whipper and Bash stood along the back wall. Moss sat in an overstuffed chair with his eyes closed.

Solomon, Still, and Crabbe came down and found a spot to lean against the wall. They wanted to stretch their legs after the cramped quarters of the helicopter. Walrus took a seat at a small writing desk that sat in front of everyone.

Chapter

Callie smiled to herself and imagined her father's delight. Re remaining members of the Circlet, except Hal, and the Expedition team were together in one place. There were new additions, but he'd have approved.

Isley frowned and studied the newcomers. "I'm glad Sumo told us that Solomon was alive and well. If you'd pop up out of nowhere, someone would've shot first. My blood pressure is high enough. Is my blood pressure going to skyrocket enough to cause a heart attack?"

Solomon's voice answered, "You have the same knowledge as the rest of us. Callie seems to have most of the answers."

Callie took a bottle of water that Lion handed her but didn't rise to the bait.

Moss sighed. "Solomon, please, play nice. We're going to be awhile. Ms. Rivera?"

"Call me Callie. Are we recording our little conference?"

Moss explained. "No. After we leave here, yes. I took a huge gamble on your note. I had to trust your word that you had hard evidence against the poaching network. Until you explain, there is no evidence to support or disprove allegations. If the information is pertinent, verifiable, and incriminating, we'll protect you to the best of our ability. If you want verification, Sumo put together a general blanket of immunity. Again, we need more data to deal with proper channels later. We need to do everything by the book. Enemy leaders are closing ranks and starting damage control. Pica is playing innocent and using his connections to slip through the system. When we've had some sleep and time to regroup, we'll ensure legal loopholes are covered."

Callie read through and signed the paper. "May I keep this in my pocket until after our discussion?"

Lion asked a question that worried her. "Moss, why isn't Hal here?"

Moss waved to Callie. "Talk to the girl. I went off her note on who needed to be watched and guarded."

Callie owed Hal for protecting her life. She would not betray Hal's role: past or present.

Callie took another swallow of the water and started. "Safety and protection was and is my intent. I will refer to my father as Nigel to explain. Nigel had an ability to see into a person's soul without judging. He could analyze and figure out hidden, or overt motives, in a short time. He saw hopes, dreams, fears, and burdens. Nigel accepted a person for every good or bad personality quirk. One example is Dusty. The woman never had access to his money, but she continued to maintain a relationship. Dusty had to adhere to the rules, or she couldn't visit. There were times she bent those rules depending on the situation.

"Hal is not made for the life Solomon, Sumo, Lion, Nod, or Moss chose. Nigel understood and nudged Hal to divert his path from the core group and work on the fringes. I think that Nigel's death did what he intended. Hal was content with the center of his world being family and job. He distanced himself until a call for help went out. Hal reconnected with me after I became a student. If Hal accompanied you, his entire family would have to come. Hal has a wife, children, and three grandchildren under the age of six.

"The last reason, Hal is a temperamental gambler. I'm not talking about betting money. He deals with an emotional component. The last time we were at the shooting range, one of Beau's cousins and Mr. Dew's cronies made snide remarks about female shooters. I was fine ignoring the rudeness. Hal took offense and challenged the crony. Found myself in a shooting contest."

Nod sighed. "I hate to agree, but you're right. Did you win?"

Callie smiled, and Lion made more of relieved noise. "I was afraid you were going to say Hal was compromised."

Solomon sighed. "Let's discuss Hal later, but I will say that Callie is safe due to his aid tonight."

Judge Walrus smiled and nodded in agreement.

Callie asked, "Where would you like me to start?"

Solomon's voice turned into a slight growl. "I suggest you begin with Nigel. I found and read the letter my brother left. My feelings run along the line of tired and worried. I am not sure how to protect you or anyone else from reprisals."

The young woman offered Solomon some advice. "Stop trying to control life. Stop pretending you are the only sheriff in the territory keeping order."

Moss stifled a laugh until he heard Solomon chuckling. "Go ahead and tell the story."

Callie started with Nigel's investigation into poaching and an innocent person attempting to help. The filing of the material was to protect family and friends. Callie talked about stowing away to save her father with them for the first time.

Callie took a deep breath and admitted, "I escaped the cabin but couldn't stop the accident. I was up on the hill. Saw what happened. Dad suspected where the ambush would occur and had cameras. I retrieved the devices later."

Judge Walrus asked gently. "Where are the recordings?"

"Hidden. I made sure the cameras recorded and put the footage away."

"Were you close enough to identify the driver?"

Callie nodded yes, but she couldn't bring herself to say Tort or Pitter. Those in the room erupted with questions and statements.

Solomon finally controlled his temper, and he came to sit on Callie's other side. "We will protect you."

Tears slid down her cheeks. "I….. They….."

Isley was the one who put the pieces together from his earlier conversation with Callie. "Shit! I guess you learned Dusty's lessons too well. Pitter and Tort! Guess they burned the cabin a week later. How did you continue like nothing was wrong? You had to work with the man who killed your father."

Walrus continued to keep the conversation going. "Tell us about the research."

"I never, ever told Sumo or anyone that the rest of my father's research was in my possession. My thought process was to remain clueless and not pose a threat. I took over the investigation, researched, and watched. After Sumo helped me set the snare, I relocated the entire trap to coordinates of my choosing."

A doorbell sounded in the room, and the intercom buzzed for attention.

Arc's voice wafted down through the speaker. "We are secure, but we need help with a situation. Before I come down, please inform Callie that we knew Pitter was a rotten apple. I was assigned to investigate him."

Walrus pushed a button on the desk and responded. "Rorke will come and open the door for you."

Arc entered the room and smiled at Callie. "Glad to see you have returned in one piece."

"Thank you for trying to protect me. I wasn't sure whether I could trust you until Pitter showed his true nature."

A flurry of sound from the stairwell was followed by a girl squealing in pain but triumph. "I told you! A hidden door!"

Arc muttered something unintelligible and shared, "I hate babysitting! I want to leave with the first group out."

Isley started to laugh but stopped when Moss sent him a stern look.

Arc explained the reason he crashed their meeting. "Uh, Ms. Roach had computer access at the greenhouse and downloaded files. She put together almost everything that has happened in the last few weeks. The young lady made a video with highlights. Um, the problem is that Rosa figured out what Roach was doing. Rosa made Roach share, and word spread.

"Lion's girls and Rosa have been watching Callie's adventures on the telly. Roach started with the dinner that Callie and Rorke had with Dusty and Baker. I am afraid to ask the source of the surveillance. We put a halt to the video when we landed above Nigel's hidden evidence. We knew Roach watched events on the mountaintop until the greenhouse locked up. Not sure how much you wished to share with civilians."

Mer snapped. "That two-bit hacker!"

Isley rolled his eyes. "Callie, before you ask, the girls are fine. Lion and her five juvenile delinquents saw Judge Walrus. Lion went first, and then her five girls independently. Afterward, Walrus spoke to them as a group. There will be no charges or formal reprimands. Dew and his cronies don't want to add fuel to the fire. The judge did lecture each one on behaving responsibly and listening to the supervisory adult."

Judge Walrus was trying not to smirk, "Arc, you may as well tell me why you have an unsure look on your face."

"Roach refuses to tell her source, but she has Callie's helmet footage from her helicopter escape. Callie wanted proof that she left the two alive, and she verbalized very elaborate plans for their tortures while they rotted in prison."

Callie sighed. "Should have known better than to ask Roach to do background checks. How is Gran taking all of this?"

Arc frowned. "Surprisingly well. Your grandmother hasn't seemed surprised or distressed. My opinion is that she's a little too calm. If I had a child who acted like you, I'd be in an emotional meltdown."

Rosa's voice came from behind Arc. "I'm rarely surprised by much these days. Young man, go upstairs and help Rorke. He allowed me to come down, but the girls are trying to figure out how to bypass the second door."

Arc disappeared, and Callie fidgeted for the first time. She had no idea what to say or how to react. Rosa walked over to Callie, and Solomon went to stand so that Rosa could sit.

Rosa blocked Solomon from moving and hugged them both. "The two of you certainly make a pair! Solomon, I know you are Nigel's brother. The day Callie and Brine disappeared to see the balloons in Boise was enlightening. The police escort and Nigel's state of mind scared me more than Callie's impromptu trip. The floodgates opened about events surrounding his childhood and his research into poachers.

He was terrified that the past would catch up with him and put Callie in danger. After Nigel died, I figured that Callie took over his research. Didn't interfere because you and Sumo were always there to watch over her."

Callie whispered and hugged her grandmother. "I love you! I am sorry you had to keep everyone's secrets.

"How upset will I be watching the rest of Roach's cinematic show?"

"Depends on which cameras she hacked."

Judge Walrus moved the process along. "Ms. Rosa, you have quite a family! Let's use the tunnel exit while the girls try to figure out how to access the stairs or elevator. Nod, do you feel up to walking?"

"Yes! Lion, keep that wheelchair away from me!"

Mer didn't argue or add his opinion. He only made sure Nod stood without wobbling.

Lion was not upset in the least. "Nod. Use the chair."

"I hate you right now!"

Lion patted Nod's arm. "Glad to know you are feeling better. Are you hungry?"

"Yes. Is there any pie left? I better eat before Callie raids the fridge for dessert."

Upstairs, Callie diverted the gathering's attention to her appearance. Solomon tried to keep the hugs at a minimum. He didn't want to share the injuries to her ribs. Callie decided that she'd rather lie down than watch a rerun of events. She retreated to the room that she had occupied during the scavenger hunt.

Roach followed and let her settle on the bed.

The teaching assistant grinned delightedly at Callie. "Love the setup at BE. You left your backpack with the laptop in the classroom. Payday! I had an awesome time bypassing your uncle's various passwords and spyware. Mer hasn't done too bad of a job, and it took me a couple of attempts. The only reason I could access the files was that I physically on site."

Callie's admitted with relief. "Thank you for telling me the truth. I received an alert as soon as you accessed my computer. I'm sorry. I slipped about a comment about background checks. Someone may ask you."

Roach smiled in reassurance. "Please! There is no trace to me. Every byte links to your computer system. Are you all right? That drop into the body of water looked a little rough."

Callie asked, "How did you retrieve the information from the helicopter ride? It happened after I left the mountaintop."

"I figured that you'd want a record of events. I worked backward using the frequencies on the surveillance on top of the mountain. I found the main server on the edge of BE property and the mini-relay stations that you set up on different sites around the state. Nice job disguising the frequencies on AM radio bands. The others may not have internet, but I do. Granted, I haven't shared that little tidbit."

Callie sighed tiredly. "That means you heard my conversation with Dusty. I better call and warn her that she's about to be a star. The woman never ceases to surprise or amaze me."

Roach hesitated before sharing the rest of her actions. "Ah, I phoned Dusty as soon as I had access to the recordings and watched. Also, I approached Rosa on whether to mute or delete the part about Blake. We spoke to Blake about sharing because there isn't anything incriminating. Do you think we should forewarn Solomon about your actions? The poor man has had a bad day."

"No."

Roach asked, "How bad are the injuries?"

"I'll live. Run along and restart the video so that everyone will be able to see your masterpiece. I'm taking a long winter's nap."

Arc had made Roach stop when the helicopter started smoking, and the team had moved to the rocks. This time, they continued to watch the events unfold. Everyone remained quiet until Callie was working in the back of the helicopter. Tort and Pitter were distracted in the cockpit.

Arc announced in almost disbelief. "There is a lake not far from their position. I think Callie is about to repel out over the lake. The bags went out one side to use as an anchor weight. If the lines are long enough, she could repel down to the water. Even with planning, hitting that water is going to hurt."

Blake sputtered. "What if the ropes tangle?"

Bash answered. "Tangled isn't the problem. If the rope gets caught on a corner, bolt, or bar, the line has to be cut. Even at a low speed, like 110mph, she'll be dragged while cutting the ropes. Luckily, she is wearing a helmet and goggles, but a drop is going to hurt."

The listeners could hear Callie's voice as she waited. She had to make sure that Tort or Pitter did not see the line of bags she dropped and whispered. "If you are watching, the poachers use this route regularly. The current flight path is low to avoid notice and radar. When we reach the lake, Tort will have to hover and check for air and water traffic. I'll activate a tracker and stay on the ropes until he hovers. I'm recording because I want evidence that I escaped without injury, and I disembarked leaving Tort and Pitter alive."

Callie went silent and watched the scenery. A landmark appeared, and she went out now open door. The weight of her disembarking wasn't noticeable. She was waited for Tort to hover and check the area before flying across the lake. She started repelling, and the wind sent her twisting and spinning like a leave caught in a whirlwind.

Bash's prediction was correct. A line caught somewhere above as she neared the water. Callie took her knife and severed the connection to the helicopter. She was only about twelve feet from the surface, but the landing hurt as she entered the lake. Water, bubbles, and gasping breaths were the only sounds anyone heard. The helicopter continued its journey, never suspecting it was missing a passenger.

Callie broke the surface, inflated a life vest, and rested while regaining her equilibrium. "I'd rather be spit by a canoe!"

Chapter

A motorboat neared Callie's location. Engine noise slowed to a crawl and powered off. The boat coasted a short distance away.

Dusty's voice asked from the wheel, "Do you need any help, dear?"

Callie swam to the side and grabbed a rope ladder that Dusty pushed over the side. "No. Thank you for coming to pick me up."

"Delighted to help! I'm excited that you finally called to ask me for a favor. I had to wait twenty-four years. Well, almost that long. Your birthday isn't for another eight days."

Callie took off the gear and started to pull in the line. She was hurting but wanted to be off the water as soon as possible. Pitter and Tort might realize she was gone and circle back.

The camera recording events landed with a clear view of Callie as she spoke. "Thank you for being a part of my world. Your presence in my life is the sole reason I didn't plunge a knife in Tort's heart weeks ago. How is Bree? Jedidiah?"

"They are settled in guest houses. Baker has taken quite a shine to our guests. Did you know that Bree and Orlin were orphans?"

"Yes."

Dusty spoke in her slow, precise manner. "You are dripping all over the floor. There are towels and dry clothes below."

While Callie changed, Dusty sat in the driver's seat like a queen addressing the court and asked conversationally, "Have you and Rorke had sex yet?"

"My dating life is none of your business!" Callie couldn't see Dusty and tried to soften the tone, but she started to feel the cuts and bruises.

Dusty ignored the words and continued, "Rorke is so much better for you than Linus. Glad that each of you declined the invitation to the key party. I asked Baker to broach the matter with Rorke while we were in the ladies' room. Baker was impressed at Rorke's composure and tact. I was proud of your poise because I couldn't read your true feelings. Finally! My lessons had sunk into your brain. There is so much drama surrounding a child and trying to teach one is exhausting."

Callie reemerged, and Dusty sighed at the young woman's appearance. "Well, that is a start, but you are a mess."

Callie turned the conversation away from her wet hair and bare feet. "Are you aware that my family thinks you seduced Linus?"

"Of course. Giving Linus an internship to pursue his dreams was a small price to pay."

Bluntly, Callie asked, "Did you have sex with Linus?"

"No. Linus was of legal age, but the young man was inexperienced. He needed someone with much more patience at teaching techniques in bed. Not my area. and I was married."

Callie's face went scarlet and then settled into her usual mask. "Baker seems nice, and he loves you. I would have liked him five years ago."

"Selfishly, I was afraid that you would be upset. Nigel and I were great friends, and I was the only mother figure in your life. Baker and I met after Nigel died. I have heard and read that a child may resent a parental figure who finds someone else."

Callie reminded Dusty. "Don't forget about Rosa."

"Don't be silly. Of course, Rosa helped. She's your grandmother. You had an unusual family, but it worked. Nigel trusted me enough to tell me that Solomon was his brother. They were going to be adopted together, but Solomon refused to become part of a family. After Nigel died, Solomon called every so often. Nigel's brother should learn to relax, enjoy life, and socialize instead of being such a paranoid, controlling man."

Callie asked, "Would you do me a second favor?"

Dusty sounded extremely happy but sent Callie an amused look at the request. The young woman was much too serious.

"Of course."

"Do not interfere in my relationship."

Dusty made a triumphant noise and wanted to know how to help. "I knew you loved him! Would you like me to drop a few hints? Make dinner reservations? Bribe him to take you on a few dates. May I help plan the wedding?"

Callie's tone took on a warning note. "Dusty! Stop! Those ideas count as interfering."

Dusty's hand fluttered uncharacteristically toward Callie to catch her attention. "I should not care, but you need to know something."

The tone caught Calle by surprise, and she braced herself for the news. "Yes?"

Dusty looked uncharacteristically nervous. "I have used my skills to manipulate men and women after we married, but I have never cheated on Baker. I realize the notion might be difficult for you to understand, but many people find me a challenge to be around. Rosa and your grandfather were kind to me. If Rosa felt my behavior was out of place, she spoke up. The lady never went behind my back. Any words about my character, she told me in person.

"Thessa and Mer were honest with me. If I did something to make them angry, they became mad and yelled. The first time Mer threatened to murder me, I was upset. Rosa must have sensed my discomfort because she sat me down to talk. She explained that a family, blood or otherwise, had to work at being a family. Part of that dynamic was sometimes letting out the emotions and dealing with the problem. The words weren't meant in a literal sense."

Dusty paused, and Callie tried to encourage the woman to keep talking. "Sounds like Gran."

"Ever since Nigel died, you have been so grown up and responsible. You try so hard to protect and save everyone. I did something rash and hope you'll forgive me."

Callie closed her eyes and took a slow, deep breath. "What did you do, Dusty?"

"You were hurt jumping off the roof, and I couldn't let something worse happen. I did not approve of you having dinner with Beau. Then, I watched the replay on the surveillance monitors. I understand that the real problem was Mr. Dew, Senior. So proud! I watched you playing cat and mouse with Mr. Dew's gang. You did listen and learn over the years. I decided to help Beau."

Callie muttered, "I should have known you were too quiet about my relationship with Beau. Linus became a target for your attention but not Beau. How did you come across surveillance from the restaurant?"

Dusty did pretend not to hear. "Solomon gave me an emergency number, and I asked to see the files. When Thessa got into legal trouble, Nigel and Solomon went straight to a person who had the knowledge and power to help. I went to talk to their same friend to help Blake and Beau."

Callie pinched her nose and asked, "Dusty, what exactly did you tell the friend about Blake and Beau?"

"I told the truth. Beau took Blake to the hospital after being hurt. Beau didn't know who to trust and called you. The poor child is dying a slow, painful death. Beau's dream is to live near a pond, a lake, or river and help salmon. He has little in common with his family. They ridicule him for being soft and caring.

Callie tried to cut to the core of the conversation. "Dusty, what happened to Beau?"

Dusty answered. "The charges were reduced to something, something with parole and community service. A judge overseeing his case promised to see that Solomon receives the paperwork so that Beau may do his service with fish. We'll wait to tell Solomon when he isn't so mad about your actions tonight. Mr. Dew believes that his son pled guilty and disowned him. Callie, do you want me to take care of Mr. Dew?"

"No. Please no. If Beau and Blake are safe, don't stir up a hornet's nest."

Dusty clicked her fingernails against the fiberglass side. "May I still be invited to the wedding?"

"When and if I have a wedding, you may come."

"I love you. Thank you for allowing me to be a part of your life."

Chapter

There wasn't more to Roach's show. Solomon and Walrus disappeared immediately afterward and did not return. There were no breaches in security, and the authorities cleared everyone to go home. Solomon called Callie's kin to arrange a family meeting for Sunday afternoon.

Mer met Rorke and Callie at church. Her uncle looked tired but was quite pleased with himself. Mer had been the one who put down an offer on the house. Lion wrangled a doctor's appointment for Nod on Monday, and Mer was tagging along.

Mer grinned and told them that he was crashing Solomon's family reunion to speak first.

After a quick lunch, Callie retreated to the greenhouse but kept track of the time. Mer unlocked the door for the first group of visitors. Isley and Lion remained at the front to let guests inside. Isley, true to his suspicious nature, had a tablet preloaded with names and pictures.

Rorke and Mer wandered through to join Callie in the computer office. Her uncle had changed into a suit and tie.

Callie asked, "Does crashing Solomon's meeting have to do with proposing to Nod?"

Mer grinned lopsidedly. "Yes."

Callie frowned. "Is asking in public a good idea if she's not feeling well?"

"We have plenty of help if she vomits or passes out. Isley can be as picky as Solomon about security. The man has a list of family and friends and is checking it twice. I had to rack my brain to figure out who to tell him to add."

Callie sighed. "Glad Rorke warned me that the family meeting is turning into a public gathering. I've seen individuals from the lodge, Roach, Cattail with her boys and parents, and various family members. I guess you had better use the public announcement system."

Mer glanced at the monitors. "I see Wither arrived and want to have a last-minute word. He's checking in with Isley. Thanks! Love you."

Rorke thought Callie had forgotten his presence until she turned to him. "You are in charge of the first aid kit."

Judge Walrus knocked and leaned on the door jam. "Hello!"

Callie tried to gauge if the man's appearance meant good or bad news. He looked relaxed, but he was also blocking the door with his body.

Walrus spoke to Rorke and Callie. "Many facets of life are about to change drastically, while other parts remain the same. We are setting up a joint task force to deal with the research on poaching. Solomon will lead the task force. Whipper, Still, Bash, Arc, and Crabbe agreed to join the team. If agreeable, Rorke will join as well. We have a lot of material to cull through. Callie, we'd like you to work as a consultant."

Callie asked, "Is Solomon aware of these plans?"

"Yes." Walrus turned and locked eyes with Rorke. "Moss and I are very serious about you proposing to our girl."

Rorke rolled his eyes. "Callie is not the only person who everyone ignores discussing certain topics. We have not had a proper date. My choice would be a nice romantic evening that is not interrupted. Let's deal with Mer and Nod's engagement today."

Walrus smiled. "I am glad Nod and Mer finally worked up the gumption to talk to the family. They are a good, solid couple. Now we have to work on Isley and Lion."

Callie laughed. "People accuse me of meddling in lives, but you are worse."

"I appreciate the compliment coming from you. We'll discuss details about work later."

Walrus disappeared, and Dusty appeared in the doorway. Callie did a double-take to make sure the woman was Dusty. She wore jeans, boots, and a comfortable looking top. Makeup was minimal but tastefully done.

Callie smiled. "Hello! You look different today but nicely put together."

Dusty ignored the compliment and frowned.

Callie offered to give Dusty privacy for the conversation. "Rorke, would you show Uncle Mer how to wear and use the equipment? It's the same system that we use in class. Give Solomon the second headset since he wants to address the family."

Rorke disappeared.

Dusty closed the door behind him. "Callie, we need to talk before Solomon addresses the family. Last night, Solomon phoned and asked me to meet in person."

The implications of that one sentence made Callie decide to have a seat. Her chest felt worse as she tried to take air into her lungs.

Dusty did not beat around the bush. "Solomon shared that you are aware that we are your biological parents. How long have you known?"

"I think a part of me always knew, but Nigel confirmed the relationship the night he died."

302

"Do you understand why Nigel, Solomon, and I made our decisions?"

"Yes. Ah, wait. The three of you?"

Dusty smiled, but it was a tense, unsure expression. "You know the truth. I suppose it won't hurt to answer. Solomon and I met, but he used Nigel's name. We fell in love, and he told me the truth about his life. Solomon never shared any details about his childhood, but he did tell me about his brother. We loved each other, but Solomon had responsibilities. I never felt those obligations were more important, but then his friend died. Solomon felt responsible, but he wasn't. His friend was in the ocean and far away. I wanted to give Solomon a family, but there was no way I could be a mother. After I became pregnant, we went to Nigel and formed a plan. Nigel and I married so that he could be the father of record. The last time that I saw Solomon was when you left the hospital with him and Nigel."

Callie exclaimed, "Who took care of you?"

"I was fine, but thank you for thinking of my health."

Dusty was as closed about her past as Solomon. Details would not be forthcoming.

Dusty continued. "Last night, Solomon let us know the outcome of events. Callie, I'll never recognize the biological connection, and I request that you never do either. You are the one secret that I never shared with Baker. If my husband suspects a relationship, he's never commented. My husband knows that my past is not a danger to our love or marriage."

Callie asked a question that had nagged at her. "Why did Thessa go to you for help? Why are Bree and Orlin hiding at your house?"

"I see you figured out that Orlin is alive. Thessa is my sister. We couldn't stay together. Rosa and Nigel, Senior, adopted her."

Callie decided to see how much Dusty might impart about the past. "Solomon used to sneak out to my grandparent's farm to see his brother, Nigel. Did you meet Solomon trying to visit Thessa secretly?"

Callie finally dented Dusty's outward façade, and her expression turned to one of shock. "How do you know?! We never told anyone. Not even Nigel."

Callie didn't answer.

Dusty took a deep breath and composed herself. "Well, don't tell Solomon or Bree. If you tattle, Solomon will relocate my sister far away. I wouldn't be able to keep an eye on her or visit."

Callie promised not to share her knowledge. "The past is safe with me. Why is Solomon calling a family meeting?"

"I'll let Solomon have the spotlight today. Come on."

Callie walked with Dusty to the Turtle Pond.

Mer tested the sound system by announcing, "Please join me at the Turtle Pond. Solomon would like to make an important announcement after me."

Solomon was talking to Baker, which didn't bother Dusty one bit.

Callie found Solomon handing her the second headset back. "I don't need a voice magnifier."

Callie smiled shyly at Baker. "Thank you for taking care of Bree, Orlin, and Jedidiah. I'm hoping that I'll be able to visit soon."

Baker shared. "Jedidiah and the puppy went back up the mountain. He invited me to come anytime, but I don't know the area. I'd love to hike up with you to see his place."

"I'd be happy to take you. Dusty, you are welcome as well."

Blake bounded over and asked, "May I talk to you?"

Callie directed Blake to the side door.

Outside, Blake danced around her happily. "My grades posted, and I have all A's."

"That is a wonderful start. Why the fidgeting of concern?"

"A friend let me have their old computer when they bought a new one, and the laptop started doing strange things. The school refunded my housing money. There is a little left after paying Lion for apartment expenses. I thought about buying a new one, but I went into the store and left overwhelmed. Do you think you or your uncle would mind helping?"

Callie had no problem volunteering her uncle. "Asking Mer to help you is fine. Blake, don't be afraid to ask, talk to us, or tell us to mind our own business. You do not owe us. We need you as much as you need us. Four years down the road, our relationship will change. You'll head to Boise, Idaho Falls, or Twin Falls to work in a hospitality venue. Your parents will recognize their daughter is safe, happy, and doing all right. We'll stay in touch, visit every so often, and be there for support to celebrate happy occasions or help in a crisis."

"Part of life is constant change, and a person grows or alters with time. Ah, Blake, let's go inside."

Blake looked to where Callie spied a large dog running around the corner.

Blake smiled. "That is Crabbe's dog, Hermes. Hermes has been here with Crabbe's parents. They are staying a couple of days this trip. Hermes knows not to pee in the greenhouse."

"That is not a dog but a small horse. It's coming right for us."

304

Blake did not understand Callie's panic as she unlocked the door and shoved Blake inside. "Are you afraid of dogs?"

"You try and be hunted by a pack of wolves who are endangered and not supposed to be hurt."

"What happened?"

"Headed to a large grove of trees. Sumo made me climb the highest one and stay. They circled me while Sumo went to find all the venison steaks that he could. Set the steaks upwind. Circled downwind and used the flares to herd them to the steaks. I believe that is one of the few times that I recited the entire plant encyclopedia at once."

Callie stowed the extra mic on her belt and didn't realize that the sound system broadcasted the conversation.

Blake and Callie returned to the Turtle Garden. Sumo and Rorke came to stand by Callie, who eyed Hermes suspiciously. Crabbe had leashed the puppy, and a couple had come to stand next to Crabbe. Callie assumed it was Crabbe's parents. When it appeared most of the family and friends were in the vicinity, Mer formally proposed. He also confessed that he bought the house that Nod had on her phone. When Mer finished, he tried to hand the mic to Solomon.

Solomon ignored him. "Callie, would you join me?"

"Ah, I rather stay right here."

Solomon waited while Callie walked over and stepped up beside him. Deep breath. Smile. Friendly. No emotion.

Solomon told the curious audience. "I spoke to Rosa and made sure she was comfortable with me sharing. Keep any questions or judgments about my speech to yourself. I don't care to share more than I'm about to say."

Callie put a hand on Solomon's arm. The older gentleman covered her fingers with his and squeezed slightly. Going public with family and friends opened Solomon up to a whole different set of feelings and complications.

Solomon had thought a lot about what to say. "Recent events have made me rethink a decision that I made long ago. After our parents died, my brother and I were going to be adopted. I figured that I'd be better off on my own and disappeared. My brother swore not to tell his adopted family about me. After Callie was born, I rejoiced that our family would continue. Nigel and I discussed what to do when he became a single parent. We agreed that no matter what happened, she'd not be adopted or sent to foster care. The problem became apparent quickly. We had no idea how to take care of a baby and barely survived the first night. Nigel drove home to his parents to see if they'd help. The entire family welcomed Callie with open arms.

"When Nigel died, I moved nearby but remained out of sight. I was worried about putting Callie or her family in danger due to my work. The last week has shown me that Callie is perfectly capable of stirring up more trouble than I ever thought possible. I wanted to recognize the relationship between Callie and me. Thank you for listening."

Callie wasn't sure what to say or do, but Hermes provided a distraction. The dog heard the mother and father duck quacking along with the chicks peeping. Hermes barked and lunged into the pond. Surprised by the motion, Crabbe released the leash. Callie tried to stop the canine by grabbing him, but the dog knocked her into the water with him. Callie was able to grab the lead, but the pet was a strong swimmer. Hermes thought Callie was playing when she grabbed his leash. The dog swam and pulled her along the surface of the water. Her ribs immediately protested the action. Callie vaguely heard Rorke ordering her to turn the lead line loose.

Coughing out the water, Callie wheezed. "My ducks."

Rorke made her turn the line loose. "What happened to the ducks being wildlife and leaving them alone? Hermes, the ducks, and the turtle are friends. Well, I suppose that coexist is more the term."

Callie tread water next to Rorke. Breathing was difficult with her injured ribs. Callie was mostly using her legs to stay on top of the water. She kept moving, so Rorke was between her and Hermes. Her pet turtle swam over. Mr. Turtle was overjoyed that Callie was in the water with him. The adult ducks and ducklings joined them.

Looking around, Callie saw Solomon was sitting at the edge of the pond. He'd tried to stop her from grabbing the leash and ending up in the water. The result was Solomon landed in the muddy reeds.

Sumo smiled and quipped. "You were addressing your concerns about chaos. Are you sure you want to claim her as family and to try to keep her out of additional trouble?"

Walrus and Sumo helped Solomon to his feet.

Crabbe called his dog. The pet ignored the summons until Callie started for shore. The dog obeyed, and the turtle swam back to the island beside the ducks.

Pickle met the trio with towels and offered, "I have plastic seats and will drive you to the house. A little water and dirt won't hurt anything."

When the three were in the car, Pickle kept looking at Solomon and Callie.

Solomon finally said, "Spit it out, young lady."

"Did my finding out about Nigel's investigation put him in danger?"

Solomon paused, and his mind processed. "Give me a moment to gather my thoughts. My brain is a bit waterlogged after ending up in the pond."

Solomon paused and then explained. "Nigel was researching a dangerous group, and they have spies in many levels of society and government. He contacted the authorities before you talked to him. If Nigel had any doubt that you, Rosa, or Callie were in danger, he would have told me. The peril this week is solely due to Callie's idiocy in trying to protect everyone. There was no remorse or hesitation when Tort or Pitter acted."

Callie put a hand on her friend's arm. "I swear you had nothing to do with my father's decisions, his research, or fate."

"Thank you. I feared asking, but not knowing seems to be worse."

Pickle was relieved at the answer and smiled shyly. "Callie, do you know Crabbe's story? His parents are nice, and he was kind after the Teton debacle."

"I have no idea but could poke around."

Solomon warned. "Callie!"

Damage to Callie's ribs made breathing and talking hard, but she stated, "Stop being a sour lemon. If I find out, Hermes stays away from me."

Solomon laughed. "I can handle ulterior motives. Callie, take the prescription pain medicine. You're moving slowly, and the dog pulling you is going to hurt."

After changing, she noticed that Solomon had placed her necklace on her dresser. She put the chain back on her neck.

Rorke came back a little while later and found her in the office. She was gazing at the walls of her former bedroom and thinking.

Rorke wrapped her gently in an embrace. "I recognize your reluctance to talk about the future. When I feel the time is right, we'll talk about getting married. Solomon and Nigel were able to hold onto very few family heirlooms. One being their mother's rings."

Callie searched Rorke's face. "What about my family?"

Rorke shook his head. "Isley warned me that Mer made noises about prenup documents. No worries. If anyone wants to start matching assets, the lodge and surrounding area belong to me. Originally, Solomon signed a loan for the land. I paid him back over time, and we put everything in my name. Built a little at a time as the money became available."

Callie asked, "My inquiry is more about my unusual kindred. You were willing to raise Bree's child without pause before we knew the entire story. My heart is thankful for the support."

Rorke tried to reassure the woman he loved about his feelings. "Unusual is relative. Your uncles and aunt are present. Two uncles are without their wives and children but came for support. Solomon's cohorts trickled into the greenhouse, and they are congratulating Hal in helping to save you. I'd say that I was fortunate. Regardless of race, religion, or personal feelings, I see love, trust, faith, and hope for the future."

"Would you care if I don't travel as much?"

"Fine by me. You stay home and take care of the kids."

Callie leaned into Rorke's warmth. "Now you're walking a fine line. Dad hauled me all over in a backpack, stroller, or a trampoline type thing. I think a woman from the Nez Perce Indian tribe made him a bag. He was collecting Camas, with permission, on the reservation."

"Papoose style. Cool. Do you have the bag? Is there a board?"

"I have no idea. How do you feel about having a tea party in the Fairy Garden?"

Rorke gently turned Callie to face him so that he could look into her eyes. "I'm a guy and have never been to a tea party. I understand that you haven't contemplated a future beyond seeking justice. Now, you are overthinking. Stop worrying about the future. We'll figure life out as we go. I love you."

Callie spoke her feelings aloud for the first time. "I love you, too."